DATE DUE

OCT 1 6 2014	
NOV 2 2 2014	

DISCARD

Hampstead Lane

HEA

Parliament
Hill

Gervez's
house

Isa
Dunsta

Praise for

THE FIRST ESCAPE

(BOOK I IN THE DOPPLE GANGER CHRONICLES)

What Readers Are Saying

"I was so absorbed in this book that it only took me two days to read it (I couldn't put it down!). I loved the way it was part graphic novel and part book. That really made me understand what the characters looked like. And my favorite parts made me laugh out loud!"

"I absolutely love The Dopple Ganger Chronicles—the story line is good and exciting and gripping. I especially like Sadie and Saskia because I have a twin, so I like stories about other twins growing up."

What Teachers Are Saying

"I was a reluctant reader when I was a child, and comics were about the only thing I would read cover to cover without interruption. . . . The Dopple Ganger Chronicles will be a permanent part of my classroom for sure. I only hope it is the dawn of a new format of book so others can jump on the bandwagon."

"The children at our school have been so excited by THE FIRST ESCAPE. We have set aside twenty-five minutes every day to read it, and that is not enough, as we have children begging to take it home. We even have a waiting list of children who want to read the book. It's not often that reading can cause such a buzz."

"From the first paragraph we knew this book would be the key we needed to unlock the minds of reluctant readers. For those who already enjoy reading, this is one of the most atmospheric and enjoyable books I've ever seen. I can't wait to unleash it on my reading groups! The illustra-novella is here to stay."

What Parents Are Saying

"My son is almost thirteen, has ADHD, and has a hard time staying focused, so reading is a chore for him. But he is totally into The Dopple Ganger Chronicles! When he's not doing his schoolwork, he has his nose in that book! We're so happy to see him enjoying a book on his own!"

"My eleven-year-old daughter had a reading age of seven and would 'switch off' whenever she encountered a book, as her dyslexia and special needs made reading tedious. But G. P. Taylor's visit to her school inspired her to try THE FIRST ESCAPE. It was the first time she'd ever grasped a book, and she read it all from cover to cover and even wrote a final chapter of her own. The teachers were astonished. . . . It was the mixture of words and illustrations that made her want to read it. It's almost a miracle."

"My eight-year-old son, who has been reluctant to read chapter books despite his abilities, devoured the first Dopple Ganger book, and then his eleven-year-old brother did as well. They are very eager for the next book!"

"I want to thank you for writing The Dopple Ganger Chronicles. My son does not often enjoy reading, but he loved your book—in fact, he couldn't put it down. He keeps asking when there will be another addition to the series. I can't thank you enough; we'll be anxiously awaiting the next installment."

G. P. Taylor

DG

THE DOPPLE GANGER

CHRONICLES

BOOK II: THE SECRET OF INDIGO MOON

SALT**RIVER**®

AN IMPRINT OF

TYNDALE HOUSE PUBLISHERS, INC.

CAROL STREAM, ILLINOIS

Visit Tyndale's exciting Web site at www.tyndale.com

Visit Markosia's Web site at www.markosia.com

Visit the Dopple Ganger Chronicles Web site at www.dopplegangerchronicles.com

TYNDALE, Tyndale's quill logo, SALTRIVER, and the SaltRiver logo are registered trademarks of Tyndale House Publishers, Inc.

THE SECRET OF INDIGO MOON

Designed by Stephen Vosloo

Art directed by Jacqueline L. Nuñez

Edited by Elizabeth R. Kletzing

G. P. Taylor is represented by the Caroline Sheldon Literary Agency.

Library of Congress Cataloging-in-Publication Data

Taylor, G. P.

The secret of indigo moon / G. P. Taylor.

p. cm. — (The Dopple Ganger chronicles ; #2)

Summary: Erik Morrissey Ganger and his friend, fourteen-year-old Sadie Dopple, meet a wealthy recluse while trying to escape tunnels under Isambard Dunstan's School for Wayward children in order to pursue a former foe who has inadvertently kidnapped Sadie's twin sister, Saskia.

ISBN 978-1-4143-1948-3 (alk. paper)

1. Graphic novels. [1. Graphic novels. 2. Robbers and outlaws—Fiction. 3. Kidnapping—Fiction. 4. Orphans—Fiction. 5. Schools—Fiction. 6. Twins—Fiction. 7. Sisters—Fiction. 8. Supernatural—Fiction. 9. Mystery and detective stories.] I. Title.

PZ7.7.T39Sec 2009
[Fic]—dc22   2009005434

Printed in China

15 14 13 12 11 10 09
7 6 5 4 3 2 1

FOR

ALL CHILDREN WHO HAVE
NEVER KNOWN THEIR FATHERS

AND

ALL FATHERS WHO HAVE
NEVER KNOWN THEIR CHILDREN.

LET US KNOW WE ARE LOVED AND ADORED
JUST AS WE ARE. . . .

Contents

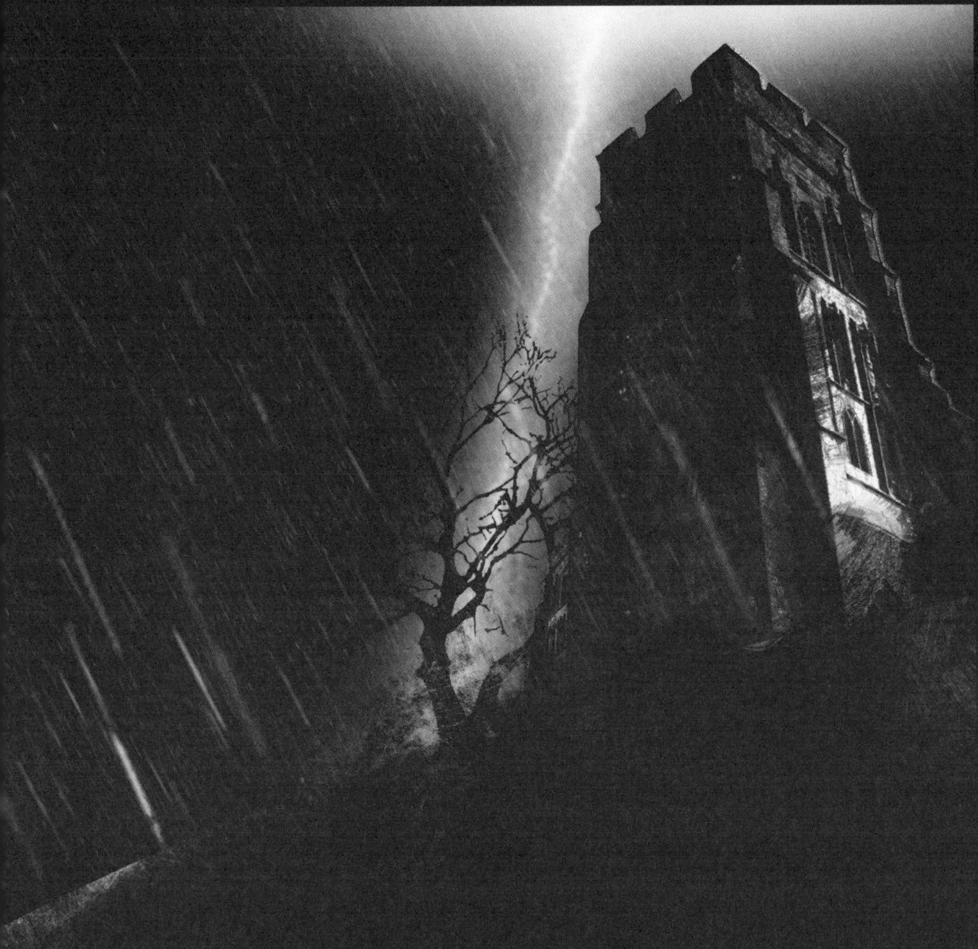

Chapter One

Night Vision

IN THE HIGH TOWER of Isambard Dunstan's School for Wayward Children, Erik Morrissey Ganger couldn't sleep. He had been counting the hours since midnight, when the storm first began to rage, by listening to the church clock woefully clanging the hours and the quarter hours like a funeral bell. Now he knew it was . . .

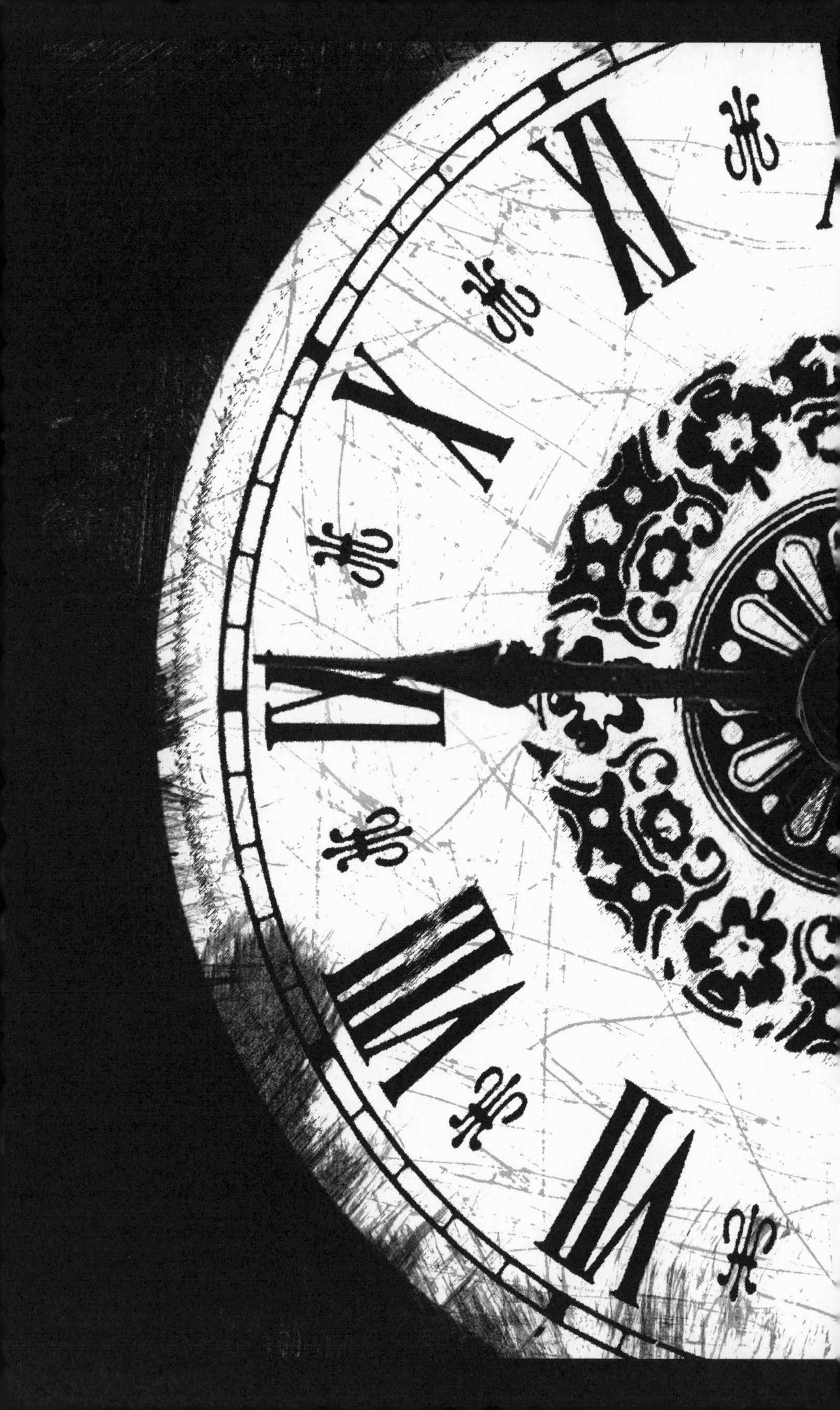

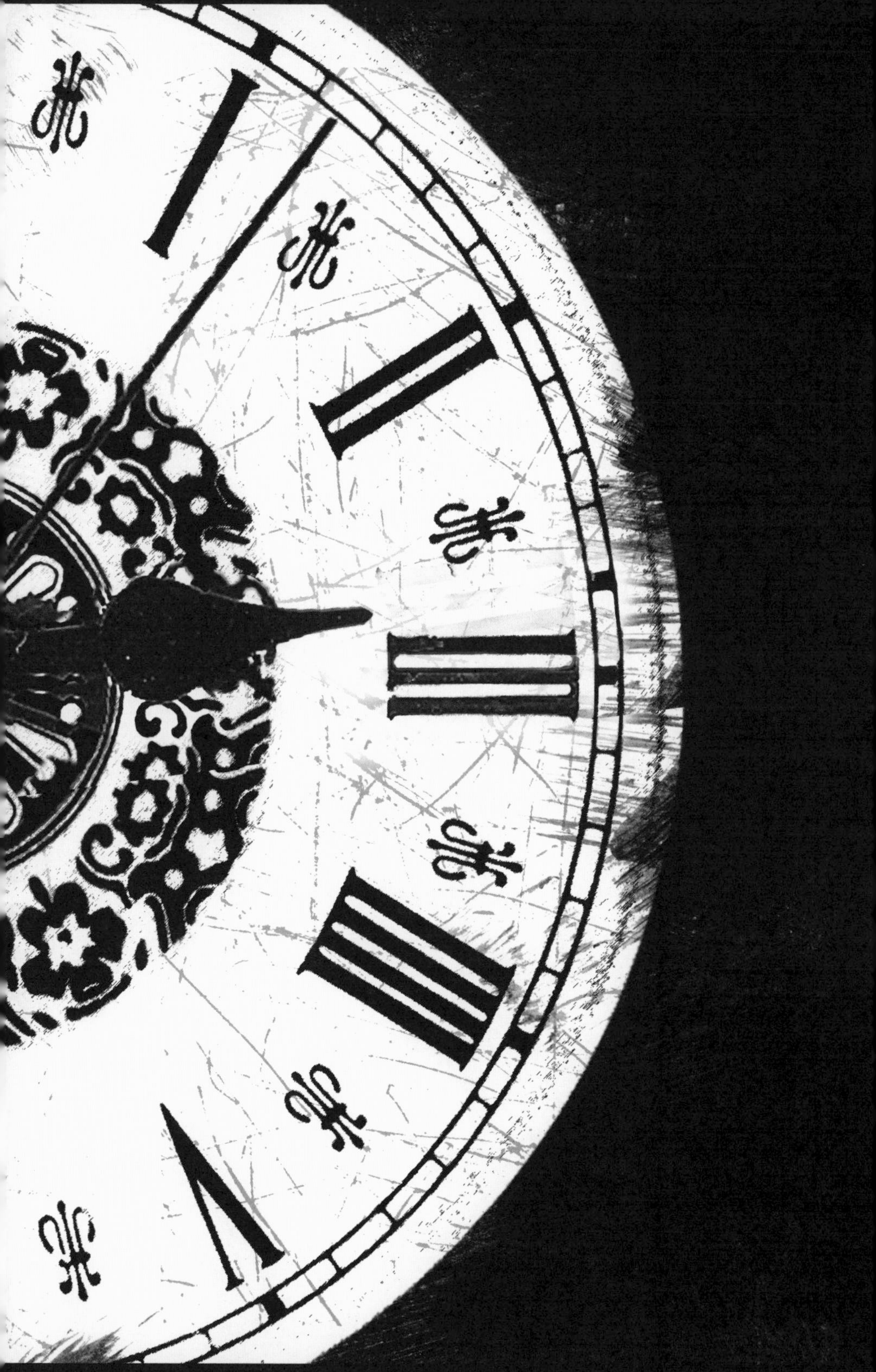

Far above Erik's room, the winter thunderstorm clattered against the roof tiles and shook the walls from side to side. Rods of black rain hammered down from the night sky like iron spikes, beating against the narrow windows and rattling the shutters. It was as if the storm had been sent to keep honest folk inside so the wicked could walk the earth unhindered as the water washed away every trace of the crimes they would commit.

Erik could hear the water glugging through the thick iron drainpipes that ran down the high stone walls to the ground far below. They coughed and spluttered like an old man wheezing his last before he gave up the ghost. The sound captured Erik and wouldn't let him go, forcing him to listen to every detail so he couldn't sleep.

Without warning the window burst open, blasting a frigid wind around the room.

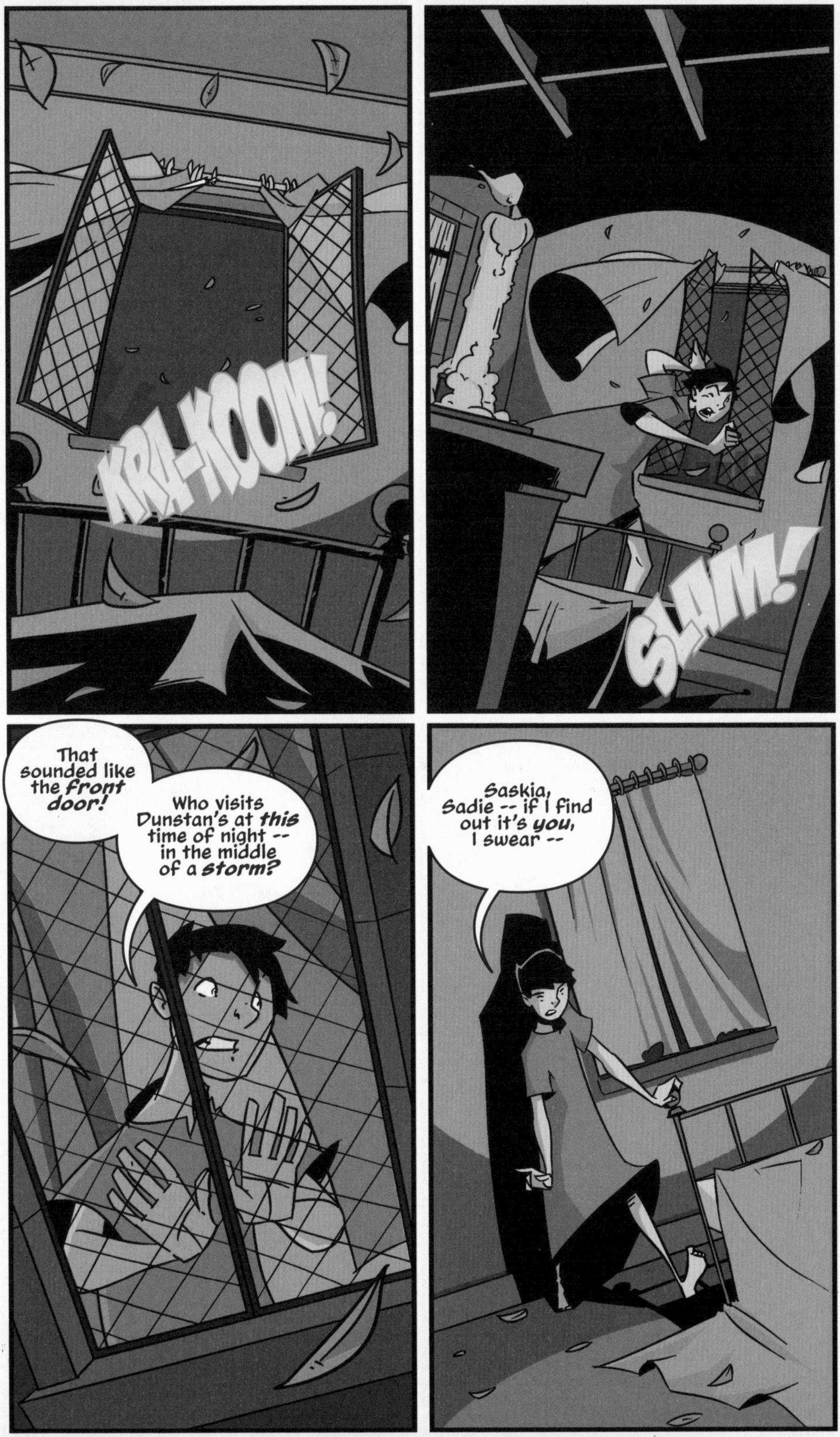
KRA-KOOM!
SLAM!
That sounded like the front door!
Who visits Dunstan's at this time of night -- in the middle of a storm?
Saskia, Sadie -- if I find out it's you, I swear --

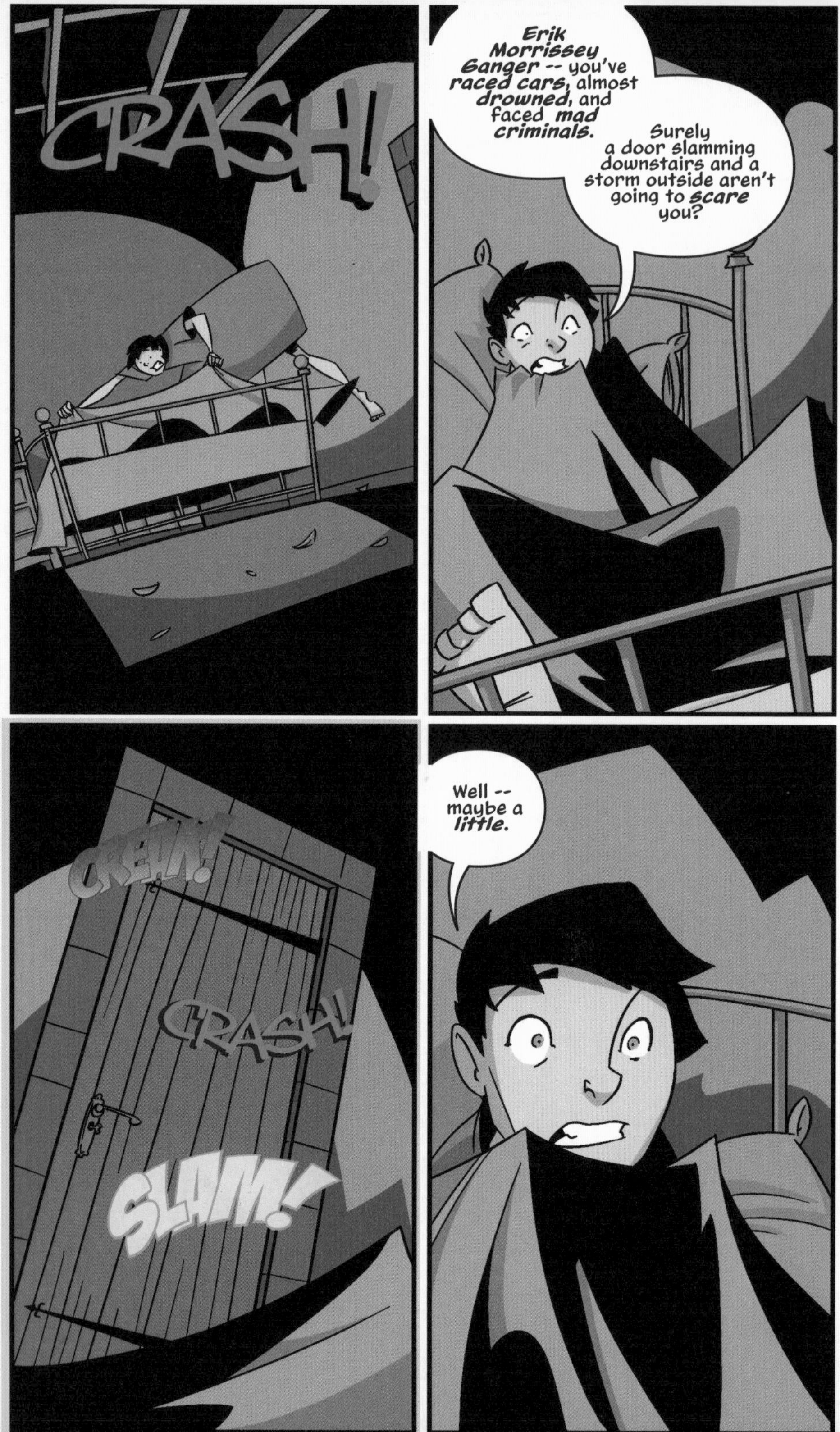
CRASH!
Erik Morrissey Ganger -- you've raced cars, almost drowned, and faced mad criminals.
Surely a door slamming downstairs and a storm outside aren't going to scare you?
CREAK!
CRASH!
SLAM!
Well -- maybe a little.

Erik stared at the door to his room. In the candlelight the door handle shimmered for a moment as if it had been shaken by an icy hand. He was not sure if he had really seen it happen or if this was part of a waking dream. A sudden, sharp  **bang**

echoed up the spiral staircase and then down again. Erik leaped from his bed and grabbed the poker from the fireplace as the storm outside began to roar like a hurricane.

Erik could feel his heart beating with panic in his chest, his blood pulsing heavily through the veins in his neck. He walked to the door of the room, twisted the key in the lock, and with trembling fingers turned the handle.

"Is there anybody there?"

he asked as he opened the door and peered into the short corridor that formed a narrow landing outside his room. "Is there—"

His words were cut short by another loud bang, and this time Erik recognized the angry sound of a door being slammed shut. The echo ran swiftly up and down the spiral staircase like an unseen creature. Suddenly Erik was pushed back into his room by a gigantic gust of wind that blew open his door and made the flames of the fire leap up the chimney. As he lay on the floor, poker in hand, he heard above the wind the sound of something being dragged over the cold stone entrance hall below. Jumping to his feet, he pushed against the door and the howling gale that screamed and hissed around him. The door held fast as if the weight of a strange beast were being forced against it.

The wind tore about the room, sending up books, papers, and anything in its way. Flames and coal were sucked slowly up the chimney as Erik strained against the door.

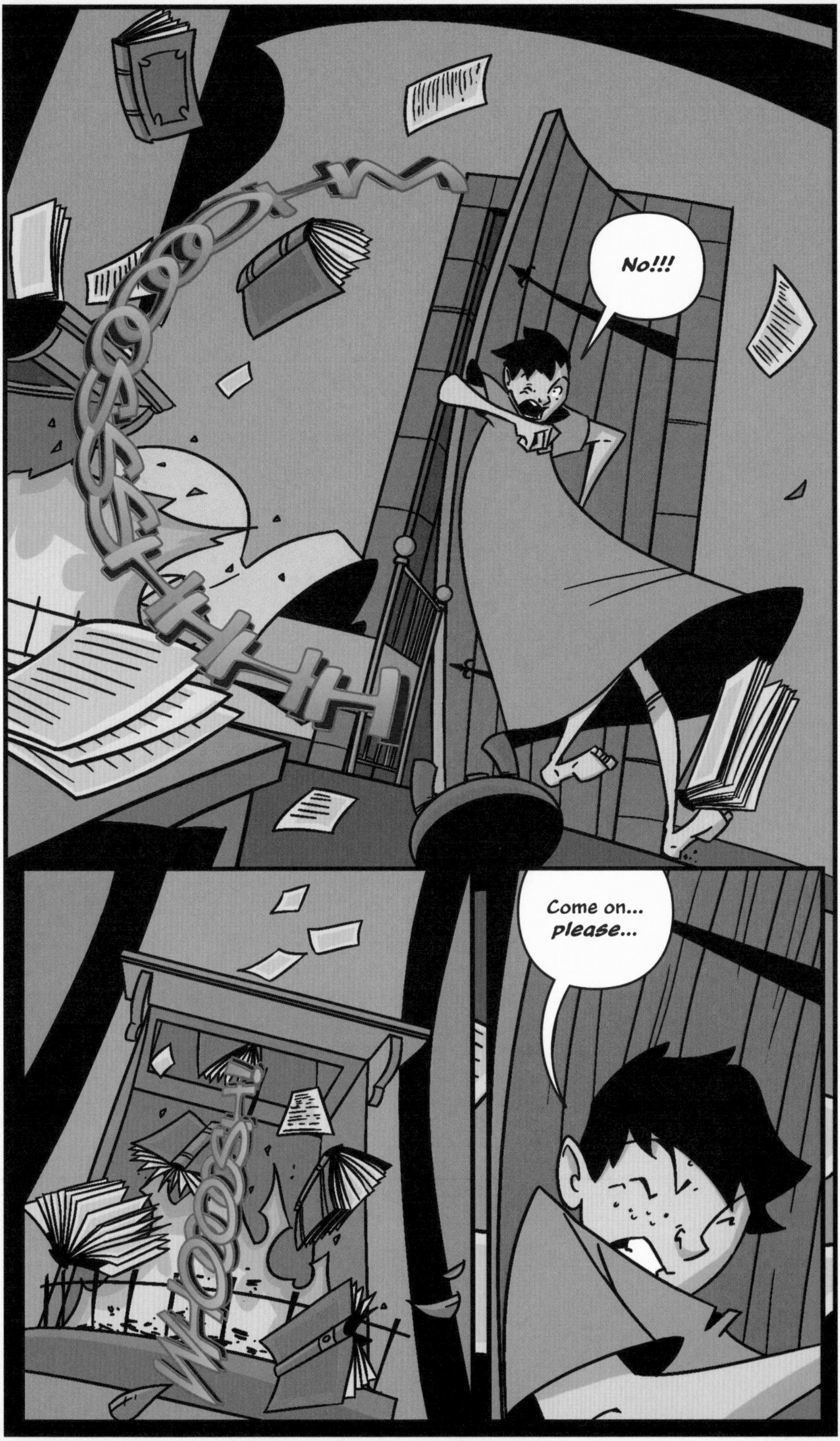
No!!!
Come on... please...

Erik pushed and pushed. The wind beat against him as it rushed up the high tower like a spiraling cyclone. Coal and ash flew up the chimney as the flames disappeared, leaving an empty grate. He pushed harder. The door moved slowly. Then all at once it flew back and slammed shut. Erik fell to his knees. He rose quickly, turned, and locked the door. Then as fast as he could, he took the old wooden chair from beside his bed and wedged it under the handle. He waited for a moment, listening to the rain. Outside, the wind howled viciously as though trying to break through the shuttered window again. His door shook once more, and then as quickly as the fury had come, it was gone. The rain fell softly as the howling wind seemed to just die away.

Unsure as to what had happened, Erik dressed quickly. He pulled on a starched shirt, itchy pants, sturdy black shoes, an overcoat, and a hat. He grabbed a flashlight and faced the door, hesitating for just a moment, wondering if the wind would return. Then he strode forward, removed the chair, and reached for the key.

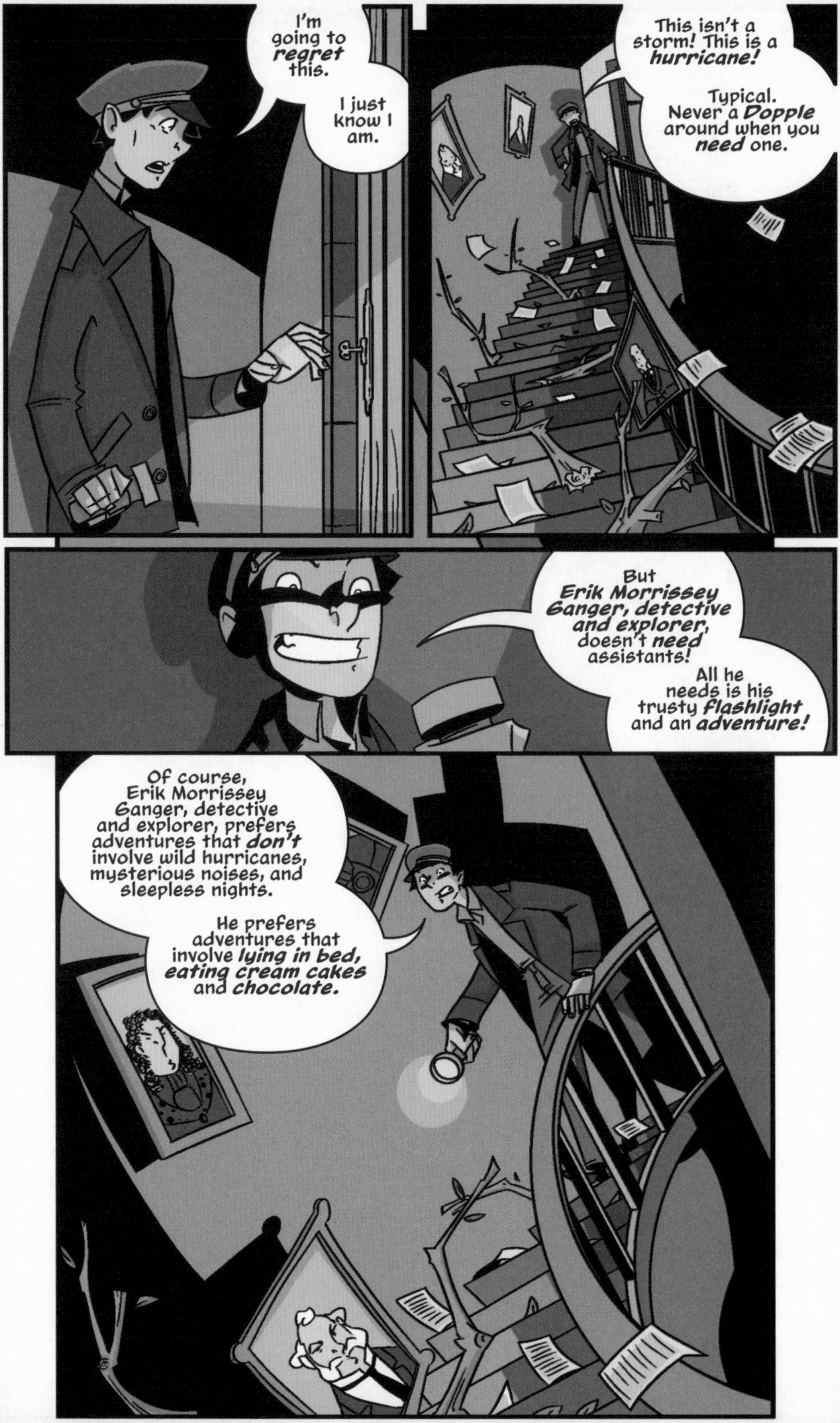
I'm going to *regret* this.
I just know I am.
This isn't a storm! This is a *hurricane!*
Typical. Never a *Dopple* around when you *need* one.
But *Erik Morrissey Ganger, detective and explorer,* doesn't *need* assistants!
All he needs is his trusty *flashlight* and an *adventure!*
Of course, Erik Morrissey Ganger, detective and explorer, prefers adventures that *don't* involve wild hurricanes, mysterious noises, and sleepless nights.
He prefers adventures that involve *lying in bed, eating cream cakes* and *chocolate.*

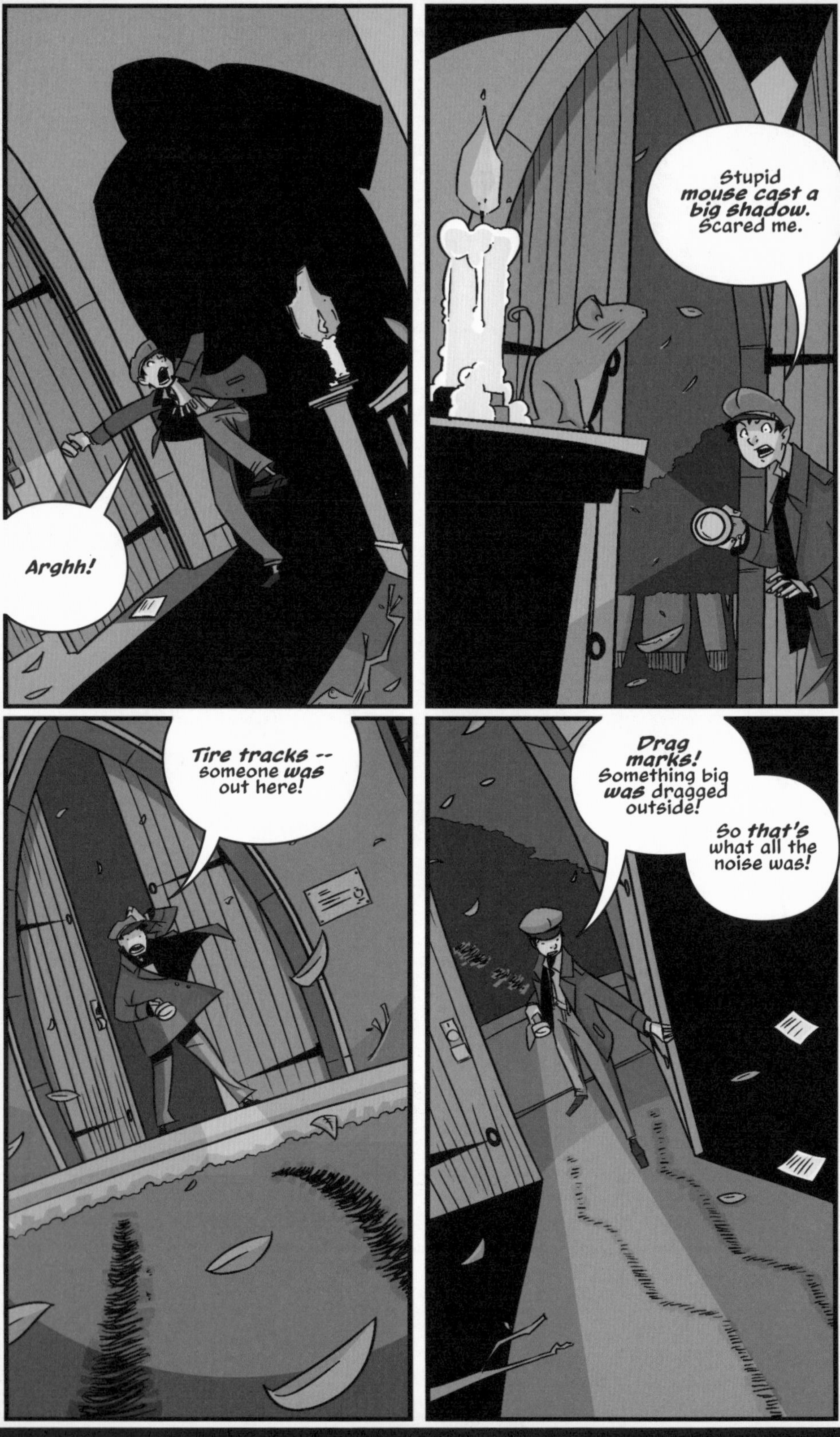
Arghh!
Stupid mouse cast a big shadow. Scared me.
Tire tracks -- someone was out here!
Drag marks! Something big was dragged outside!
So that's what all the noise was!

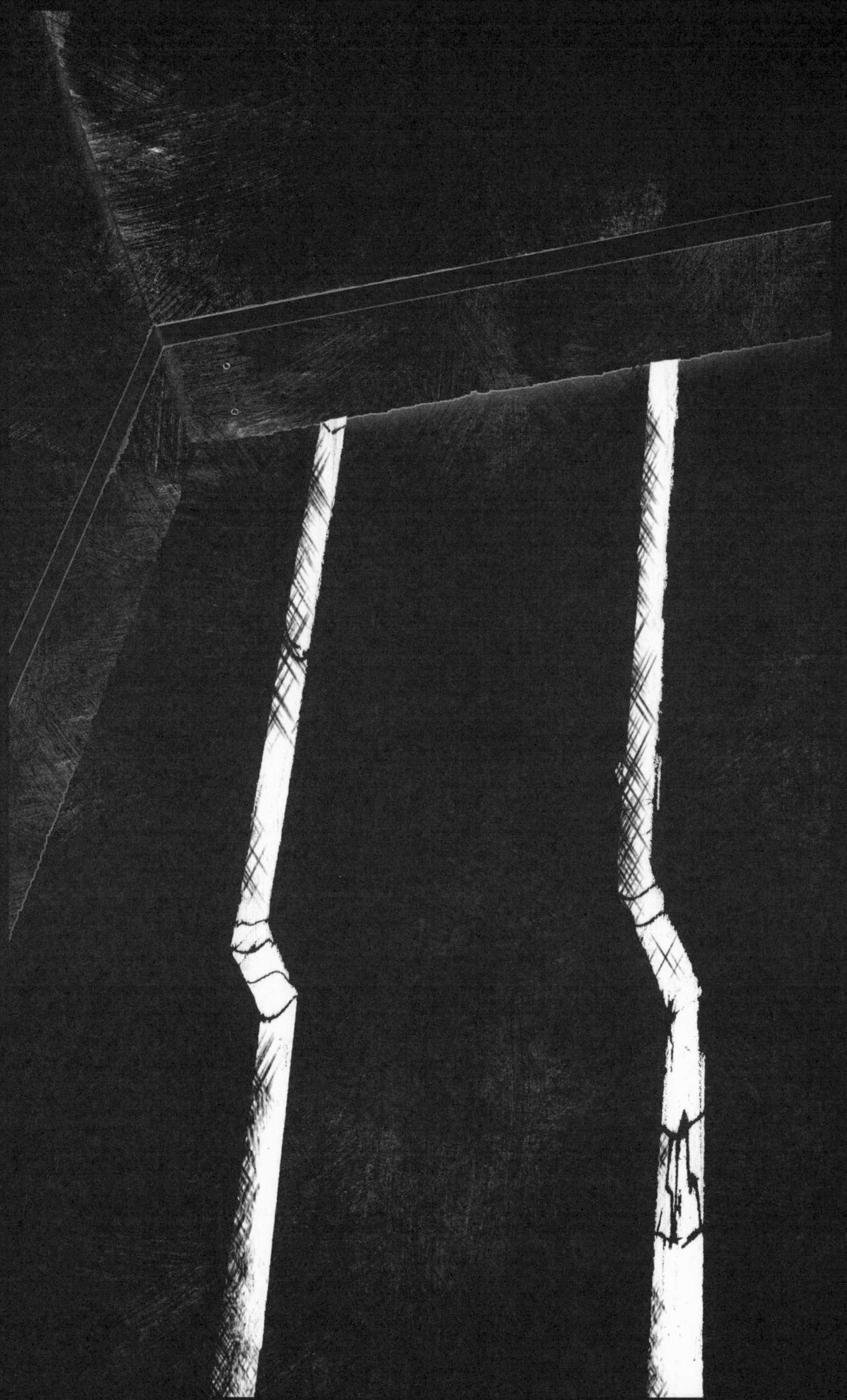

The drag marks ended at a solid stone wall and seemed to disappear behind it. It looked like some large object had been miraculously pulled through solid stone, across the slab floor, and then outside. Nervously Erik went to the wall and examined the marks. Each was exactly an inch wide. With a long finger he rubbed the stone. The marks had scraped the surface.

"Heavy," he said in a whisper, not sure if whoever had dragged the object away was still nearby. "It must have—" Erik stopped abruptly. From outside he heard the sound of footsteps on the gravel drive. Someone was coming. Quickly and quietly, he switched off his flashlight, sank back into the dark alcove under the stairs, and pressed himself against the cold stone as he held his breath.

He knew that no one from Isambard Dunstan's should be out at that time of night. The headmistress, Miss Rimmer, would see to that. All children must be in bed by seven o'clock and all staff must be in their rooms by ten, she always said. Any child caught out of bed after lights-out would be sent to the tower and locked in the cold, dank room at the very top until morning. It was Erik's job to make sure that no child escaped from the tower. Apart from sweeping, cleaning, and attending the occasional class, Erik Morrissey Ganger, the only boy at Isambard Dunstan's School for Wayward Children, was to keep the tower room ready and guard it.

But when a wayward child was being punished, Erik had been known to sneak up the tower stairs to make sure she was comfortable and to keep her from growing afraid. Occasionally he would even give the offender a spare key so she could come and go as she wished.

Now, as Erik hid in the shadows, he thought about the last time he had freed someone from the tower. Sadie Dopple and her identical twin sister, Saskia, were well known at Dunstan's for creating mischief and causing destruction, and they had become the bane of Miss Rimmer's existence. When Saskia was sent to live with Muzz Elliott, the famous but eccentric author, at Spaniards House, Erik had rescued Sadie from the tower so they could find Saskia. Disrupting the whole school in their escape, the pair had been chased across Hampstead Heath by Mr. Martinet, the vilest teacher at Dunstan's, and Hercules Kobold, a nasty man with a gigantic bloodhound. Then they were kidnapped by the Great Potemkin, the magician of Hampstead; they escaped in a police van, crashed into a pond, and then rescued Saskia and Muzz Elliott from some vicious treasure seekers who wanted them dead.

It had been two weeks since Erik and the Dopples had returned to Dunstan's. Muzz Elliott had sent them back to the school so she could finish her latest novel. But she had invited Erik and the twins to Spaniards House every weekend since their return.

Now, from the darkness of his hiding place, Erik's thoughts were interrupted by the sound of the footsteps getting closer. They crossed the gravel drive, seemed to stop momentarily on the bottom step, and then continued up the three stone stairs and through the large wooden door.

Erik listened intently, trying to picture who it might be. He imagined a short man as wide as the door, in a long, dirty coat with a wet, dripping hat. He pictured the man's thickset face with gloating eyes.

Erik waited. He could hear the man breathing heavily.

"Can't be hanging around," the man whispered as a gentler, lighter scurry of footsteps crossed the gravel. "I got the car out of the way. I don't think we need it to get the rest of the stuff."

There was a grunted reply, almost like a cough.

"We'll have to be quick. The storm has stopped, and we can't have anyone interfering," the first man said sharply.

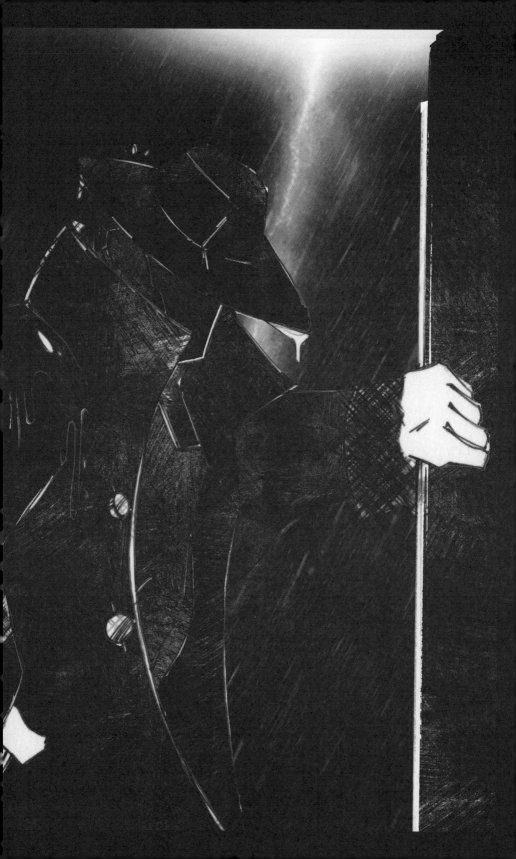

"Villains," thought Erik.

The boy held his breath and waited for them to move.

"No one will interfere tonight," said a second, softer voice. "Sleeping like babies, the lot of them."

Crouched in the dark, Erik remained still, thinking hard. He wasn't sure if he had heard the voice before, but it sent a chill up the back of his neck.

"Just one more trip and we'll be away for good," said the first man. Judging from the sound of the conversation, Erik figured the men were coming up the steps and into the hallway of the tower.

"Don't like this place.

Gives me the creeps," the first man said under his breath.

In two paces the man was right next to Erik. In the dim light from the open door, Erik could see a pair of black boots. They were worn down at the sides, as if the man walked in a peculiar way. The bottoms of his trousers were neat and trimmed with leather, and just as Erik had imagined, the man was wearing a long coat that nearly touched his boots.

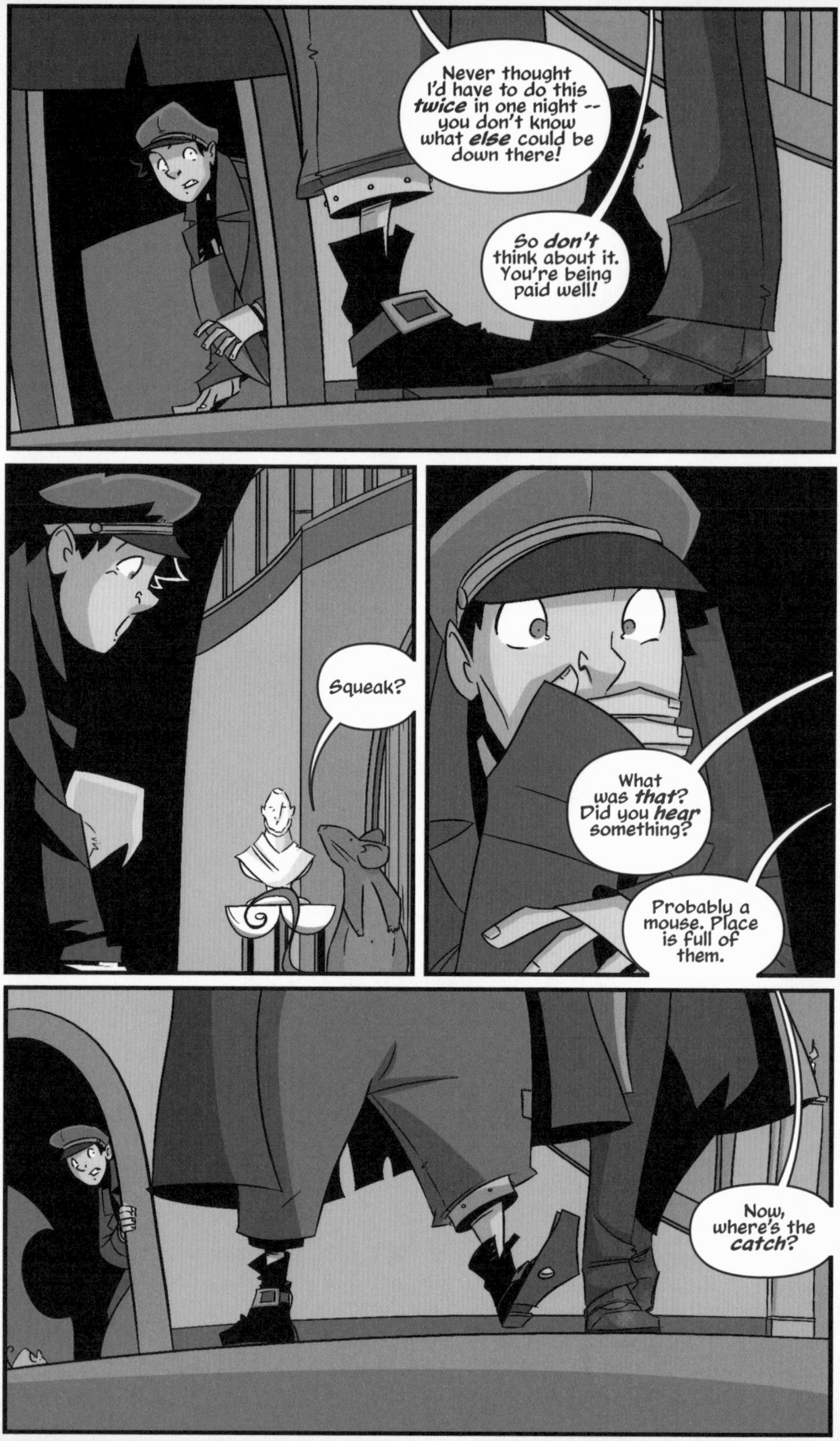
Never thought I'd have to do this *twice* in one night -- you don't know what *else* could be down there!
So *don't* think about it. You're being paid well!
Squeak?
What was *that*? Did you *hear* something?
Probably a mouse. Place is full of them.
Now, where's the *catch*?

"It's just here," the man in the boots said. The hem of his coat rose slightly, and Erik thought he must be reaching for something.

"Be quick," came the reply. Erik saw the patent leather shoes of the other man dancing excitedly upon the stone floor. His shoes were polished nicely but were flecked with spots of mud. As the man jigged from one foot to the other, something that looked like a feather fluttered to the ground beside him.

Erik couldn't see what the man in boots had done, but suddenly the wall began to move and a secret entrance appeared. It was just wide enough for the man to get through if he turned sideways and crouched down. Both he and his companion quickly disappeared through the opening, and Erik could see their backs crisscrossed by the shadows of the iron stair railing. He again felt unsettled, like he had seen the man with the patent leather shoes before.

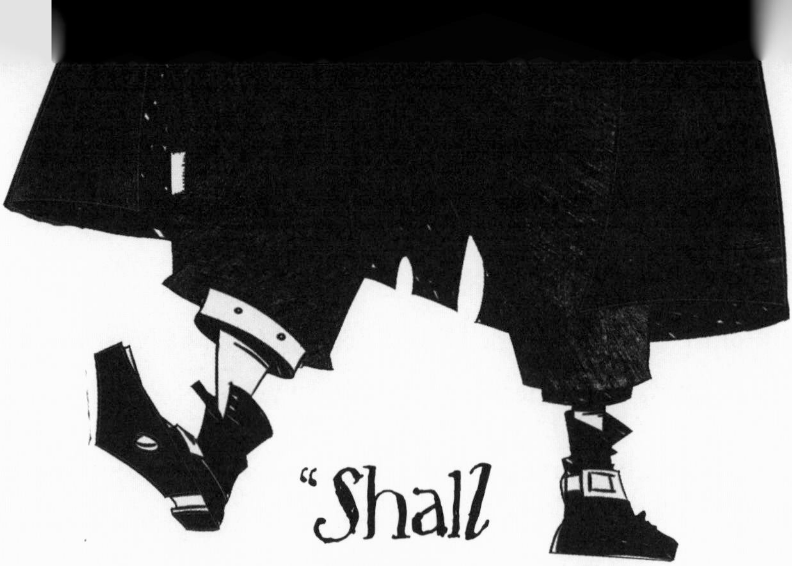

"Shall we leave it open?" The voice of the man in the boots floated back through the doorway.

"Best if we do," replied his companion.

"I don't like it in here," grumbled the man in boots. "There is something wicked about this place. Think of it: she was here for all that time. . . ." His whisper fell away, covered by their echoing footsteps.

Erik stayed hidden in the alcove until he could wait no longer. He slipped from his hiding place, through the portal, and inside the secret passageway. All was dark. From far away he could hear footsteps coming back toward him.

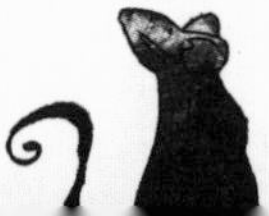

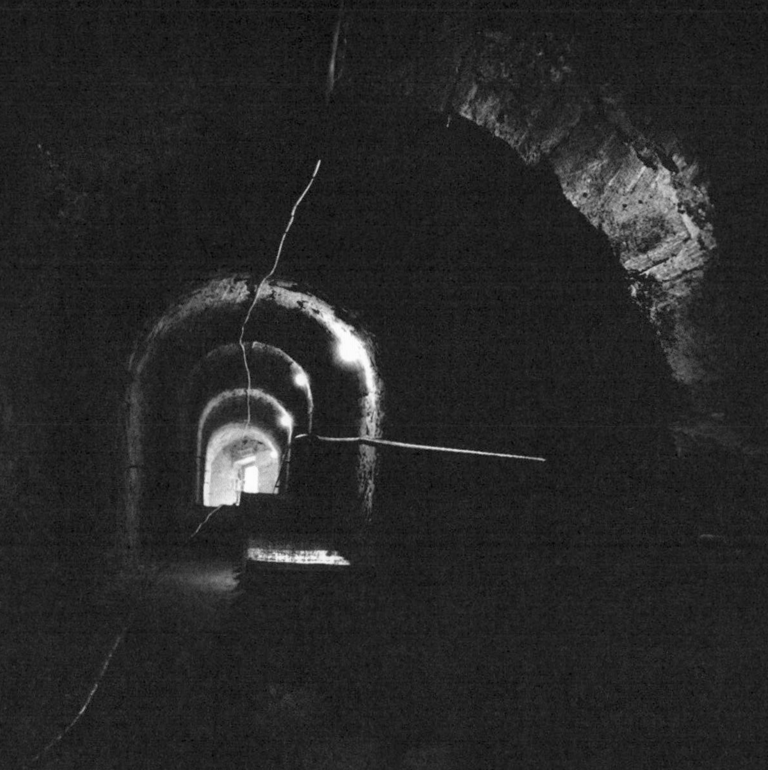

Chapter Two

A fear of Dark Places

IN THE DARK TUNNEL Erik could hear the sound of something being dragged along the floor; it sounded heavy and cumbersome. It rattled and clanged as it was pulled in his direction. Erik felt around and found a pile of what appeared to be rolled carpets, tied with twine. Quickly he ducked behind the pile. The rattling grew louder, bouncing off the tunnel walls in distorted echoes. It mingled with the muttering and wheezing of the two men and the steady drip of icy water falling from the vaulted roof.

drip

drip

drip

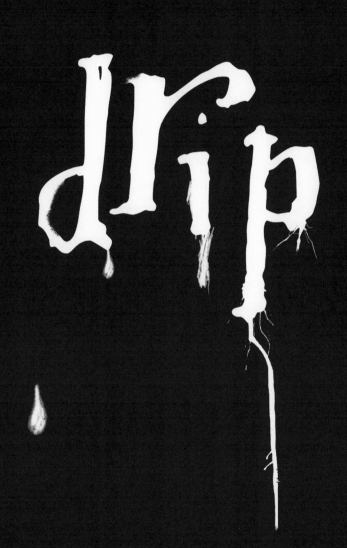

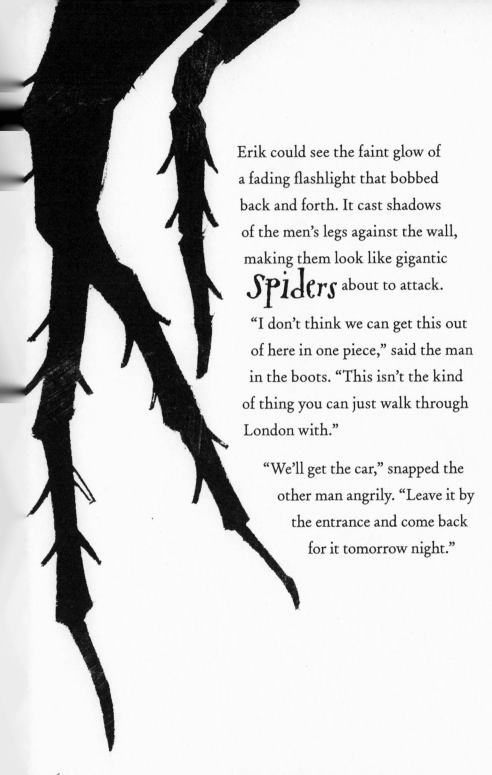

Erik could see the faint glow of
a fading flashlight that bobbed
back and forth. It cast shadows
of the men's legs against the wall,
making them look like gigantic
Spiders about to attack.

"I don't think we can get this out
of here in one piece," said the man
in the boots. "This isn't the kind
of thing you can just walk through
London with."

"We'll get the car," snapped the
other man angrily. "Leave it by
the entrance and come back
for it tomorrow night."

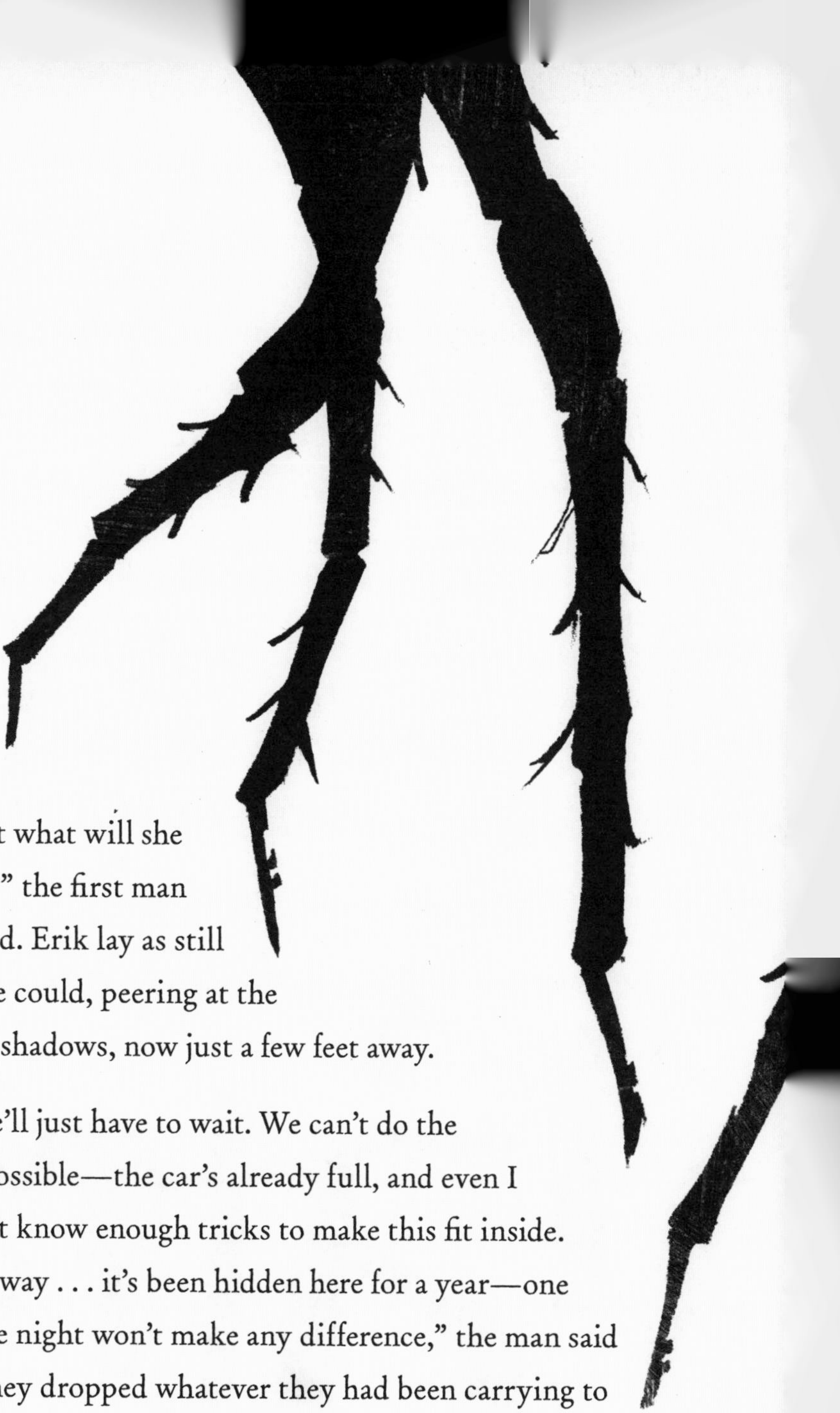

"But what will she say?" the first man asked. Erik lay as still as he could, peering at the two shadows, now just a few feet away.

"She'll just have to wait. We can't do the impossible—the car's already full, and even I don't know enough tricks to make this fit inside. Anyway . . . it's been hidden here for a year—one more night won't make any difference," the man said as they dropped whatever they had been carrying to the floor.

Erik leaned forward and squinted in an effort to see the mysterious object. His shoulder nudged one of the carpet rolls loose. He grabbed for it but missed, instead knocking another roll. Suddenly, everything that had formed his hiding place fell apart around him.

"What was that?" called the man in the patent leather shoes.

"Take a look yourself," said his companion, shining the fading light almost to where Erik crouched, motionless.

"Can't see a thing," came the reply. "Could be . . .

rats?"

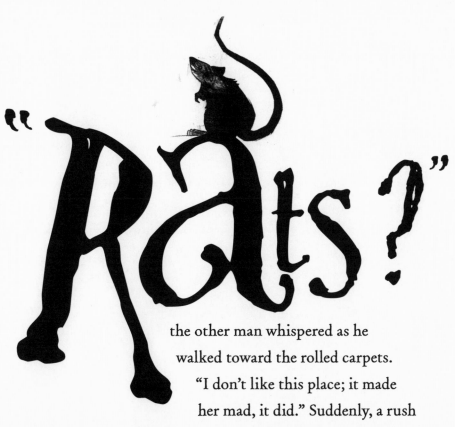

"Rats?"

the other man whispered as he
walked toward the rolled carpets.
"I don't like this place; it made
her mad, it did." Suddenly, a rush
of wind blew through the tunnel, and the man stopped
to listen. "Was that you?" he asked his companion. He
stooped and hefted up a large, coffin-like box, propping it
against the wall. "I hate the dark—there are things hiding
in the dark. . . ."

"We'll come back tomorrow—make sure the coast is
clear—that's what we'll have to do. Can't be staying here
much longer," said the man in the patent leather shoes.

His companion didn't reply. Erik saw the flashlight beam
shimmer and then fade as the two men left the tunnel.

A deep

sense of

dread

welled up in the pit
of Erik's stomach, as he
knew he was soon to
be trapped. The sound
of the wall sliding
back into place
confirmed his
fears. Any trace of
light that had come
from beyond the
passageway was
now gone as Erik was
smothered in darkness.

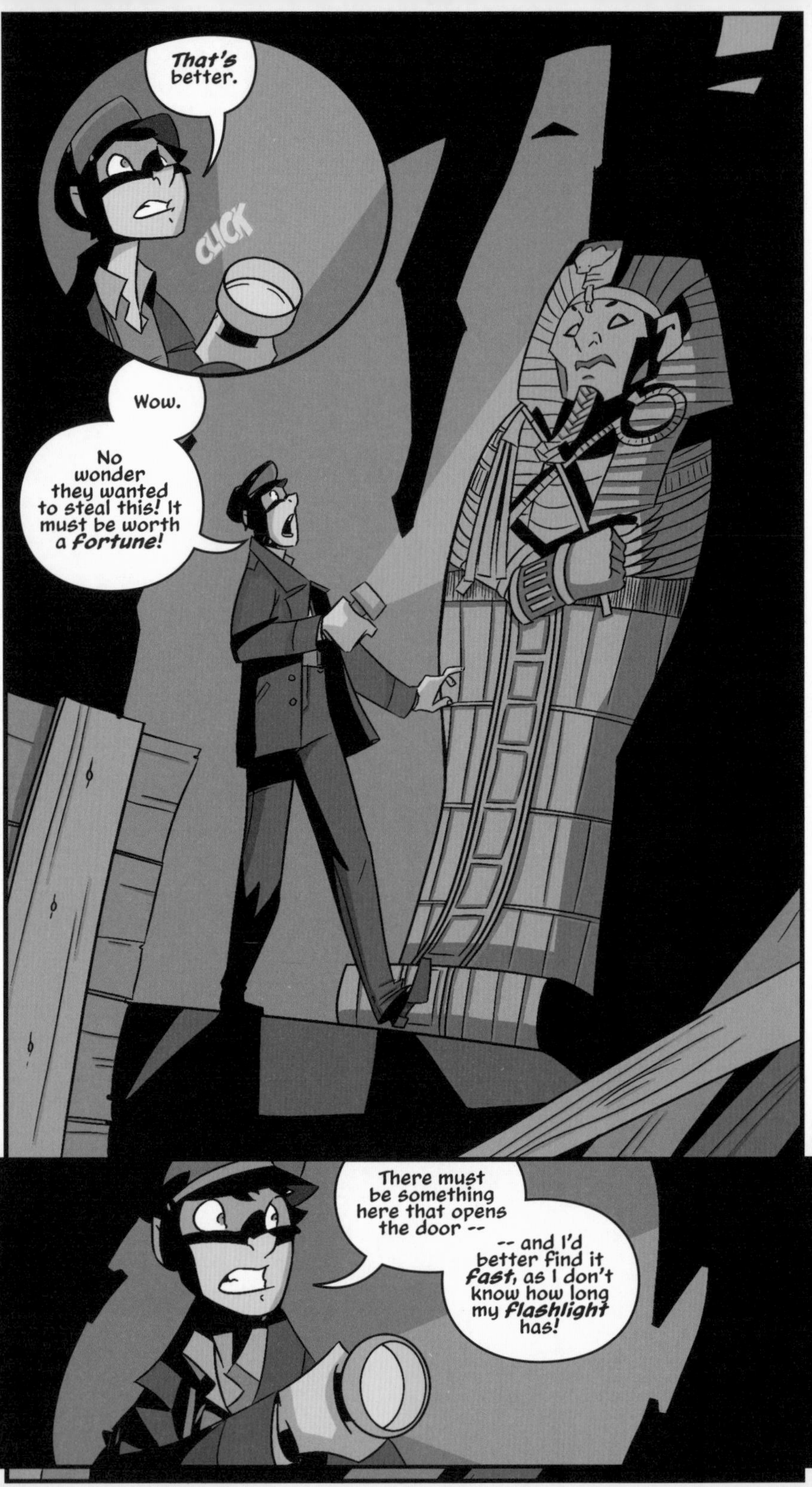
That's better.
CLICK
Wow.
No wonder they wanted to steal this! It must be worth a fortune!
There must be something here that opens the door --
-- and I'd better find it fast, as I don't know how long my flashlight has!

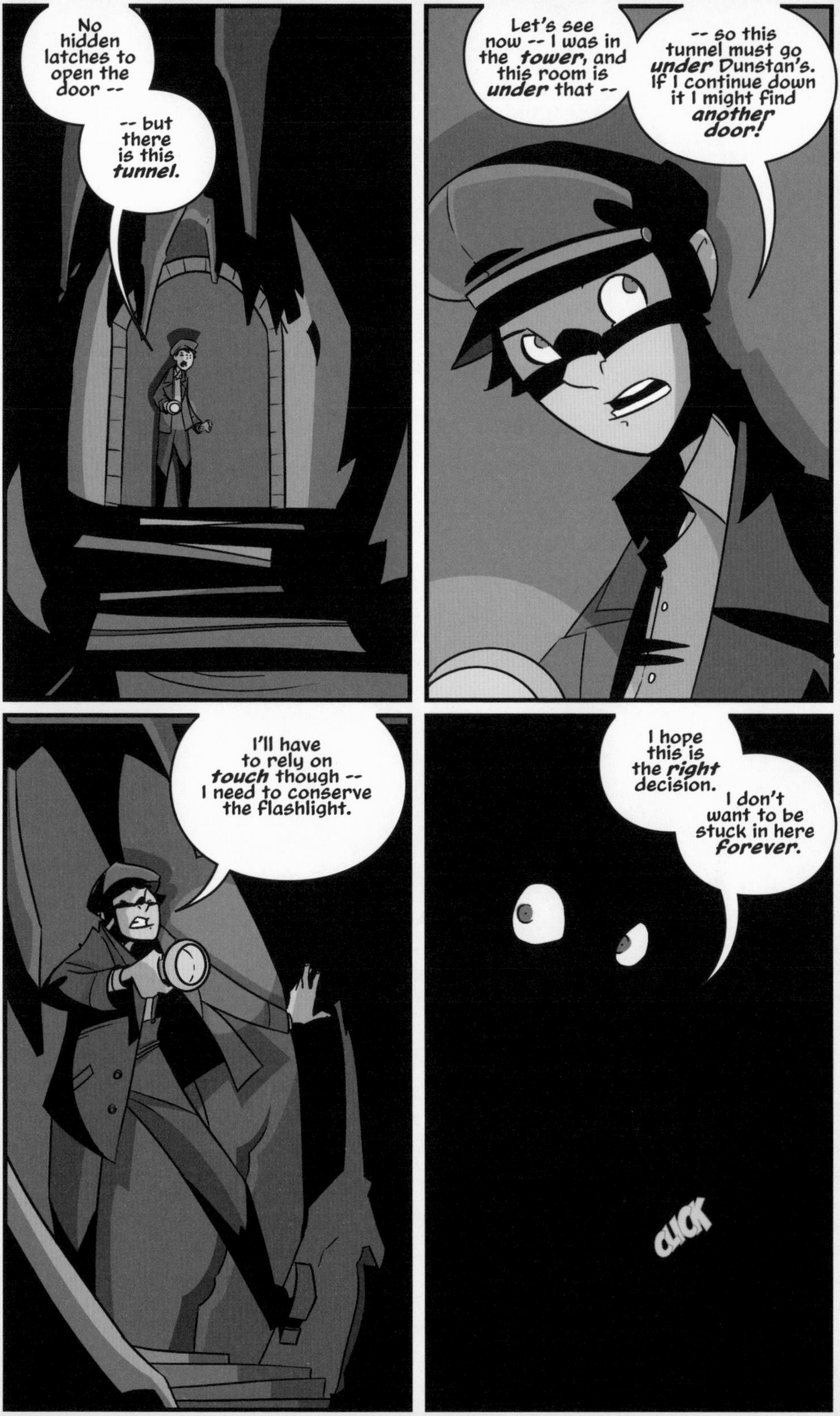
No hidden latches to open the door --
-- but there is this tunnel.
Let's see now -- I was in the tower, and this room is under that --
-- so this tunnel must go under Dunstan's. If I continue down it I might find another door!
I'll have to rely on touch though -- I need to conserve the flashlight.
I hope this is the right decision.
I don't want to be stuck in here forever.
CLICK

Erik walked on. He ran his hand along the damp wall
to find his way as he counted the paces. He walked in
complete blackness. Every now and then he would switch
on the flashlight and check the way ahead.

"I must be right under the hall by now," he said in a
whisper to break the silence.

Several more paces and two more bursts of light brought him to a bend in the tunnel. Erik fumbled his fingers along the wall and then stopped, trying to figure out what to do next. With his thumb, he etched out the shape of a brick as he scraped at the mortar.

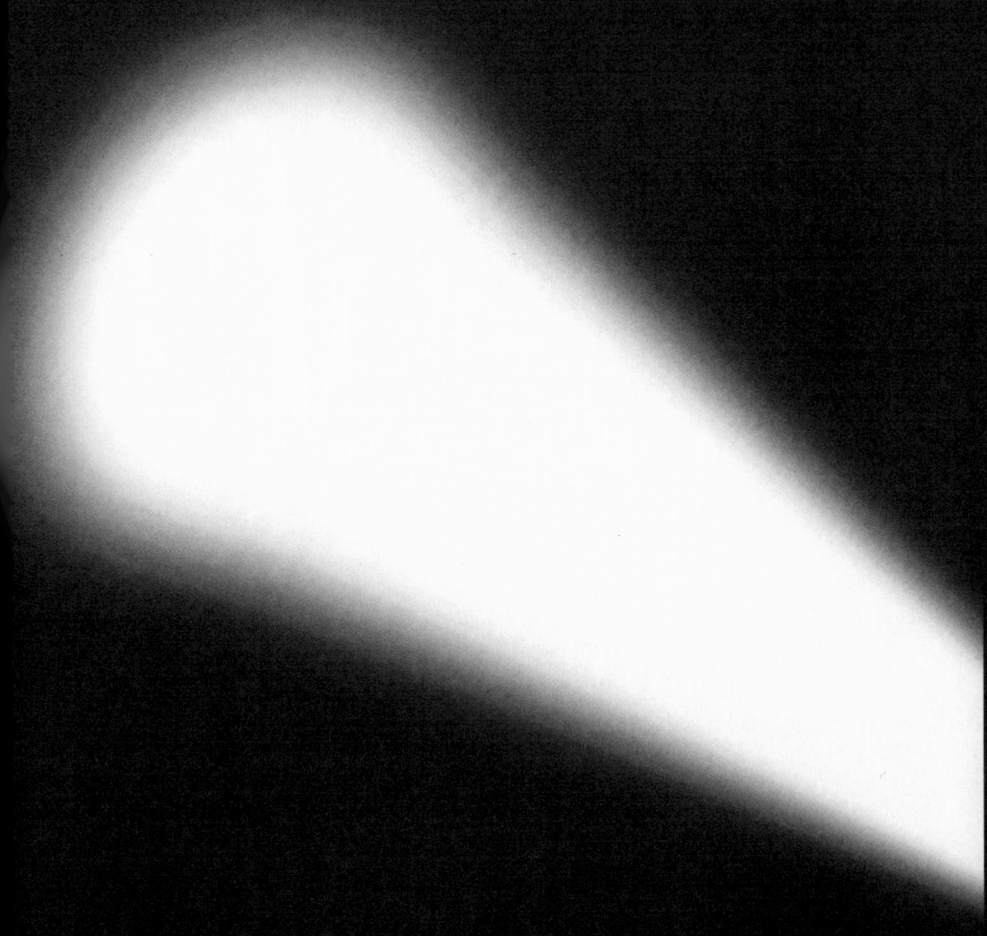

"What if I

can't get out?"

Erik said aloud. His fear echoed
through the tunnel and came
back as eerie half words.

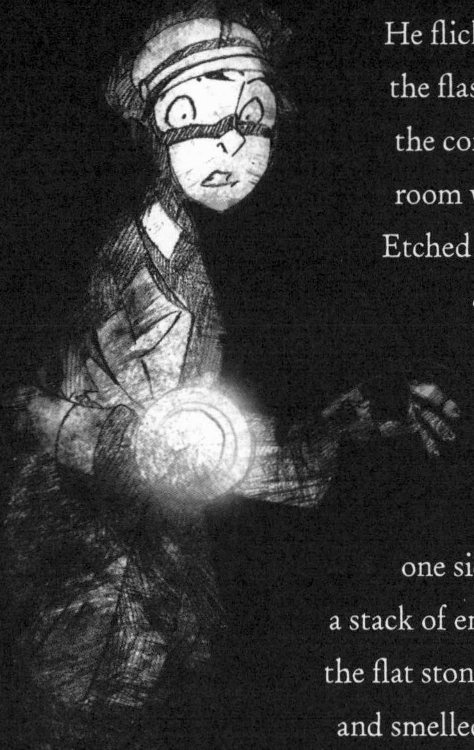

He flicked the switch on the flashlight and turned the corner. A long, low room was to his right. Etched into the jagged outline of the rocky wall, he could see the shape of what seemed to be a doorway. To one side of the doorway was a stack of empty shelves bolted to the flat stones. The room was cold and smelled of boiled cabbage. In the corner was an old desk. On the wall was a badly drawn picture of a boy, mounted in a gilded frame. The boy stared back at Erik with a lopsided smile as though he was the first visitor the boy had seen in many years.

Erik put his fingers in the crack that formed
the outline of the door. He pulled as hard as he
could, hoping that it would suddenly open and
he would be free. It held fast. He looked around
for something to trigger the lock and move the
stones. He could see nothing. Then, as he moved
his hand down the crack, his fingers touched
something sharp. Whatever it was had been forced
into the gap between two stones. It felt like crisp,
folded paper.

"What's this?" Erik asked as he pulled the paper
from the cranny.

Written on a faded envelope in black smudged ink
were the words, "To whom it may concern."

"It concerns me," Erik said, opening the envelope.

Inside was a letter written in the same neat
handwriting. In the dimming light of the
flashlight, he read as quickly as he could.

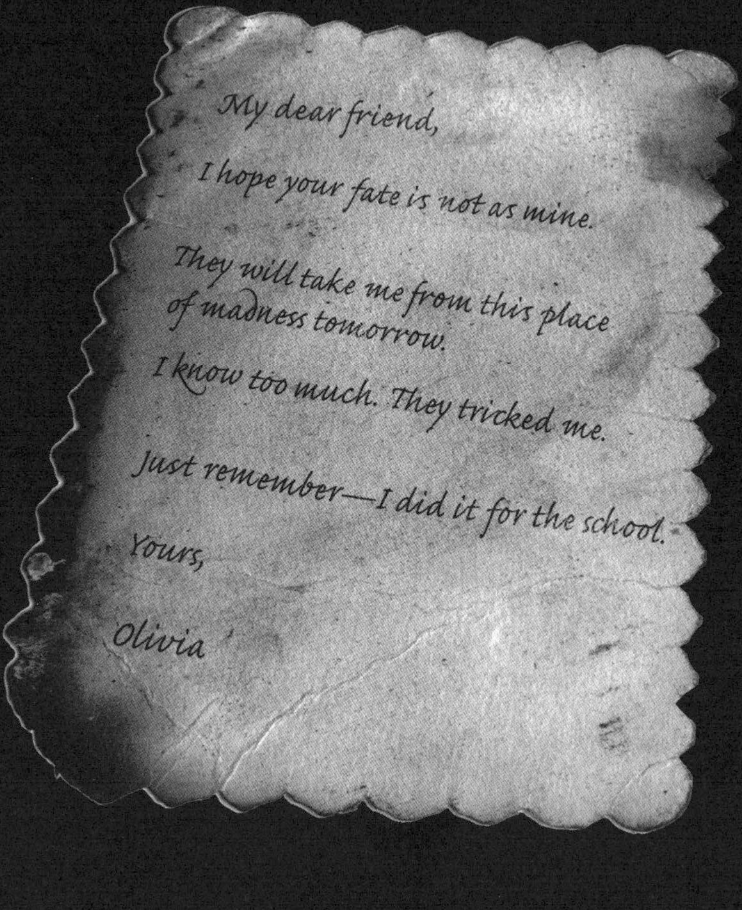

My dear friend,

I hope your fate is not as mine.

They will take me from this place of madness tomorrow.

I know too much. They tricked me.

Just remember—I did it for the school.

Yours,

Olivia

Erik read the letter over again until he had taken in every word. He knew he had seen the writing before.

"Olivia?" he asked out loud as the beam of his flashlight grew even dimmer. "It could only be . . ." He stopped, remembering the former headmistress.

Olivia Dart-Winston had disappeared from Isambard Dunstan's a year ago, on the day before Christmas Eve. In her room, all was as she had left it. There had been no note telling where she had gone. The police had been called, but a search of the ponds on Hampstead Heath had revealed nothing. Miss Olivia, as she was fondly known, had simply vanished.

Life at Dunstan's had been happy under the kind old woman's care—even Sadie and Saskia had managed to keep their mischief making under control and had exploded only once she was out of sight. Most people suspected that Miss Olivia had taken the train to Edinburgh and then into the Highlands to live with her nephew, but Sadie and Saskia presumed she had been murdered.

"It's her!"

Erik exclaimed as he read the name once more. His flashlight was now fading to its last glimmers of light. "Sadie and Saskia said Miss Olivia was dead. She'd been kidnapped and trapped down here. . . ."

As he spluttered the words, Erik was plunged into complete darkness. He shook the flashlight, hoping it would give just another second of light so he could find a way of escape. But it was too late. Erik turned in the blackness. He stumbled, then fell against an empty shelf. The shelf gave way and pushed down like a handle.

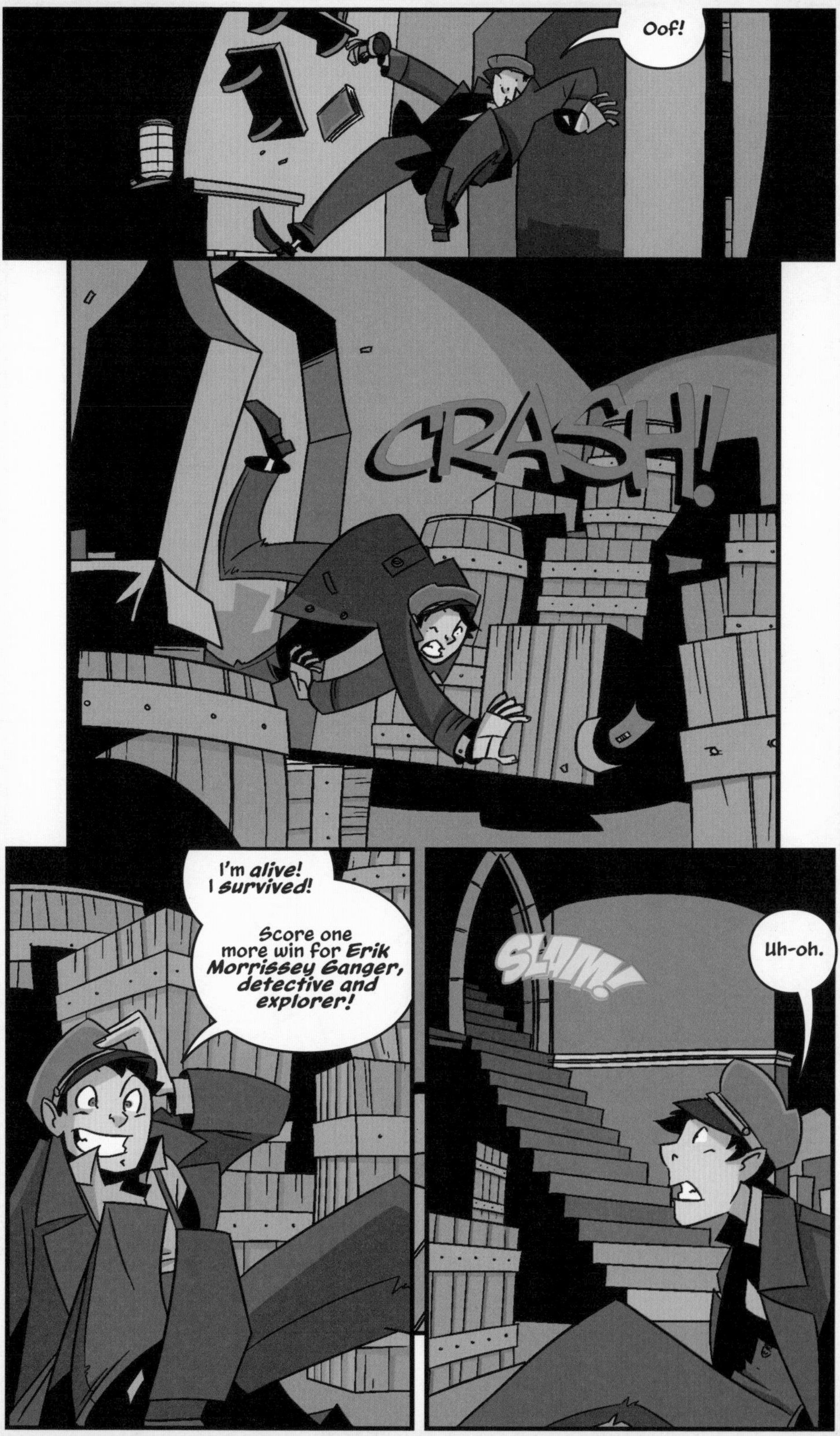
Oof!
CRASH!
I'm *alive!* I *survived!*
Score one more win for ***Erik Morrissey Ganger,*** ***detective and explorer!***
SLAM!
Uh-oh.

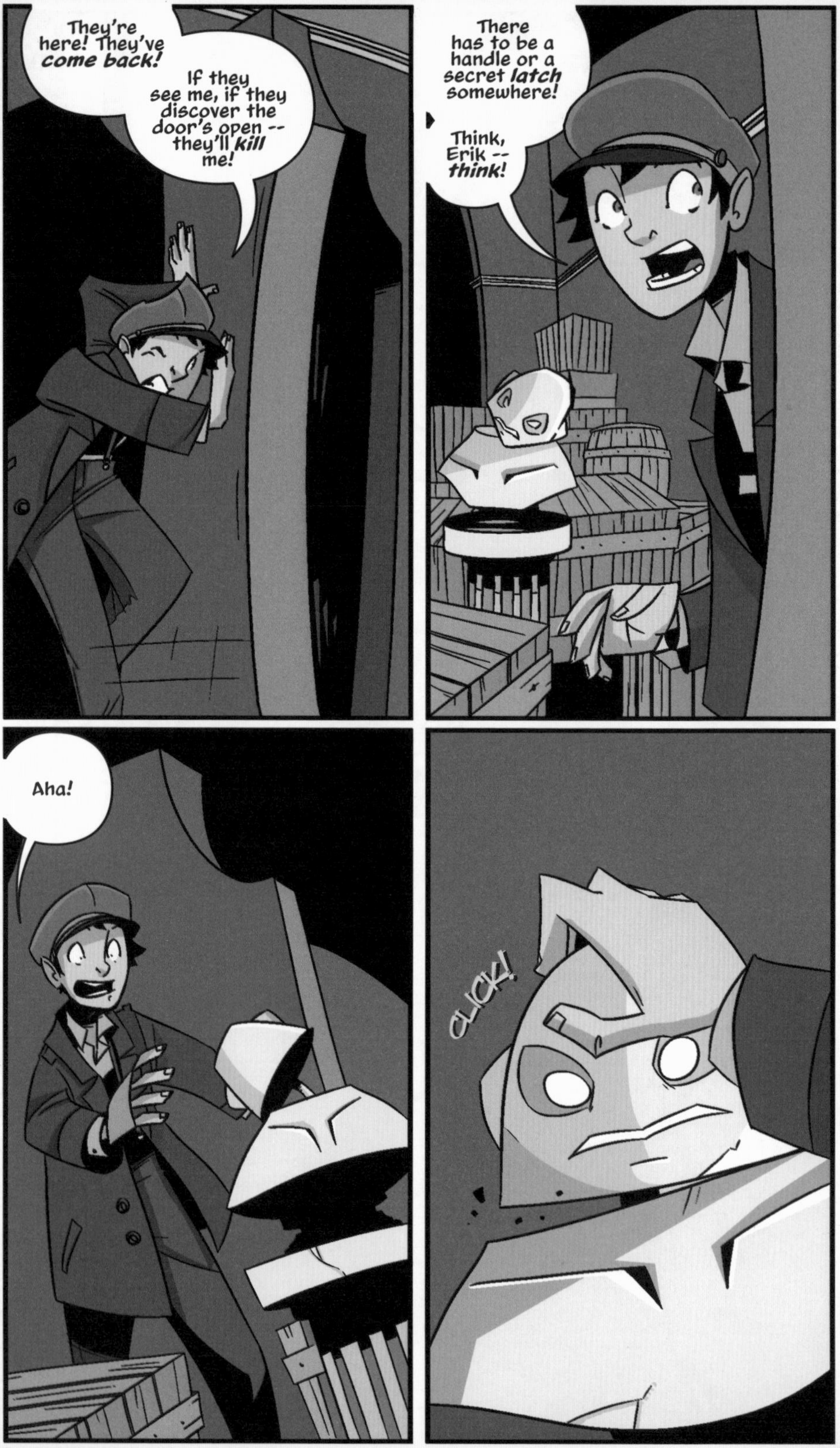
They're here! They've *come back!*
If they see me, if they discover the door's open -- they'll *kill* me!
There has to be a handle or a secret *latch* somewhere!
Think, Erik -- *think!*
Aha!
CLICK!

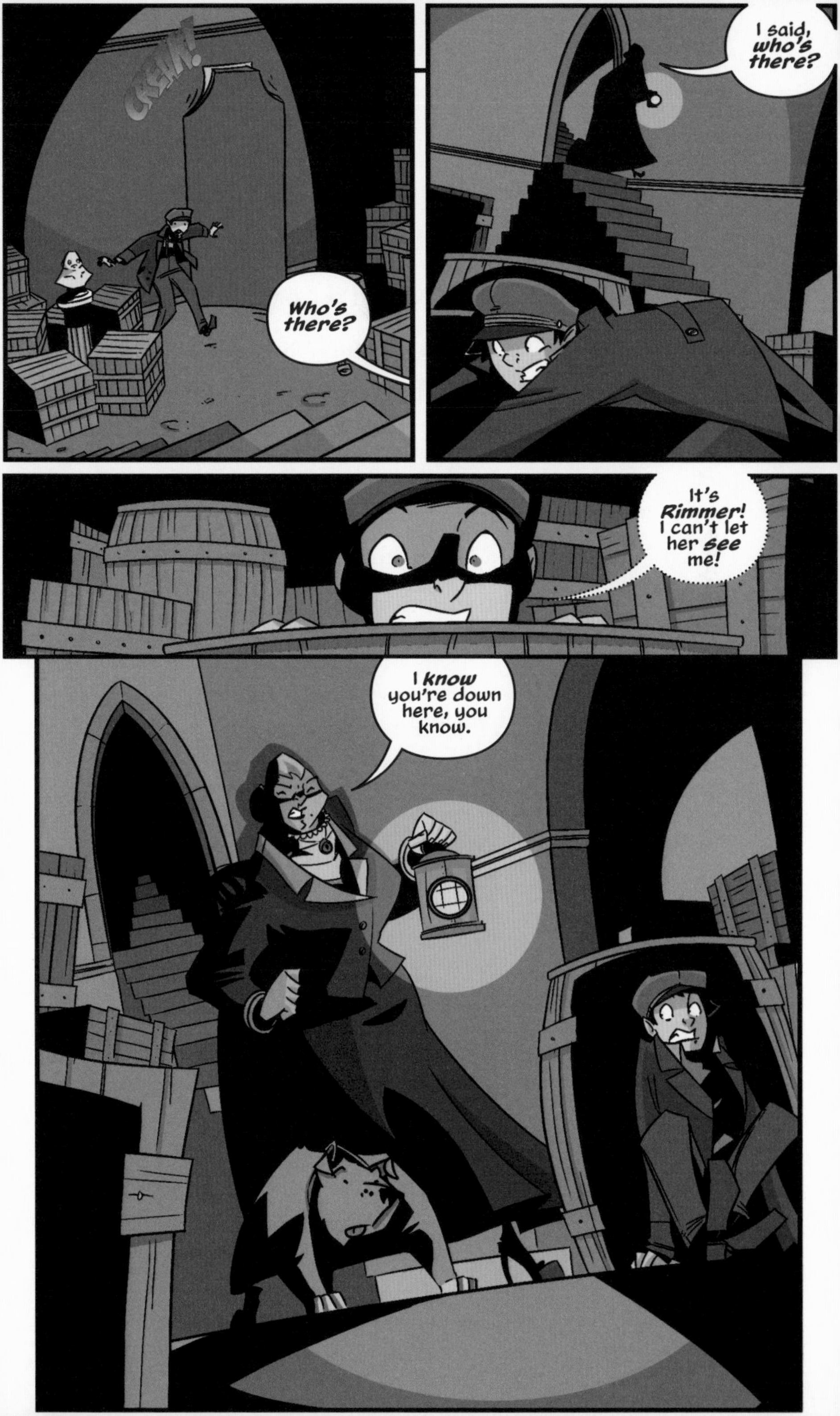

CREAK!
Who's there?
I said, who's there?
It's Rimmer! I can't let her see me!
I know you're down here, you know.

Erik remained motionless behind the barrel as Miss
Rimmer walked slowly toward him. Her ugly dog, Darcy,
led the way, constantly sniffing the ground. When she was
two feet from Erik's hiding place, Miss Rimmer stopped.
Erik heard the dog growl.

"What is it, Darcy?" Miss Rimmer asked in a cold,
quiet voice. "Have you found someone?" Erik hardly
dared to breathe.

Suddenly the dog yelped and ran off.

"Only a mouse," said Miss Rimmer quietly. She followed
her pet and soon disappeared into the darkness.

Chapter Three
Dorcas Potts

ERIK DIDN'T SLEEP for the rest of the night.
He sneaked back to his tiny room, avoiding Miss
Rimmer and her dreaded dog. Once there, he propped
himself against the wall and stared through the small
window at the trees that surrounded Dunstan's and the
road that ran along Hampstead Heath. The sycamores
seemed to reach up like long hands with gnarled bones.
The wind rattled their branches, and in the growing light
the twigs looked like thin fingers clacking together.

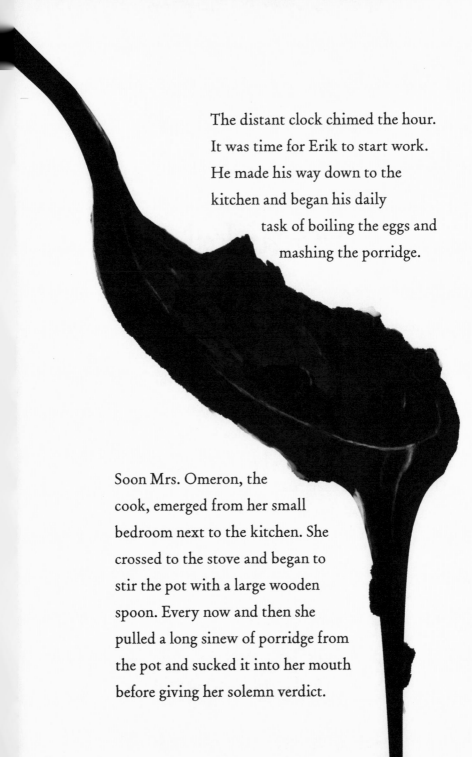

The distant clock chimed the hour. It was time for Erik to start work. He made his way down to the kitchen and began his daily task of boiling the eggs and mashing the porridge.

Soon Mrs. Omeron, the cook, emerged from her small bedroom next to the kitchen. She crossed to the stove and began to stir the pot with a large wooden spoon. Every now and then she pulled a long sinew of porridge from the pot and sucked it into her mouth before giving her solemn verdict.

"Lumpy,"

she barked at Erik as she fussed over the pots. She grumbled to herself as she worked. "Never trust a boy to make porridge when a woman can do it better."

Erik kept silent. He knew better than to say anything to her just yet. It was not safe to speak to Mrs. Omeron until she had drunk thirteen cups of tea and had taken her fill of three fried eggs and several slices of toast. To have a conversation before that time would be risking death, or even worse, imprisonment in the vegetable pantry. The pantry was situated by the cellar steps and had the smell of a vile, smoldering compost heap.

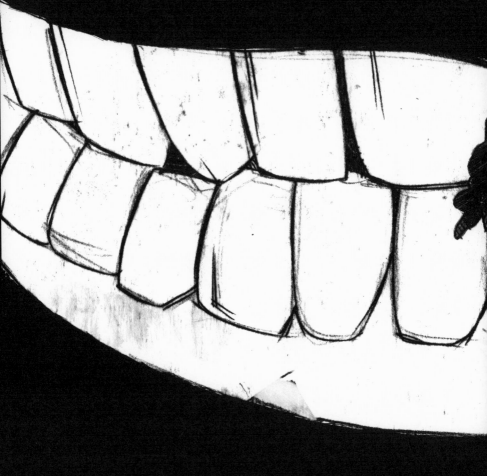

"I feel much better," announced Mrs. Omeron, gulping down several bites of toast. Erik put the thought of spending time in the stinking pantry from his mind. "You look like you've seen a ghost or something," she went on as she drank the dregs of her last cup of tea and picked a piece of egg from the gap between her teeth. "What have you been up to?" she asked, giving Erik a look with what she called her "all-knowing eye."

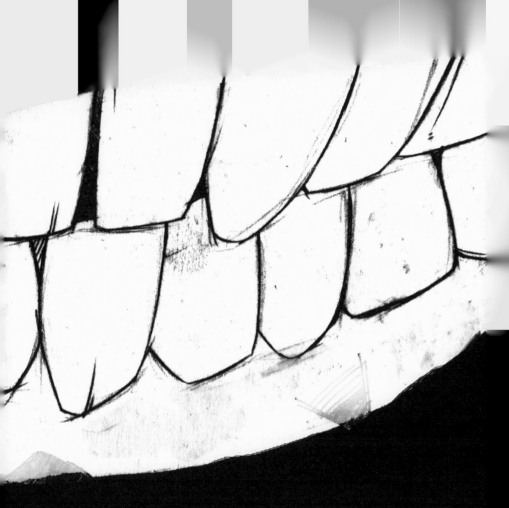

"Nothing," he muttered. Mrs. Omeron's eye followed him around the kitchen like a persistent wasp. "Bad storm last night kept me awake, that's all," he continued quickly. She handed him the bubbling porridge to carry into the refectory.

"Storm?" she inquired vacantly. "I never heard a thing."

"Rained a lot . . . thundered . . ." He paused before he asked, "Have you ever wondered what happened to Miss Olivia?"

"Miss Olivia?"

Her face had the panicked look of someone who had just been told she was going to die there and then. "Why should you want to know about Miss Olivia?"

"I was just curious," Erik muttered, wishing he had never said a word.

"Can't talk about her—forbidden by Miss Rimmer. What's done is done, that's what Rimmer said. Olivia's gone to Scotland to see some nephew of hers."

"But why didn't the police find her?"

"Police? Police?" she snapped. But then, lowering her voice, she added, "Some people think they were too busy trying to find the burglars who'd been robbing Lord Gervez next door. That's why they never found Miss Olivia. Couldn't be bothered with a poor old headmistress. Always the same: rich people snap their fingers, and the world comes running."

"What happened at Lord Gervez's house?" Erik asked casually, trying not to sound too interested.

"Ransacked. Things were taken—valuable things. But they never found out who did it, or how. I heard it was like the stuff just disappeared. Happened a little over a year ago now."

Mrs. Omeron stopped and raised her brow as she looked at Erik. He decided he'd better get moving before Mrs. Omeron scolded him for his curiosity. With his foot, he pushed open the door that led from the kitchen into the refectory. There was a rush of noise as he was greeted by the shrill voices of nearly two hundred girls impatiently waiting to be fed.

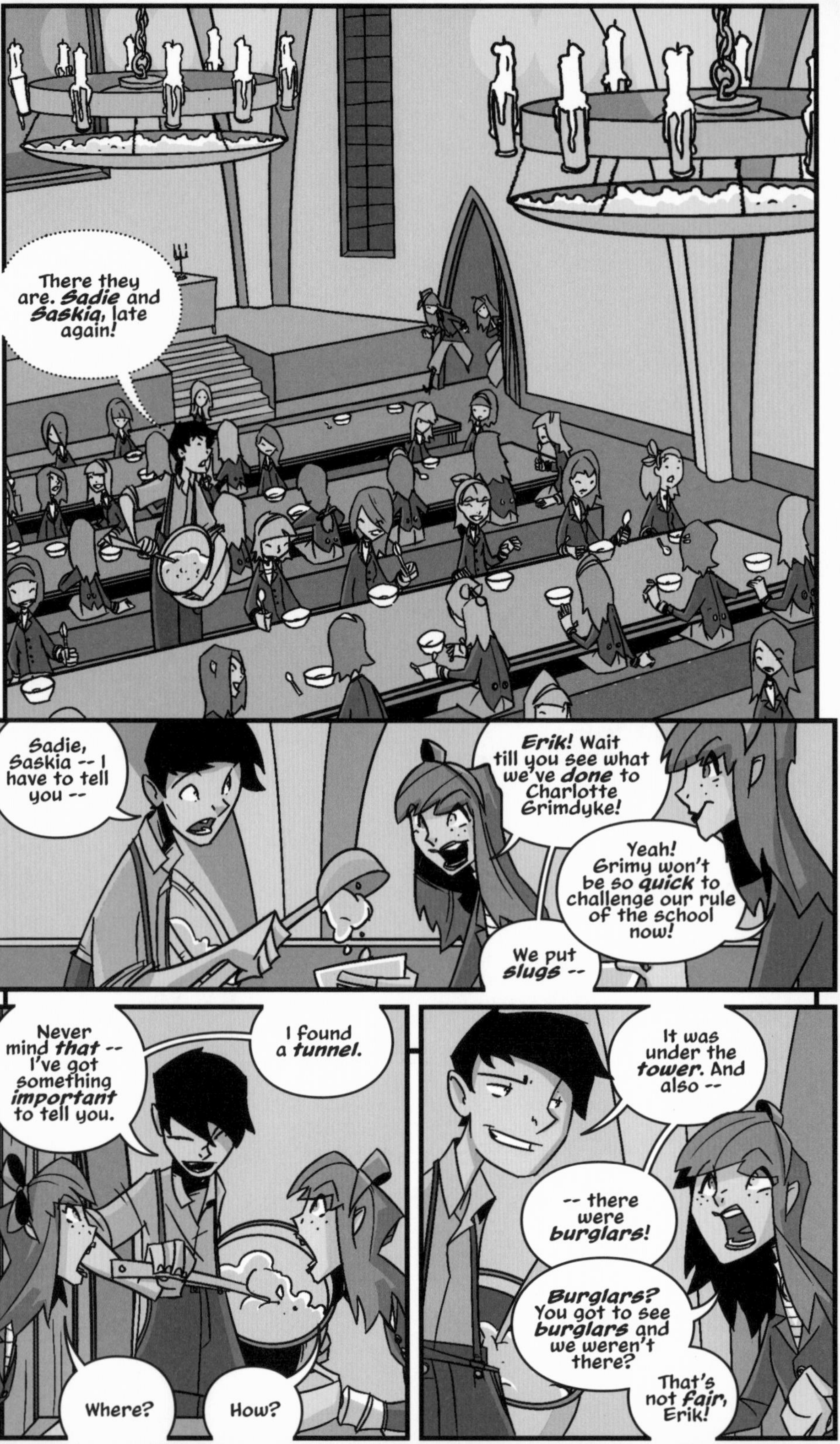
There they are. *Sadie* and *Saskia*, late again!
Sadie, Saskia -- I have to tell you --
Erik! Wait till you see what we've *done* to Charlotte Grimdyke!
Yeah! Grimy won't be so *quick* to challenge our rule of the school now!
We put *slugs* --
Never mind *that* -- I've got something *important* to tell you.
I found a *tunnel.*
Where?
How?
It was under the *tower*. And also --
-- there were *burglars!*
Burglars? You got to see *burglars* and we weren't there?
That's not *fair*, Erik!

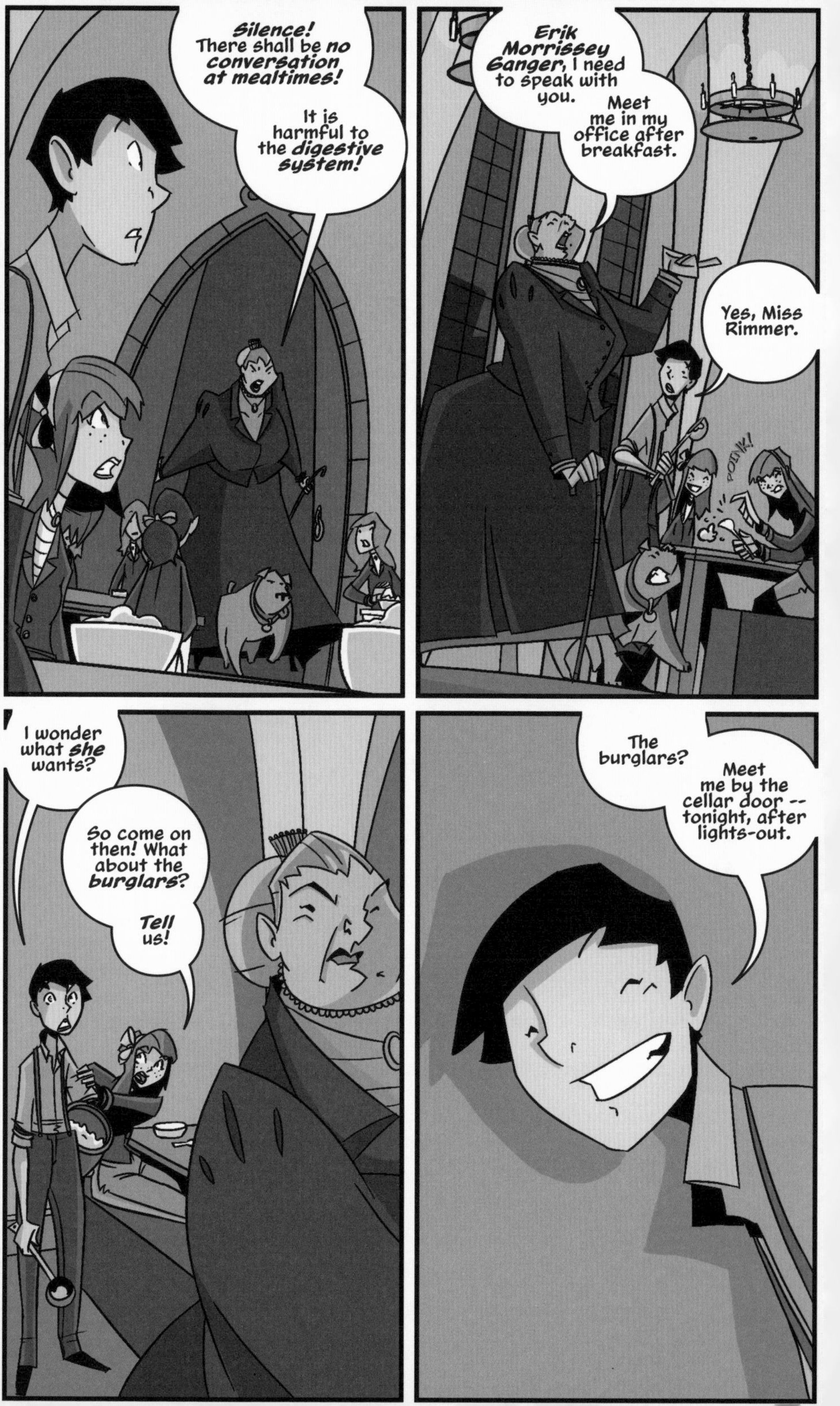
Silence! There shall be no conversation at mealtimes!
It is harmful to the digestive system!
Erik Morrissey Ganger, I need to speak with you.
Meet me in my office after breakfast.
Yes, Miss Rimmer.
POINK!
I wonder what she wants?
So come on then! What about the burglars?
Tell us!
The burglars?
Meet me by the cellar door -- tonight, after lights-out.

An hour and a half later, Erik finished up the breakfast dishes and made his way to Miss Rimmer's office.

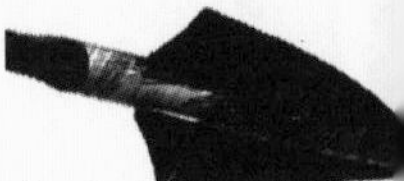

"Erik," said Miss Rimmer as she opened the door and peered at him with a half smile, "I am so glad that you have come to see me."

Erik shrugged his shoulders, suspicious of Miss Rimmer's sudden attempt at friendliness.

"I have something to ask you—a favor—a little job that you might be interested in doing."

"Yes, Miss Rimmer," he replied dutifully as he looked out the window. Saskia Dopple was on the lawn outside. She was holding a large wooden bow with an arrow expertly fitted to the string. With a look of complete concentration, she pulled back the cord. Then with a flick of her fingers, she released the arrow. It flew through the air and hit the target with a loud thud that caused Miss Rimmer to turn to see what was happening.

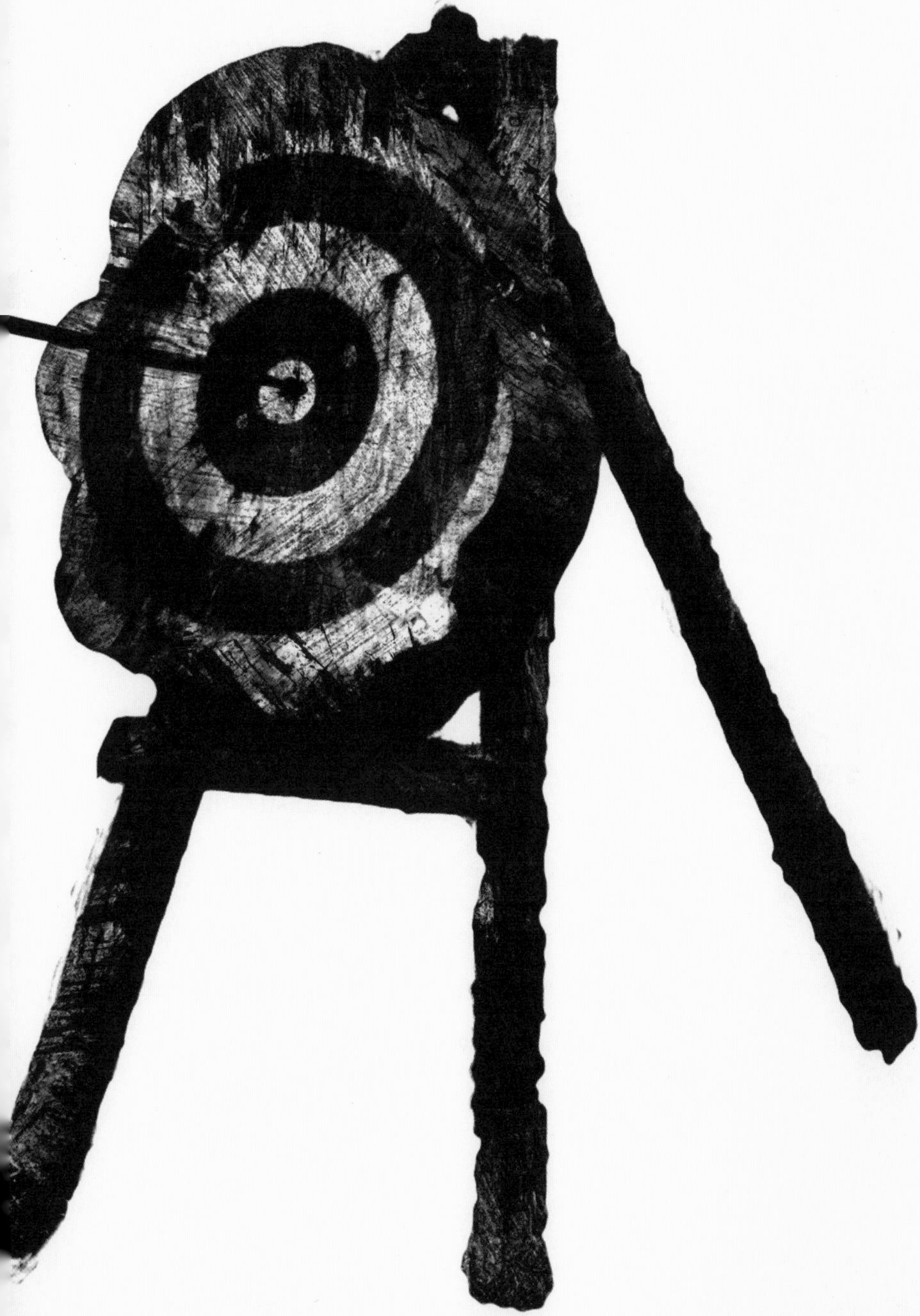

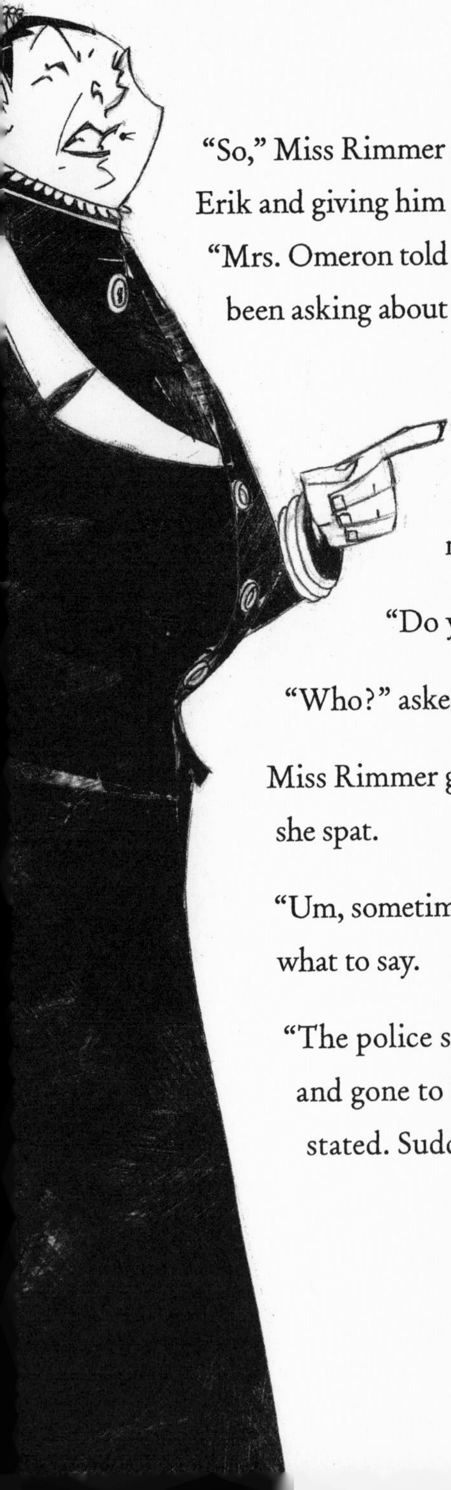

"So," Miss Rimmer said, returning her gaze to Erik and giving him another sugary sweet smile, "Mrs. Omeron told me at breakfast that you had been asking about Miss Olivia. Is that true?"

"Yes," he replied quietly.

Outside, Saskia fired yet another arrow, this time missing the target.

"Do you miss her, Erik?" she asked.

"Who?" asked Erik, distracted.

Miss Rimmer glared at him. "Miss Olivia," she spat.

"Um, sometimes," he faltered, unsure of what to say.

"The police say she has gone to Scotland, and gone to Scotland she has," Miss Rimmer stated. Suddenly her voice grew hard.

"There shall be no talk of Miss Olivia while I am here, or you will end up on the street—understand?"

Erik nodded vigorously and took a step backward.

"Good," she said, her voice softening as she reached out and patted his cheek. "Now . . . I have a job for you. There is a journalist coming from the TIMES newspaper. She wants to talk to you and the Miss Dopples about what happened at Spaniards House. It would appear that Muzz Elliott has told the journalist all about you. How you and the Dopple girls saved her life. I have arranged an interview at ten o'clock. Be careful what you say, Erik. Don't forget that you and that Dopple girl ran away from school, and it was only my charity that allowed you to return."

Erik disguised a snort. After he and the girls had returned from Spaniards House, Erik had seen Miss Rimmer counting a pile of gold coins in her office—coins that looked suspiciously like those discovered in the library at Spaniards House. And two days later she had announced that Muzz Elliott would be buying new uniforms for all the girls.

The first weekend they were at Spaniards House,
Erik and the twins had tramped all over the house,
trying to find a lock that fit a key given to Saskia
by a mysterious visitor named Madame Raphael.
Saskia believed Madame Raphael to be an angel
and was convinced she would return to Spaniards
House, but there had been no sign of the woman.
Erik thought that it was all in Saskia's imagination.
Surely no angel or ghost had given her a key,
vanished through walls, or taught her how to eat
peas with a fork, as Saskia claimed.

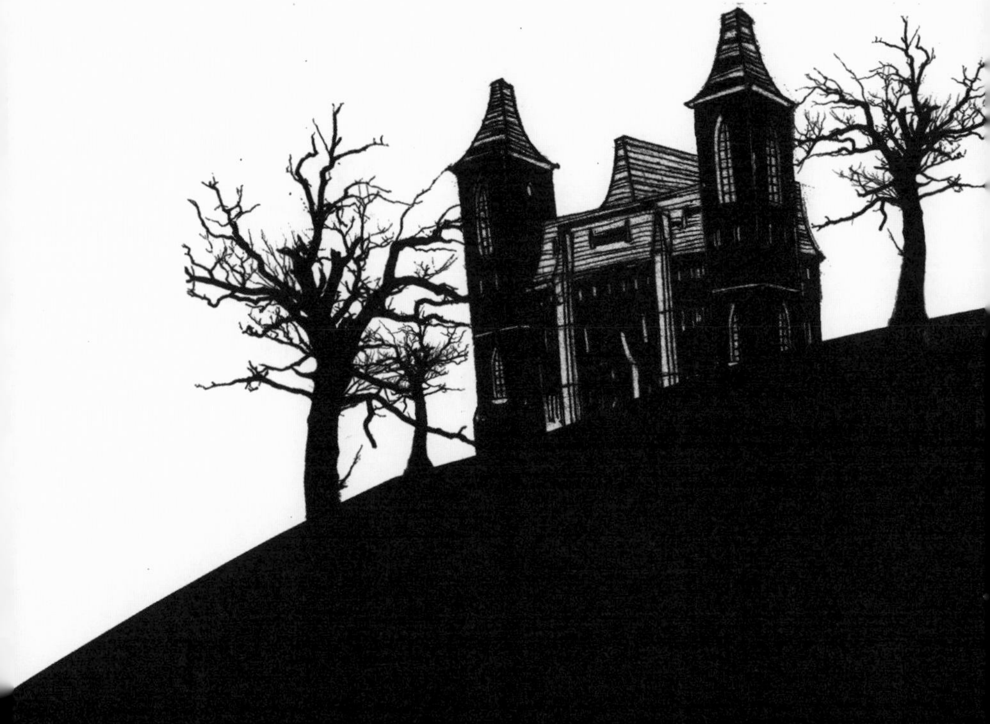

But Saskia insisted that it was all true and furiously argued that Madame Raphael had appeared before her and spoken to her on several occasions.

To Erik, the key looked like it would open an ordinary door—nothing exciting at all. After many hours of trying every door in the house they could find, Erik had eventually told the girls that it was no use. He remembered how Saskia had cried, gripping the key in her hand and demanding that they tell no

"If you say a word, Erik Ganger, you will eat frogs

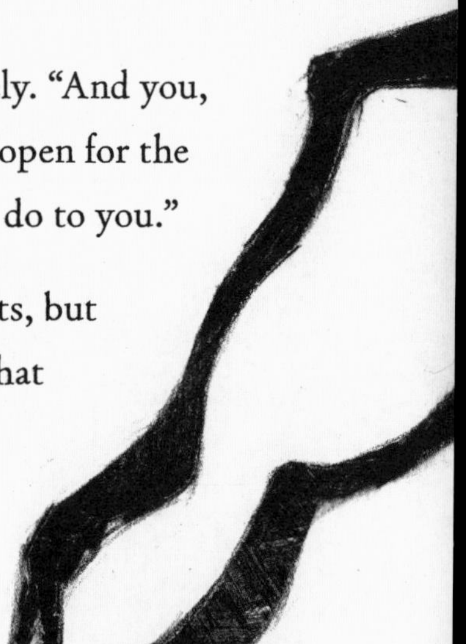

while you sleep," Saskia had said irately. "And you, Sadie, will have to sleep with one eye open for the rest of your life for fear of what I will do to you."

Sadie had laughed at her sister's threats, but Erik was not too sure. He had seen what Saskia could do, and the thought of having a host of squirming frogs pushed down his throat left him feeling quite sick. Saskia was capable of anything, and he did not want to become her next victim.

Miss Rimmer broke into Erik's thoughts. "Now go. Tell the twins to come here with you—and no more talk of Miss Olivia."

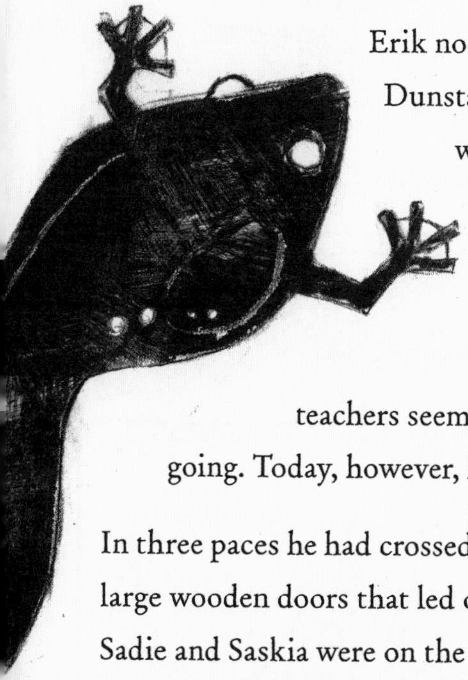

Erik nodded as he left the room. Dunstan's was quiet. All the girls were in lessons, and as the only boy in the school, he could do what he wanted. Sometimes he joined the girls in class; none of the teachers seemed to mind his coming and going. Today, however, he had a job to do.

In three paces he had crossed the hallway, opened the large wooden doors that led outside, and jumped the steps. Sadie and Saskia were on the lawn just ahead of him.

As he walked down the gravel drive toward them, he was startled by an ear-piercing wail coming from the direction of the school. Erik stared back at the front doors he had just exited.

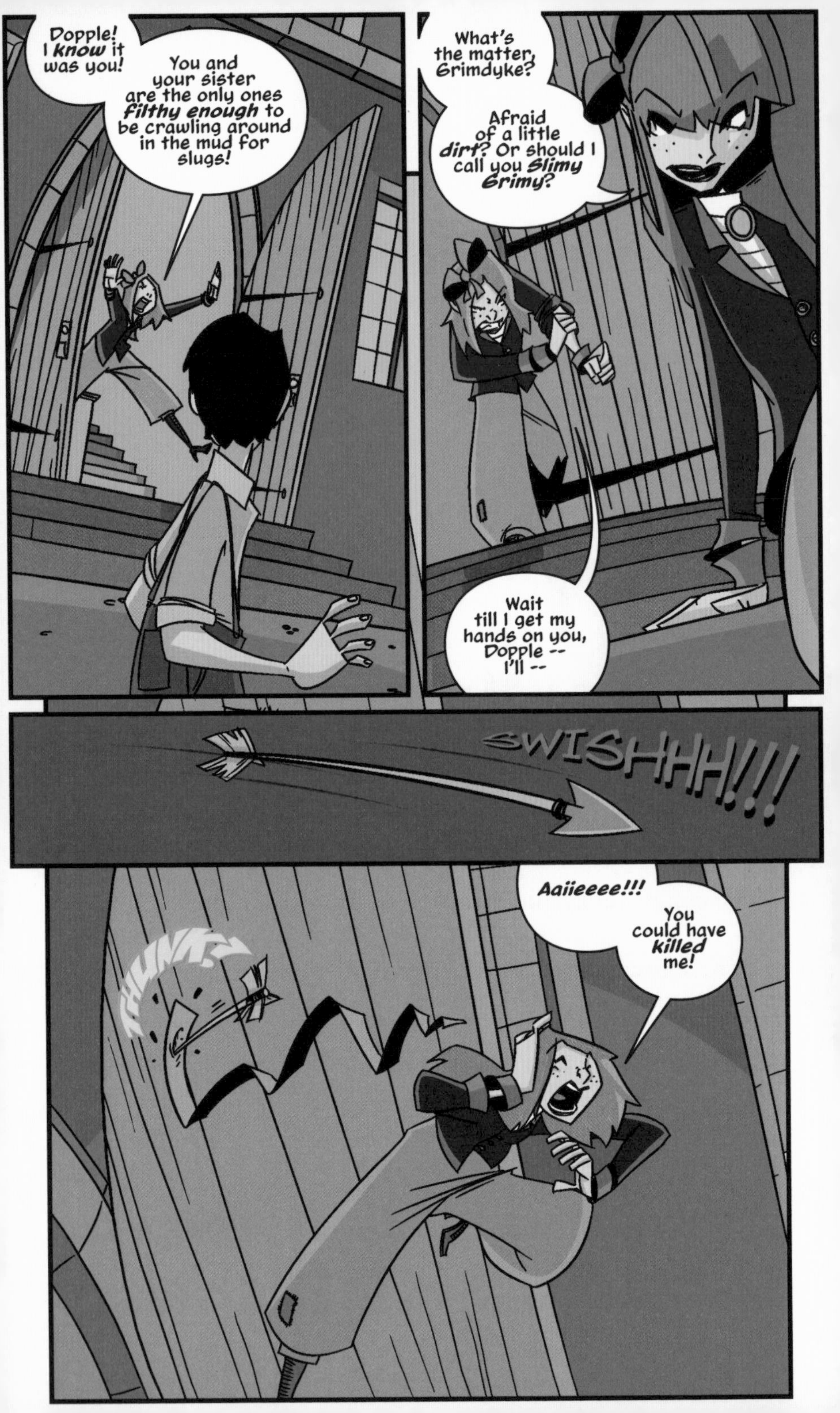
Dopple! I *know* it was you!
You and your sister are the only ones *filthy enough* to be crawling around in the mud for slugs!
What's the matter, Grimdyke?
Afraid of a little *dirt?* Or should I call you *Slimy Grimy?*
Wait till I get my hands on you, Dopple -- I'll --
SWISHHH!!!
THUNK!
Aaiieeee!!!
You could have *killed* me!

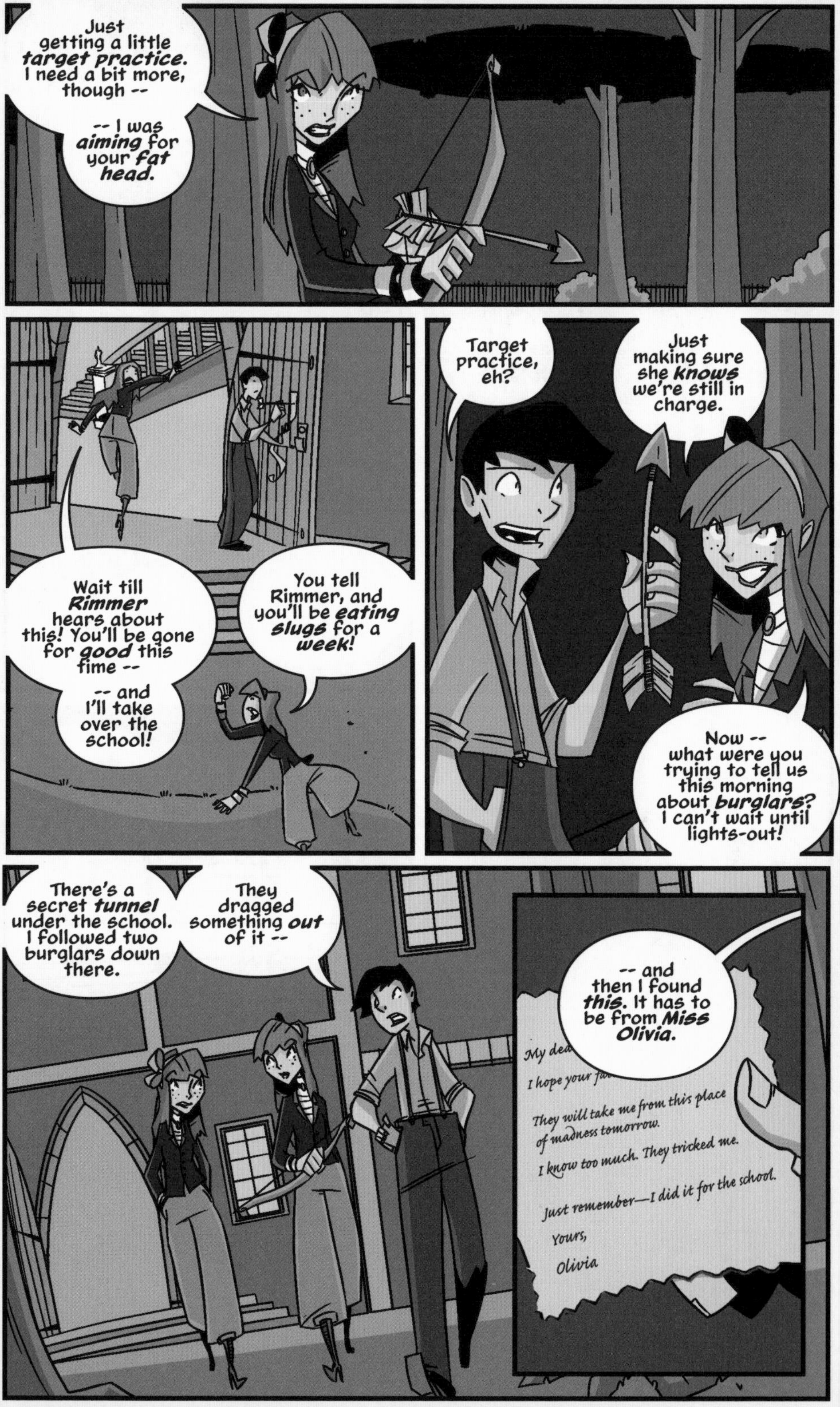
Just getting a little target practice. I need a bit more, though --
-- I was aiming for your fat head.
Wait till Rimmer hears about this! You'll be gone for good this time --
-- and I'll take over the school!
You tell Rimmer, and you'll be eating slugs for a week!
Target practice, eh?
Just making sure she knows we're still in charge.
Now -- what were you trying to tell us this morning about burglars? I can't wait until lights-out!
There's a secret tunnel under the school. I followed two burglars down there.
They dragged something out of it --
-- and then I found this. It has to be from Miss Olivia.
They will take me from this place of madness tomorrow.
I know too much. They tricked me.
Just remember—I did it for the school.
Yours,
Olivia

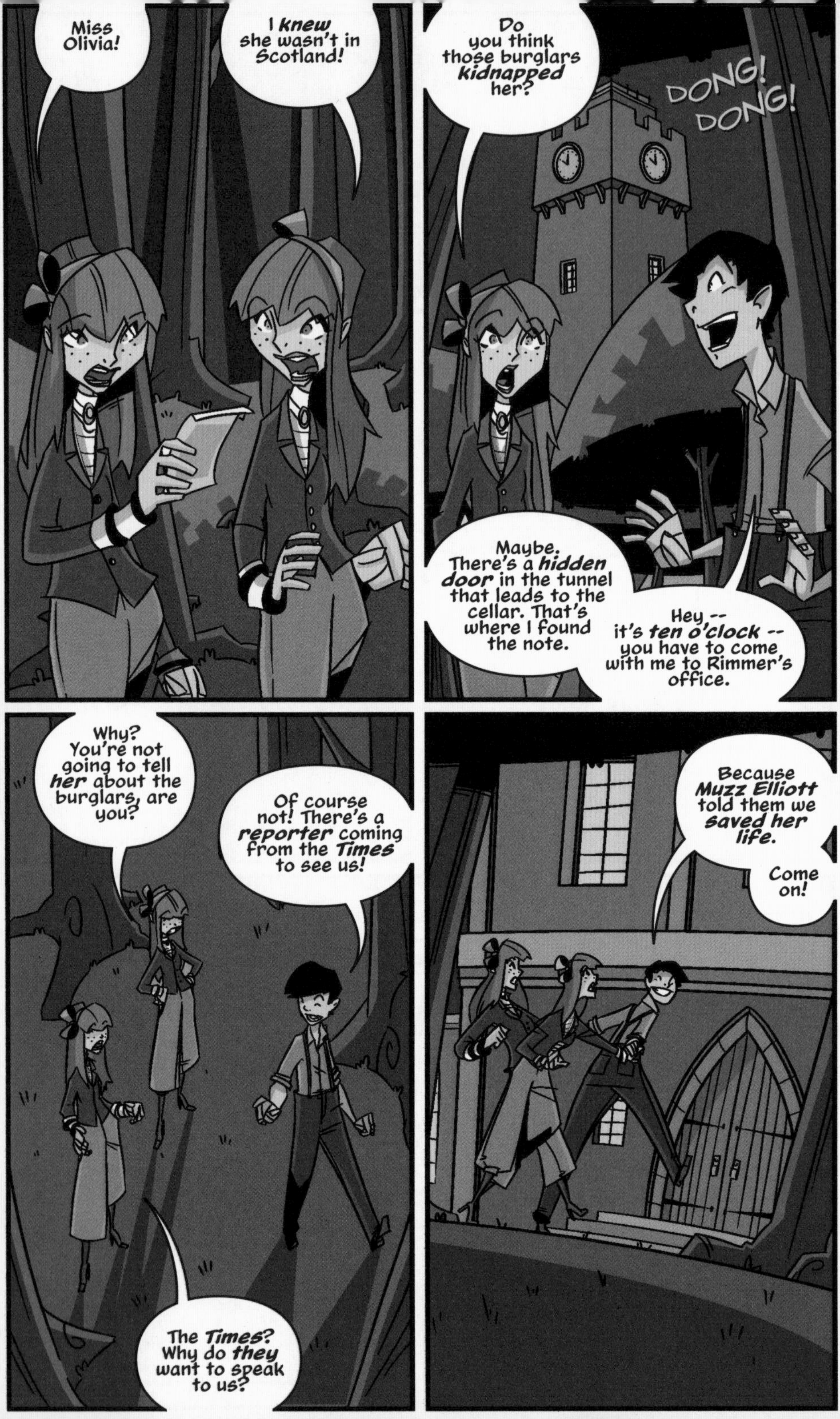

Miss Olivia!
I knew she wasn't in Scotland!
Do you think those burglars kidnapped her?
DONG! DONG!
Maybe. There's a hidden door in the tunnel that leads to the cellar. That's where I found the note.
Hey -- it's ten o'clock -- you have to come with me to Rimmer's office.
Why? You're not going to tell her about the burglars, are you?
Of course not! There's a reporter coming from the Times to see us!
The Times? Why do they want to speak to us?
Because Muzz Elliott told them we saved her life.
Come on!

The clock was still striking the hour as Erik bolted across the grass, pulling the Dopple twins along behind him. Their feet pounded on the gravel as they raced toward the school. Erik could see the large front door standing open. Miss Rimmer was on the front steps, greeting a tall, thin woman in a dark suit with a pointy hat and even pointier shoes. In the driveway a London cab was waiting with its engine running. As Erik and the twins approached the steps, the woman looked up.

"Bravo! Bravo!" she said excitedly, as if greeting long-lost friends. "These must be the heroes of Spaniards House." Her loud, crisp voice stopped them in their tracks.

"Sadie, Saskia, Erik," said Miss Rimmer, smiling uncharacteristically. "As I said, my favorite children—Erik is already fifteen, and the girls have only two years left at Isambard Dunstan's School, a place that has really changed their lives. Wouldn't you all agree?" Miss Rimmer's tone was such that they knew better than to refuse.

"Indeed," replied Saskia, looking the visitor up and down suspiciously. "Two years left—what a shame for us."

"But what wonderful years they will be!" Miss Rimmer cut in. She turned and bustled back into the entrance hall, leaving the journalist behind.

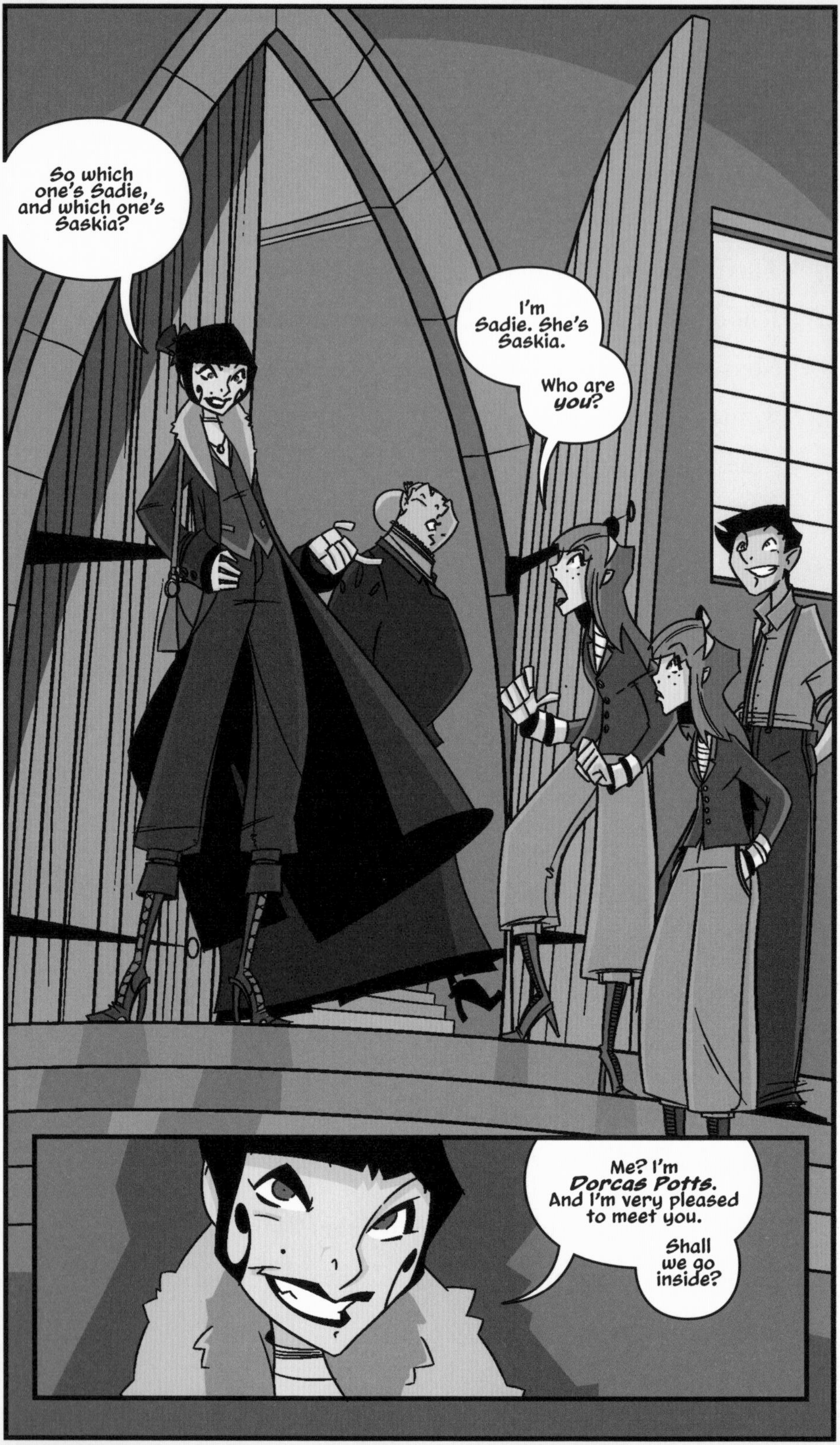
So which one's Sadie, and which one's Saskia?
I'm Sadie. She's Saskia.
Who are *you*?
Me? I'm *Dorcas Potts*. And I'm very pleased to meet you.
Shall we go inside?

Outside the school, in the woods at the bottom of the drive, a black car was parked, almost completely hidden by the surrounding trees. A man in a tall hat was framed in a side window, a pair of binoculars in front of his eyes. He lowered the binoculars from his face, twirling his wrist as though waving a magic wand, and turned to his companion.

"I don't like this," he said slowly. "Not when Dorcas Potts is sniffing around."

Chapter Four
Crimes and Questions

ERIK, SADIE, AND SASKIA were ushered into the
library. It was a grand room in the west wing of the school.
The shelves bulged with dusty, unread books all about
uninteresting things; they gave off the smell of dead, rotting
mice. Tall windows overlooked the trimmed meadows that
surrounded Isambard Dunstan's. Through the glass, Erik and
the Dopples could clearly see the perpendicular roof of the
grand house next door.

"I am so excited," said Dorcas Potts in an accent that Erik
knew was not from London. "I finally get to meet the people
who saved the life of Kitty Elliott."

"It wasn't like that," Sadie protested, but Dorcas Potts
rushed on.

"But it was—it has to be. There wouldn't be a story if you
hadn't saved her life. After all, she wrote one of the most
incredible books of all time. It changed my life." She spoke
confidently, as if she were never wrong and never corrected.
"THE WOLVES OF TANKERVILLE was the best thing I ever
read," she insisted. "I think everyone should be made to read

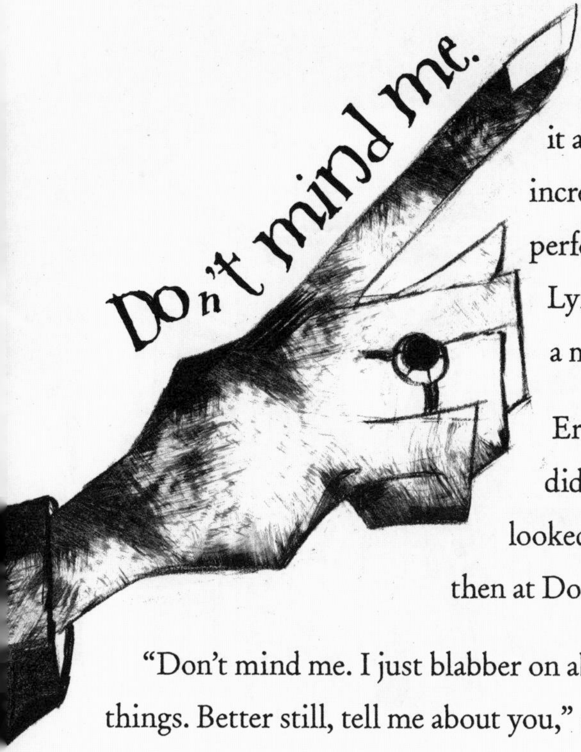
Don't mind me.

it at least once. I saw the incredible Mr. Edwards perform it last year at the Lyric Theatre—what a masterpiece."

Erik, Sadie, and Saskia did not reply. They looked at each other and then at Dorcas Potts.

"Don't mind me. I just blabber on about all sorts of things. Better still, tell me about you," she said as she thrust a pointed finger toward Erik.

"Are you American?" he asked curiously.

"Why ever do you ask?" she inquired, sounding surprised by the question.

"It's just the way you speak and—"

"I'm from Danvers, Massachusetts," she interrupted. "We just love children in Danvers—they are just so special." There was something about the way she looked at Erik that made him feel very uncomfortable.

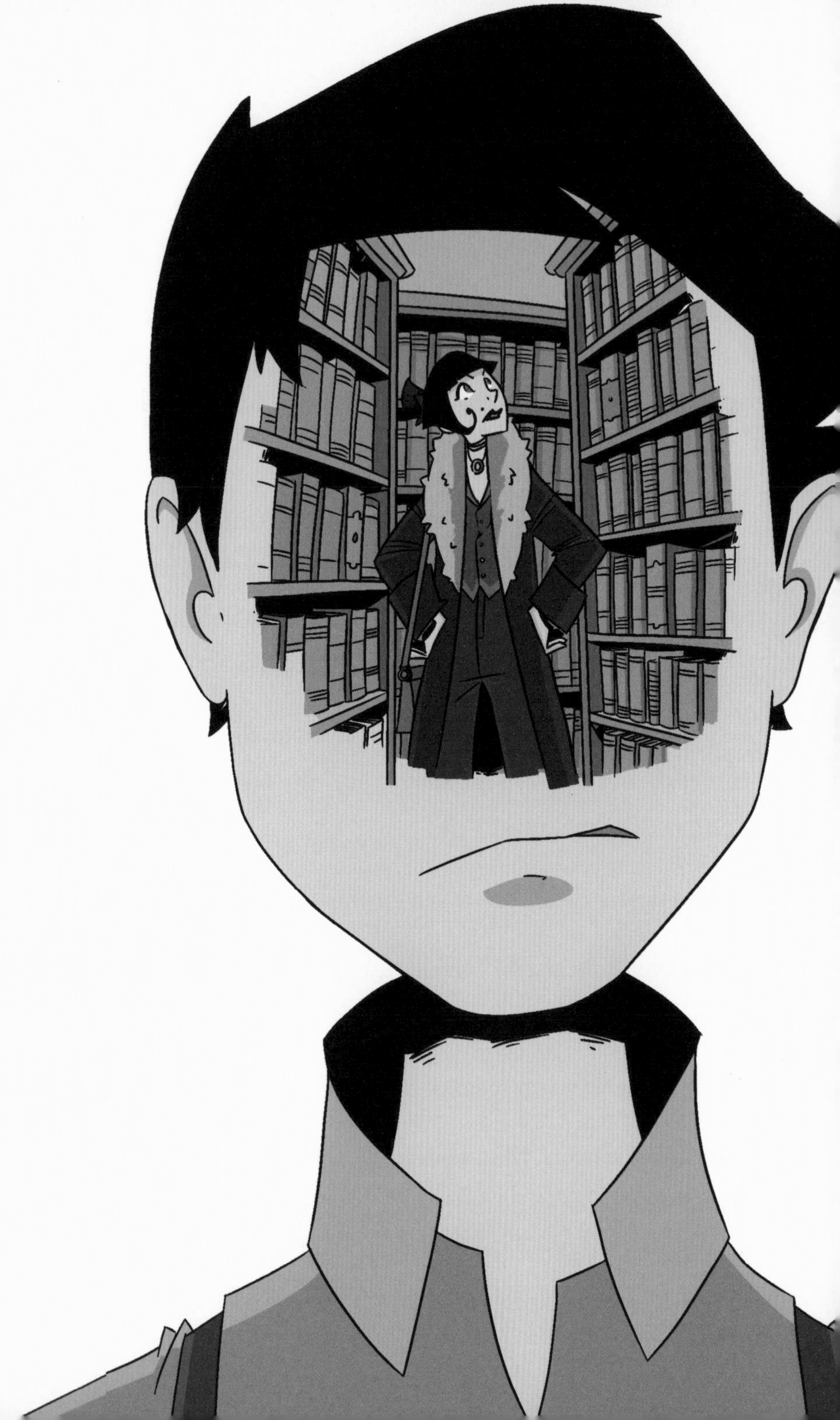

She kept staring at him, even after she had finished speaking, as if she were examining the contents of his mind.

"Has your family lived there a long time?" Miss Rimmer asked, breaking the strange silence.

"A very long time, Miss Rimmer. One of my ancestors was Giles Corey—perhaps you have heard of him?" asked Dorcas Potts, already knowing by the vague look on Miss Rimmer's face that she had no idea what Potts was talking about.

"Yes . . . of course," said Miss Rimmer hesitantly.

"Is it hard being a journalist?" Saskia broke in.

"Hard? Hard?" asked Potts with an intense look on her face. "As long as you know a story when you see one, it's as easy as apple pie."

"Mrs. Omeron makes incredibly hard apple pies," Sadie commented mischievously. "Whitney Harris broke her tooth on one last year—made her look like a vampire until they got it fixed."

"But she is all right now, Miss Potts," barked Miss Rimmer, knowing where the conversation was about to be taken. "Lunch approaches, and we haven't long for questions."

"That's fine by me," replied Dorcas Potts. "I'll just hang around for a while. You don't mind that, do you? I would simply like to get a feel for the place and get to know our heroes."

"Certainly," said Miss Rimmer. She narrowed her eyes and tightened her lips, giving the impression that she had just sucked the juice of a lemon. "I think they will love it."

"It'll be good, Miss Rimmer. We can show Miss Potts the

school and tell her all about what happened," Saskia said quickly. "We can start now and then take Miss Potts for lunch and give her a tour."

Before Miss Rimmer could say no, Saskia had rushed from the library, with Erik and Sadie following behind.

"Looks like they have a plan already." Dorcas Potts laughed as she went in pursuit.

"Most irregular . . ." Miss Rimmer started, not bothering to finish her thought since there would soon be no one left to hear it.

"An exploration into the human mind," Dorcas Potts sang out from along the passageway, "just like THE WOLVES OF TANKERVILLE."

"Quite . . ." replied the fading voice of the bemused headmistress.

Saskia waited in the corridor for Sadie, Erik, and Dorcas Potts to catch up.

"So, where are you going to take me?" the journalist asked as she pulled an engraved notepad from a small bag slung over one shoulder.

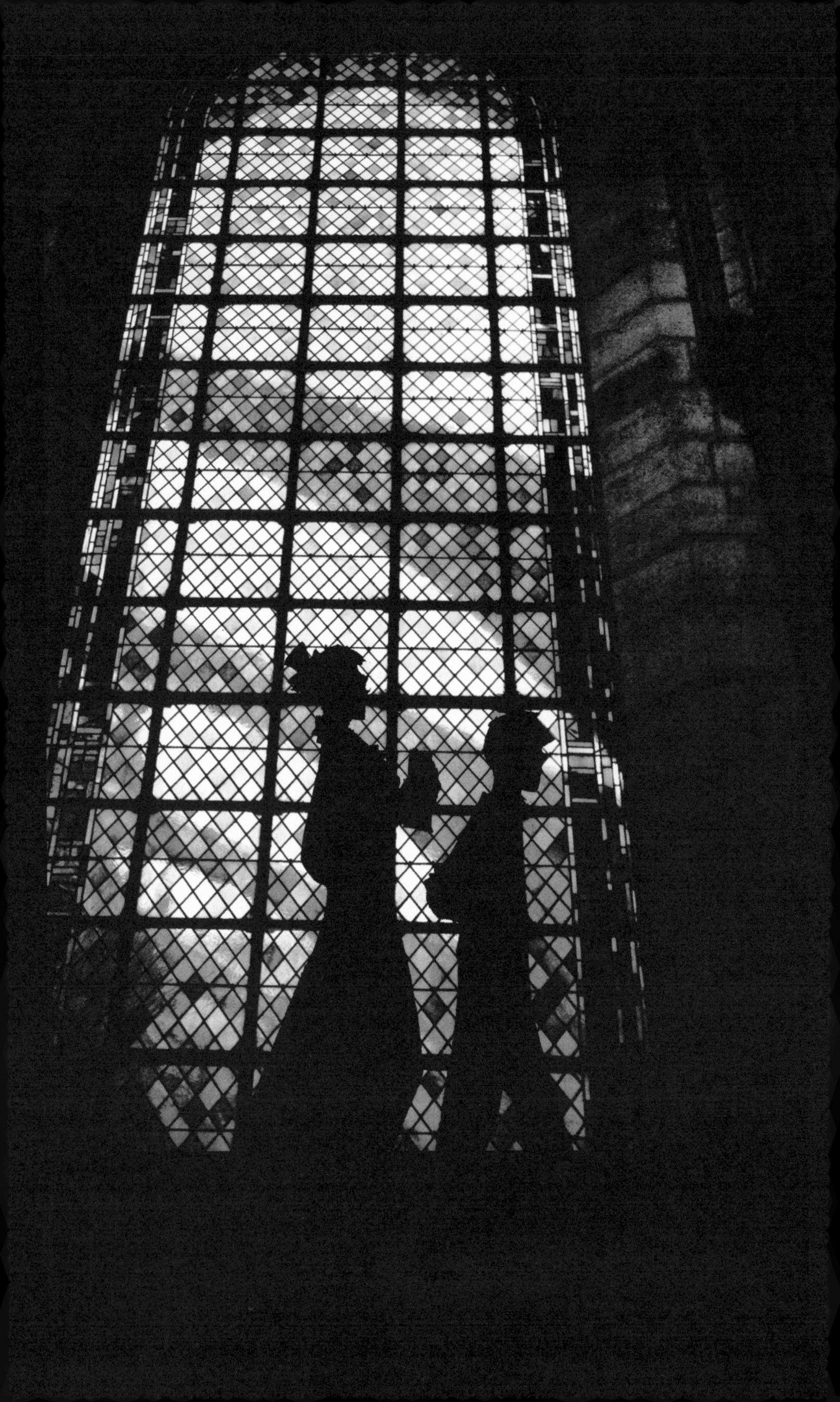

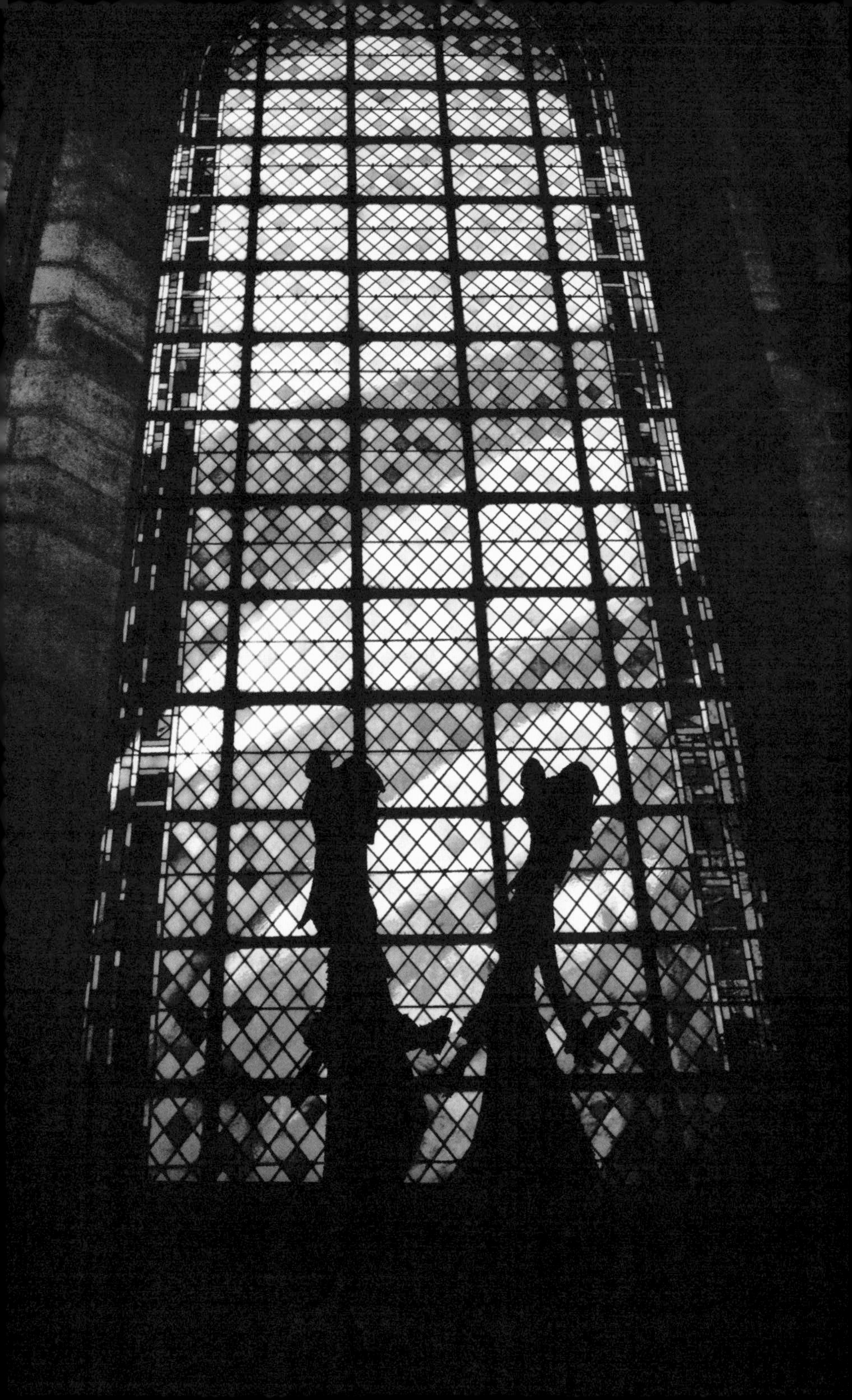

"The tower?" whispered Erik to the girls.

"Sounds good to me," answered Potts, who had heard him clearly. "Let's start there—is it someplace special?"

"It's where Erik and I began our journey to rescue Saskia," Sadie replied as they headed toward the tower.

"How did you know Saskia was in trouble?" asked Dorcas Potts.

"We always know," Sadie replied. They marched along the drab corridor, passing arched windows of dingy glass.

"Two heads and one brain—that's what our mother said," Saskia remarked cheerily as the smell of cabbage stew rolled toward them from the refectory.

"Just like Kitty Elliott and Cicely Windylove?" asked Dorcas Potts.

"I could never say what Muzz Elliott thought, and Cicely Windylove . . . escaped," Saskia replied, thinking about Muzz Elliott's twin who had nearly killed them all.

As Erik followed the twins down the corridor, he wondered what the journalist would ask. He had once seen a copy of the TIMES. It had been wrapped around a portion of fish and chips that his father had bought the night Erik was abandoned at Dunstan's. He remembered the way the oil and vinegar had seeped through the paper wrapping.

"Such a nice class of paper to have your food wrapped in," his father had joked as they walked through Hampstead. "I do believe it makes the food taste even better. I once had oyster wrapped in the NATIONAL ENQUIRER—I am sure it made me sick for a week." His father had finished the food without sharing it with Erik, scrunched up the wrapping, and thrown the paper behind a hedge.

The memory had never gone away. It was so vivid that Erik even thought he could smell the scent of fish and chips coming from the refectory. He shook his head to clear his thoughts.

"Erik, are you all right?" Sadie asked.

"I'm fine," said Erik, quickening his pace.

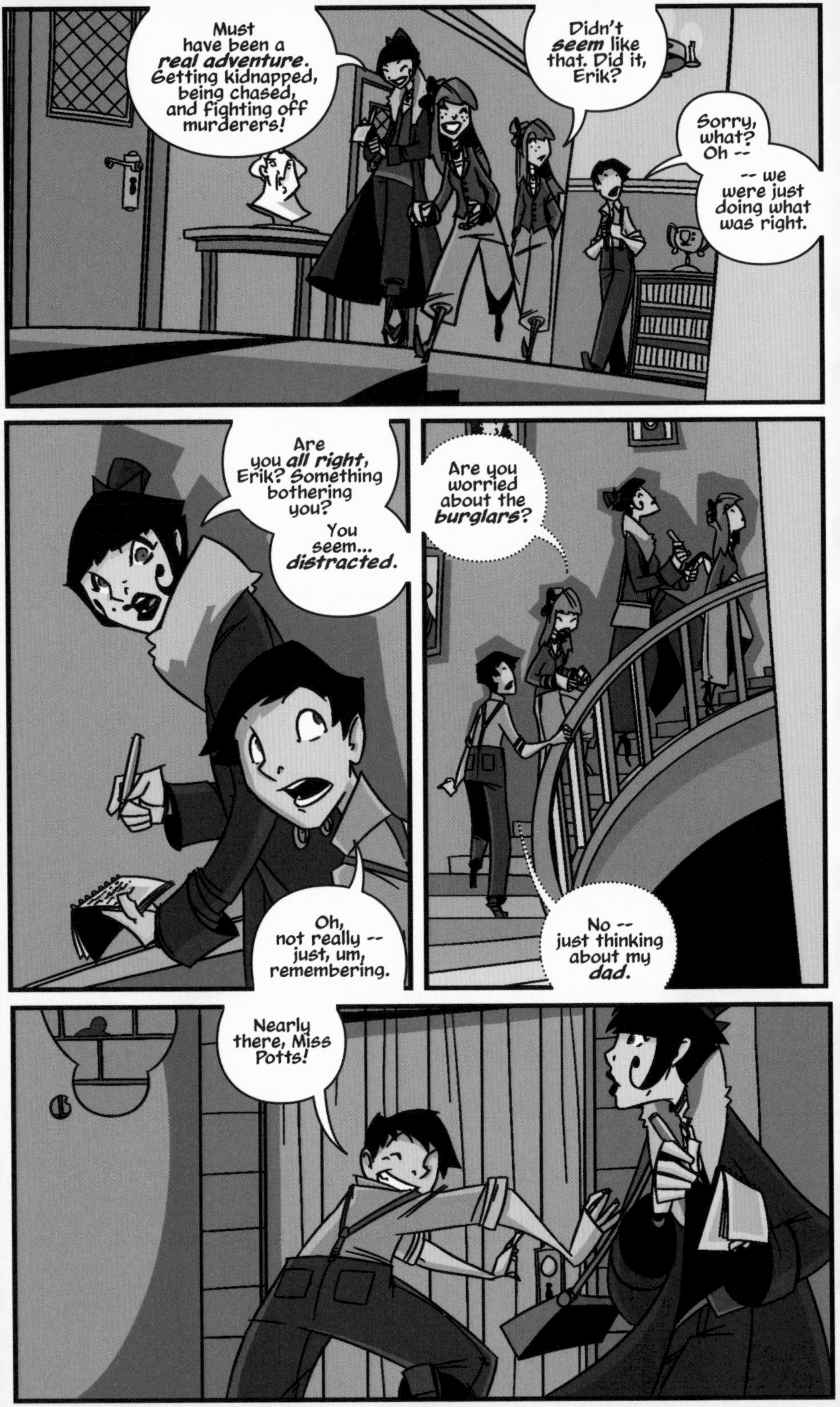
Must have been a ***real adventure.*** Getting kidnapped, being chased, and fighting off murderers!
Didn't ***seem*** like that. Did it, Erik?
Sorry, what? Oh --
-- we were just doing what was right.
Are you ***all right,*** Erik? Something bothering you?
You seem... ***distracted.***
Oh, not really -- just, um, remembering.
Are you worried about the ***burglars?***
No -- just thinking about my ***dad.***
Nearly there, Miss Potts!

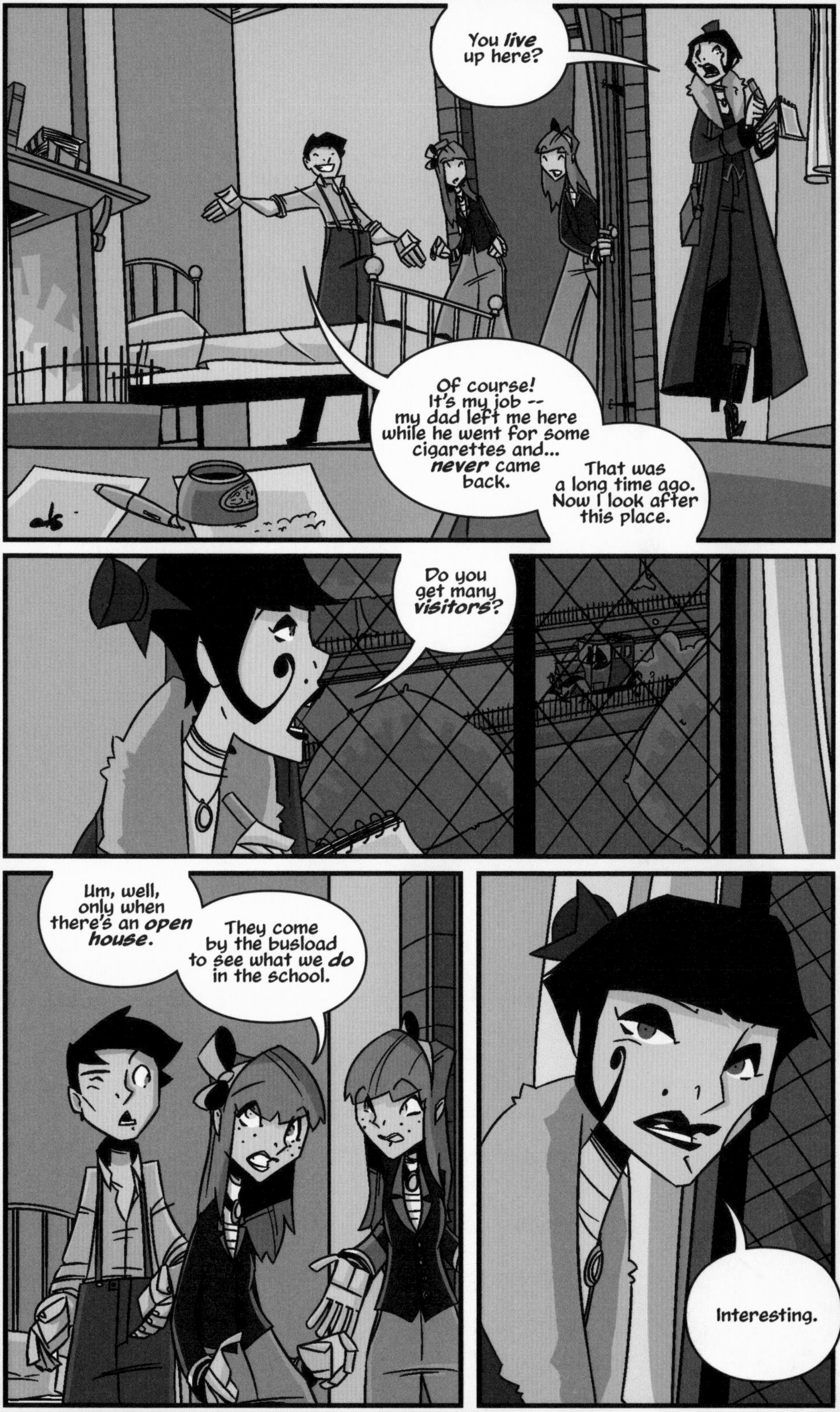
You *live* up here?
Of course! It's my job -- my dad left me here while he went for some cigarettes and... *never* came back.
That was a long time ago. Now I look after this place.
Do you get many *visitors*?
Um, well, only when there's an *open house*.
They come by the busload to see what we *do* in the school.
Interesting.

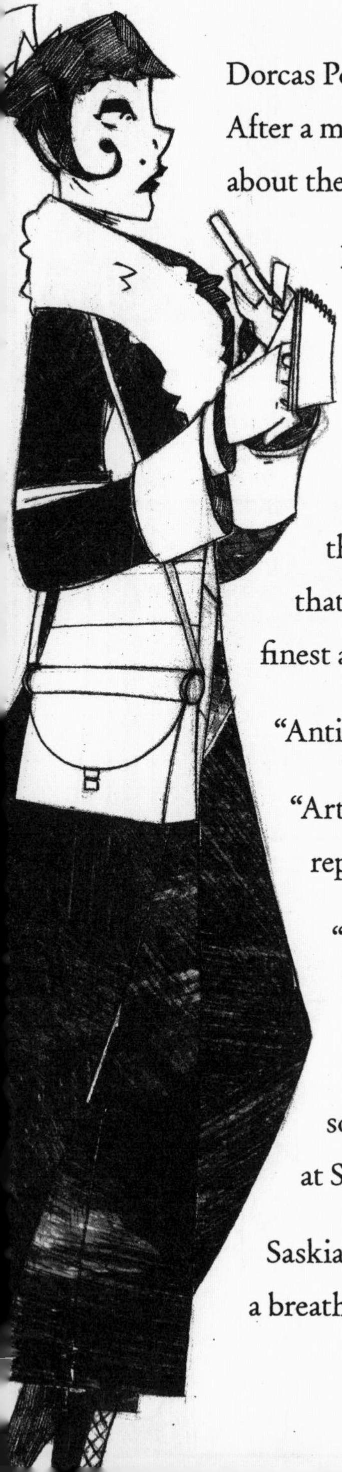

Dorcas Potts continued to stare out the window. After a moment she asked, "Do you know much about the man who lives next door?"

Erik responded, "Mrs. Omeron told me his name is Lord Gervez, but I've never seen him."

"Not many people have," said Dorcas Potts. "He keeps himself locked away in that place and never comes out. I once heard that Lord Gervez has collected some of the finest antiquities the world has ever seen."

"Antiquities?" asked Erik.

"Artifacts . . . things of great beauty," she replied.

"Treasure?" Saskia asked, coming up behind the journalist to peer over her shoulder.

"Anything is treasure if it is desired by someone else. Tell me, Saskia, what happened at Spaniards House?"

Saskia was happy to share the story. She took a breath and began to recount the details of the night they saved Muzz Elliott from certain death at the hands of her twin, her niece, and her butler. She talked for the next twenty minutes, stopping only to let Erik and Sadie fill in bits of the story here and there. Dorcas Potts took out her notepad and appeared to write down every word. The journalist did not speak but occasionally glanced up at Erik, Sadie, and Saskia as she filled the pages of her notebook. Finally, Saskia finished her story and sighed.

"That's more than I need," said Dorcas Potts as she put the notepad back in her bag and slipped the pen in her pocket. "I'd best be going—can't keep you from your lunch."

"Weren't you going to stay?" asked Erik.

"I couldn't possibly. I have to file the story. It's for the crime page tomorrow."

"You're a crime writer?" Erik asked with admiration.

"Certainly am—one of the best in the business, and the only woman to hack the job this side of the Atlantic," Dorcas Potts replied, flashing a grin with her shiny, white teeth.

Sadie and Saskia looked at each other. "Do you think you could find our mother?" they asked at the same time.

"She left us here while she toured Europe," Sadie continued.

"She's an actress, and she's very good," Saskia added.

"We think she's been kidnapped—that's why she hasn't come back for us," Sadie explained with a sniff. "It's been three years."

"What's her name? I could ask our offices in Paris and Rome if anyone has heard of her," the journalist said as kindly as she could.

"Biba Dopple—the actress. She's tall and thin and has one yellow eye and one blue," they again said together, as if they had rehearsed the words a million times.

"Shouldn't be hard to find," Dorcas Potts replied.

"She once had a photograph in the HAMPSTEAD GAZETTE—it was just before she went away," Saskia explained breathlessly, excited at the prospect of finding her mother again.

"Is that what crime writers do—find missing people?" Erik asked, intrigued.

"For the most part. Sometimes we get to solve the crimes that the police can't—that's what I like the best," Dorcas Potts replied as she scrutinized his face.

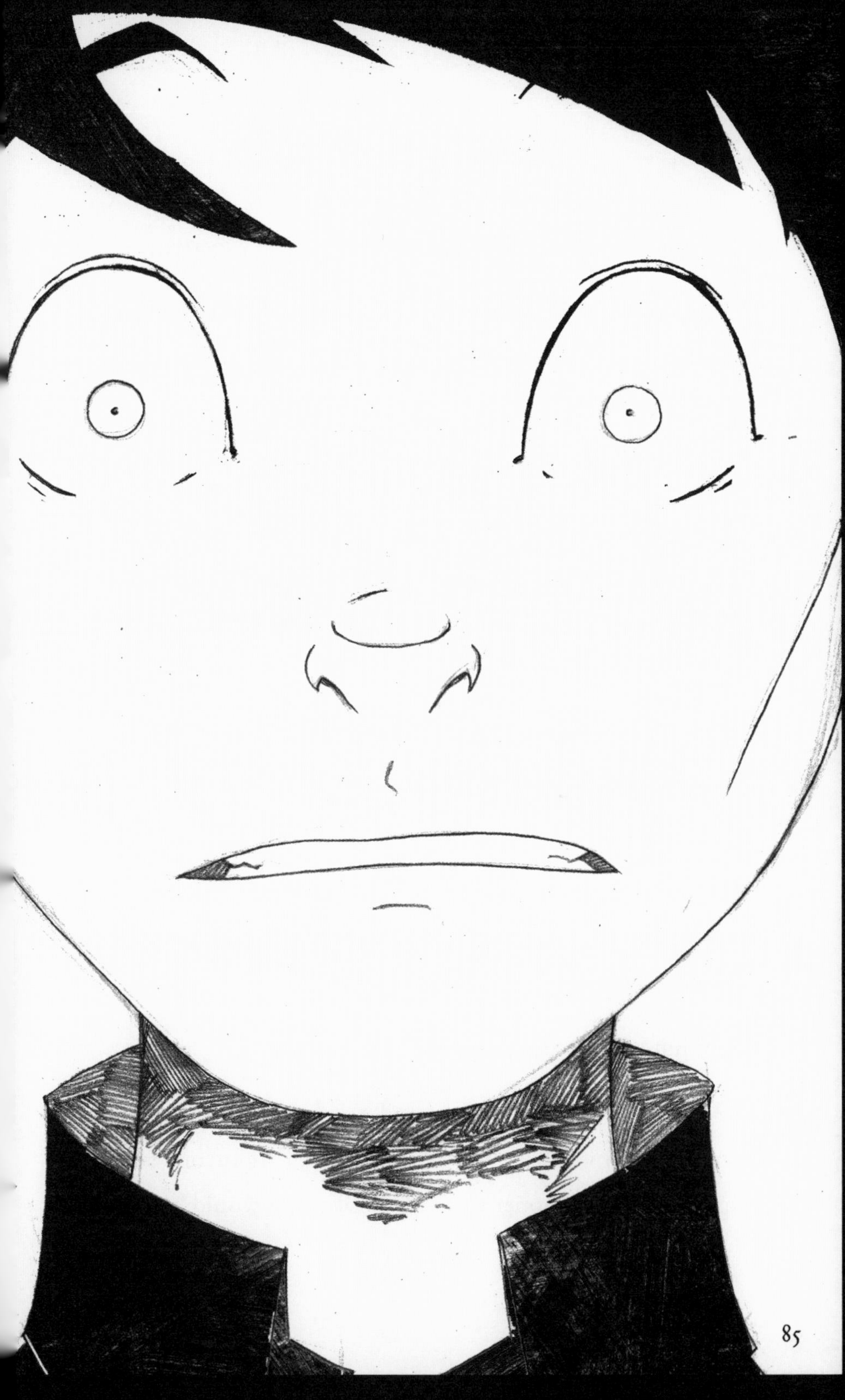

"So how do you catch burglars?" Erik asked eagerly.

"Have you got the bug for this, Erik? Saved Kitty Elliott, and now you'll take on the world?" she asked as she moved toward the door.

"Sounds fun," Sadie replied on Erik's behalf.

"Sounds dangerous," said Dorcas Potts as she opened the door and stepped outside, her bobbed hair bouncing. "Villains will do anything not to get caught. They'll even resort to murder."

With that, she turned and swirled down the stairs, her long, black coat billowing behind her like the wings of a bat.

"Do you think we should have told her about the note you found in the passageway?" Sadie asked Erik as he stood at the door looking down the stairs.

"I'm not sure we can trust her," he replied.

"Why not?" Saskia blurted out. "You heard her say she can solve crimes that even the police can't! If anyone could figure out what happened to Miss Olivia, it would be her."

"She did say she would help us find our mother," put in Sadie.

"She could have just been saying that," Erik argued.

"I'm going to tell her about the tunnel," Saskia announced. She pushed past them both and ran down the stairs.

"She can't do that—no one will believe us," Erik protested as he rushed after her, followed closely by Sadie. "Come back, Saskia!" he yelled angrily.

The door to the school closed just as Erik and Sadie reached it. They twisted the handle and then ran outside. Dorcas Potts was in the back of the taxicab, waving good-bye to Saskia, who was chasing the car down the drive toward East Heath Road.

"Saskia, wait!" shouted Sadie as she ran after her sister. "Did you tell her?" she asked, panting and out of breath when she finally caught up with Saskia.

"Didn't get the chance. She was already in the taxi. I tried to shout, but she didn't listen—just waved and off she went," Saskia replied glumly.

Around them the trees that lined the driveway to the road seemed to wave their empty, lifeless branches in deep melancholy. A single magpie screeched above their heads before darting down to dance in the twigs of the hedgerow.

Erik stared at the taxi as it turned from the drive and onto East Heath Road. It accelerated suddenly and then stopped just as abruptly in front of Lord Gervez's house.

"That's odd," he said. "She's getting out." He set off toward the hedge. "I'm going to find out what she's up to," he announced.

As Erik, Sadie, and Saskia ran along the gravel drive, they could see Dorcas Potts close the door of the cab and walk across the empty road. They hid behind the dead, dangling leaves of the beech hedge and peered through.

"She's going in," Sadie whispered as they watched her take a key from her bag, place it in the gilded iron gate, and unlock it with a twist of her wrist.

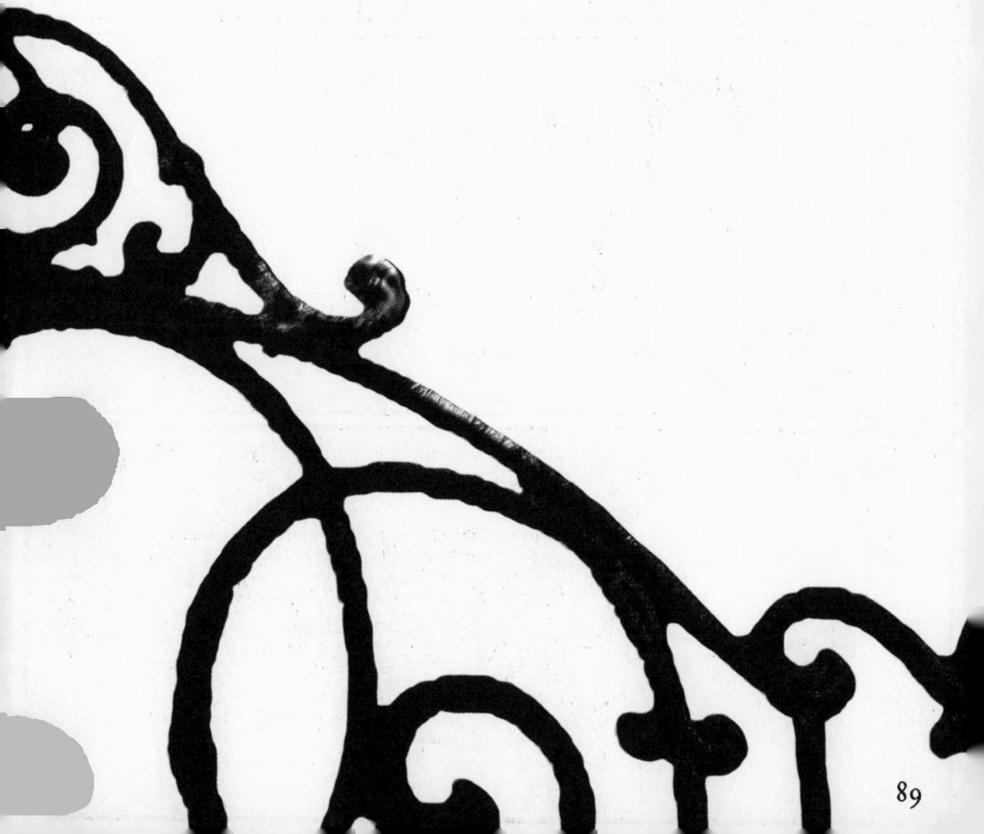

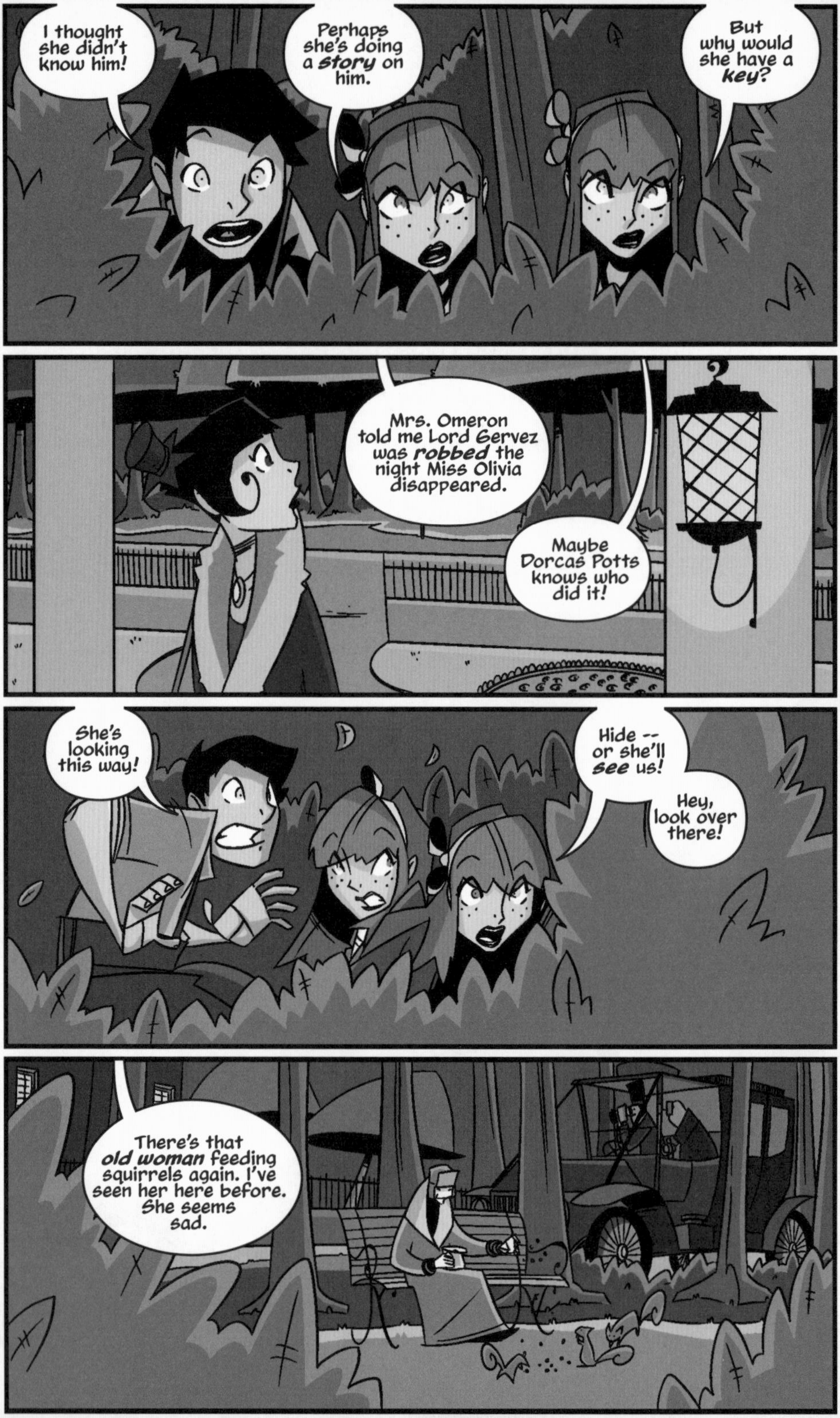
I thought she didn't know him!
Perhaps she's doing a *story* on him.
But why would she have a *key?*
Mrs. Omeron told me Lord Gervez was *robbed* the night Miss Olivia disappeared.
Maybe Dorcas Potts knows who did it!
She's looking this way!
Hide -- or she'll *see* us!
Hey, look over there!
There's that *old woman* feeding squirrels again. I've seen her here before. She seems sad.

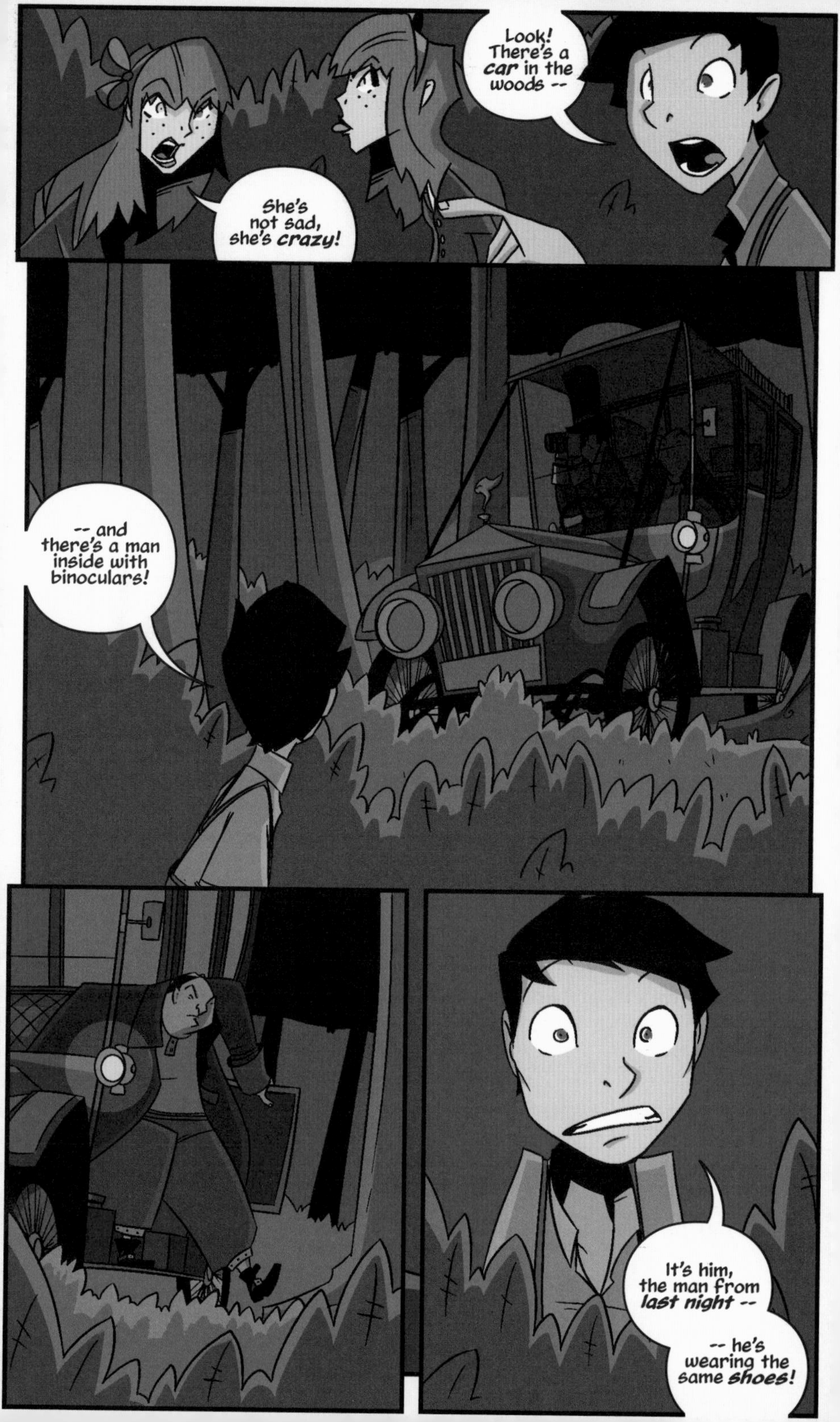
Look! There's a car in the woods --
She's not sad, she's crazy!
-- and there's a man inside with binoculars!
It's him, the man from last night --
-- he's wearing the same shoes!

Erik stared at the man's boots. He had no doubt it was the same man he had seen the night before. He turned to Sadie and Saskia to explain his discovery and noticed that Sadie was staring openmouthed in the direction of the man. She raised her hand and pointed. Erik looked back at the car and realized she was pointing at the other man who was still inside the vehicle.

"It's Potemkin!" said Sadie.

Erik felt a jolt of horror at the name of their old enemy. "No . . . it can't be!"

"He was in prison," Saskia said, bewildered.

The Great Potemkin, the magician of Hampstead, looked across the heath.

Sadie caught her breath. "He must have escaped. But why has he come back here?"

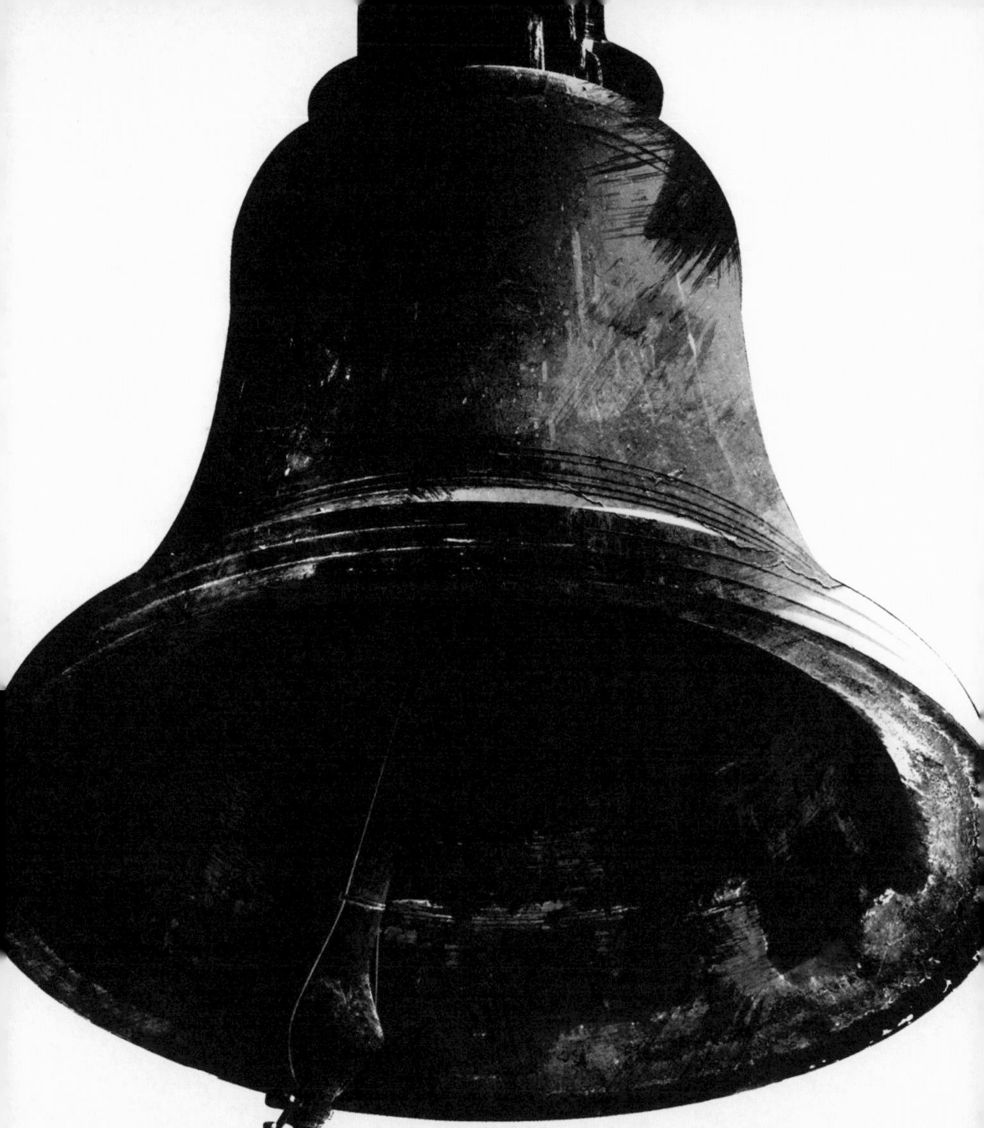

Chapter Five

An Old Enemy

WHILE DORCAS POTTS was still inside Lord Gervez's house, the bell for lunch rang, and the door of the school opened to reveal Miss Rimmer.

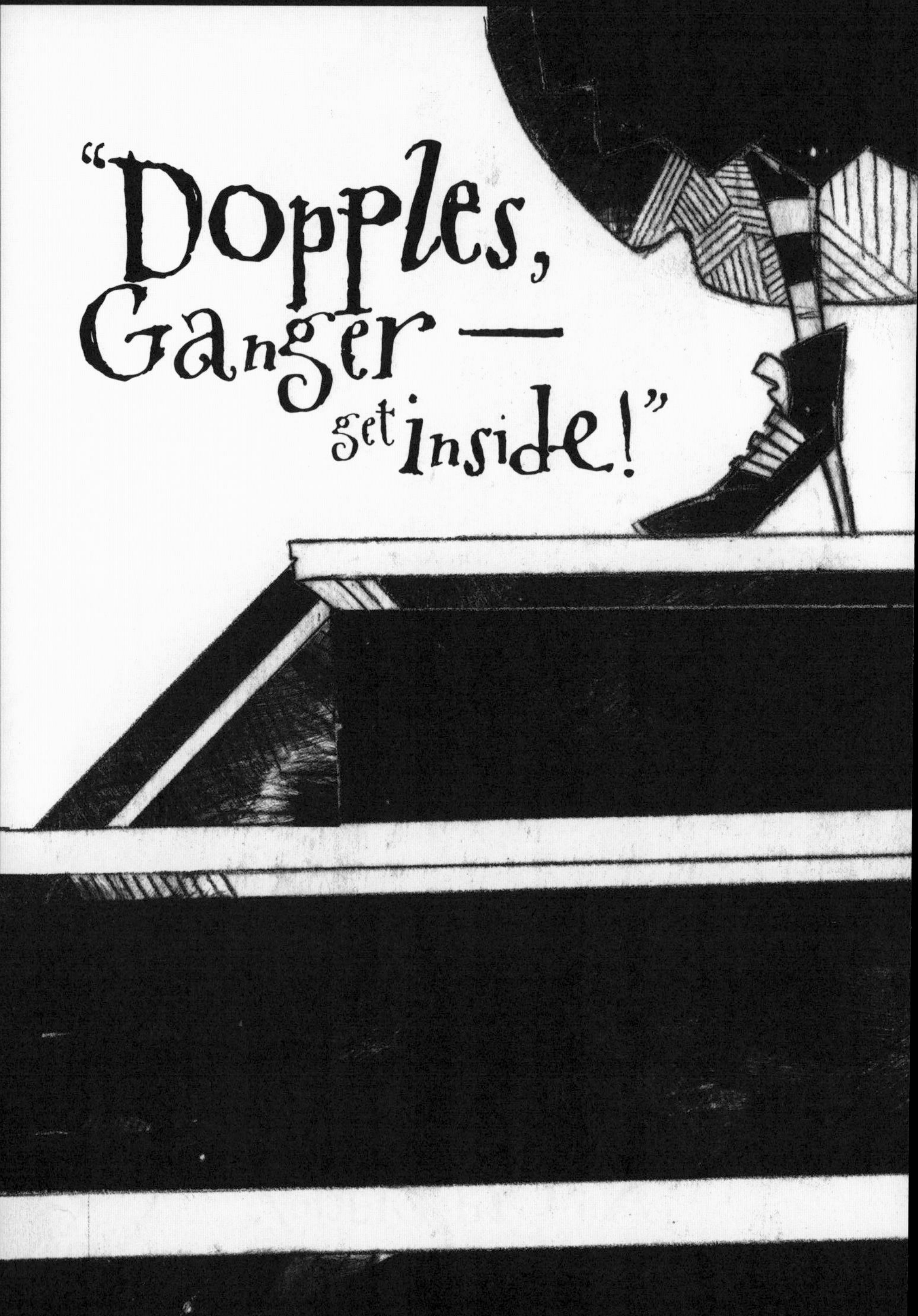
"Dopples, Ganger — get inside!"

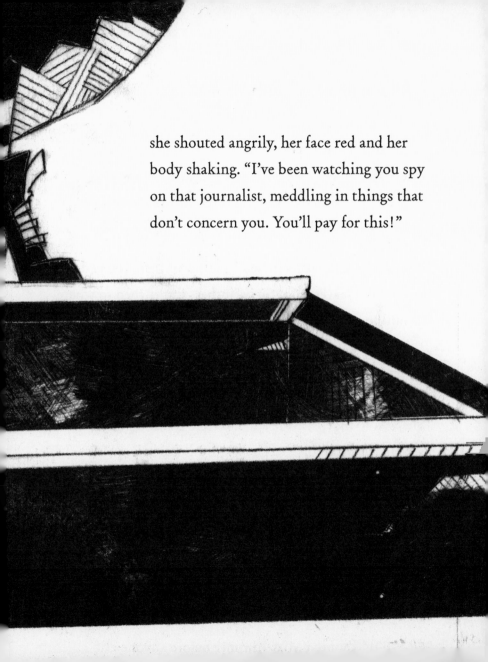

she shouted angrily, her face red and her body shaking. "I've been watching you spy on that journalist, meddling in things that don't concern you. You'll pay for this!"

The sound of her shrieking voice carried far across Hampstead Heath. The short, fat man leaped back inside the car and quickly rolled the darkened windows firmly shut. Within seconds, the long black Rolls-Royce had sped off down the road.

Erik, Sadie, and Saskia pulled themselves from the hedge, brushed the leaves from their clothes, and turned to where the bullhorn-like voice shouted at them.

"We were just watching her go," Erik explained feebly, knowing he could make no excuse.

"She was so nice," Saskia added as she tried to pull a particularly stubborn beech twig from her hair.

"NICE?" yelled Miss Rimmer. Spit flew from her teeth. "She's a snoop, and I'm glad she's gone."

"She only asked about what happened at Spaniards House, nothing about—" Erik stopped before he said the words "Miss Olivia."

"GOOD!" shouted Miss Rimmer before anyone else could speak. "That was an important interview. It could find the school a patron, and any child without a parent needs a patron or she will starve and then she will DIE."

Sadie nodded to Saskia. They both knew in their unspoken way that now was not the time to say or do anything that would make Miss Rimmer more upset. But Erik did not.

"Is Lord Gervez a patron?" he asked quite innocently.

Miss Rimmer stopped in her tracks. Her mouth dangled open in surprise. "Gervez?" she asked. "How do you know of him?"

"Dorcas Potts. She mentioned him—said he lives next door."

"What else did Dorcas Potts tell you?" Miss Rimmer snapped. Her face turned the brightest red, and her eyes bulged in their sockets. She stared at Erik and the twins. "Keep your noses out of other people's business," she said. She turned on her heels and hobbled as quickly as she could back inside.

"What did I say?" Erik asked the twins.

"Maybe she doesn't want us to know anything about Lord Gervez," Saskia replied as they all crept in through the creaking door behind Miss Rimmer.

"I think she's up to something," said Sadie. "Let's follow her and find out."

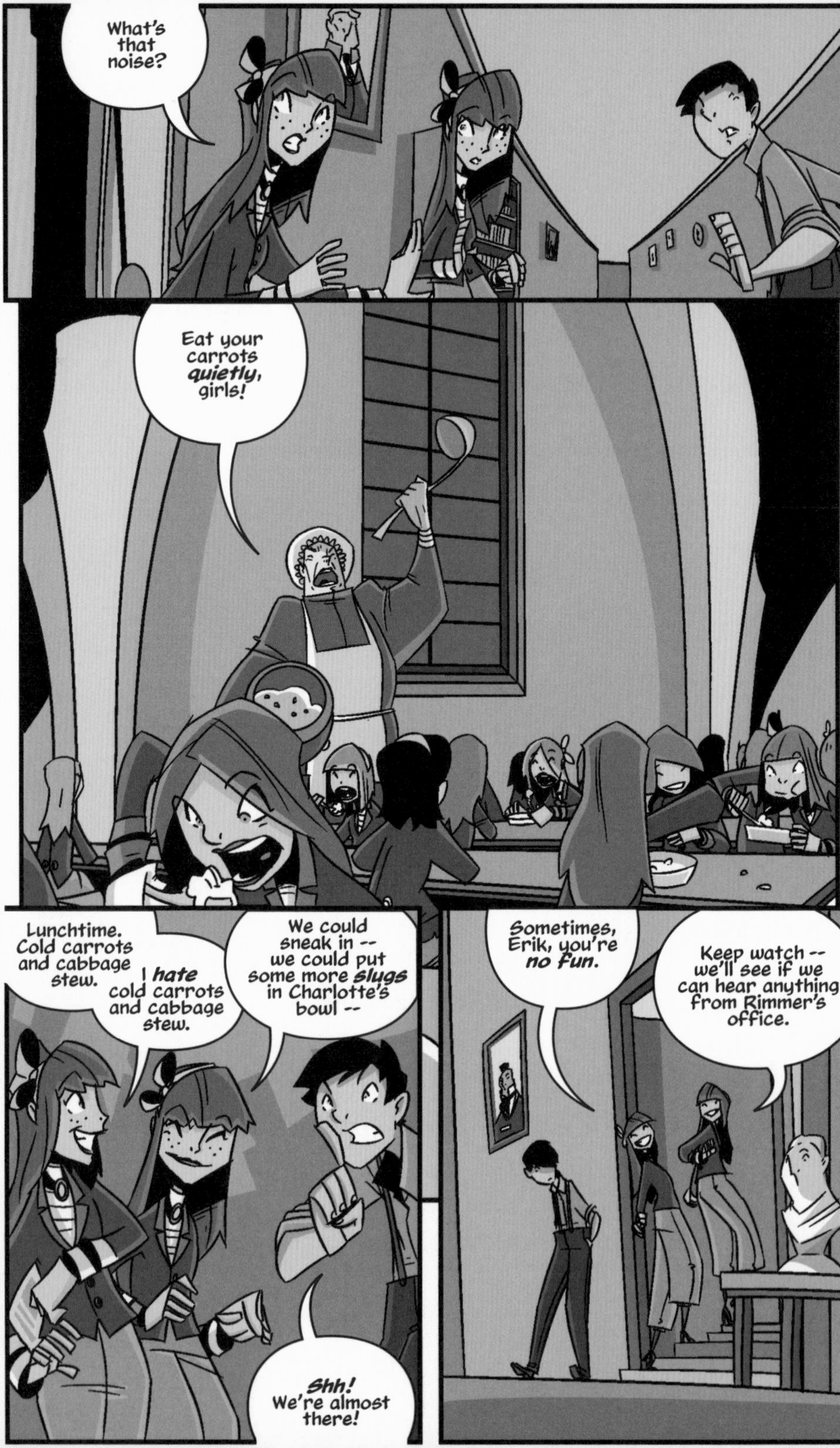

What's that noise?
Eat your carrots *quietly*, girls!
Lunchtime. Cold carrots and cabbage stew.
I *hate* cold carrots and cabbage stew.
We could sneak in -- we could put some more *slugs* in Charlotte's bowl --
Shh! We're almost there!
Sometimes, Erik, you're *no fun*.
Keep watch -- we'll see if we can hear anything from Rimmer's office.

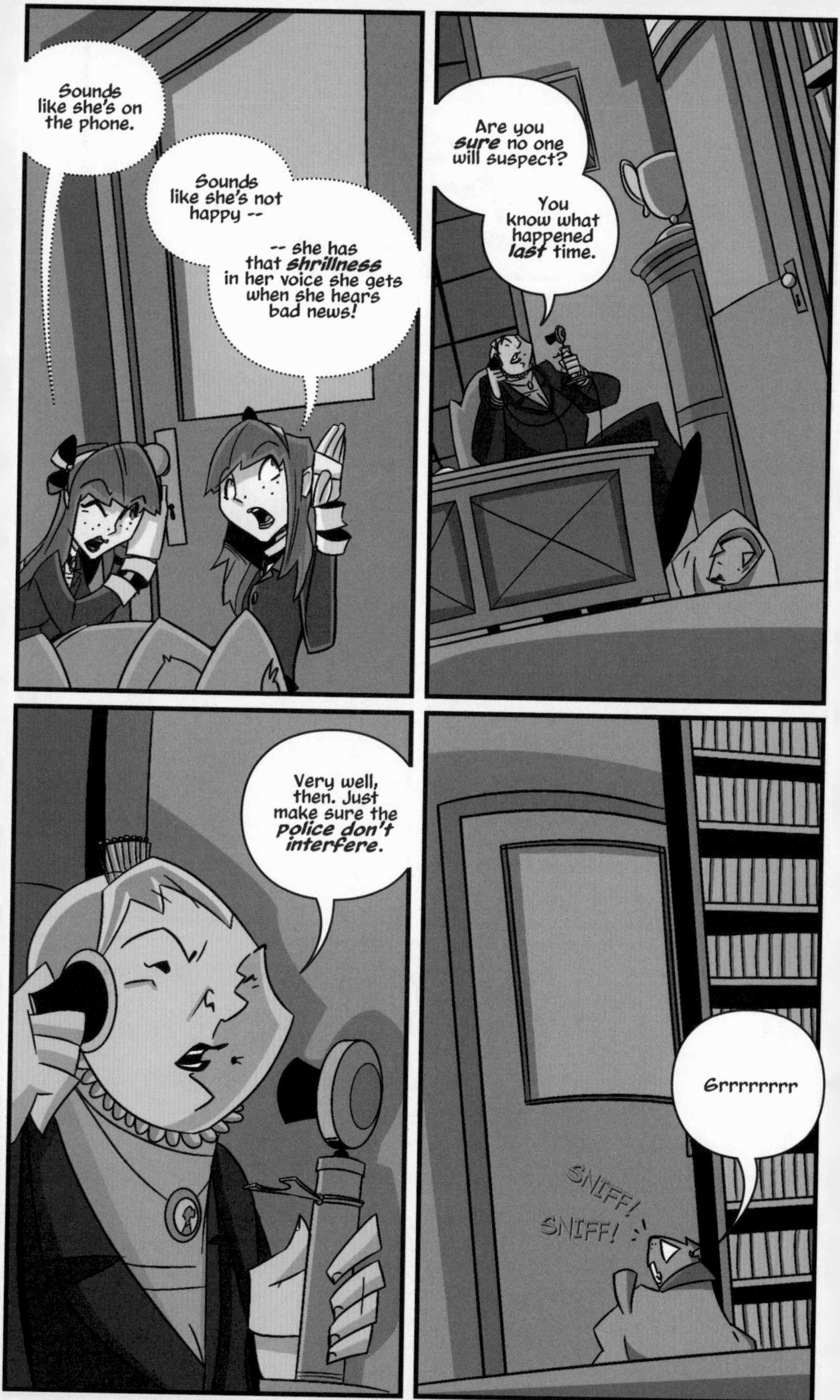
Sounds like she's on the phone.
Sounds like she's not happy --
-- she has that shrillness in her voice she gets when she hears bad news!
Are you sure no one will suspect?
You know what happened last time.
Very well, then. Just make sure the police don't interfere.
SNIFF! SNIFF!
Grrrrrrrr

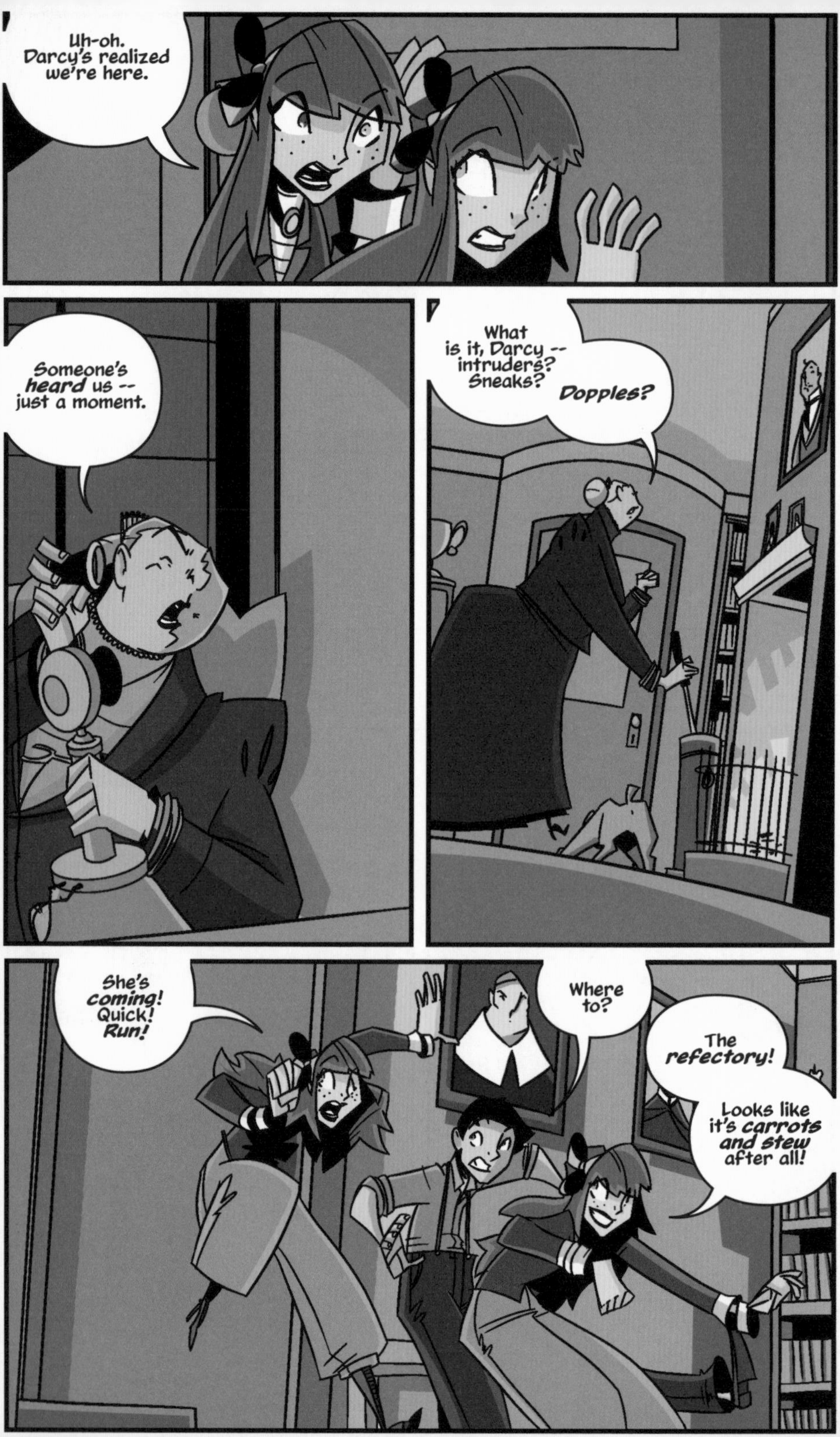
Uh-oh. Darcy's realized we're here.
Someone's *heard* us -- just a moment.
What is it, Darcy -- intruders? Sneaks? *Dopples?*
She's *coming!* Quick! *Run!*
Where to?
The *refectory!*
Looks like it's *carrots and stew* after all!

In an instant they were gone. By the time Miss Rimmer arrived in the refectory, two of the girls who had been sitting at the farthest table had mysteriously disappeared, and Sadie and Saskia were in their place, finishing off two plates of raw carrots and cold stewed cabbage. Erik was sweeping quietly in the corner.

From the doorway, Miss Rimmer stared at them suspiciously. She whispered to Mrs. Omeron, who looked up from the bowls of what only she would describe as stew and then nodded. Miss Rimmer tut-tutted in disappointment and then turned and walked away.

"Can we come out?" squeaked a voice from under the table.

"Stay where you are," Saskia insisted as she watched Miss Rimmer walk down the corridor back to her office.

As soon as the door slammed shut, Sadie and Saskia let go of the two girls they had been holding under the table. One at a time, the girls slid out from underneath the long bench.

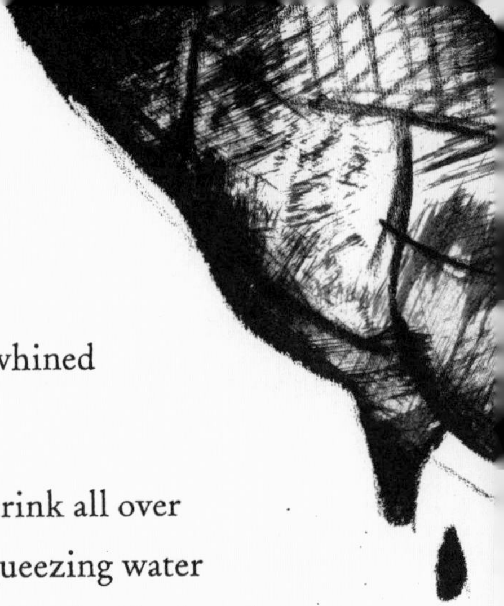

"You've eaten half my dinner," whined Sarah Sotheby.

"And you've made me spill my drink all over myself," added Jenny Paxton, squeezing water from her long braids. She reached under the bench and picked up her now empty cup.

"It would have given you pimples," Sadie whispered. Sarah snatched the plate from Sadie and glared at her in anger. "Or should I say MORE pimples?"

Sarah looked at the remaining cold carrots, gravy, and stewed cabbage and then at Sadie. For the slightest second she seemed tempted to push the plate firmly in Sadie's face and then run.

"I wouldn't do that, Miss Sotheby," Saskia warned, smiling. "You wouldn't get very far."

"I wasn't going to do anything," Sarah replied as she walked off, her white, trembling fingers squeezing the plate until it nearly snapped in two. Jenny, suddenly realizing she was alone with her captors, bolted from the table and hurried after Sarah.

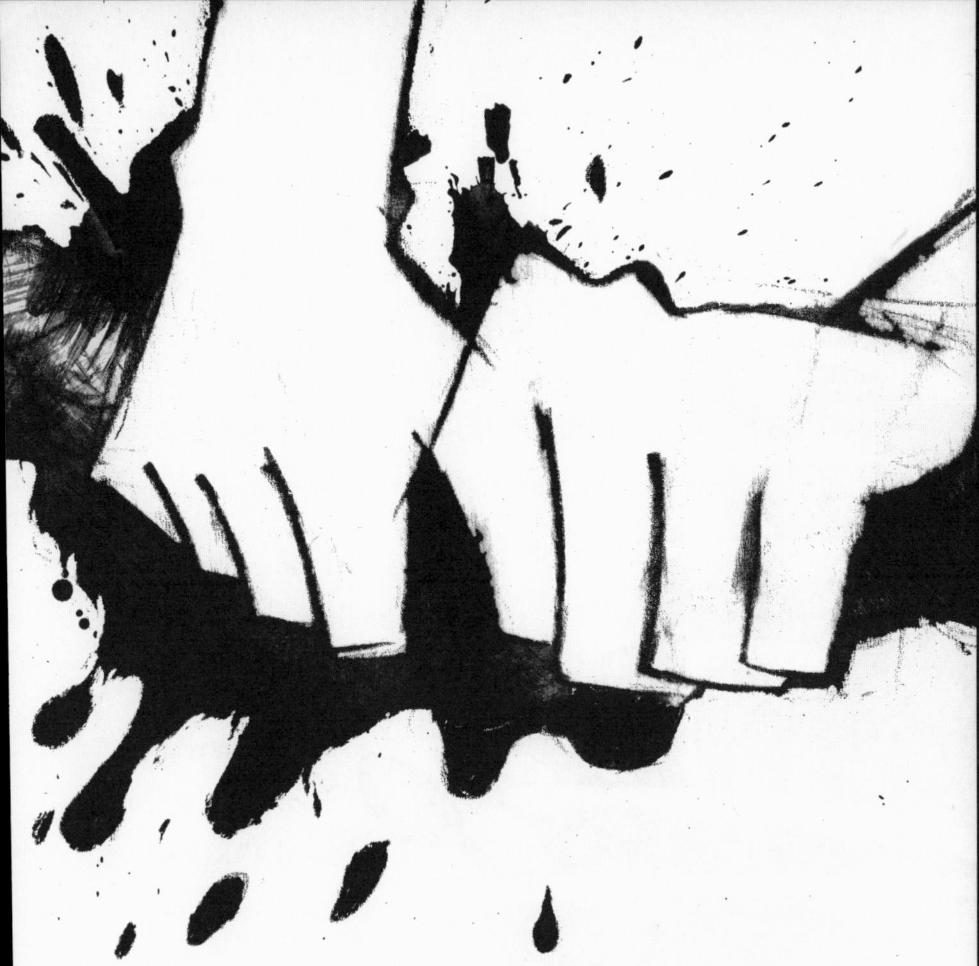

As the Dopples watched the two girls leave, Erik sidled up to the table and leaned on his broom. "Do you think Rimmer knew it was us outside her office?" he asked as the refectory began to empty.

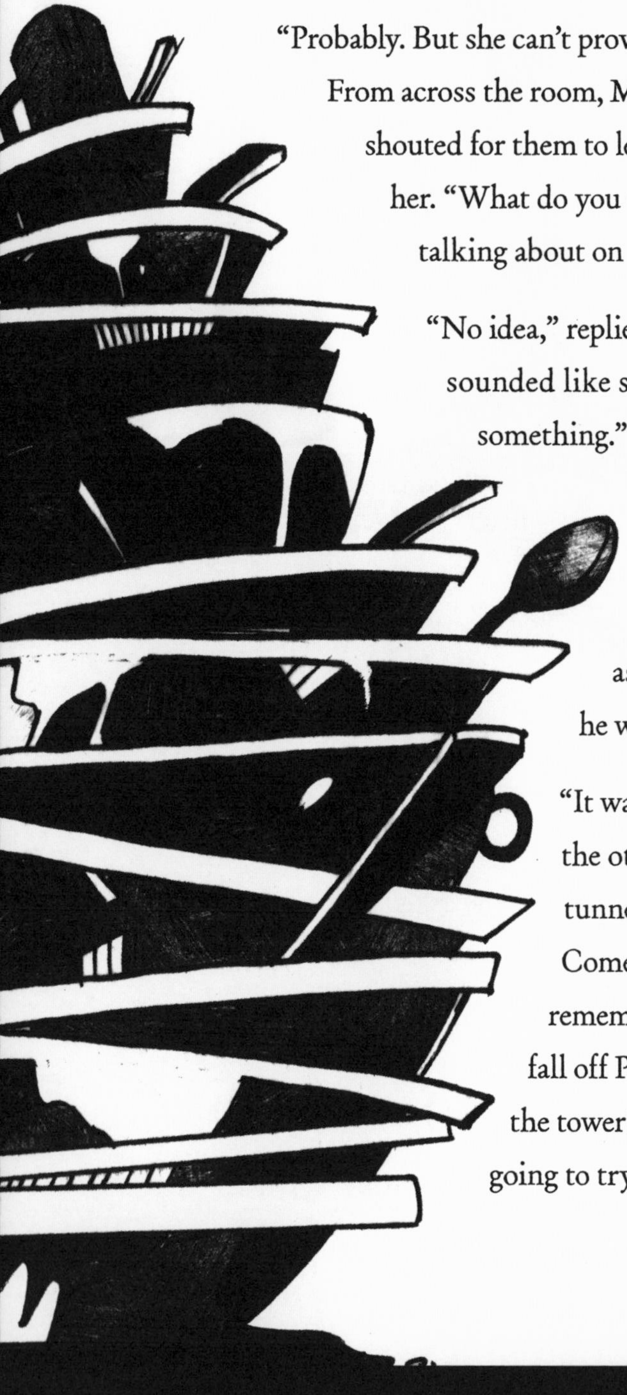

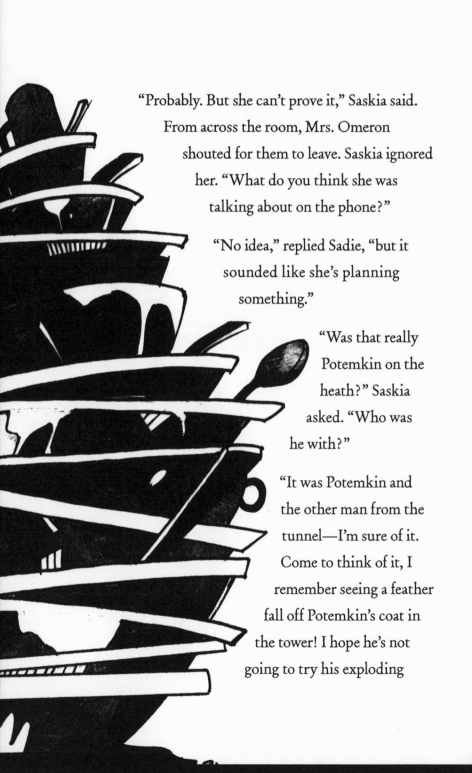

"Probably. But she can't prove it," Saskia said. From across the room, Mrs. Omeron shouted for them to leave. Saskia ignored her. "What do you think she was talking about on the phone?"

"No idea," replied Sadie, "but it sounded like she's planning something."

"Was that really Potemkin on the heath?" Saskia asked. "Who was he with?"

"It was Potemkin and the other man from the tunnel—I'm sure of it. Come to think of it, I remember seeing a feather fall off Potemkin's coat in the tower! I hope he's not going to try his exploding

chicken trick again. . . ." Mrs. Omeron rattled the dishes
in an attempt to rouse the three from the table.

"Don't you have somewhere to go, Miss Dopples?" she
bellowed. "And you, Erik Morrissey Ganger—pick up that
broom. You have work to do and a pile of dishes higher
than your head."

Erik raised one eyebrow and looked at the twins. "I'll see
you tonight in the tower—try to sneak out after lights-
out. Be careful."

With that, Erik grabbed the broom, cleared the bowls
from the table, and followed Mrs. Omeron into the
kitchen. Sadie and Saskia remained at the table.

Saskia's eyes followed a cobweb as it floated gently through
the air toward them. Her gaze rested on the scowling face
of Isambard Dunstan, glaring at her from the stained-glass
window in the refectory wall. He was the school's original
patron and had left the house to be used as a home for
children abandoned by their parents. Children just like
Saskia and Sadie Dopple.

Neither Saskia nor her sister liked to think that they had been abandoned; they had merely been temporarily forgotten. However, it was at times like these, when they were alone in the refectory with the mess of the school all around them, that they realized they were just that: abandoned. Saskia longed for her mother to hold her in her arms again—just as she had on the day she left the twins, promising to return.

And then Saskia thought of someone else who had been like a mother to her, for a little while. She took a breath and said slowly, "I know one thing."

"What's that?" Sadie asked as she flicked a forgotten carrot across the table.

"Since I met Madame Raphael, I haven't felt as lonely."

"Are you trying to tell me again that she was real?" Sadie asked suspiciously.

"She is real. And something she said has sort of, well, changed me," Saskia replied nervously, afraid that her sister would scoff at what she was about to say. "She told me the Companion would always be near when I needed him, so . . . I've been praying." Saskia rushed on, "And I know those prayers have been listened to. I can feel it. I know we'll see our mother again. It's like a promise that's been made inside me . . . and it'll be kept."

Sadie snorted jealously. "Wishful thinking—poppycock—you've eaten too many carrots . . . or been brainwashed by Muzz Elliott and all that fine living. You're as batty as that old woman feeding the squirrels."

"It's not that, Sadie. I'm starting to believe what she said," Saskia replied, knowing her words had unsettled her sister. "I don't want to leave you behind in this. I want you to meet her so she can tell you, too. It works—really works—"

"Meet a ghost who'll teach me to pray?" snapped Sadie.

"She's not a ghost—she's an angel."

"Angel?" Sadie laughed. "Next you'll be telling me that old Dunstan up there in that window can tell us what we're thinking."

Saskia ignored what Sadie said. "We can go back to Spaniards House this weekend and see Muzz Elliott—we'll wait for Madame Raphael to appear, and then—"

"We'll be as mad as Cicely Windylove," Sadie replied.

"So you'll give it a chance?" Saskia asked her sister.

Sadie shrugged her shoulders. She watched Erik return to the refectory and pick up the dishes from a table at the other end of the room. "Perhaps a chance and nothing more than that," she replied with a half smile.

The rest of the day passed slowly. Sadie and Saskia finished their lessons distractedly, ate another tasteless meal, and spent the evening watching Charlotte Grimdyke search for her pencil case while they passed it back and forth under the table.

At last the girls were all in their beds and Miss Rimmer had gone to her room, after threatening to lock them in the tower for a month if they said another word past lights-out. The twins got up, stuffed some clothes under the sheets to make it look like they were still in bed, and crept down the silent hall. They reached the tower in no time and began the climb up to Erik's room.

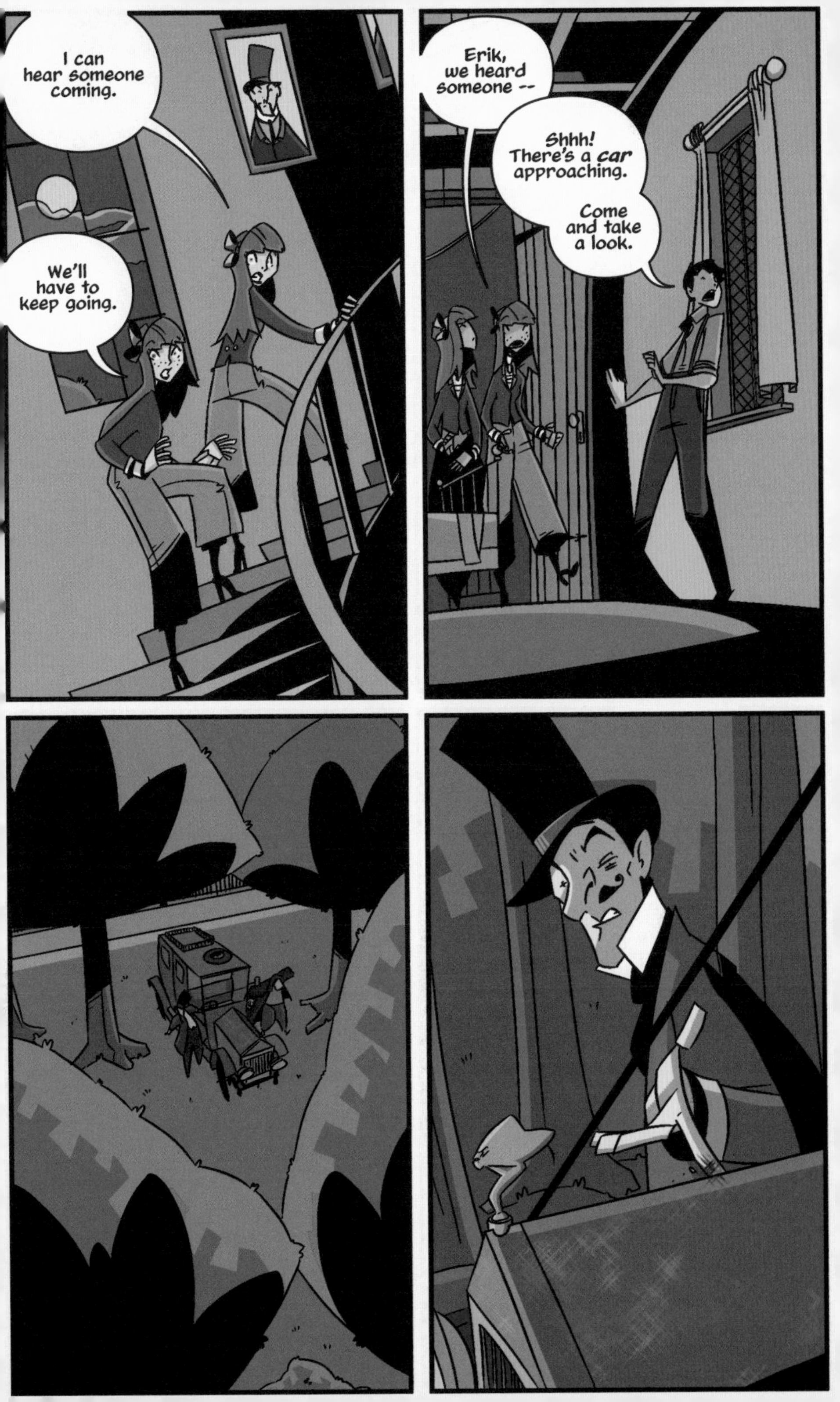
I can hear someone coming.
We'll have to keep going.
Erik, we heard someone --
Shhh! There's a *car* approaching.
Come and take a look.

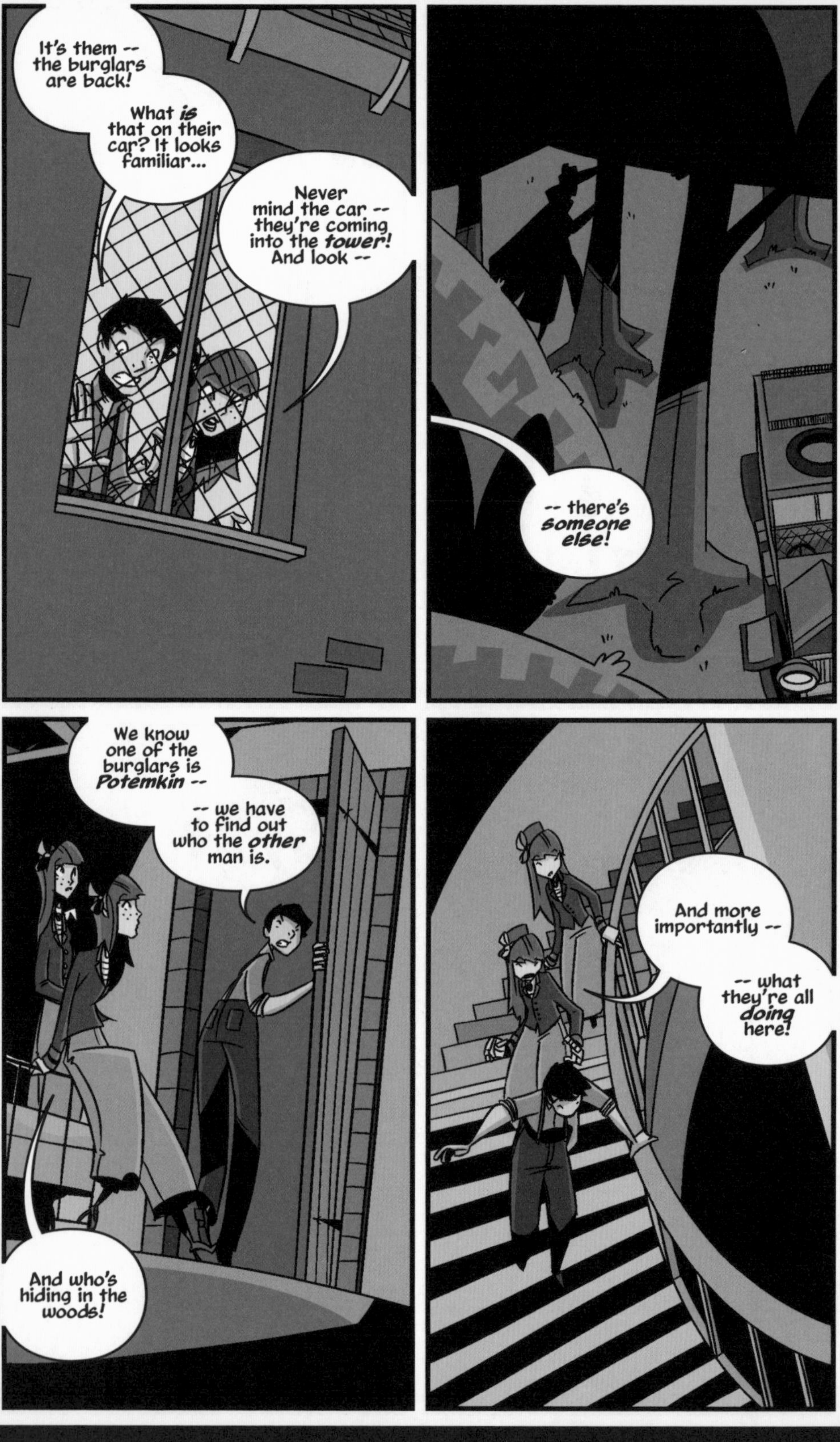
It's them -- the burglars are back!
What *is* that on their car? It looks familiar...
Never mind the car -- they're coming into the *tower*! And look --
-- there's *someone else*!
We know one of the burglars is *Potemkin* --
-- we have to find out who the *other* man is.
And who's hiding in the woods!
And more importantly --
-- what they're all *doing* here!

Together they slipped quietly down the stairs and held their breath. They could hear the scraping of the stone as the wall slipped from its place to reveal the hidden tunnel.

"Gotta keep quiet," said one of the men.

"The boy will be asleep by now—it's after lights-out, and I'm certain there is no one else in the tower tonight," replied the other man.

It was a voice that Erik and Sadie knew well.

"It's Potemkin," Sadie whispered, stifling a scream.

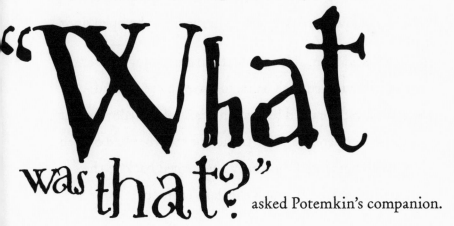 "What was that?" asked Potemkin's companion.

"Wind . . . just the wind," Potemkin replied with a touch of annoyance. "This is the last time we'll have to do this, and I'm not going to be stopped by the wind."

The Dopples and Erik clung tightly to the walls and kept still. They could hear the men's footsteps fading as the two burglars went into the tunnel. They waited until all was silent. Saskia gripped Sadie's hand as all three crept toward the entrance.

"We'll have to go inside," Erik said quietly. Night shadows were streaming in through the open door.

Erik glanced from side to side, then darted forward and slipped into the tunnel. Sadie followed close behind. Saskia moved forward but caught sight of a shadow moving outside the open door. She turned to see what had caused it but saw nothing. Cautiously she turned back to the tunnel and passed through the dark entrance.

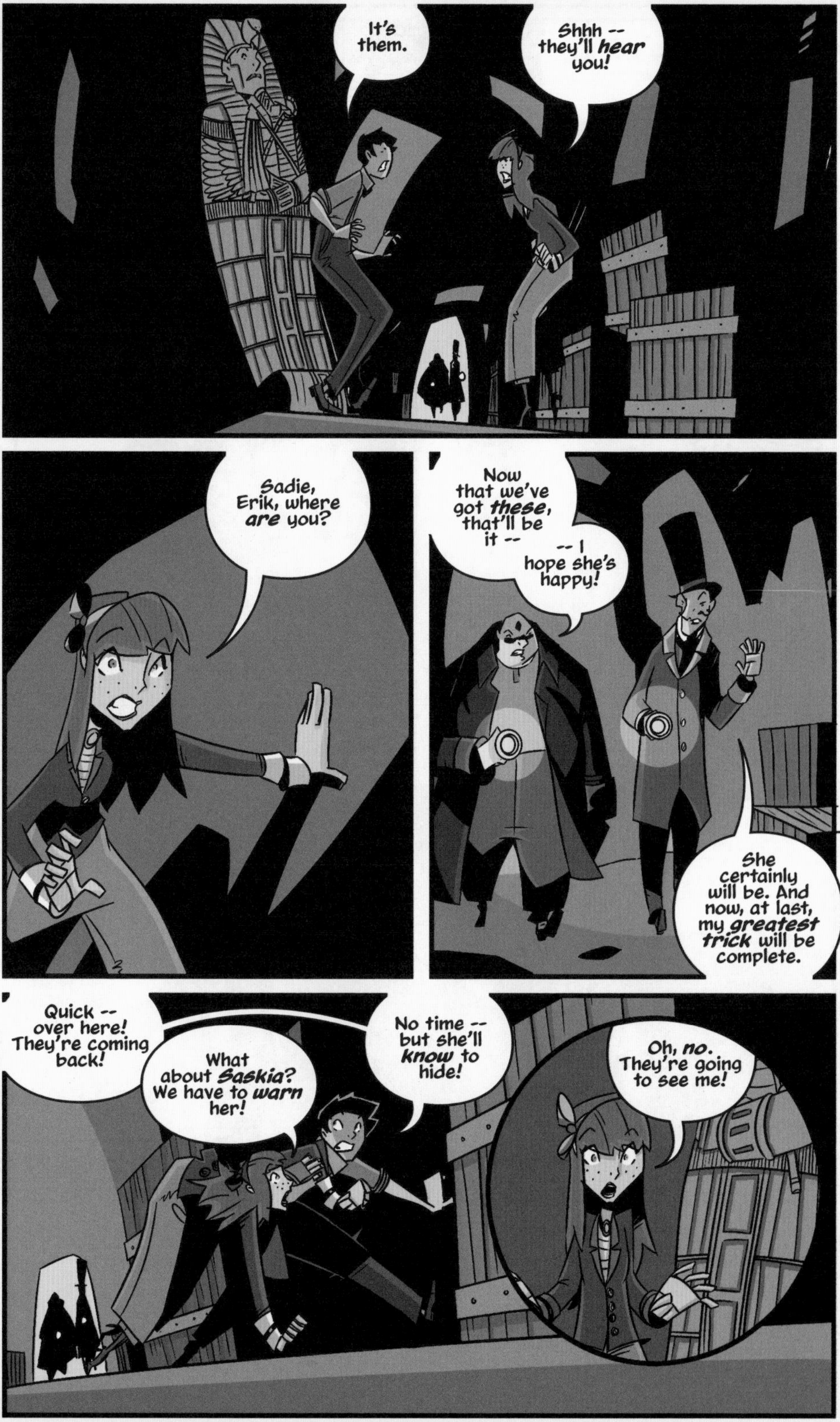

It's them.
Shhh -- they'll *hear* you!
Sadie, Erik, where *are* you?
Now that we've got *these*, that'll be it --
-- I hope she's happy!
She certainly will be. And now, at last, my *greatest trick* will be complete.
Quick -- over here! They're coming back!
What about *Saskia*? We have to *warn* her!
No time -- but she'll *know* to hide!
Oh, *no*. They're going to see me!

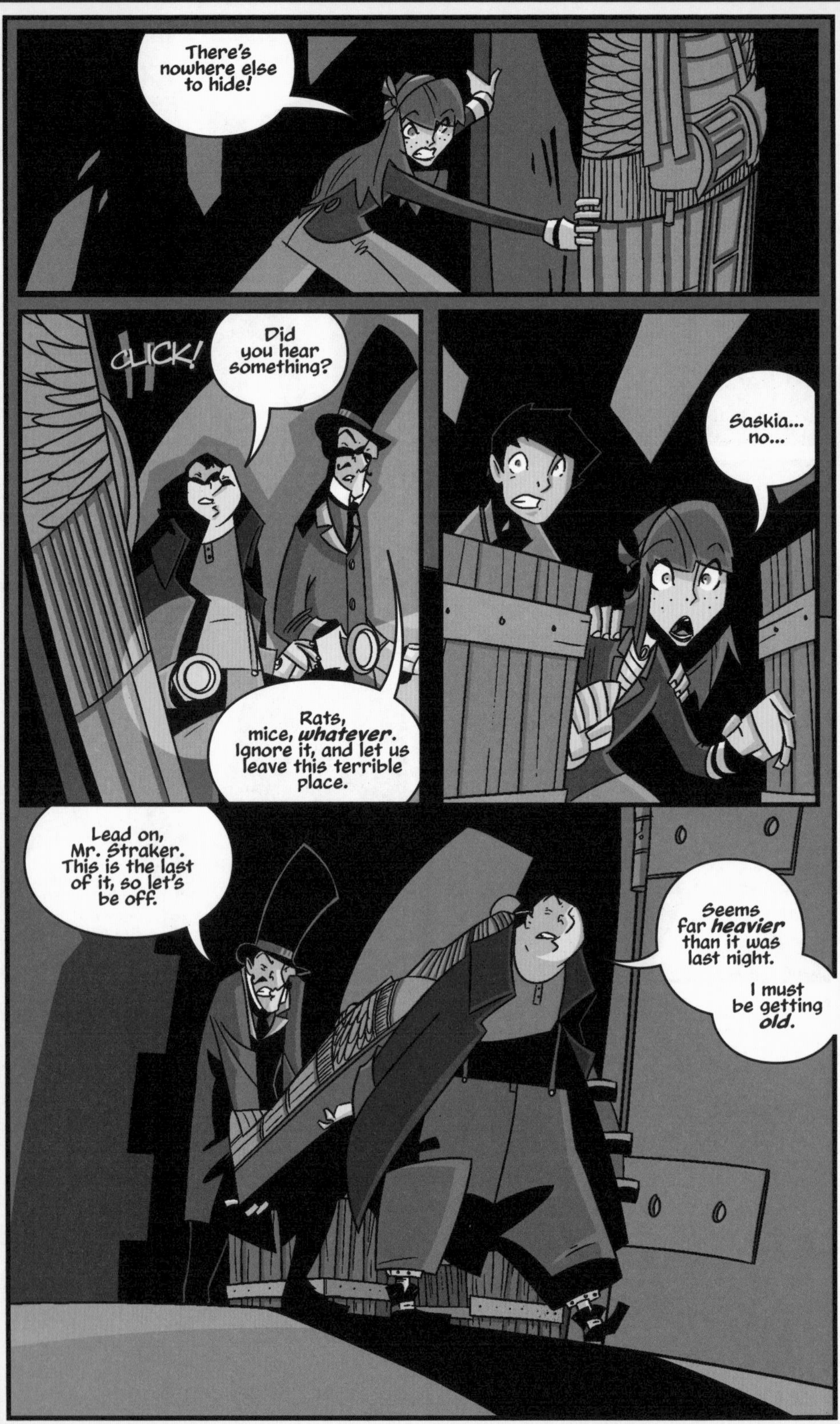
There's nowhere else to hide!
CLICK!
Did you hear something?
Rats, mice, whatever. Ignore it, and let us leave this terrible place.
Saskia... no...
Lead on, Mr. Straker. This is the last of it, so let's be off.
Seems far heavier than it was last night.
I must be getting old.

Sadie held her face in her hands and tried to hold back the tears. The last she had seen of Saskia was her shadowy figure pulling open the lid of the sarcophagus and slipping inside before Potemkin and Straker carried it away.

"She's gone, Erik. They've taken her,"

Sadie moaned, her words
echoing through the tunnel.

Chapter Six
Mutterings of a Madman

THE WALL SLID shut, blocking out the light from the hallway. There was an eerie silence. A dull emptiness filled the tunnel.

Finally Erik spoke. "We'll find her. We can track down Potemkin and then rescue Saskia."

"Why didn't they lock him up better? The police saw him escape their van. He is a magician, after all!" Sadie protested. She squeezed her fingertips into her palms in frustration.

"There has to be a way to open this door from the inside," Erik said as he shone his flashlight at the rock wall and traced the outline of the tunnel door with his finger. "It must be here somewhere."

"They've taken her, Erik!" Sadie wailed. "They don't even know she's in that thing. She could . . . she could . . ."

"Don't even think it. We'll find her. We have to believe we will."

"And what will they do to her when they find her? Potemkin was going to electrocute us—so what will he do to her?"

"We'll get her before then. We have to—" Erik didn't finish his thought.

From the dark distance came a strange sound. At first it was a whisper and then a whistle. Then it was like the mutterings of a madman dragging a long chain across the stone floor. Sadie looked at Erik. Her eyes glinted with fear. Every thought conjured the impossible. Whatever was making the sound was coming closer; whatever was coming closer would soon find Sadie and Erik.

"What is it?" asked Sadie, her mouth close to Erik's ear.

"I'm not sure. It could be—"

"A ghost?"
Sadie asked.

"I-I-I don't believe . . ." Erik stammered, trying to think of what to do.

"What else would make a noise like that?" Sadie asked in a rising panic as a sudden chill wind swirled through the tunnel around them.

. . .

Saskia lay on her back in the sarcophagus, listening to the muffled crunch of feet on gravel below. She swayed and bounced with each footstep as she was carried away by Potemkin and the man Potemkin had called Mr. Straker.

A stale, musty odor filled her nose. Saskia tried not to imagine who the previous occupant of the

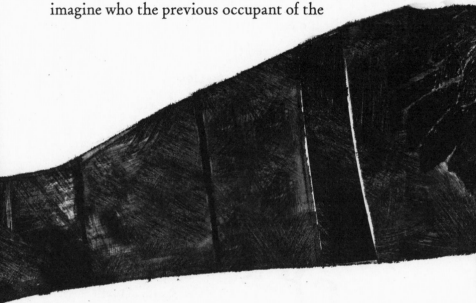

coffin had been . . . or how long the body had been encased in the box. She suddenly felt very cold.

The two men stopped. Saskia heard a car door open and felt herself slide jerkily forward as the sarcophagus was pushed across a rough surface. Then the door closed and all was quiet. After a moment, she heard the engine start noisily.

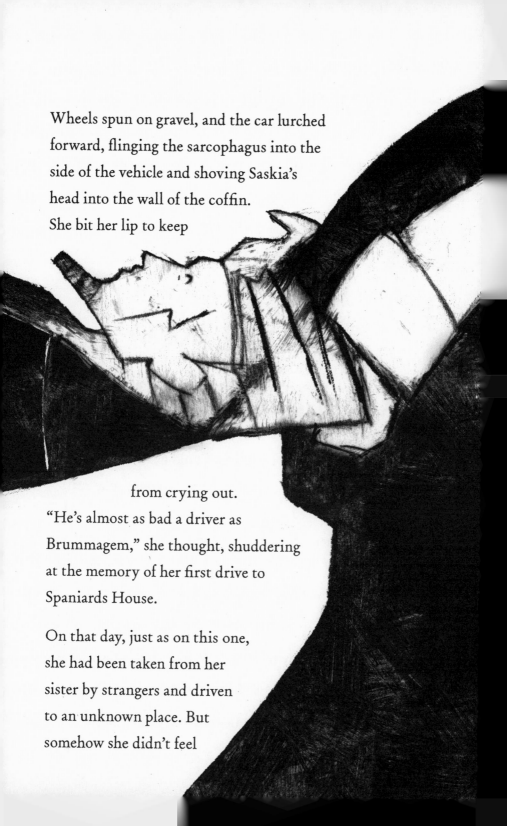

Wheels spun on gravel, and the car lurched forward, flinging the sarcophagus into the side of the vehicle and shoving Saskia's head into the wall of the coffin. She bit her lip to keep

from crying out. "He's almost as bad a driver as Brummagem," she thought, shuddering at the memory of her first drive to Spaniards House.

On that day, just as on this one, she had been taken from her sister by strangers and driven to an unknown place. But somehow she didn't feel as afraid as she had when she was first driven to Muzz Elliott's. She couldn't explain it, but she had a new sort of strength growing inside her, like an elegant swan rising from a still pond.

Saskia took a deep breath and slowly exhaled.

"Madame Raphael?" she mouthed. "Can you hear me?"

She listened, straining, but all she could hear was the whirring of the engine. She thought, "I know you're real. I know you appeared to me at Spaniards House. You said you would be here when I needed you, and I need your help now. I'm locked in a coffin, in a car with two burglars, and I don't know how I'll ever get back to Erik and Sadie. . . ."

Tears came to Saskia's eyes as she thought of her sister and Erik. She blinked them away furiously. "Why won't Sadie believe me?" she thought. "I've shown her the key—and the note!

And Erik's no help either. Sadie's my own sister, but she

would believe Erik sooner than me. Madame Raphael, why can't you appear to them, too?" she called out with her thoughts. "Then they would know I'm not lying. If only you would show yourself to them just once. . . . If only you would show yourself to me again . . . just once."

As if in answer, a loud whistle pierced the night.

Saskia heard a rumbling growing louder, until at last she recognized the steady th-thunk of a passing train. The car slowed and came to a stop. Above the rumble of the train, Saskia could make out the muddled voices of Potemkin and Straker. She put her ear next to the crack that formed the opening of the sarcophagus and listened.

"I'm glad not to be going back to that place again," came the coarser voice of Straker.

"You should be more grateful that the headmistress entrusted you with such an important job," said Potemkin. "Don't forget that none of this could have been done without her help."

Saskia froze. "Headmistress?" she thought. A chill ran up her spine. "So that's what Rimmer's been up to! I have to get back—I have to warn the others!"

* * *

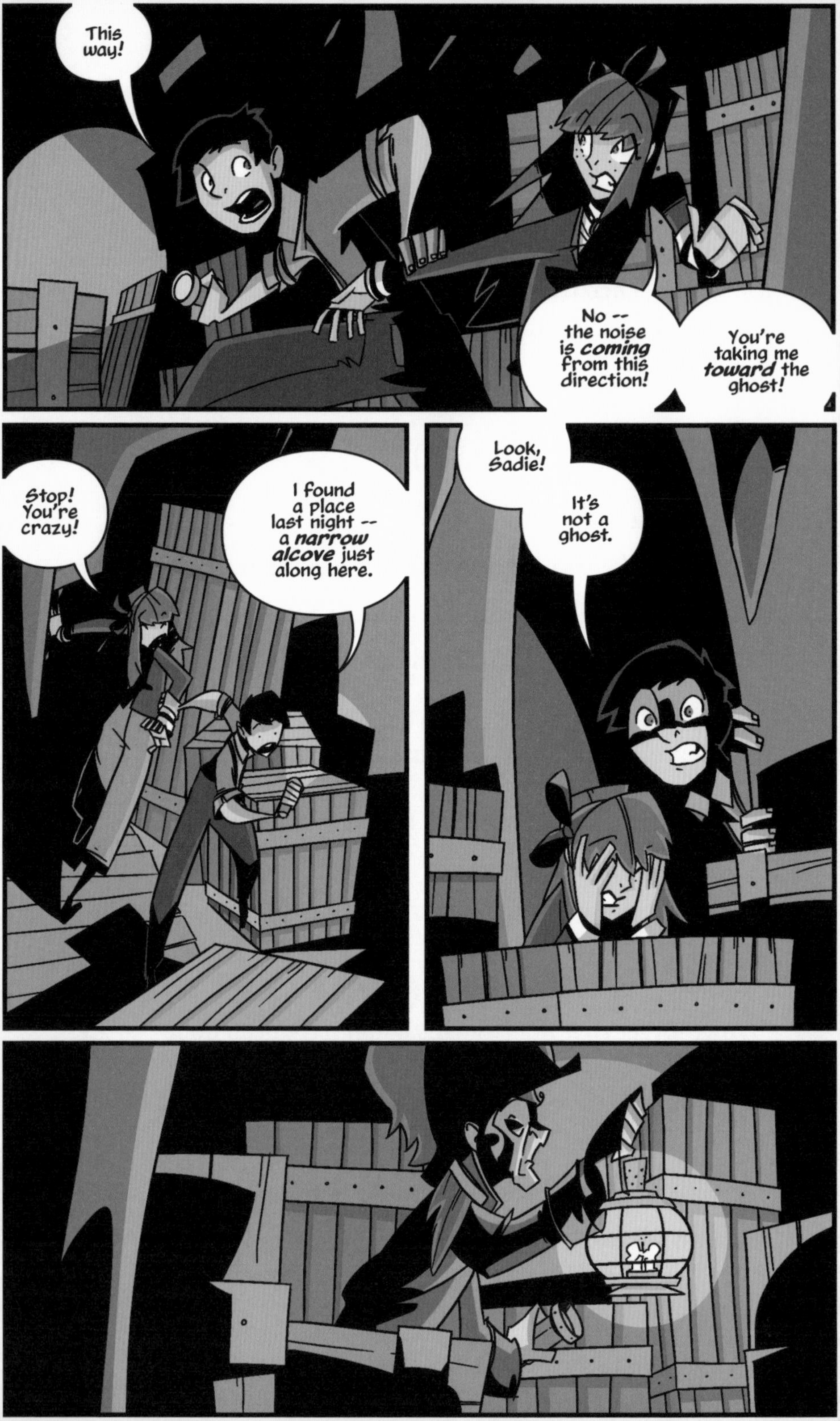

This way!
No -- the noise is *coming* from this direction!
You're taking me *toward* the ghost!
Stop! You're crazy!
I found a place last night -- a *narrow alcove* just along here.
Look, Sadie!
It's not a ghost.

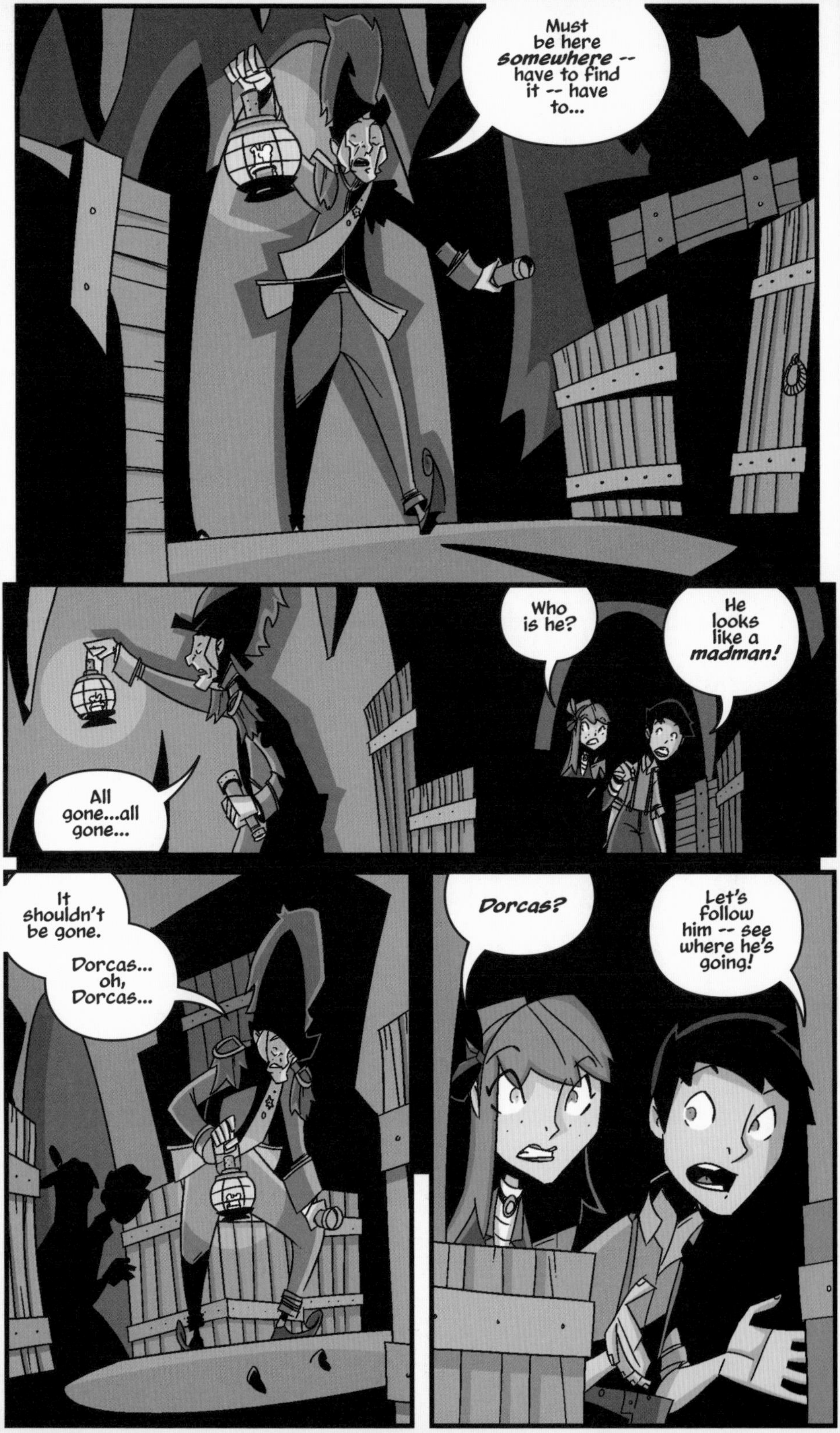
Must be here *somewhere* -- have to find it -- have to...
Who is he?
He looks like a *madman!*
All gone...all gone...
It shouldn't be gone.
Dorcas... oh, Dorcas...
Dorcas?
Let's follow him -- see where he's going!

Erik and Sadie crept out of the alcove and followed cautiously after the strange man. Soon he was nothing but a distant amber glow in the dark tunnel. His mutterings could no longer be heard as he disappeared into the blackness. Erik paused for a moment and switched on the flashlight. He looked in the direction the man had gone.

"The passage is leading away from the school," he said.

"To the heath?" Sadie asked.

"No," said Erik slowly.

Suddenly he turned to face Sadie. "I think it's him."

"Who?" asked Sadie anxiously.

"Lord Gervez. He was looking for something, but he wasn't acting like a burglar."

"We did see Dorcas Potts go into Lord Gervez's house—that might explain why he was asking for her," Sadie reasoned. "But Lord Gervez or not, that doesn't change the fact that we have to find Saskia. The burglars are probably miles away by now!"

Erik thought for a moment.

"There **must** be a way out through Gervez's house," he said.

"If we go through the school, Rimmer could find us. She was prowling around last night. But if that was Lord Gervez, he looked pretty harmless. If he stops us, then we'll just make a run for it. It's the only way we'll get away from this place. Then we'll go after Potemkin. He shouldn't be hard to find."

"Hard to find?" Sadie laughed. "The man's an escaped convict—he's not going to be hanging around on the street corner waiting for us to walk up and catch him, is he?"

"I saw their car. There can't be many like that one—even in the whole of London," Erik said as he smiled at her in the dim light.

"So we go after Lord Gervez, get out through his house, and search London for a car?" she asked disbelievingly.

"Yes," he said simply. "We can find Saskia by following Lord Gervez."

In the glow of the flashlight, Erik saw Sadie raise a skeptical brow over her yellow eye. "I guess it's better than standing around here," she said quickly, her voice breaking from a whisper and echoing far along the corridor.

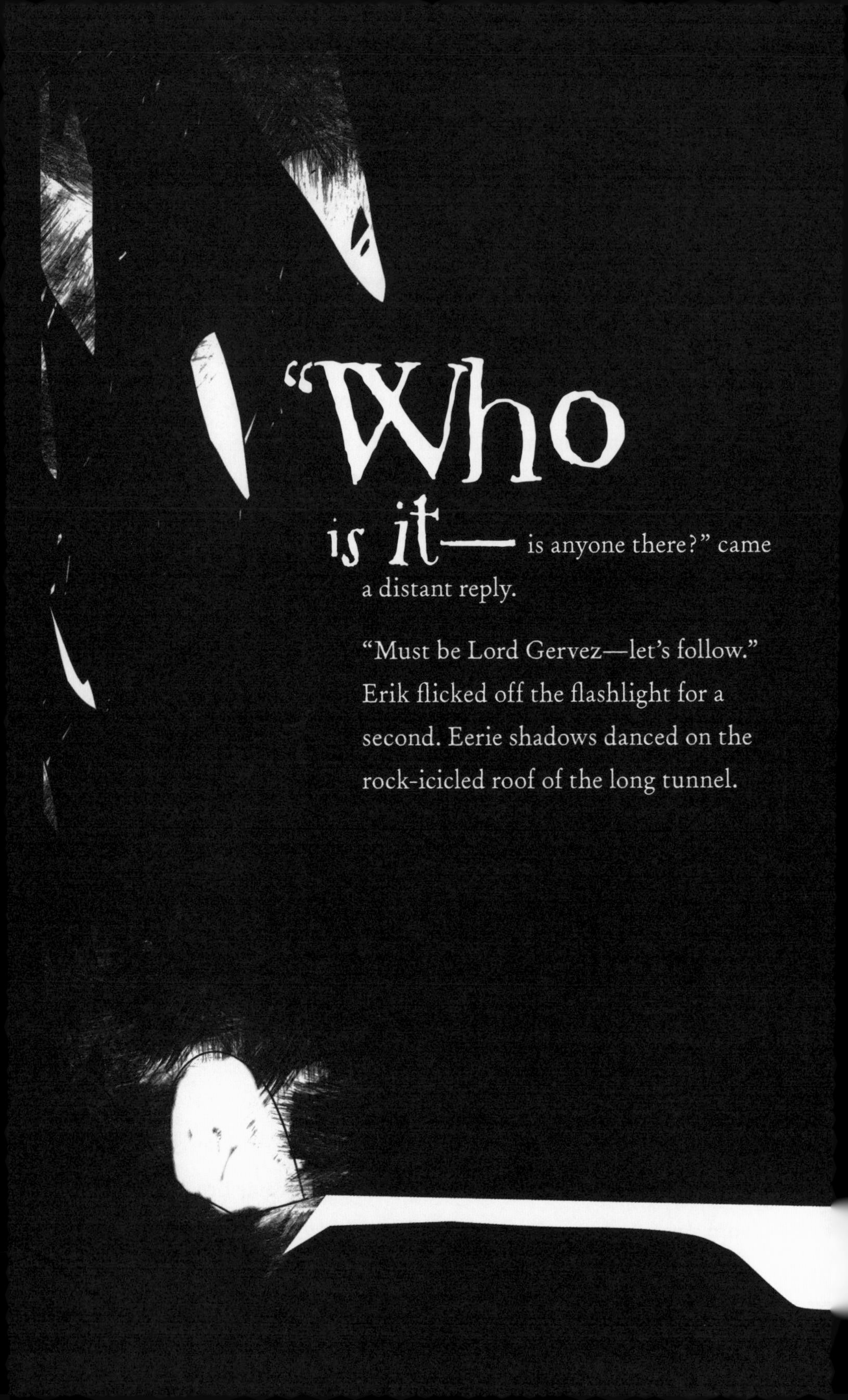

"Who is it— is anyone there?" came a distant reply.

"Must be Lord Gervez—let's follow." Erik flicked off the flashlight for a second. Eerie shadows danced on the rock-icicled roof of the long tunnel.

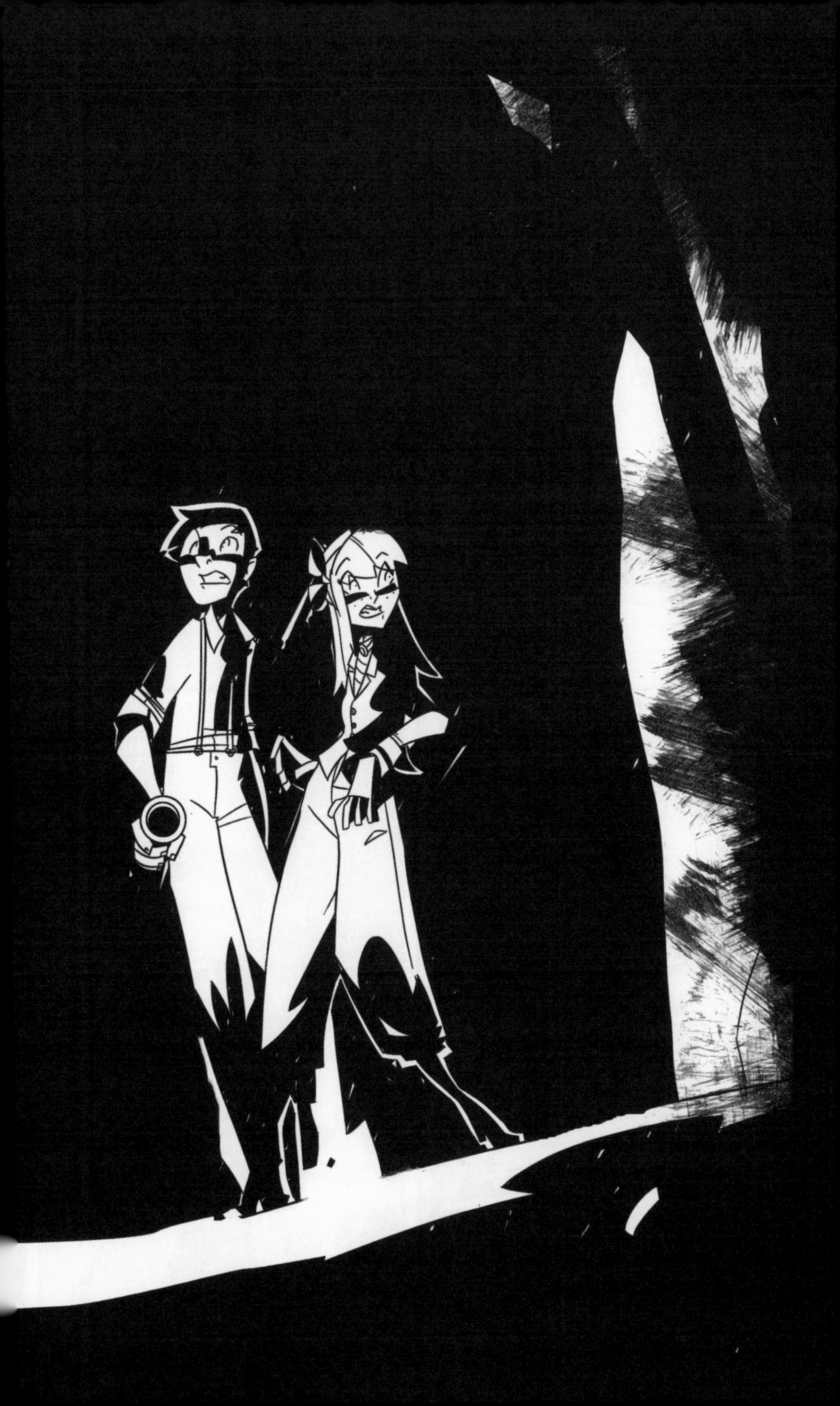

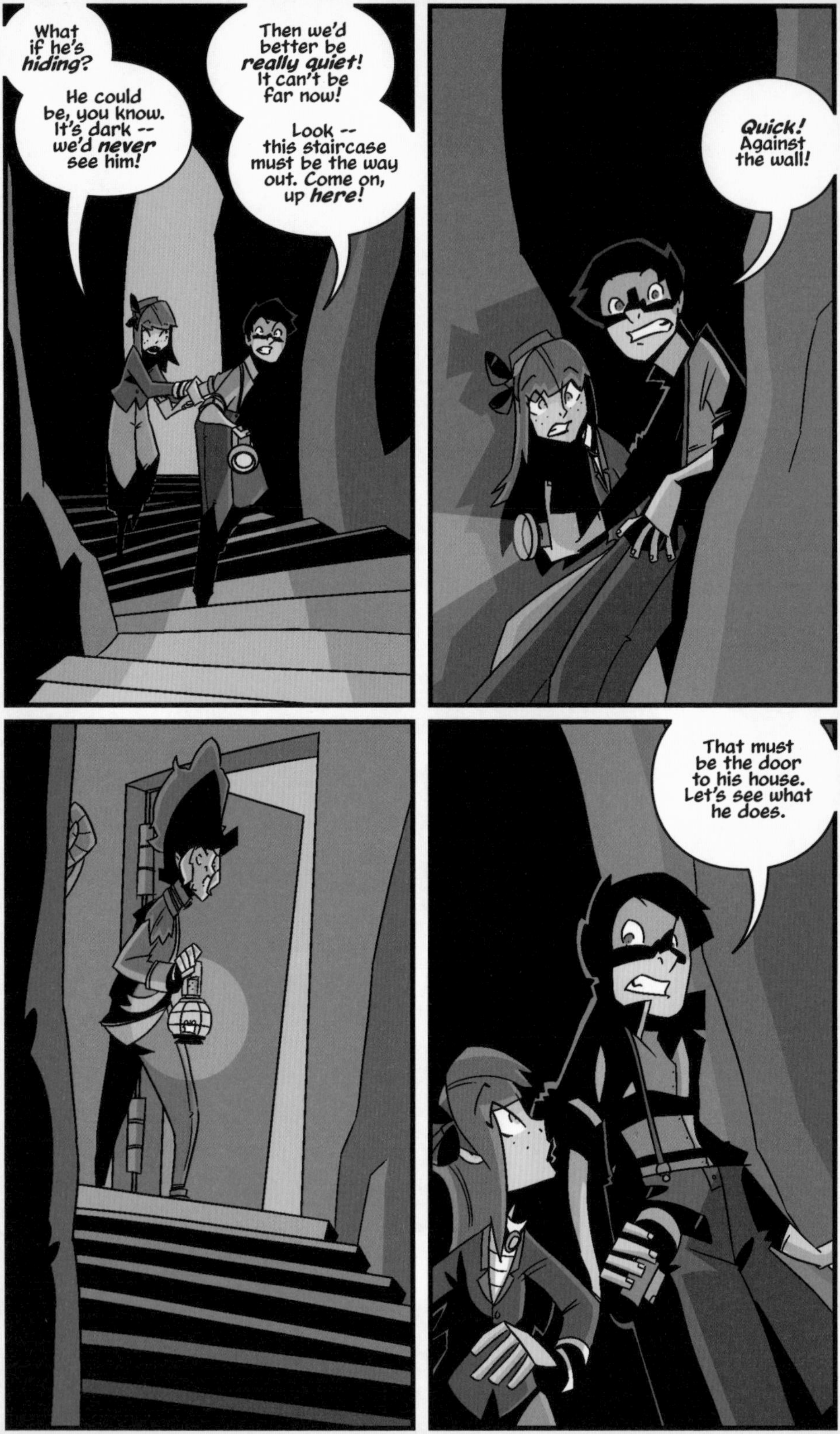
What if he's *hiding?*
He could be, you know. It's dark -- we'd *never* see him!
Then we'd better be *really quiet!* It can't be far now!
Look -- this staircase must be the way out. Come on, up *here!*
Quick! Against the wall!
That must be the door to his house. Let's see what he does.

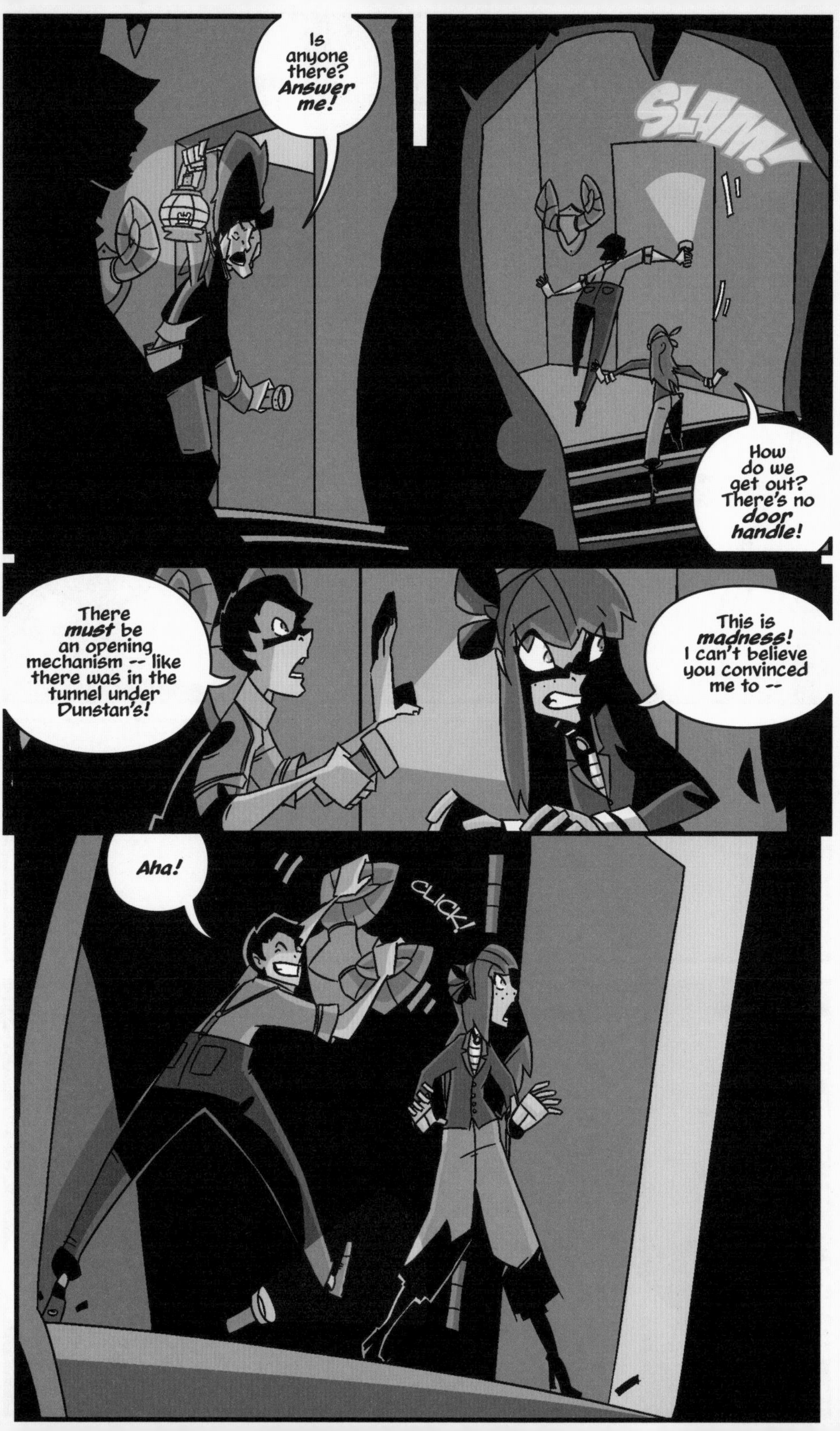
Is anyone there? *Answer me!*
SLAM!
How do we get out? There's no *door handle!*
There *must* be an opening mechanism -- like there was in the tunnel under Dunstan's!
This is *madness!* I can't believe you convinced me to --
Aha!
CLICK!

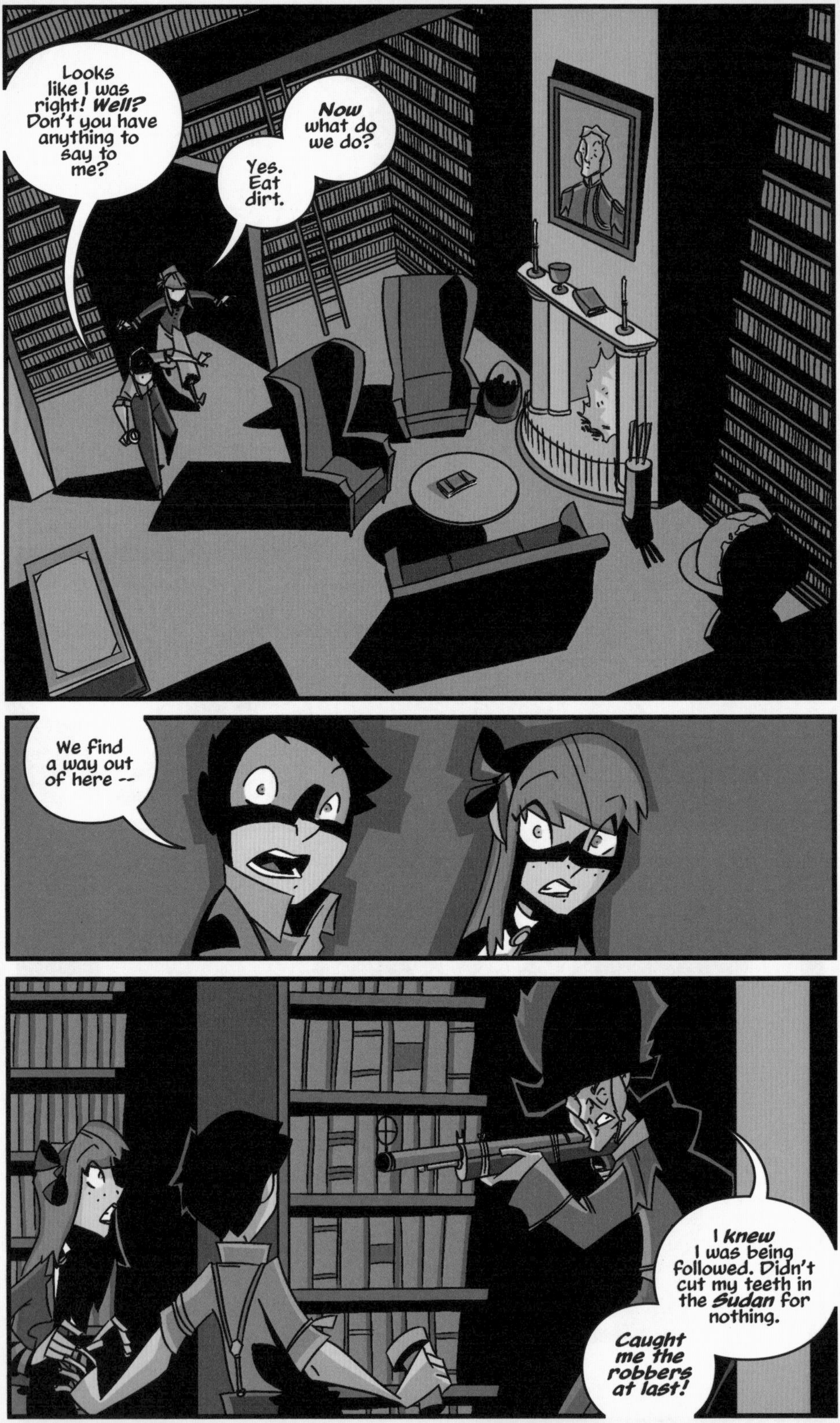
Looks like I was right! *Well?* Don't you have anything to say to me?
Now what do we do?
Yes. Eat dirt.
We find a way out of here --
I *knew* I was being followed. Didn't cut my teeth in the *Sudan* for nothing.
Caught me the robbers at last!

The man looked down the barrel of the rifle. He aimed the muzzle at Erik, his finger trembling over the hair trigger.

"We're not robbers," said Erik.

Sadie butted in. "I lost my sister—the burglars have taken her."

"Burglars . . . taken your sister?" the man asked, turning toward Sadie so the gun was now aimed at her. "Was she valuable? Never heard of a burglar stealing a sister before. Was she made of gold? Did she have precious jewels as eyes, or onyx teeth?"

"She was hiding," Sadie said.

"Hiding? And they still managed to steal her?" he asked, at last lowering the weapon. "Happened to me once. Well, not the stealing part. I was hiding in a swamp, and a crocodile bit me in the Congo."

"Congo?" Erik asked, wondering what part of the body that could possibly be.

"Bad location to be bitten—not a hospital for miles," the man said. "But burglars—burglars make my blood boil, and if you are caught in my house when candles have been lit and children should be in bed, that can make you only one thing: burglars!"

He raised the rifle again and took aim.

"What did they take from you?" Erik asked as he saw the man's finger reach for the trigger.

"You should know; you did it," the man replied. "I have never met a burglar dressed in a school uniform. Did Miss Rimmer train you for this? Is it to pay for that madhouse she calls a school? I've been watching her ever since she took over as headmistress—a power-hungry tyrant, if you ask me."

"So you are Lord Gervez?" Erik asked, shooting Sadie a sideways glance.

"Indeed I am," replied his lordship.

"Then you have to believe us," Sadie said urgently. "We found the tunnel when the burglars were taking away a large coffin—"

"A sarcophagus," Erik said quickly, hoping Lord Gervez would believe them.

"Sarcophagus?" Lord Gervez asked.

"It's what they took my sister in—she was hiding inside so they wouldn't find her, but now they've taken her away."

Lord Gervez looked even more confused. His eyes widened, then scrunched tightly shut, then opened again.

"Honestly, we're not burglars," Erik repeated as Lord

Gervez dithered with the rifle. "We found the tunnel and followed you here."

Lord Gervez sighed. He lowered the rifle to the ground.

"Then—then who are you?" he asked quietly, as if the sigh had taken away the last of his aged voice.

"This is Sadie Dopple, and I am Erik Morrissey Ganger. We live at Isambard Dunstan's," Erik said.

"We followed two burglars into the tunnel under the school, and then we had to hide. They got my sister, and then we saw you, so we followed you here," Sadie continued.

"I saw the burglars last night," explained Erik. "They were taking things from the tunnel —they said they would come back tonight, so we waited for them."

"What kinds of things?" Lord Gervez asked expectantly.

"Treasure, that's what it was," Sadie said without thinking or even knowing what had been taken. "It was Mr. Potemkin and a man called Straker—they took it."

"Treasure? Oh dear." Lord Gervez sighed and sat down in one of the leather chairs by the fireplace. He set down his gun and motioned toward a leather sofa opposite him. "You may as well have a seat," he told them.

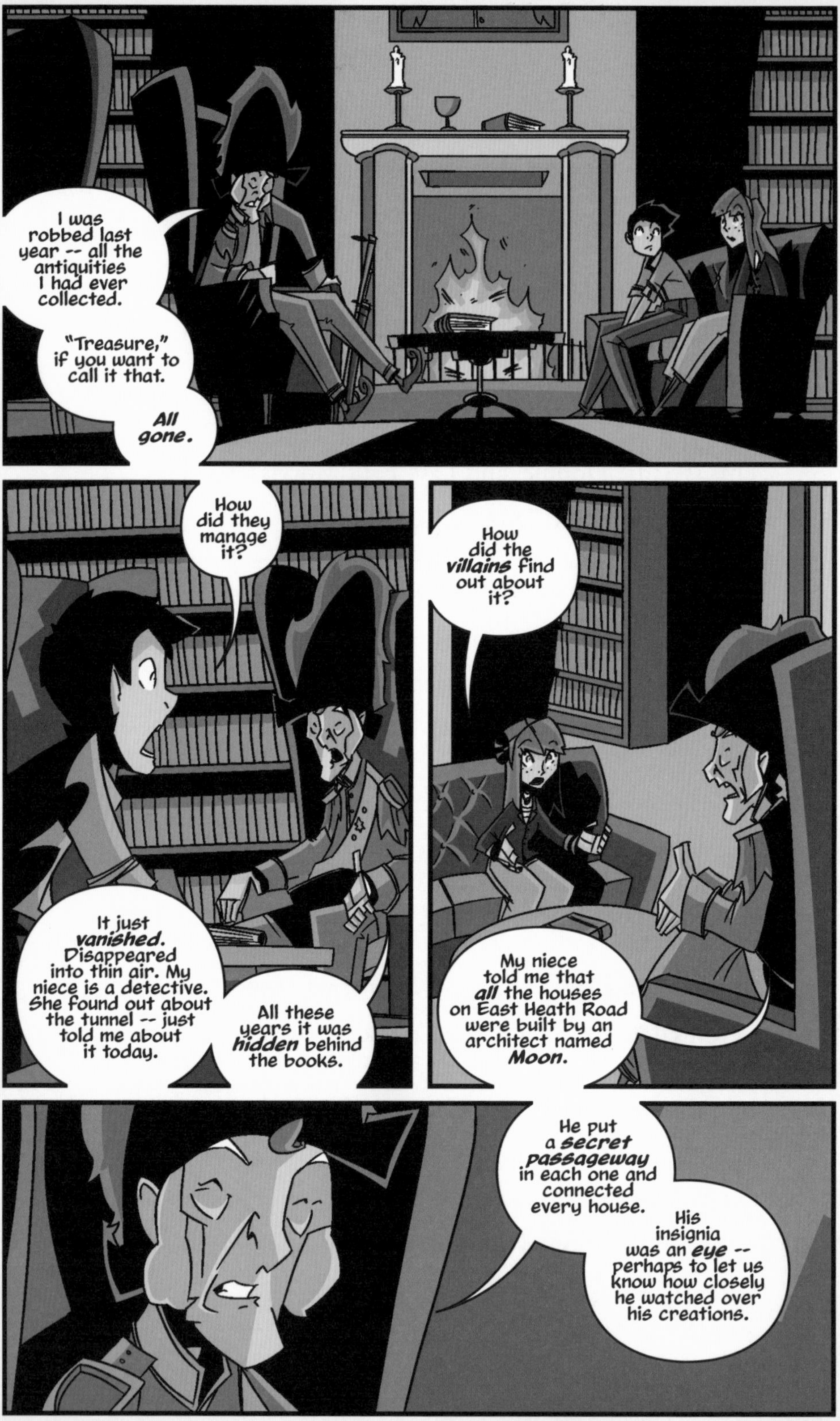

I was robbed last year -- all the antiquities I had ever collected.
"Treasure," if you want to call it that.
All gone.
How did they manage it?
It just vanished. Disappeared into thin air. My niece is a detective. She found out about the tunnel -- just told me about it today.
All these years it was hidden behind the books.
How did the villains find out about it?
My niece told me that all the houses on East Heath Road were built by an architect named Moon.
He put a secret passageway in each one and connected every house.
His insignia was an eye -- perhaps to let us know how closely he watched over his creations.

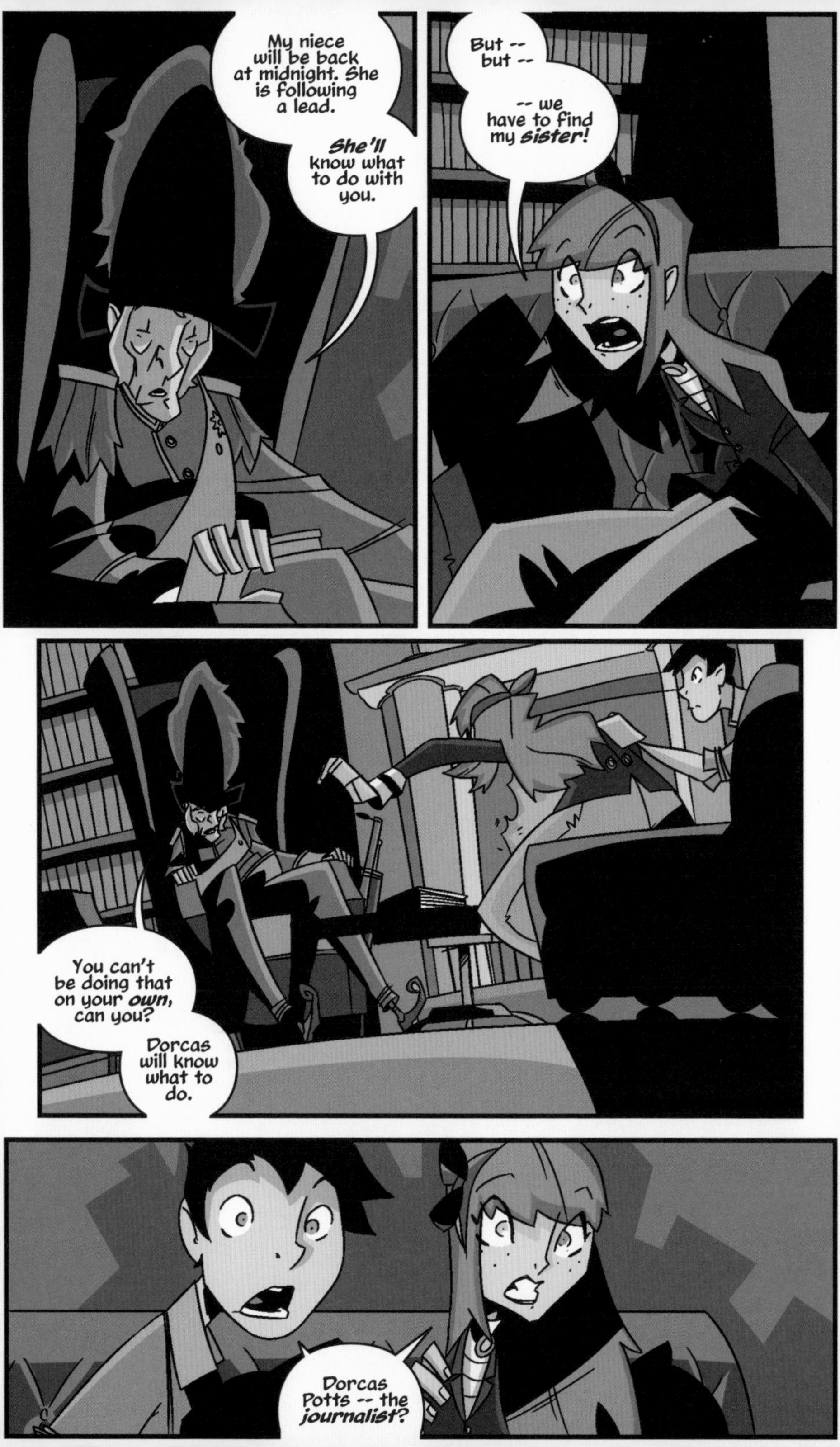
My niece will be back at midnight. She is following a lead.
She'll know what to do with you.
But -- but --
-- we have to find my *sister*!
You can't be doing that on your *own*, can you?
Dorcas will know what to do.
Dorcas Potts -- the *journalist*?

"You knOW her?" asked Lord Gervez sleepily.

"We have heard of her," Sadie replied. She looked at Erik wide eyed in the hope he would say no more.

"I think that under the circumstances you should wait here until she returns." He reached out and tapped the barrel of the gun.

Sadie protested, "But we have to—"

"Delightful," Erik interrupted quickly. "That would be fine—we would love to meet such a famous detective."

"And that she is, that she is," Lord Gervez said with a yawn.

Erik raised one eyebrow and looked first at Sadie, then at the door of the room, and finally at Lord Gervez. Sadie smiled in agreement.

"Wait," he whispered as Lord Gervez began to snore.

They waited. The grandfather clock in the corner of the room chimed the quarter hours until it reached eleven-thirty. Lord Gervez continued to snore heavily. His hand slipped from the armrest and dangled by the side of the leather chair.

Erik slowly got to his feet and beckoned for Sadie to follow. As he took a step, he noticed Lord Gervez's big toes twitching uncontrollably in his curly-toed slippers.

"Is he asleep?" Sadie whispered as quietly as she could.

Erik nodded, but just as he was about to set foot on the Persian carpet in front of the fire, they both heard a familiar sound. From outside the house came the revving of an engine. It clunked and rattled in the manner of a London taxicab. Erik and Sadie quickly tiptoed over to the window and peered through the heavy drapes. They heard the squealing of brakes as the cab pulled up to the large iron gates in front of the house.

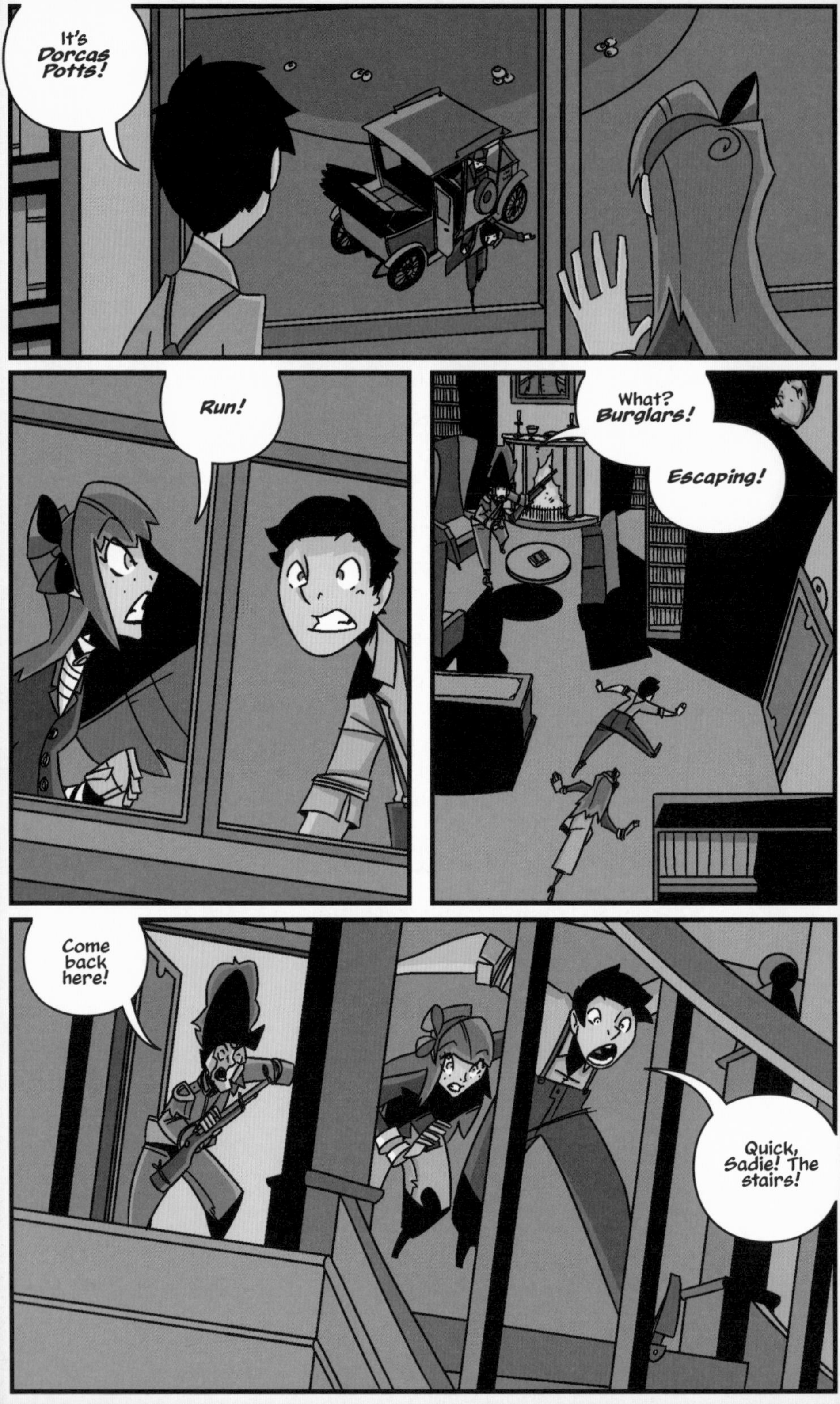
It's Dorcas Potts!
Run!
What? Burglars!
Escaping!
Come back here!
Quick, Sadie! The stairs!

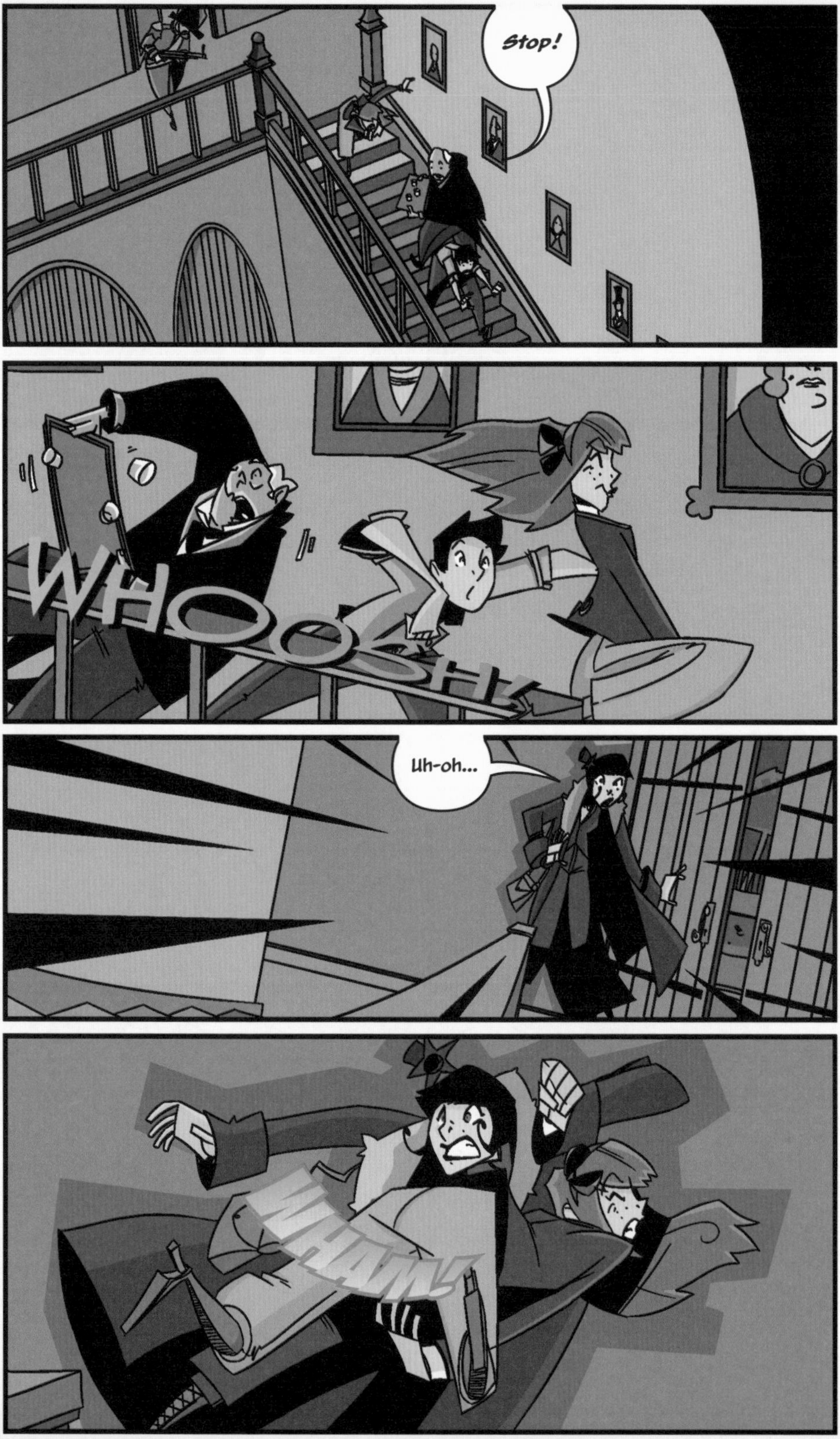

Stop!
WHOOSH!
Uh-oh...
WHAM!

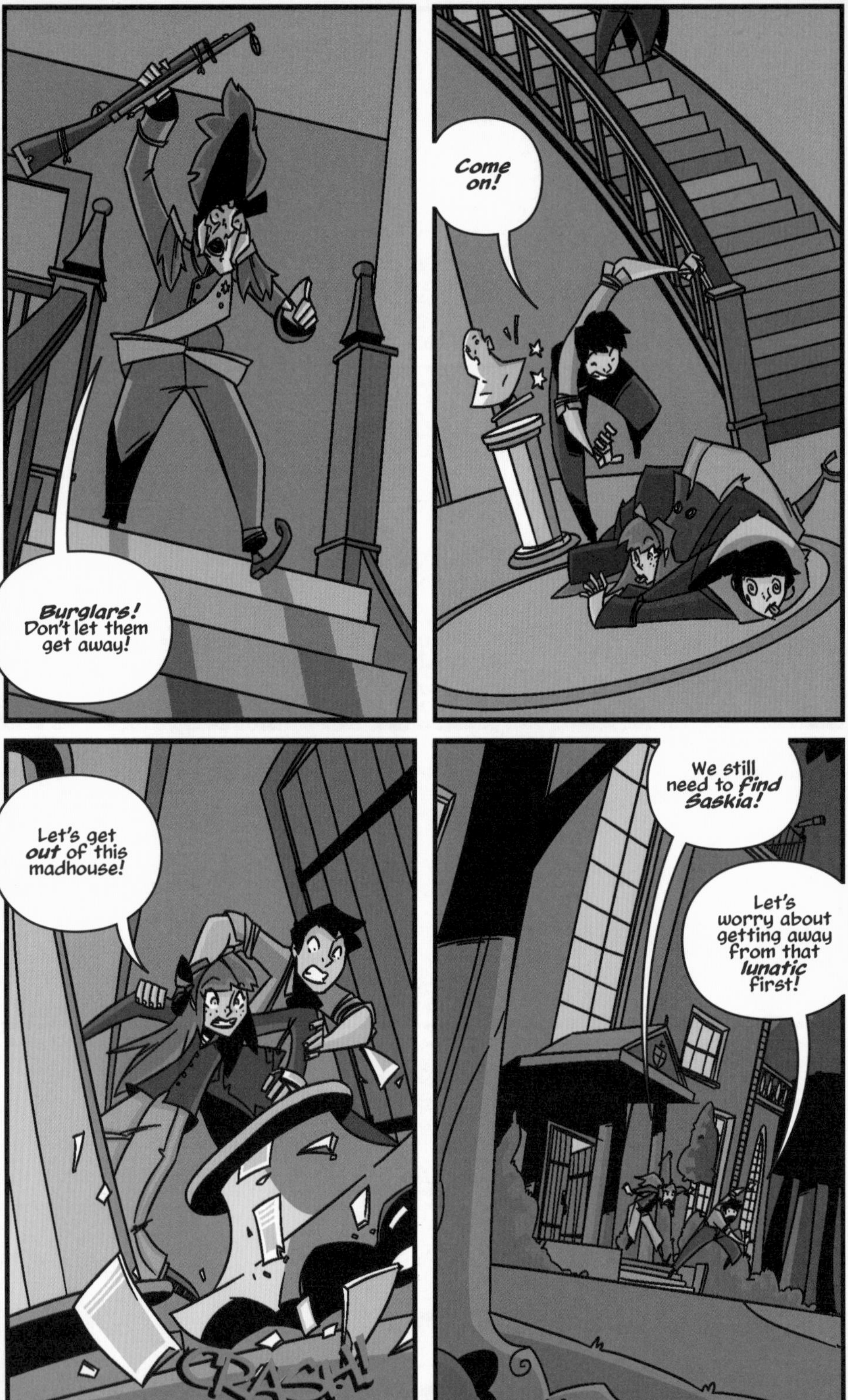
Burglars! Don't let them get away!
Come on!
Let's get out of this madhouse!
CRASH
We still need to find Saskia!
Let's worry about getting away from that lunatic first!

Lord Gervez bent down slowly and helped Dorcas Potts to her feet.

She turned to him with a concerned expression on her face. "Uncle Abyssinia—

are you all right?"

Still breathing heavily, Lord Gervez replied, "It was the burglars from the tunnel: Potemkin and Straker. Strange names for children."

Dorcas Potts looked out the open door in the direction Erik and Sadie had gone. Her eyes narrowed almost to slits as she said, "Burglars, no, but definitely meddlers. Something will have to be done about them."

Chapter Seven

Pursuit

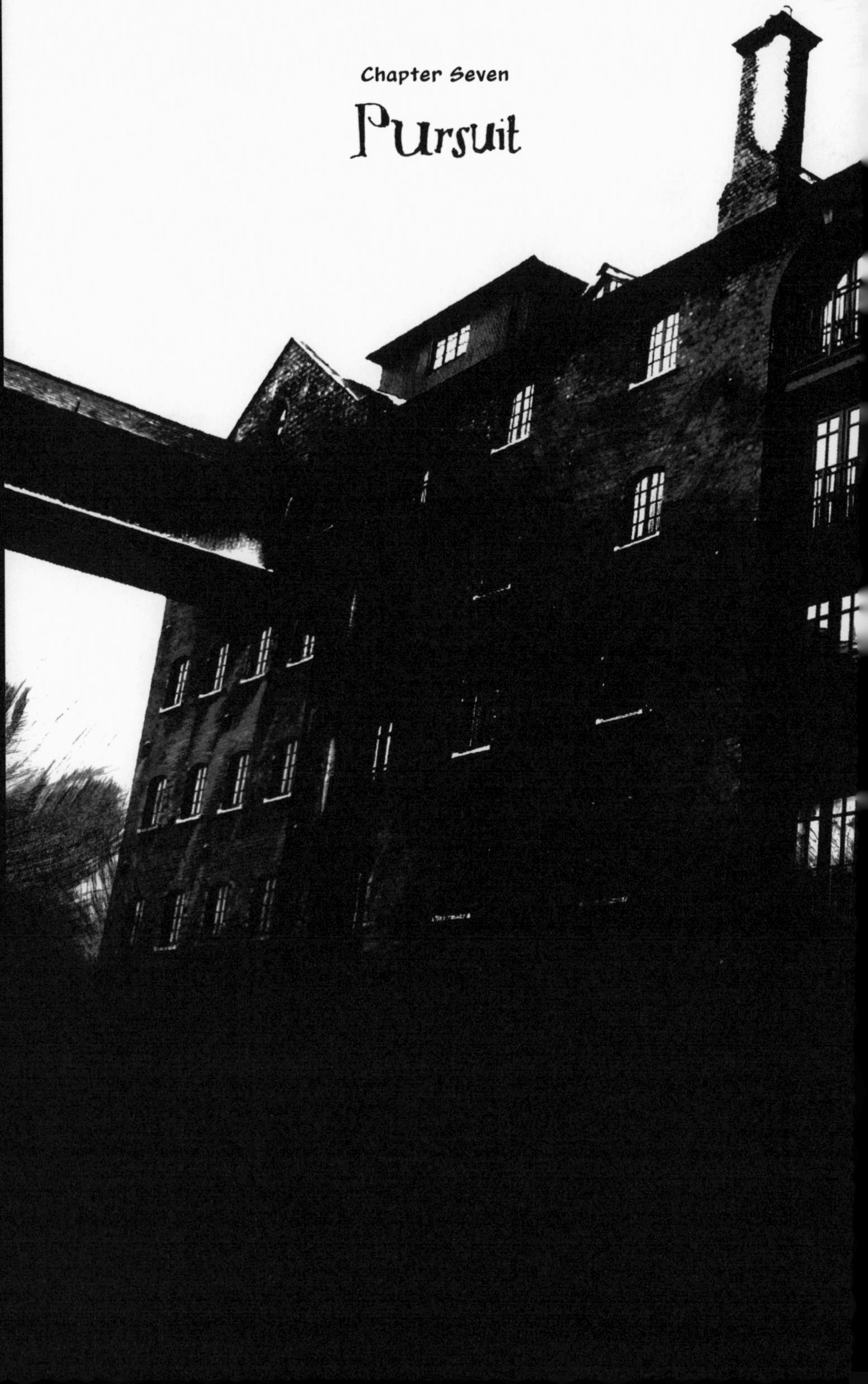

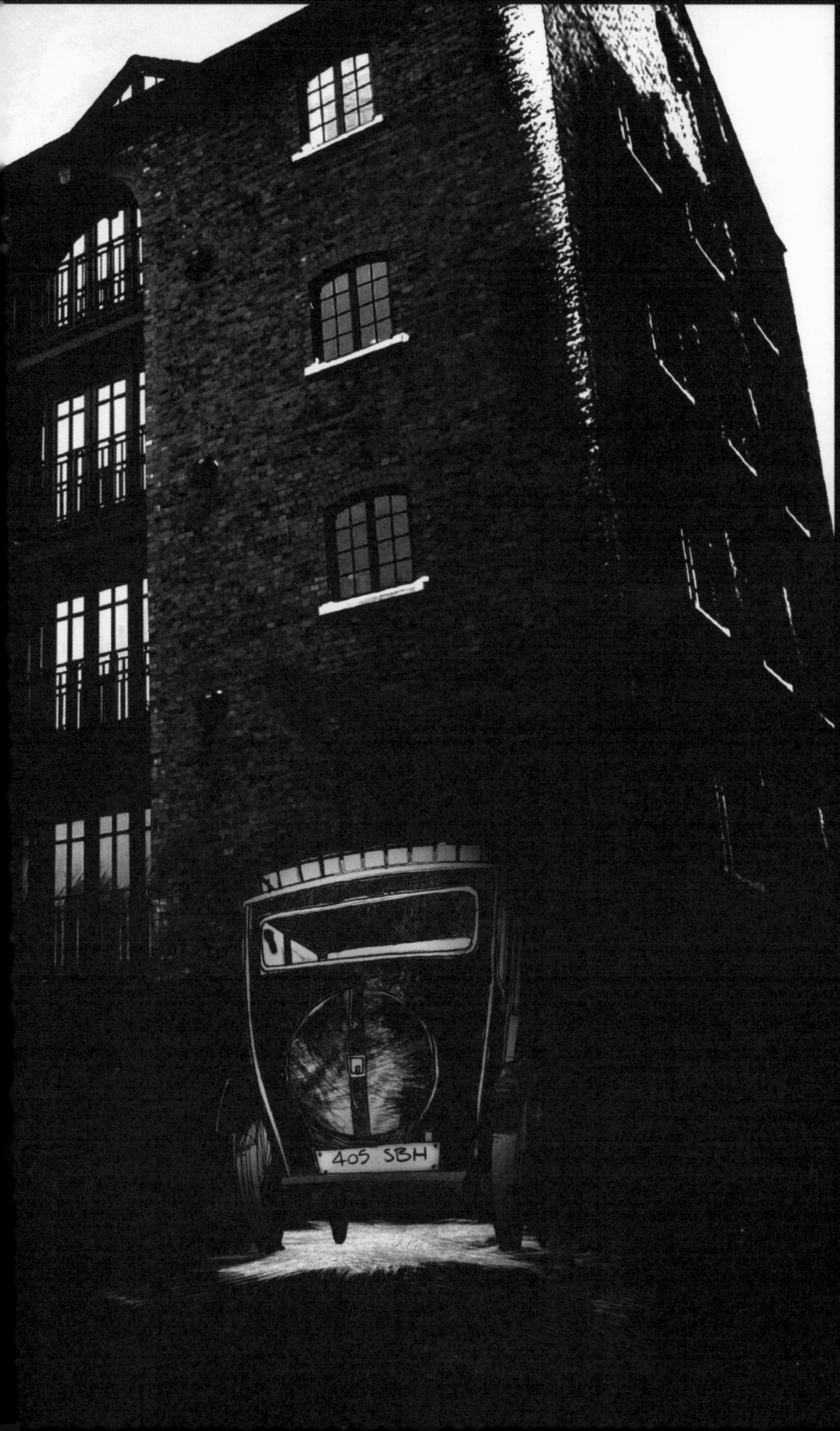
405 SBH

SASKIA LAY STILL in the sarcophagus as the chugging of the train died away. Potemkin's sharp voice called out, "Let's get the stuff inside." Two car doors slammed, one after the other. The sound echoed inside the coffin.

"Where are we?" Saskia wondered.

She was jolted from her thoughts as the sarcophagus was pulled from the back of the car and hoisted into the air at a sharp angle. Her face smashed into the side of the box.

She heard the gruff voice of Straker quite close, asking, "Where do we take this one?"

"Upstairs," Potemkin replied.

Saskia's elbow banged against the box with each jolting thud of the burglars' feet. She could hear their heavy breathing. Their steps halted briefly, a man grunted, and suddenly she felt herself being tipped sideways, her feet rising into the air. Blood rushed into her head as the coffin was turned nearly vertical.

Suddenly the burglars came to an abrupt stop, and Saskia's feet rose even higher. For a moment, she was turned completely upside down. Her scalp was flattened against the rough edge of the box, and her temples pounded. Her palms grew moist, and her breath came faster as fear began to take hold.

All at once the box swung completely around. There was a jarring thud as it dropped to the ground and Saskia again smashed into the side of the coffin.

"Quickly," came the voice of Potemkin. "We must finish unloading the car while there is still time." Saskia heard the sound of footsteps fading. A door closed. And then she was alone.

Immediately Saskia began searching for a way out of the sarcophagus. She braced herself against the back of the coffin and pushed on the lid with all her strength, but it held fast. She felt along the crack between the lid and the rest of the coffin, hoping to find a catch of some kind, but she felt only the rough wood of the box.

Saskia kicked the lid in frustration. The sarcophagus wobbled dangerously from side to side, threatening to tip over. But the lid remained tightly closed.

"Madame Raphael," she whispered desperately, as tears filled her eyes, "help me find a way out of here!" The words echoed inside her mind. She strained to hear an answer. But there was only silence.

. . .

Sadie and Erik ran down the road from Lord Gervez's house in the opposite direction of the school. They reached the town and continued for several minutes through the wet streets and damp alleyways. Erik never stopped in his pursuit of Sadie, who seemed to get a yard ahead with every long stride she took.

"I don't think they're following us," Erik gasped as they finally stopped at the bottom of Parliament Hill. He listened to the panting steam engine as it chugged along the iron rails that led to Belsize Park.

"Good," Sadie replied. "We have to look for Saskia. She could be anywhere."

"We'll just have to walk the streets around here until we find the car," Erik said.

"But that could take forever." Sadie snorted. "We have to think. Have you seen that car anywhere before?"

At first Erik didn't reply but watched the steam rising from the railroad tracks and floating above the nearby houses. Suddenly he realized what he was looking at.

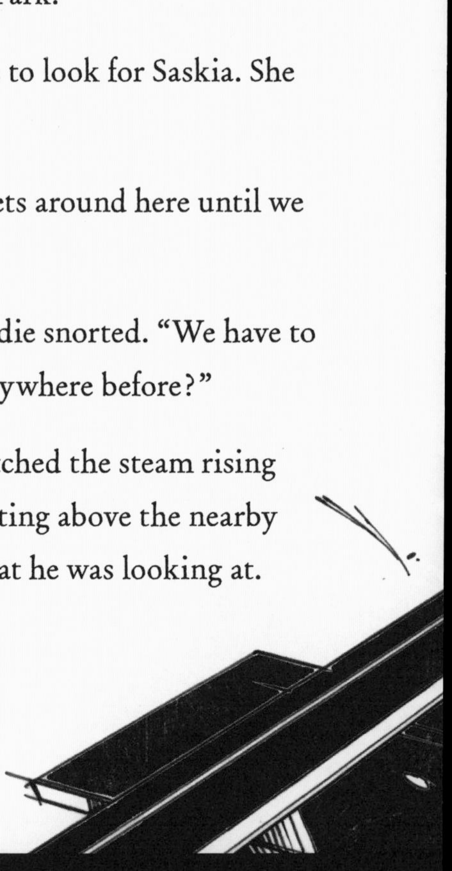

"The train," he cried. "That's it!" A whistle blew as the train went into the tunnel at Belsize Park. "Where can you keep a sarcophagus without it being found?" Erik asked excitedly.

"A big house—a museum?" Sadie responded, confused.

"Or a factory," Erik replied triumphantly. "Follow the train!"

"What are you talking about?" Sadie questioned, but Erik had already begun to race along in the direction of the train.

"Hurry!" he called over his shoulder.

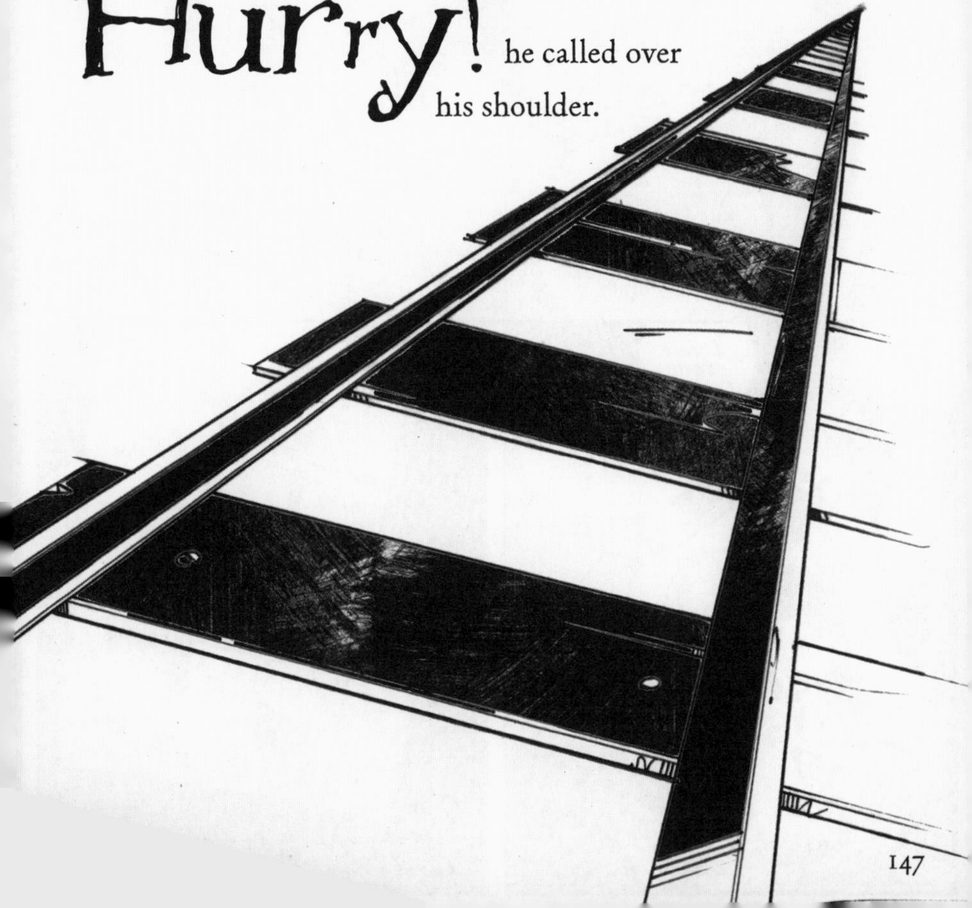

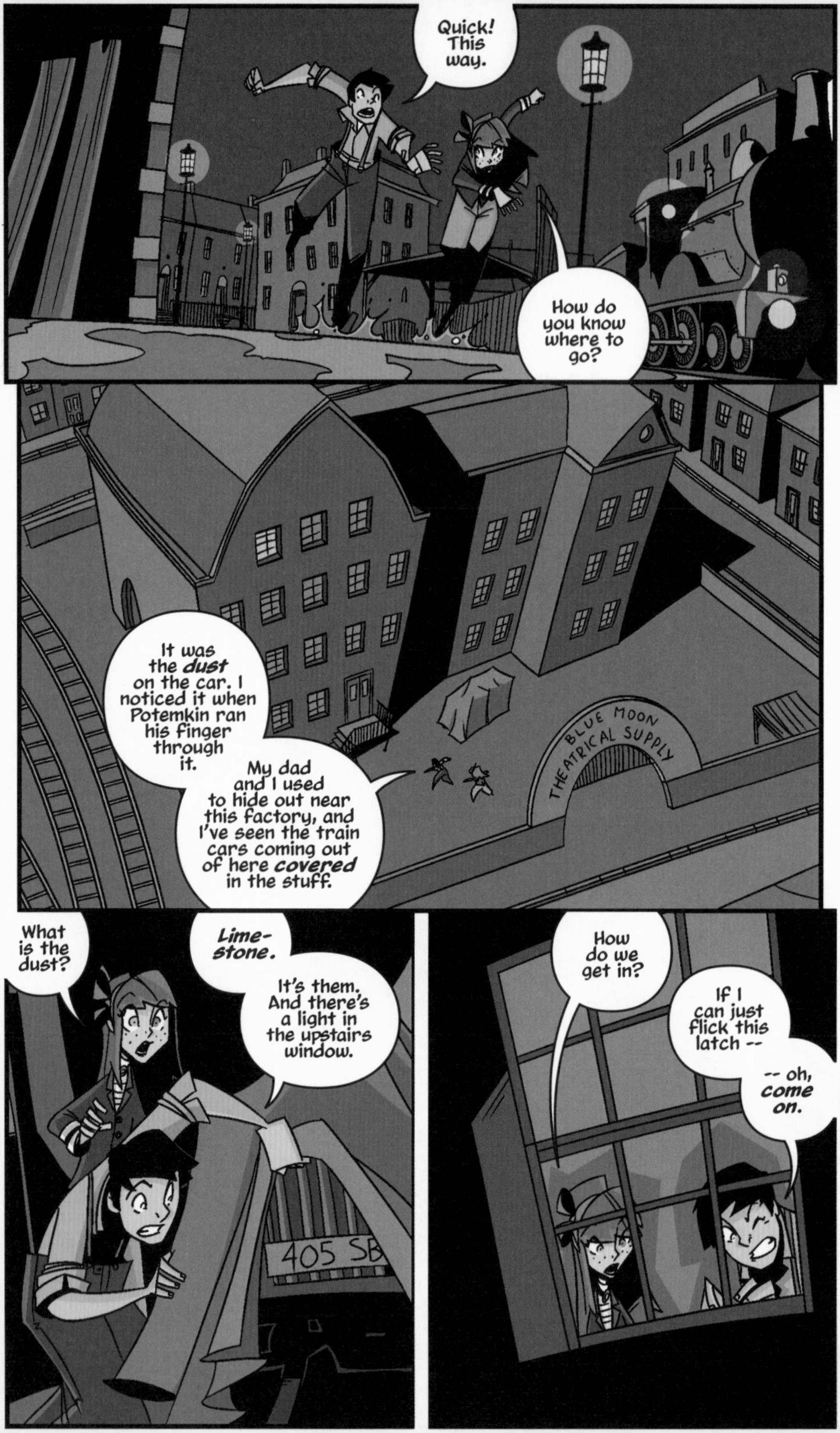
Quick! This way.
How do you know where to go?
It was the *dust* on the car. I noticed it when Potemkin ran his finger through it.
My dad and I used to hide out near this factory, and I've seen the train cars coming out of here *covered* in the stuff.
BLUE MOON THEATRICAL SUPPLY
What is the dust?
Lime-stone.
It's them. And there's a light in the upstairs window.
405 SB
How do we get in?
If I can just flick this latch --
-- oh, *come on.*

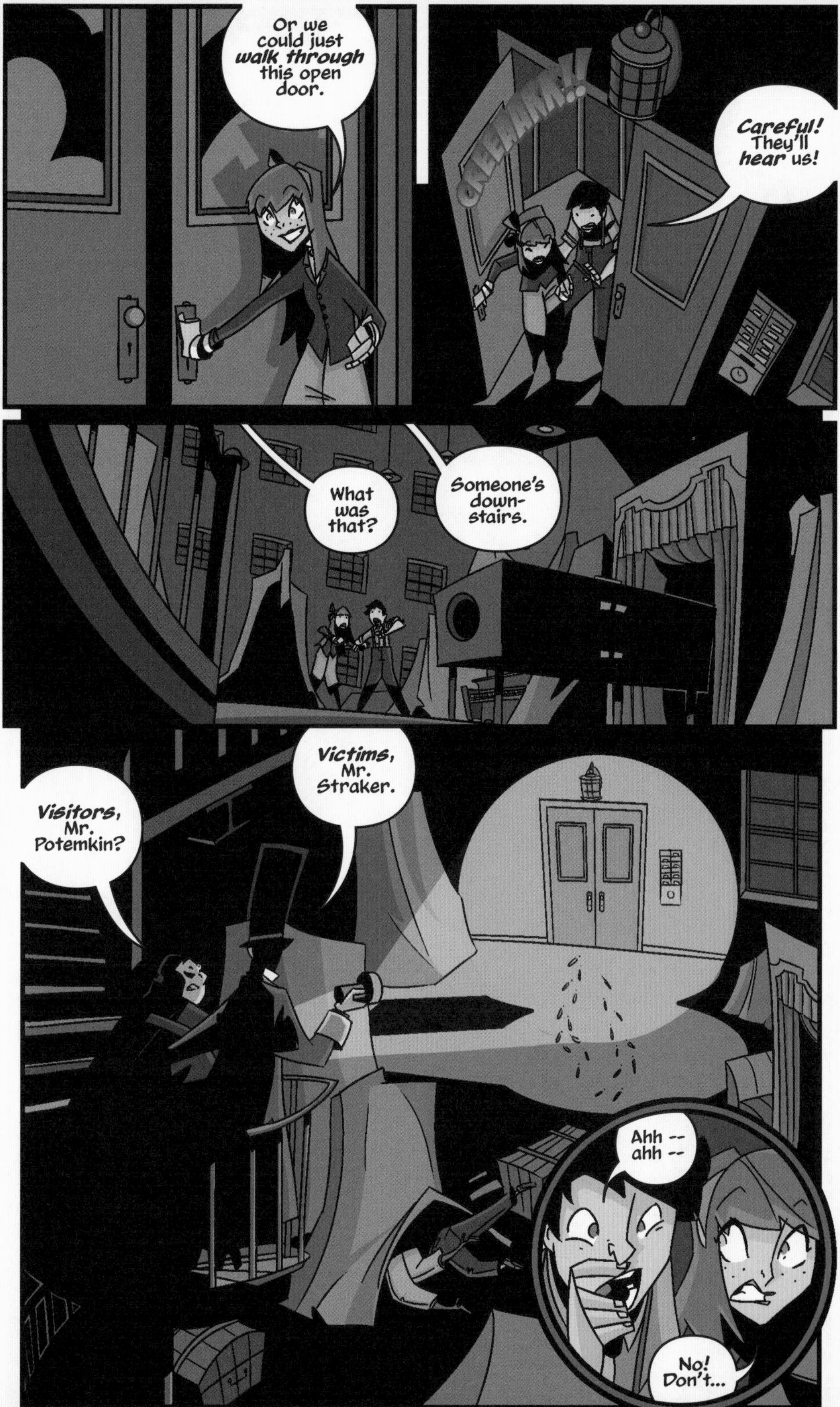
Or we could just *walk through* this open door.
CREEEAAANK!!
Careful! They'll *hear* us!
What was that?
Someone's down-stairs.
Visitors, Mr. Potemkin?
Victims, Mr. Straker.
Ahh -- ahh --
No! Don't...

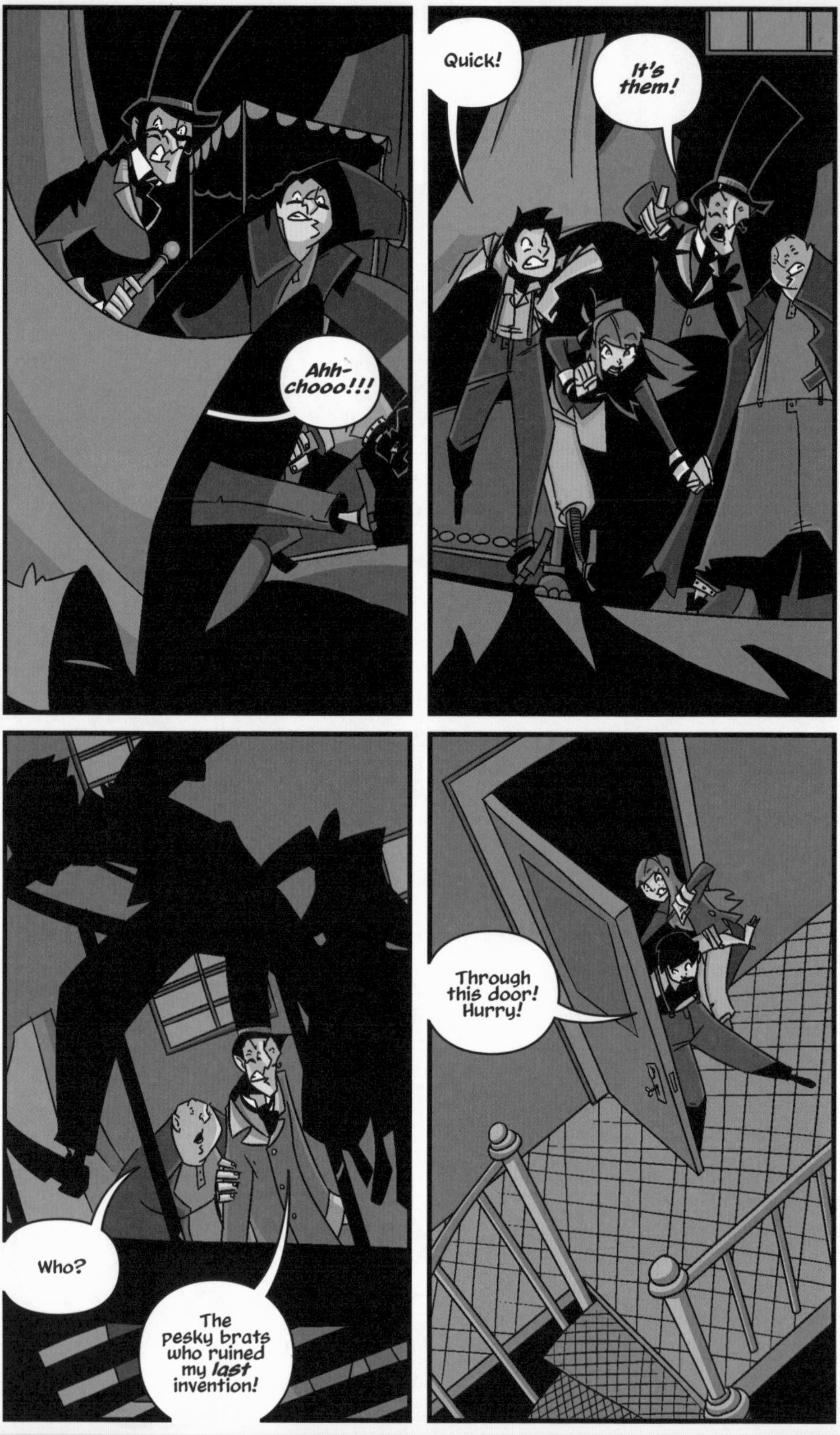
Ahh-choooo!!!
Quick!
It's them!
Who?
The pesky brats who ruined my last invention!
Through this door! Hurry!

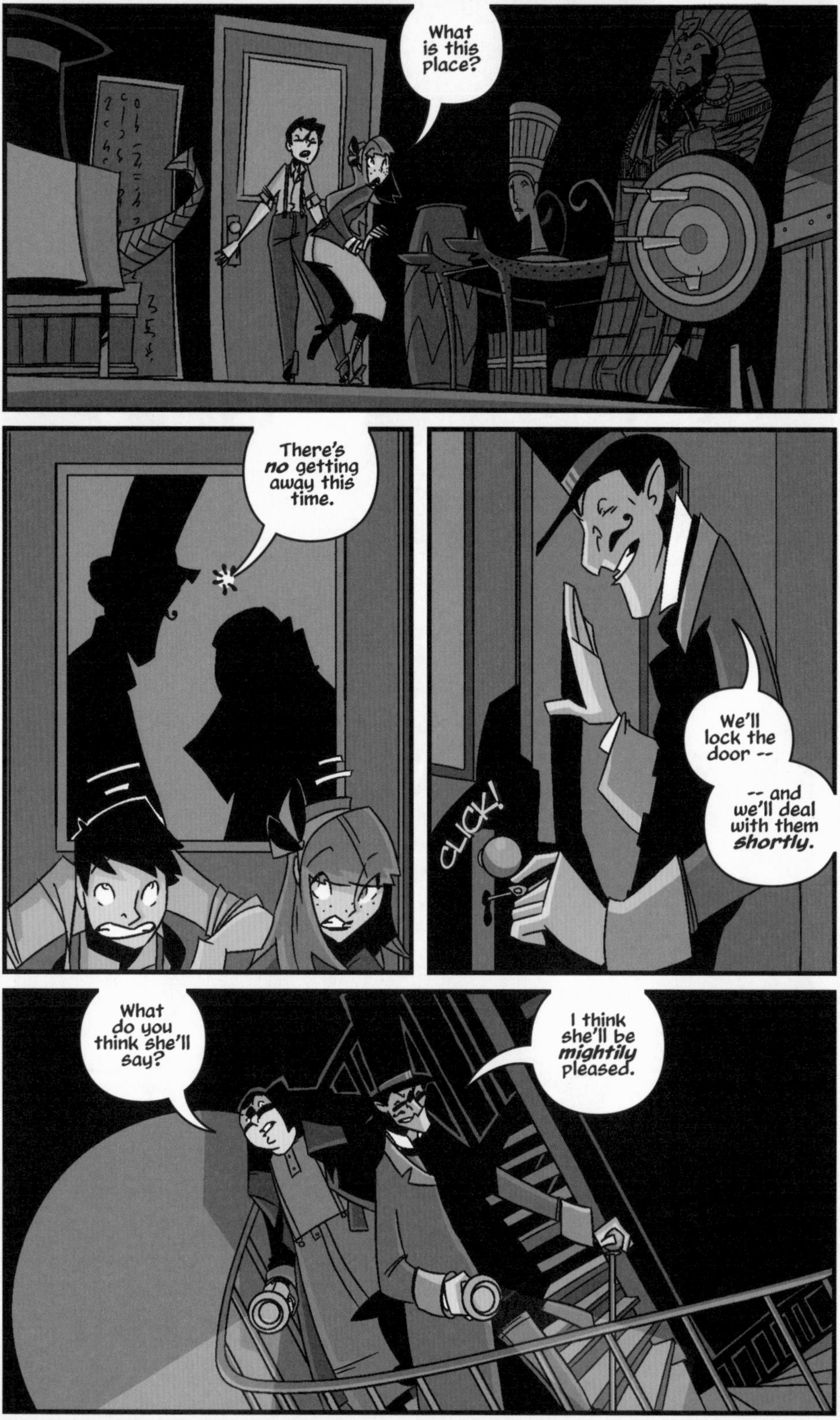
What is this place?
There's *no* getting away this time.
We'll lock the door --
-- and we'll deal with them *shortly*.
CLICK!
What do you think she'll say?
I think she'll be *mightily* pleased.

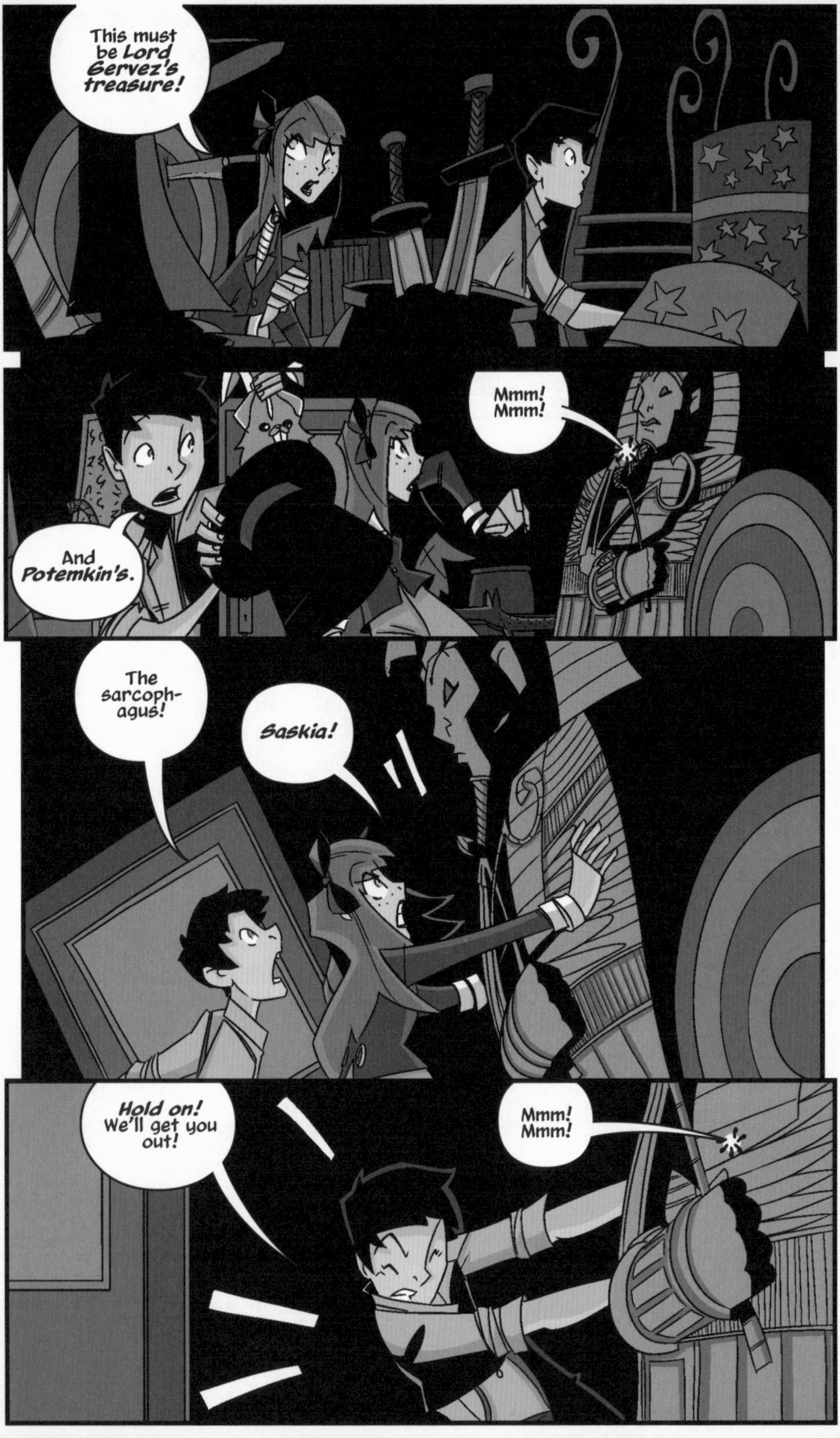
This must be Lord Servez's treasure!
And Potemkin's.
Mmm! Mmm!
The sarcophagus!
Saskia!
Hold on! We'll get you out!
Mmm! Mmm!

Erik pulled at the lid of the sarcophagus as hard as he could. It wouldn't budge. His fingers slid down the narrow crack that cut through the wooden box. He could barely see what he was doing. The room was dark, lit only by an oil lamp in the corridor that shone in through the frosted-glass panel of the door.

"If I can just do this," he said as he fought to open the lid.

From inside, the muttering got louder. Saskia started to kick at the lid of the coffin.

"**Get me out!**" came a muffled yell as Saskia pushed from inside.

"Quiet," Sadie whispered. "Potemkin is outside."

Erik pulled even harder, but the lid held fast. It was then that Sadie noticed a small metal catch on the bottom of the lid. Without saying a word, she reached over and pulled the lever. The lid flew open. Erik fell to the floor, and Saskia tumbled on top of him.

"Erik! Sadie! I'm so glad you're here," Saskia said as she got to her feet and looked around the darkened room. And then she added, almost to herself, "Maybe Madame Raphael did hear me."

Erik snorted.

"Not that angel nonsense again," he scoffed. "She's been shut in that coffin too long—it's affected her brain," he said to Sadie.

But Sadie was not listening. She ran to her sister and pulled her into a hug. "I was so worried!" Sadie exclaimed. "What were you thinking when you got in that thing?" But then, seeing the look on her sister's face, she quickly added, "At least Potemkin and Straker don't know you're here—do they?"

"No, I don't think so," said Saskia. "Where are we, anyway? And how did you get here?"

"In a factory by the train station. It was Erik who figured it out," Sadie answered. "We saw Lord Gervez in the tunnel and followed him to his house. This treasure was stolen from him. He accused us of stealing it and chased us out of his house! Then Dorcas Potts came—she's his niece, and she's been working on the burglary case. . . . We managed to escape them both and then found our way here," Sadie whispered as quickly as she could.

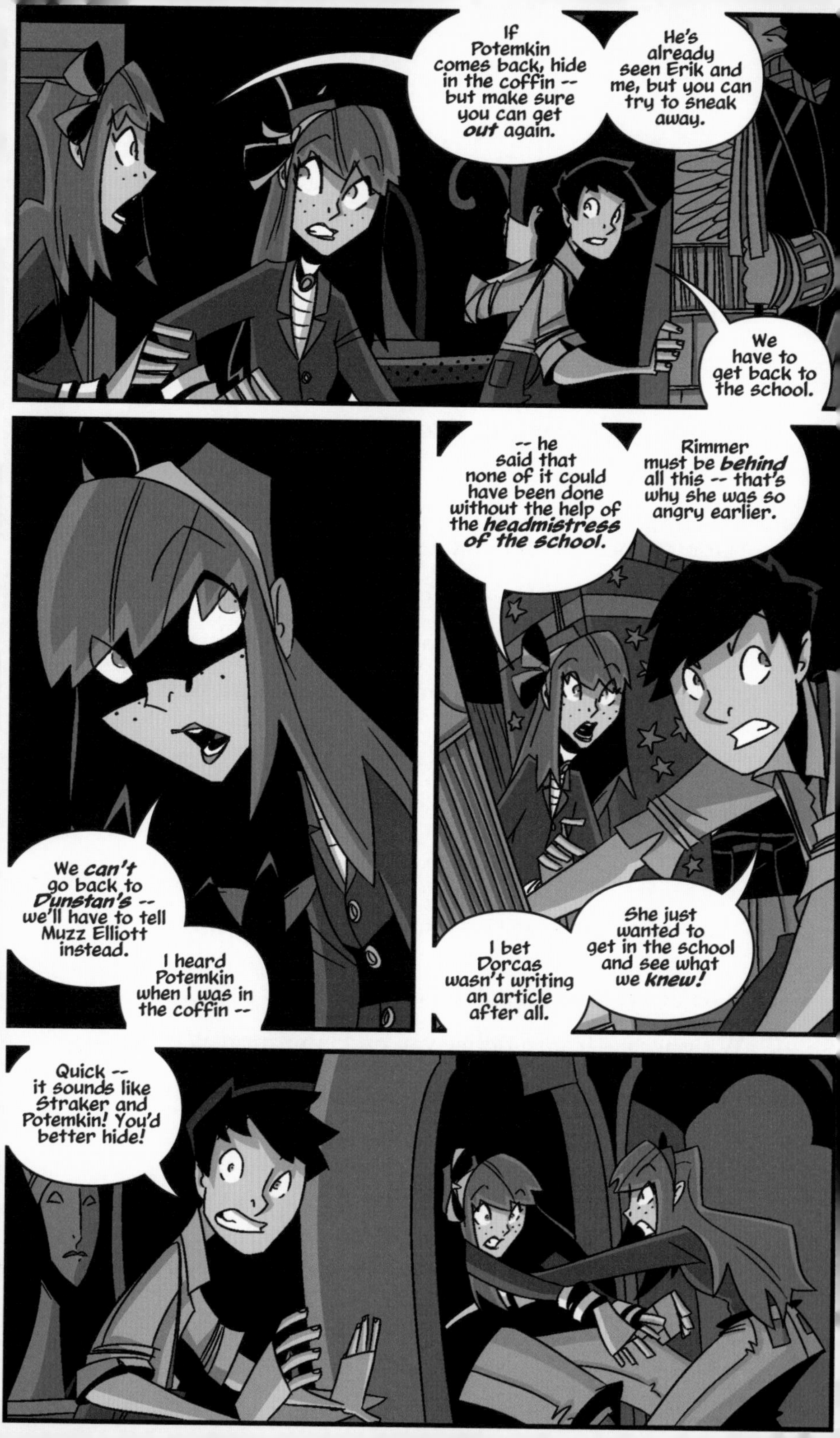
If Potemkin comes back, hide in the coffin -- but make sure you can get *out* again.
He's already seen Erik and me, but you can try to sneak away.
We have to get back to the school.
-- he said that none of it could have been done without the help of the *headmistress of the school*.
Rimmer must be *behind* all this -- that's why she was so angry earlier.
We *can't* go back to *Dunstan's* -- we'll have to tell Muzz Elliott instead.
I heard Potemkin when I was in the coffin --
I bet Dorcas wasn't writing an article after all.
She just wanted to get in the school and see what we *knew!*
Quick -- it sounds like Straker and Potemkin! You'd better hide!

Just as Sadie managed to close the lid of the sarcophagus without locking Saskia inside, the door opened. Straker stood in the doorway, his fat, bald head shining like a full moon. Erik stared him in the eyes.

"You won't do anything to us. Dorcas Potts knows you're here!" he shouted.

"Dorcas Potts . . . did you hear that, Mr. Potemkin? They're friends of Dorcas Potts. Pity that, pity that. And pity that she can't be here to see what will happen to you," Straker grunted, his thick brows twitching intensely.

"Such a shame." Potemkin laughed and then stepped into the doorway. "To think we could have dealt with three at once."

"You won't get away this time," said Sadie firmly.

"Get away, Miss Dopple? Getting away is what I do best. Whether it's from a police van on Hampstead Way or Pentonville Prison. There are no walls, no bars, no doors that can keep me locked away for long."

"And how did you escape from Pentonville? No one gets out of there," Erik said.

"Tsk, tsk, Mr. Ganger, you know a magician never reveals his tricks.

"But since you will never be able to repeat this to anyone else, I shall consider it your last request and satisfy your curiosity. I simply asked my dear friend Mr. Straker to bring me some sherbet. It was the finest treat a man could ask for, made from my own secret recipe.

"All it took was a teaspoon in the lock, and it blew the door clean off. No one was looking for poor old Potemkin in the mayhem that followed. They all presumed I was blown to pieces—just like my old friend Mr. Woss. But unlike my unfortunate assistant, I am a true magician."

Potemkin stepped forward and reached behind Sadie's ear, pulling out a silver coin. "I can make things appear—" he twirled his wrist and the coin vanished—"and disappear at will." He smiled secretively. "The police think I am dead and no longer care to find me."

"They will when we tell them you're here," Sadie said.

Potemkin laughed. "Too late for that, dear Sadie. . . . And to think I once considered making you two my apprentices. I would have taught you everything I know, but all you did was beat me over the head and leave me for dead."

"You would have killed us. Your Matter Illuminator didn't work," Erik protested.

"Sadly I was robbed of the chance to perfect it," Potemkin replied. "But now I have invented something far more spectacular. It is a creation of beauty and of power. Millions will be attracted to it, and I will again become famous through my invention—though no one will ever see my face."

"You're quite mad," Sadie said.

"Perhaps," Potemkin replied. "But at least I will still be alive in the morning—which is more than I can say for you two."

"You'd kill us?" Erik asked.

"So I would. It's an order."

"From the headmistress?" Sadie asked.

Potemkin looked at Straker.

"Never said a thing," Straker mumbled.

"So you know of my employer?" Potemkin asked coolly.

"And Lord Gervez knows of you!" Erik shouted desperately. "We saw you in the tunnel. I watched you take the artifacts, and we waited for you to come back."

"It was all necessary for my invention," Potemkin explained. "Sometimes there has to be a sacrifice for art . . . and tonight it will be you."

With a sparkling flash, a pistol appeared in his hand. Potemkin smiled at Straker.

"I will telephone the headmistress and tell her there has been a change of plan.

Take them to the GaraZello."

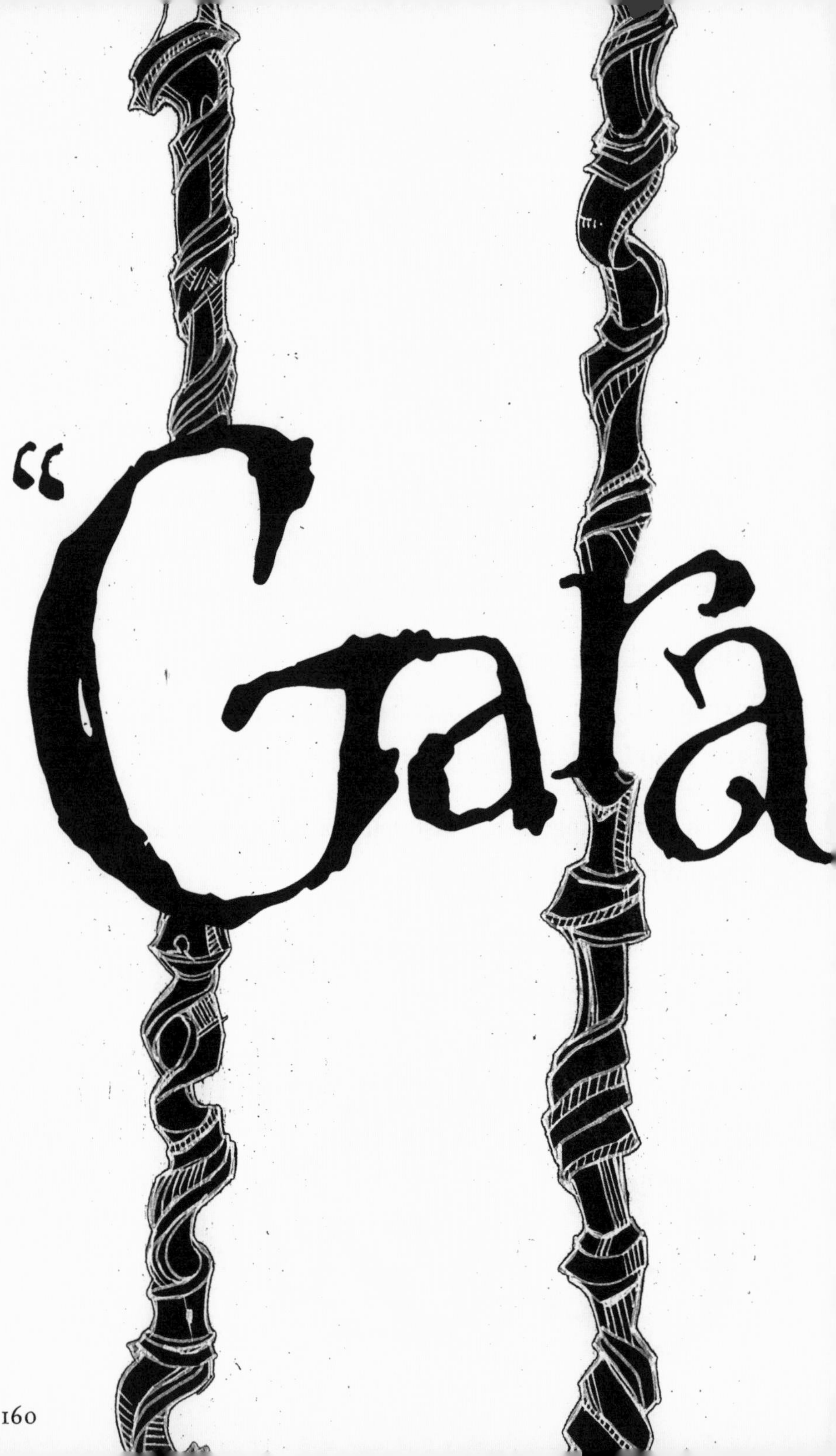
“Gara

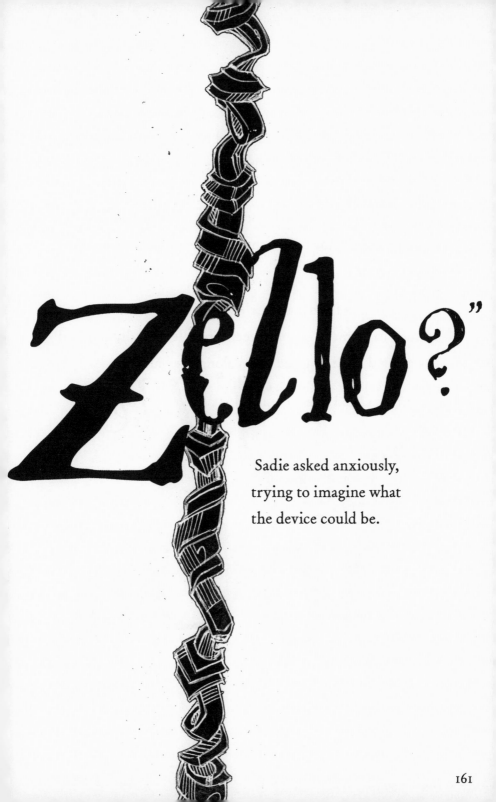

Zello?"

Sadie asked anxiously, trying to imagine what the device could be.

"Monsters—strange creatures and galloping horses—all created from his lordship's fine collection. It shall be an amazing experience—the ultimate way to leave this world," Potemkin replied. "Struggling is futile, and we have plenty of time before that Potts woman finds out where we are."

Straker grabbed Sadie and Erik at the same time. His arms seemed to be made of solid steel. Their feet hardly touched the ground as he dragged them along the hallway.

Potemkin called after them, "I'll be there soon.

Don't start without me.

The Garazello is the verve—the vim and vigor of our mundane life."

As Straker dragged Erik and Sadie along the passageway, he threatened, "Don't try anything—I would hate to drop you."

Sadie whispered to Erik, "What do you think the Garazello does?"

"I don't know," answered Erik, "but I hope it isn't like the Matter Illuminator. He nearly electrocuted us with that thing."

Straker cut off their conversation. "The Garazello is Mr. Potemkin's greatest invention yet. Only he can't seem to get the speed right—the Garazello has an odd effect on everything he puts on it."

Ahead of them, Sadie and Erik could see the open doors of a gigantic hall. Just inside the doors stood a carousel, larger and more menacing than any carnival ride they had ever seen. A feeling of dread washed over them.

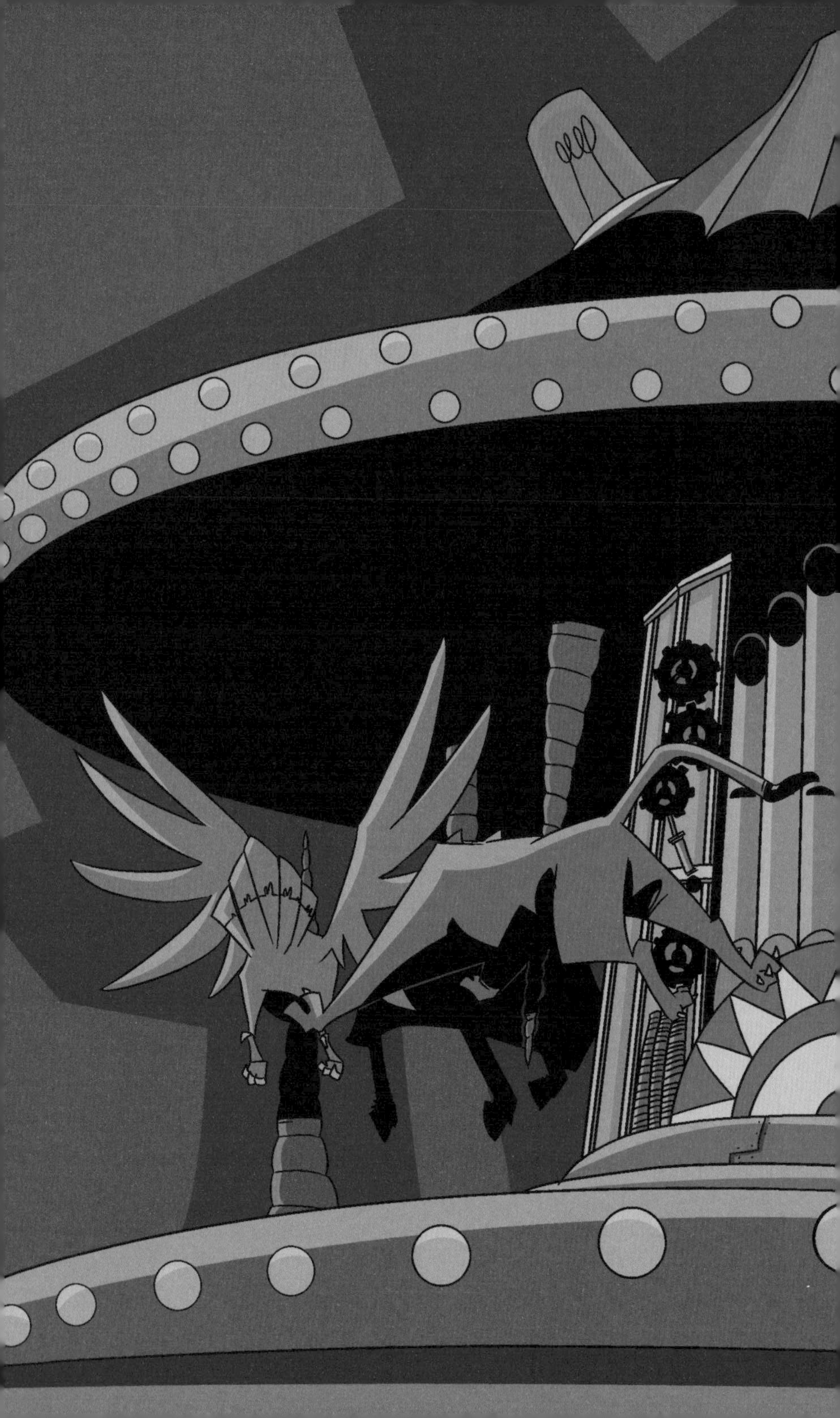

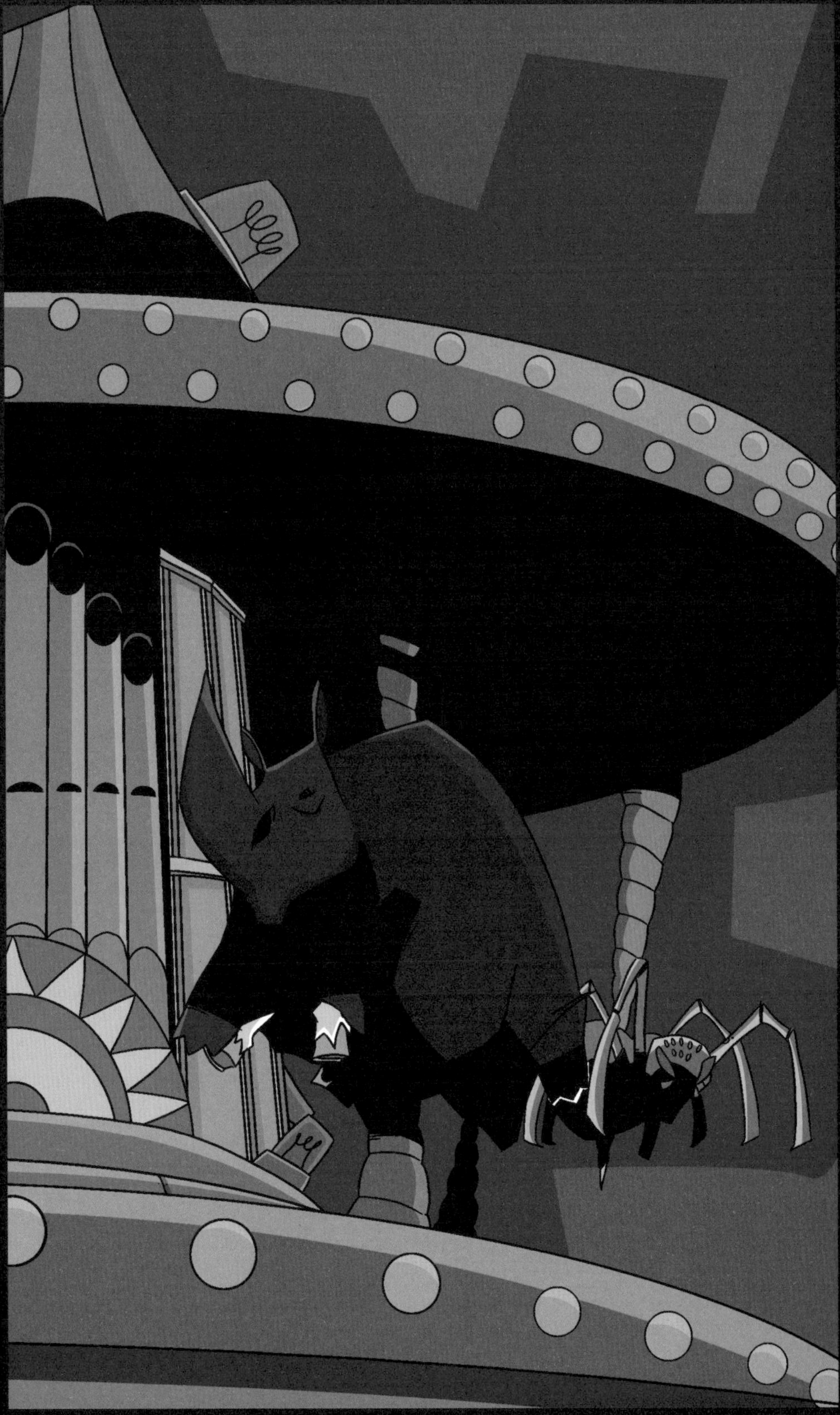

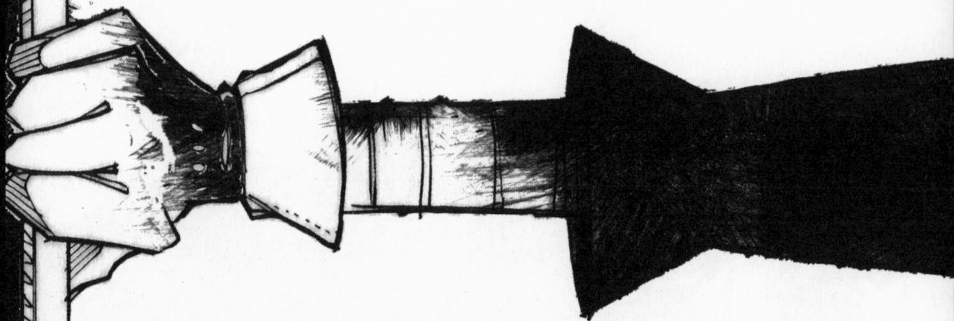

As they passed through the doors, Sadie grabbed at the door frame in a desperate attempt to escape the strange machine.

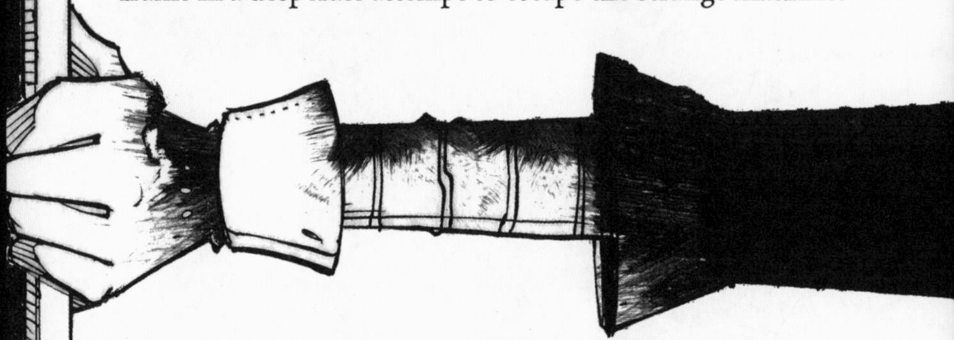

"It's no use hanging on," Straker chided, pulling her away. "The Garazello can't be kept waiting."

Chapter Eight
The Gluttonous Garazello

IN THE ROOM BEFORE him, Erik could see a gargantuan machine. It towered above him like a vast ship ready for sail. In front of him was an immense carousel painted in yellow and red, with gold twisted spikes hanging from the roof. The spikes spiraled down and looked like they had been speared through the writhing backs of a host of mythical creatures. Rabid horses, frogs with bulging throats and eyes, manic geese with razor teeth, ferocious cats, and colossal spiders stared at him. Each beast was suspended mid-leap from the eerie merry-go-round with legs outstretched and mouths gaping wide. They all hung as if frozen in time, waiting for a magician to bring them to life.

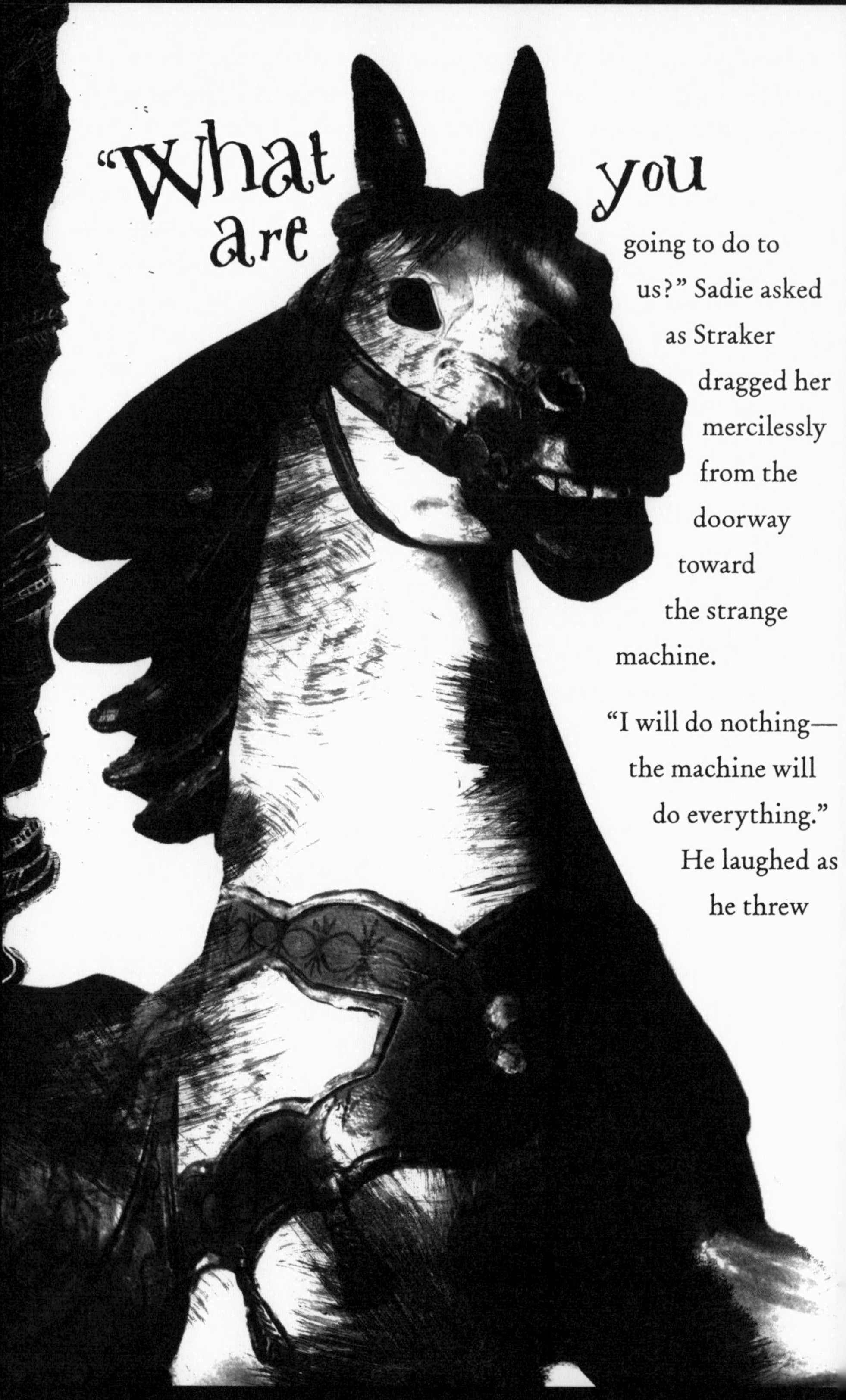

"What are you going to do to us?" Sadie asked as Straker dragged her mercilessly from the doorway toward the strange machine.

"I will do nothing—the machine will do everything." He laughed as he threw

Erik onto the polished wooden platform that appeared to support the creatures. "Just pick a beast to ride upon—that is all you have to do."

"And what if we don't?" Erik asked.

"Then I will shoot," Potemkin said as he appeared at the door and aimed his gun at them. "I will give you both a chance. Survive the Garazello, and I will set you free—how much fairer is that?"

"You expect us to trust you?" Sadie shouted as she, too, was thrown onto the machine.

"Trust, no. Obey, yes." Potemkin smirked. "Your choice: spin and risk the effects of the machine, or be shot like dogs."

"Let's take the chance, Sadie. It's just an overgrown spinning top."

"A brave man or a fool—which are you, Erik?" Potemkin asked.

"If you keep your word, then we'll take our chance," Erik replied as he glanced at Sadie and tried to smile.

"Very well," Potemkin grunted. "Pick the creature on which you will ride, and I will start the Garazello."

Erik and Sadie looked about them. On all sides were animals so intricately detailed that it seemed they could come to life at any moment. They were beautiful and horrible at the same time.

Sadie reached out to touch what looked like a warhorse. It hung from the roof of the Garazello by a gold twisted spike. The beast was pure white and wore a leather saddle and battle armor that had no doubt once been part of Lord Gervez's prize collection. The horse's teeth were bared, and the animal's front hooves were tucked under it as though it were about to kick forward. Sadie reached out a shaky hand and gripped the mane of real hair. As she took her seat, she was sure that the reddened eye of the creature followed her.

"It feels alive," Sadie said as she settled into the soft saddle and held tightly to the twisted spike.

"Can't be," Erik replied, climbing onto the back of a horned black rhinoceros.

"Don't rule it out, my dear friends," said Potemkin with a laugh. He pocketed the pistol and walked toward a small booth in the darkened corner of the room. "This is no ordinary fairground attraction. It is something quite magical and exceedingly spectacular."

"What's he going to do?" Sadie asked as she gripped the twisted pole.

"He's going to spin you faster than you have ever gone before," Straker grunted. His whole body shook, whether from excitement or fear they could not tell. Potemkin pulled a lever and twisted a small wheel in the painted booth.

"I had a vagabond last for two minutes before he gave in to the Garazello," Potemkin shouted as a whir of electricity filled the room. "From the expression on his face as he let go of his animal, he thought he could fly just like Icarus— until the wall got in his way."

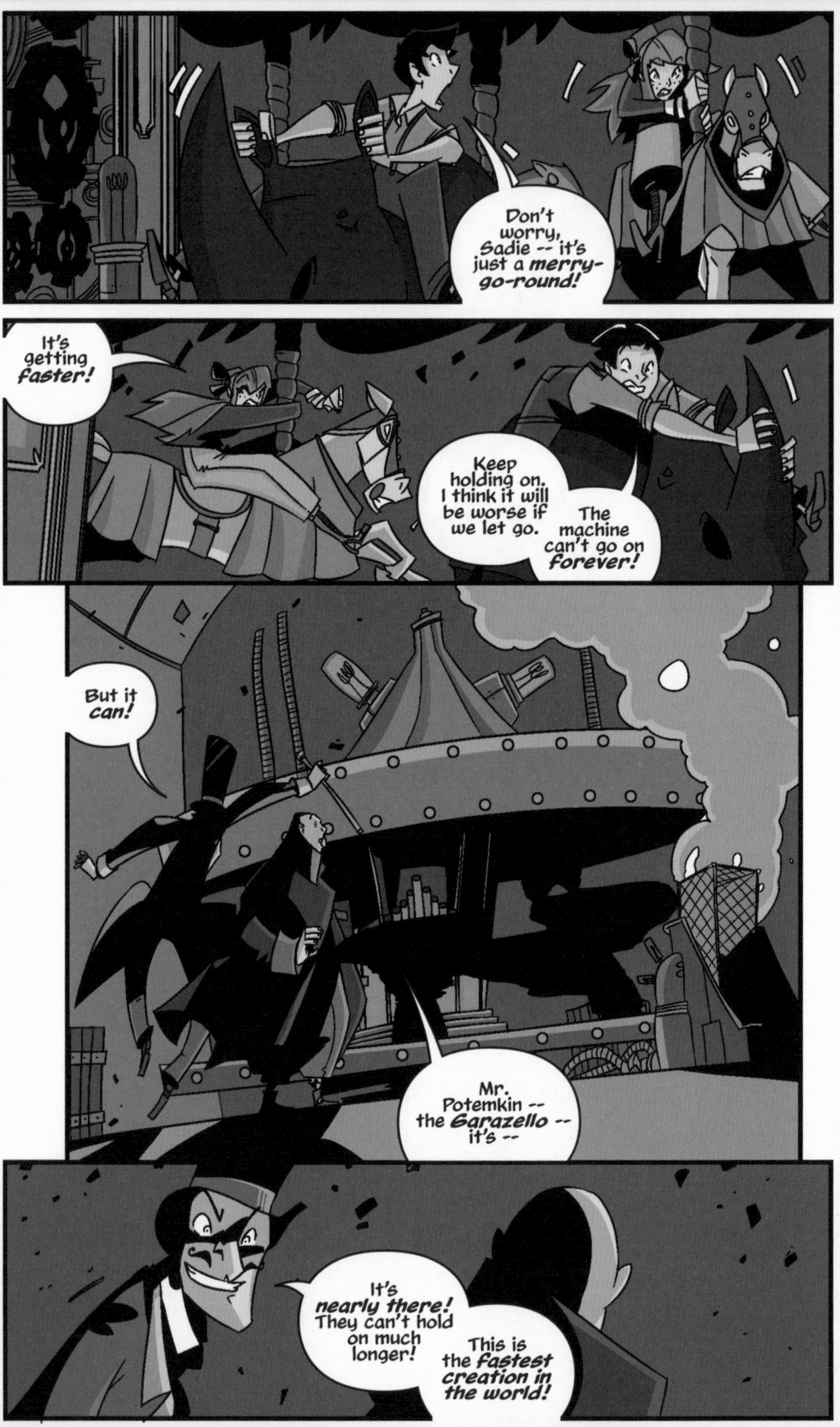
Don't worry, Sadie -- it's just a merry-go-round!
It's getting faster!
Keep holding on. I think it will be worse if we let go.
The machine can't go on forever!
But it can!
Mr. Potemkin -- the Garazello -- it's --
It's nearly there! They can't hold on much longer!
This is the fastest creation in the world!

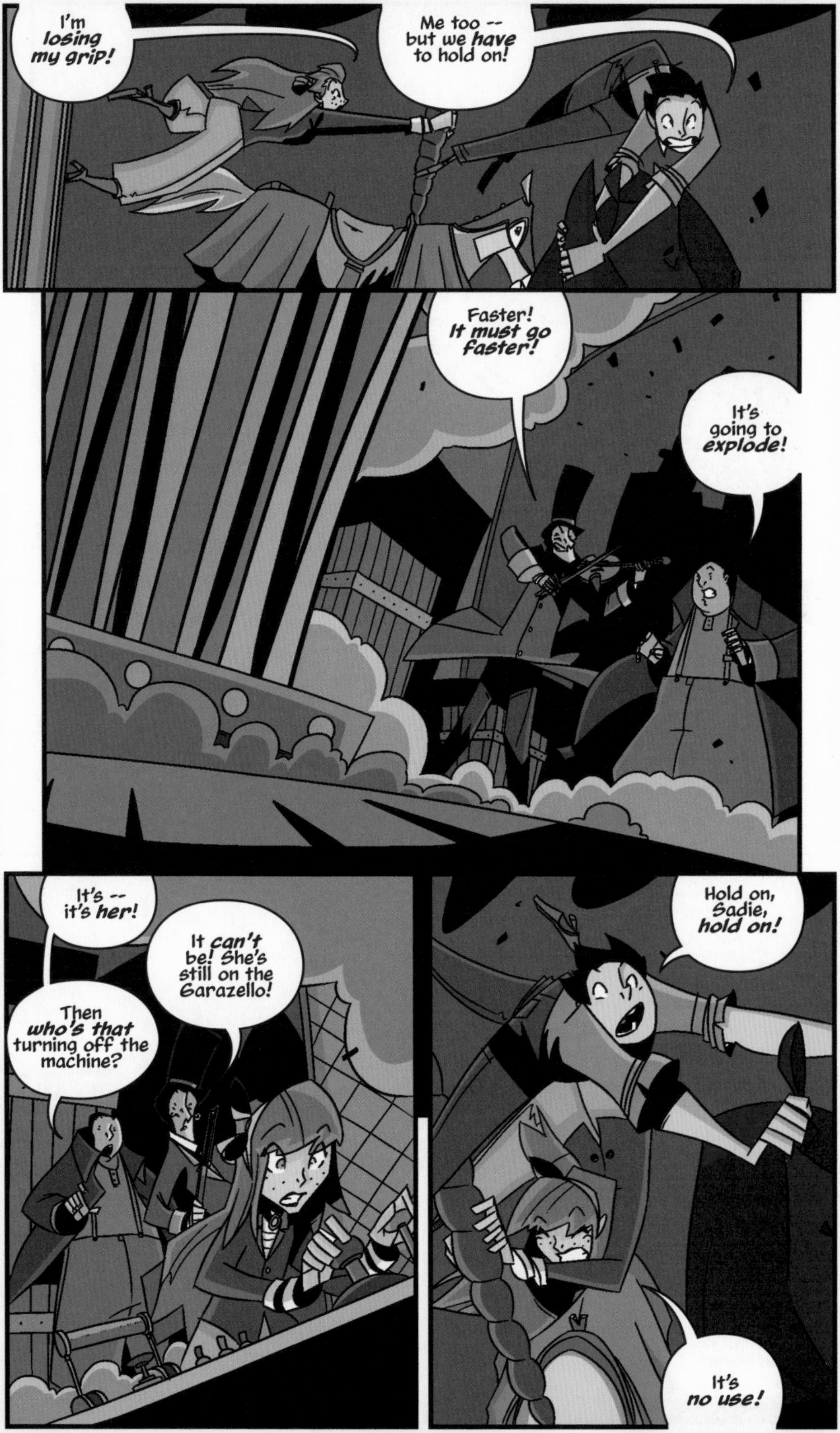
I'm losing my grip!
Me too -- but we have to hold on!
Faster! It must go faster!
It's going to explode!
It's -- it's her!
It can't be! She's still on the Garazello!
Then who's that turning off the machine?
Hold on, Sadie, hold on!
It's no use!

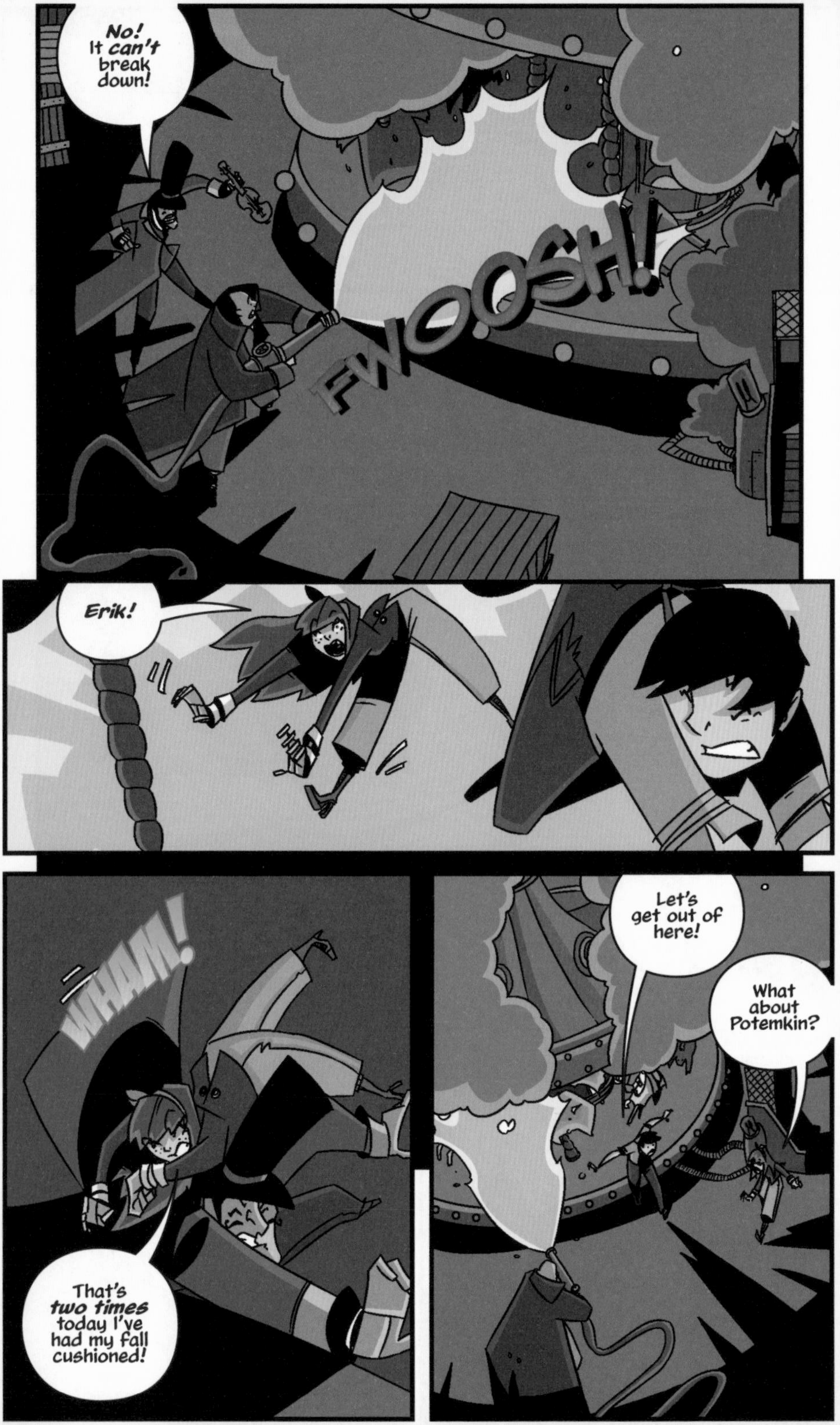
No! It can't break down!
FWOOSH!
Erik!
WHAM!
That's two times today I've had my fall cushioned!
Let's get out of here!
What about Potemkin?

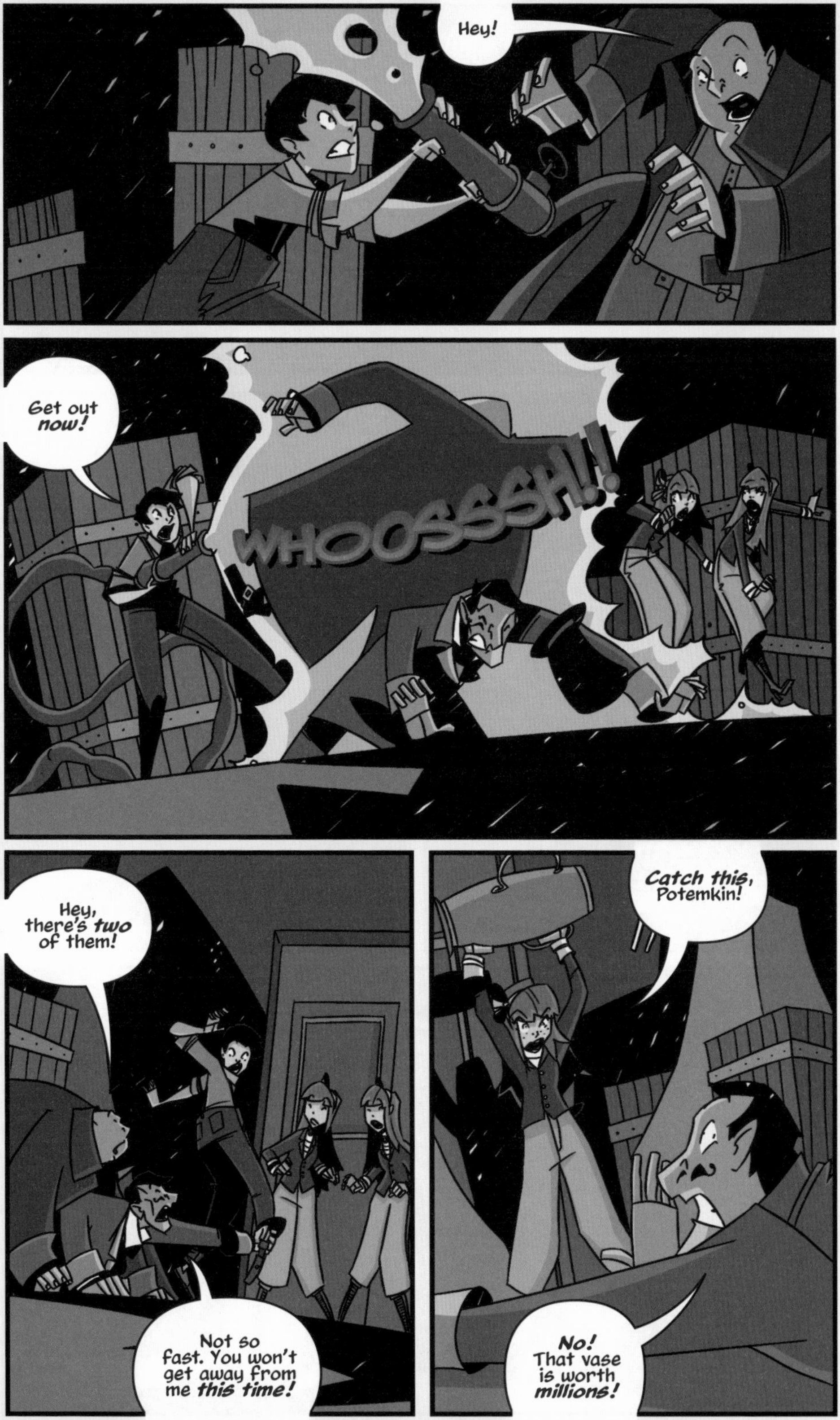
Hey!
Get out now!
WHOOSSSH!!
Hey, there's two of them!
Not so fast. You won't get away from me this time!
Catch this, Potemkin!
No! That vase is worth millions!

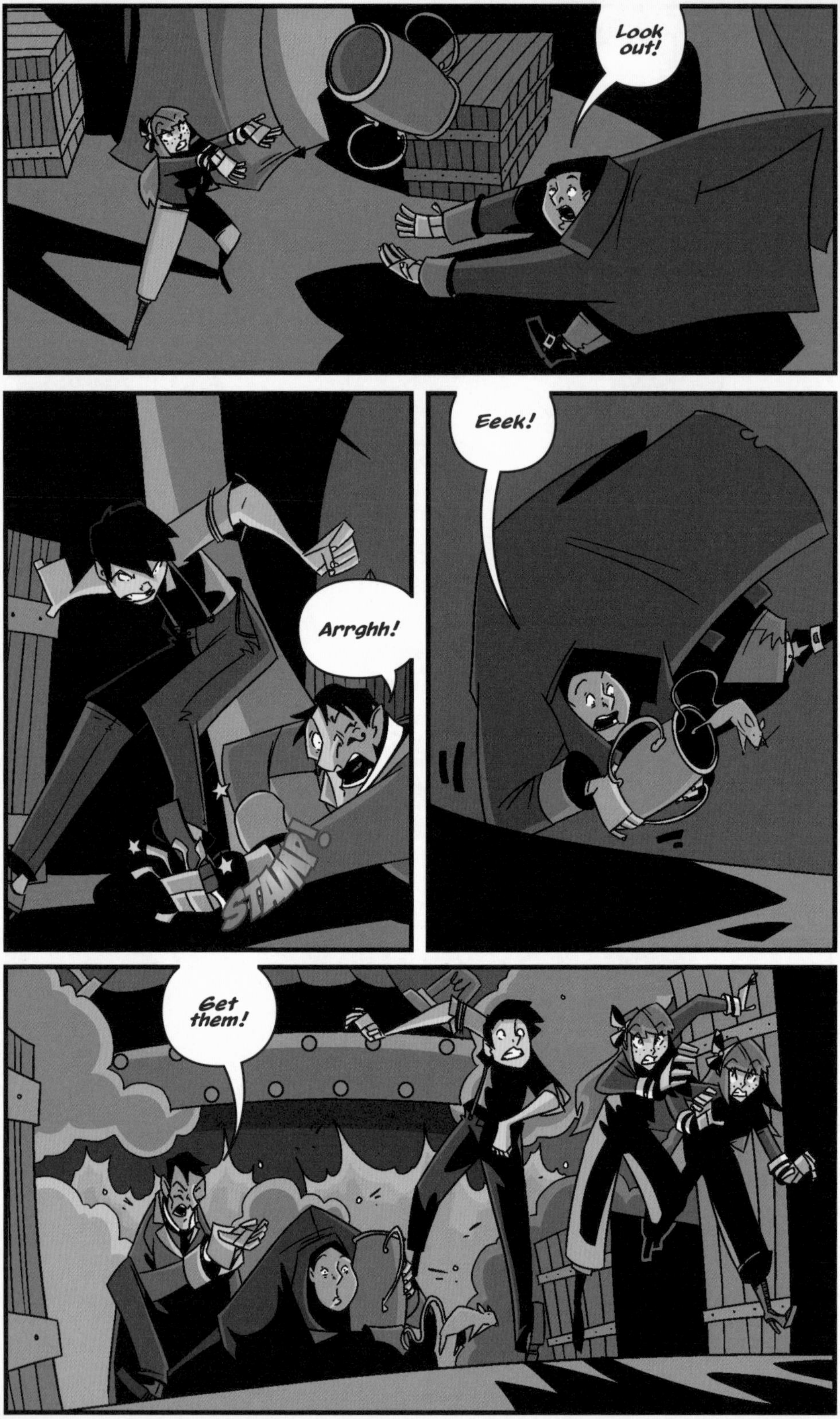
Look out!
Arrghh!
STAMP!
Eeek!
Get them!

Erik ran along the dark hallway, following the twins. He turned a corner and came to a spiral staircase. He could hear two sets of wet feet squelching along the landing behind him, and Sadie and Saskia's footsteps beating against the metal stairs ahead.

"Wait for Erik!" he heard Saskia shouting to Sadie on the stairs below him.

"No, keep going," Erik shouted back. He rushed down the stairs after the girls but could hear his pursuers gaining ground. "Tell Dorcas Potts—"

Erik's words echoed down the stairwell but were drowned out by a sudden cascade of fat barrels that thundered down from above. They clanged and smashed against the metal stairs as Straker threw them one by one. Each barrel bounced close to Erik, narrowly missing him.

"Get him!" Potemkin yelled as Straker picked up the final barrel, aimed it at Erik, and then hurled it with all his strength.

Erik looked up and leaped down the remaining stairs. The barrel hurtled toward him and smashed against the wall.

"You missed," barked Potemkin, drawing the pistol from his pocket and aiming it at Erik. "Should have done this before."

There was an incredible,
blinding
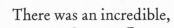flash
that tore through the darkness.
The air shook. Saskia screamed.

Then there was silence.

Erik lay facedown on the iron stairs of the factory. The remnants of the smashed barrel were all about him.

"Dead?" asked

Straker reluctantly. "I didn't know we did dead."

"He gave me no other choice," Potemkin said, walking down the stairs toward the place where Erik lay.

"Kidnapped, um . . . frightened, um . . . but not dead . . ." Straker muttered with guilt in his voice.

"My freedom is worth more than his life," Potemkin replied coldly. "Get the girls and we can do the job properly."

Straker seemed reluctant to move as Potemkin strode down the metal stairs toward Erik's lifeless body.

"What'll we do with him?" Straker asked, his voice cracking on each word.

"Making things disappear is what I do best. Get the car. We'll take his body to a place where the police will never find it."

"Are you sure that's a good thing to do?" Straker asked as Potemkin got to within two feet of Erik.

"Why do you ask?"

"Because you should never fall for the same thing twice," Erik said. He leaped to his feet like a cat, picked up a long slat of broken barrel, and lunged at Potemkin.

The magician of Hampstead jumped out of the way but tripped on a plank of wood and fell to the floor. Erik grabbed the gun from his hand. "Do you want a piece of this, Straker?" Erik challenged. "Stay back, or I'll give it to you." Straker cowered backward. Erik continued, "I know how to use this, and unlike Potemkin I always hit what I shoot at."

Potemkin grabbed for Erik, but Erik had already turned and was running after the twins.

"Stop him, Straker!" Potemkin demanded.

"He's got your gun," Straker replied warily from his hiding place.

"Idiot!" yelled Potemkin and charged after Erik.

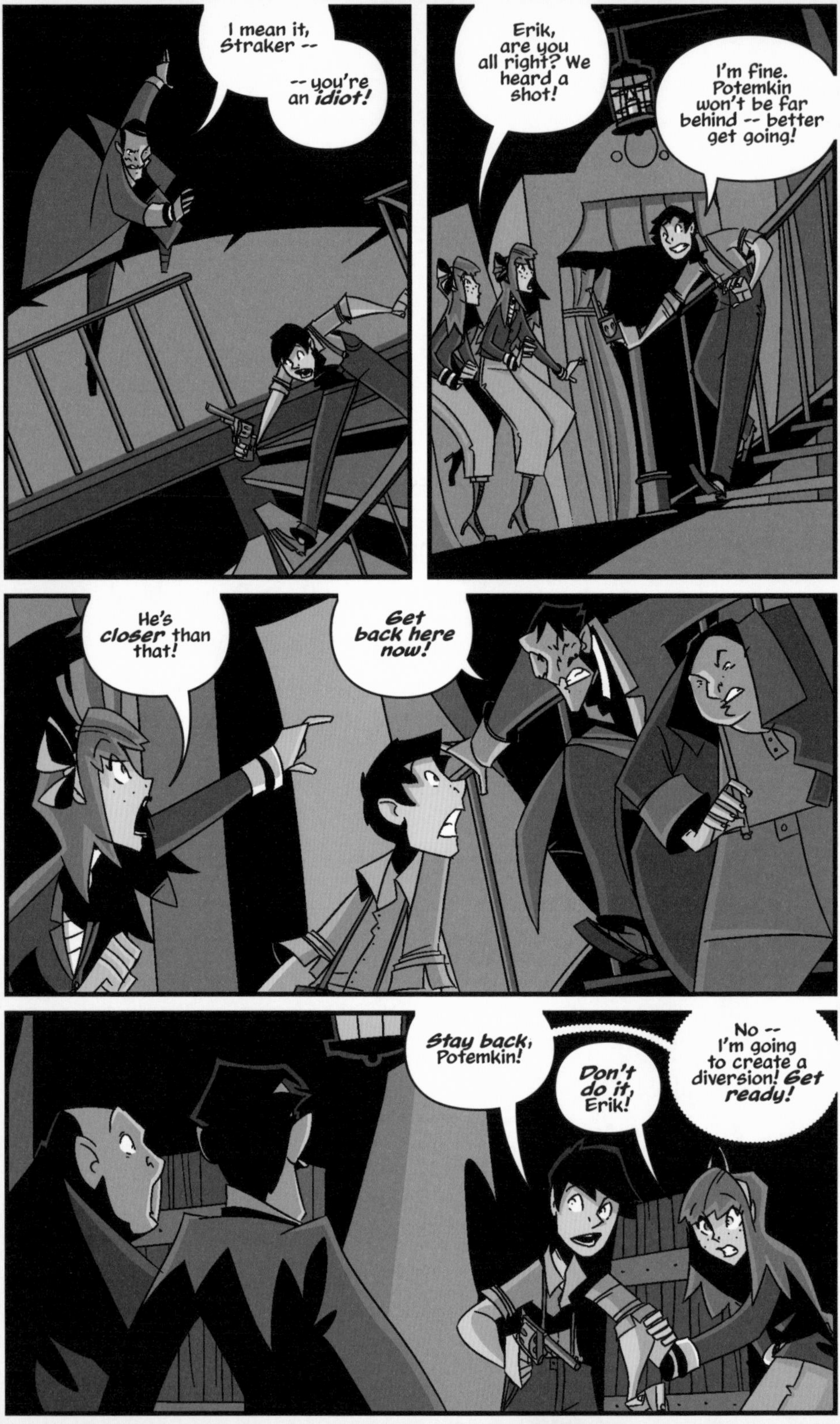
I mean it, Straker --
-- you're an *idiot!*
Erik, are you all right? We heard a shot!
I'm fine. Potemkin won't be far behind -- better get going!
He's *closer* than that!
Get back here now!
Stay back, Potemkin!
Don't do it, Erik!
No -- I'm going to create a diversion! *Get ready!*

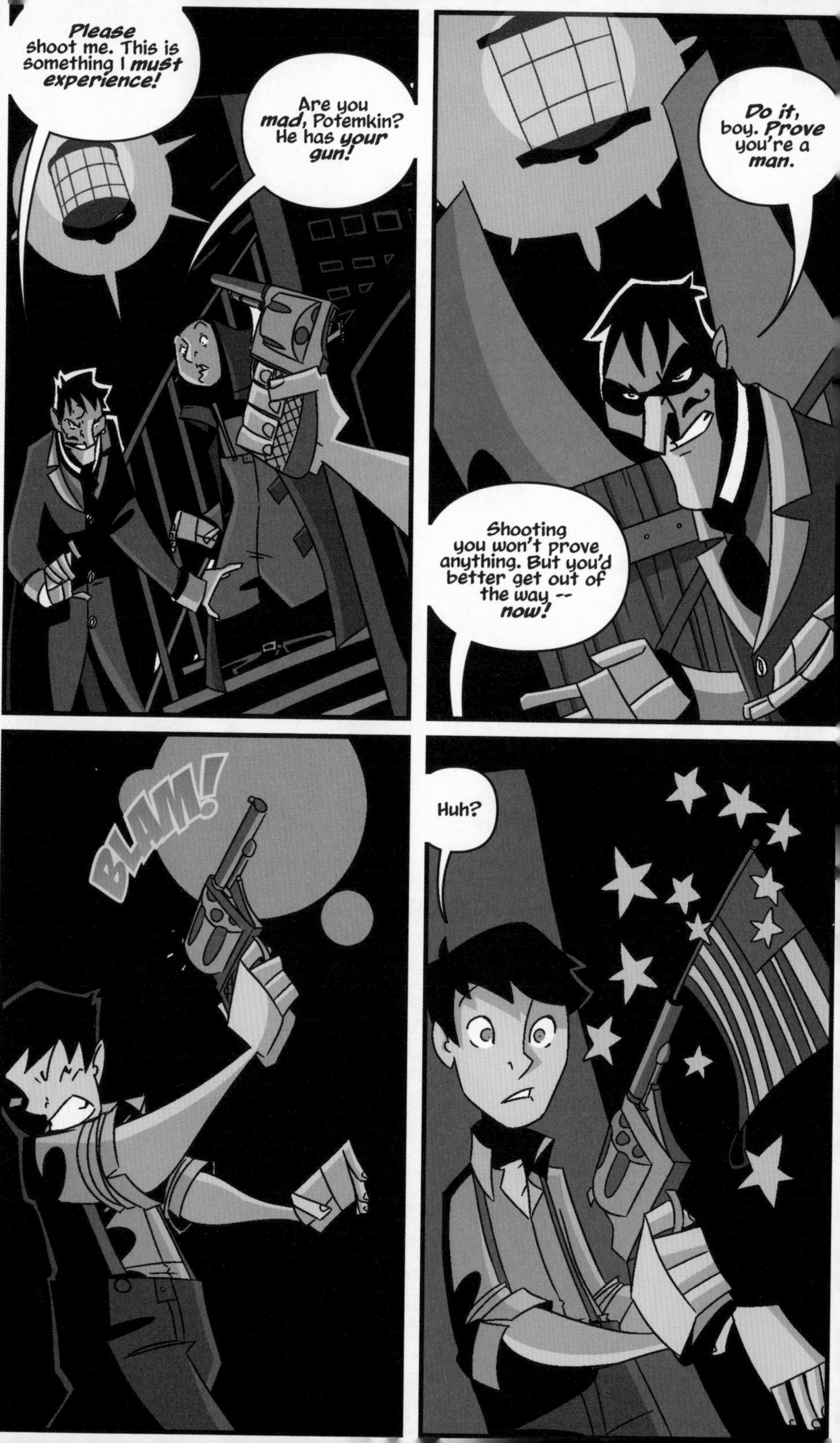
Please shoot me. This is something I must experience!
Are you mad, Potemkin? He has your gun!
Do it, boy. Prove you're a man.
Shooting you won't prove anything. But you'd better get out of the way -- now!
BLAM!
Huh?

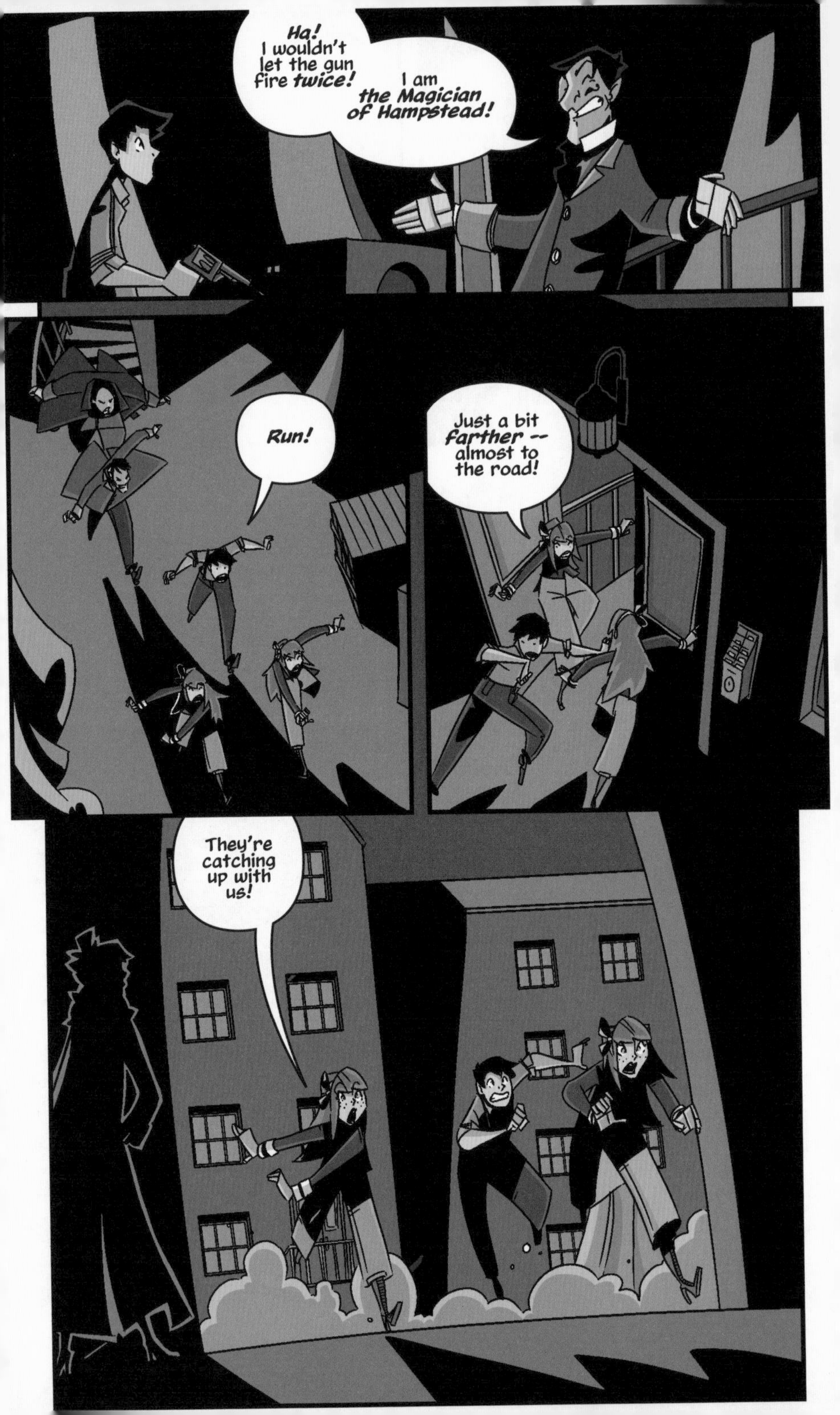
Ha! I wouldn't let the gun fire *twice*!
I am *the Magician of Hampstead!*
Run!
Just a bit *farther* -- almost to the road!
They're catching up with us!

Erik, Sadie, and Saskia ran until they were sure they weren't being followed. Erik panted for breath, unable to speak, while Saskia and Sadie looked back to see if the street was still empty.

"We lost them at the Duke of Kent Inn," Saskia said, pointing back down the street. "Potemkin couldn't keep up with us even if he conjured up a new pair of legs," she tried to joke.

"We can't stop. We have to tell someone," Sadie said as she tugged on Saskia's arm to make her run again. "We could go to Muzz Elliott, like you said—she'd know what to do."

"If only I could see Madame Raphael. I could ask her," Saskia said longingly.

"She doesn't exist, and even if she did, what good would a ghost be to us? I say we go back to Lord Gervez and ask to see Dorcas Potts," Erik said as he began to walk again, constantly looking back to see if they were being followed. "When we explain everything that's happened, they'll have to trust us. Dorcas Potts can find out everything . . . tell the police . . . get Rimmer arrested."

"It's true, I tell you—Madame Raphael is real," Saskia insisted, wanting to argue until they believed. "I saw her—she helped me. I know it in my heart."

"Then where was she when you were trapped in the coffin?" asked Sadie.

"Well," began Saskia slowly, "you found me, didn't you?"

"Look, Saskia—I think Erik's right. Our best chance is to get to Dorcas Potts. If you want to help, pray we'll find her," said Sadie. She turned and went after Erik.

Saskia sighed and followed. They walked for ten long minutes, tramping wearily through the damp backstreets of Belsize Park and the narrow alleyways of Hampstead. Saskia looked at the welcoming lights of the fine houses with their grand doorways and painted windows. Once she had been given the chance to live in a fine house and learn proper manners. Muzz Elliott had chosen Saskia to live with her for a while and Madame Raphael had taught her table manners, even showing her how to eat peas with a fork. "If only Sadie would believe me about Madame Raphael," Saskia thought. She imagined the day when the angel would appear to both of them. Maybe Madame Raphael would help them find their mother, and the three of them would be reunited at last.

It was when she heard the chiming of the church clock that she realized Erik and Sadie were no longer in sight. Had she lost them? Saskia thought of turning back, retracing her steps to see if they were waiting for her. But she knew in her heart they must have gone on ahead. They needed to get to Dorcas Potts as fast as they could—there was no time for them to turn back and look for her.

The fine rows of houses had faded without Saskia realizing it. Now she was alone in a dark, narrow alleyway that smelled of garbage. Some yards ahead she could see a broken gas lamp. It burned with a bright blue flame that spat against the night dew. With every slight breeze it hissed and gasped. "Madame Raphael," Saskia whispered, "if you can hear me, please help me find Erik and Sadie."

As she walked on, she was convinced that the alleyway was growing narrower, and for one dreadful minute she was afraid that like Alice in Wonderland she was growing bigger and bigger.

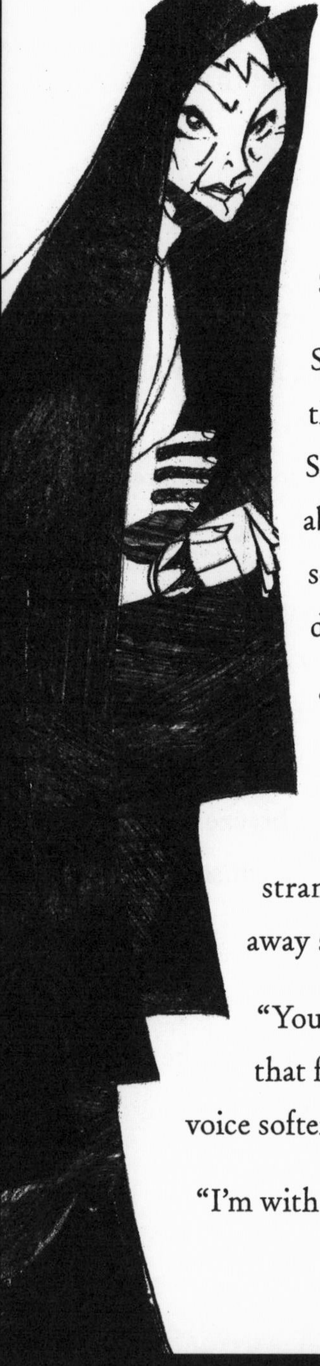

"Not a place for a lady," said a voice from the darkness. "Not in a street like this. Someone as fine as you could come to harm."

Saskia turned. There, in an alcove cut into the wall like a cave, was an old woman. She was draped in a blanket that hung about her like a shroud. Saskia could see little more than her face in the dark shadows.

"Lost for words?" the woman asked abruptly.

"My mother told me not to speak to strangers," Saskia replied, backing away slowly.

"Your mother is many miles away—I can tell that from your eyes," the woman replied, her voice softer.

"I'm with my sister and Erik," Saskia snapped.

"Looking for a friend, calling on her, and thinking she can't hear you?" The words stopped Saskia's steps. "Sometimes wisdom is closer than you think, especially when you're trying to eat peas with a fork." A gentle laugh came from the alcove.

"Madame Raphael?" Saskia asked and peered deeper into the shadows.

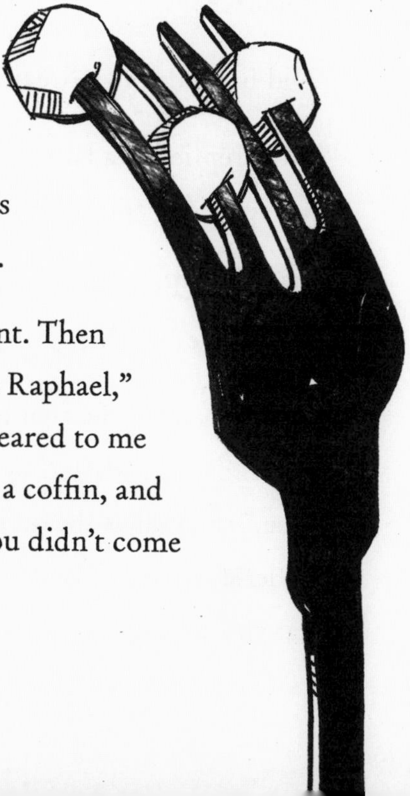

"Best not to make too grand an appearance—once I frightened the life out of some shepherds and only said the words 'Fear not,'" the woman explained.

Saskia was speechless for a moment. Then she looked down shyly. "Madame Raphael," she began, "Why haven't you appeared to me again until now? I was trapped in a coffin, and I asked you to help me get out. You didn't come . . . but you're here now."

"The answer you seek is not always the answer you are given," said Madame Raphael gently. "But I did hear you in the coffin, and as you say, I am here now."

Saskia hurried on. "And at Spaniards House I came looking for you—looked in every room—used the key."

"Sometimes to find wisdom you have to look beyond locked rooms," Madame Raphael said slowly. "I once knew a man who searched for insight into the ways of the world and only found it when he slept under an apple tree."

"Did he find it in a dream?" Saskia asked.

"No," replied Madame Raphael with a smile on her lips. "An apple fell and hit him on the head."

"Sadie and Erik don't believe you are real. They say I imagined everything."

"If I am real to you, that is enough for now. I will pray for a time to come when they, too, shall see me and hear my voice," she said as she pulled Saskia into the shadows and sat her down on the cold stone step next to her. "It's not me that you should be searching for but the one who sent me.

The Companion knows all that you need, Saskia. He is the one who can answer your prayers."

"But who is the Companion?" Saskia asked as she leaned against Madame Raphael.

There was no answer. There was no blanket. There was no Madame Raphael.

And then Saskia heard a familiar voice from around the corner. "She must be here somewhere—why did she come this way?" Sadie turned into the alleyway with Erik not far behind.

"How can you get lost in Hampstead?" Erik shouted just as Saskia stepped from the shadows.

"I'm not lost. I was here all the time," Saskia said. She wanted to tell them about Madame Raphael, but she was afraid they would just laugh at her again. Madame Raphael had left no note or key as proof of her visit this time.

"What have you—" Sadie started to ask, but suddenly a long, black car pulled up at the end of the alley. In an instant they were engulfed in a bright, white light that burned their eyes.

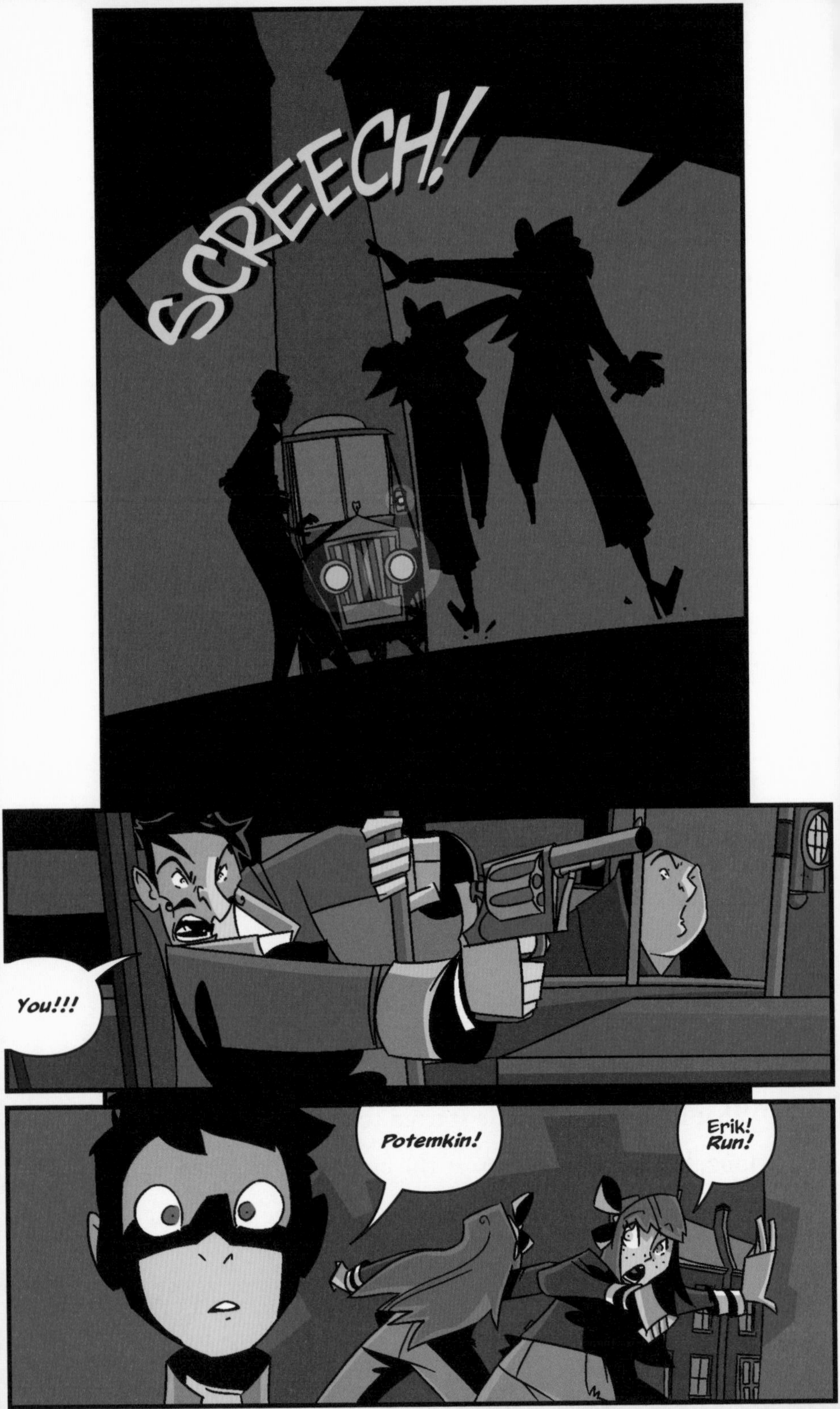
SCREECH!
You!!!
Potemkin!
Erik!
Run!

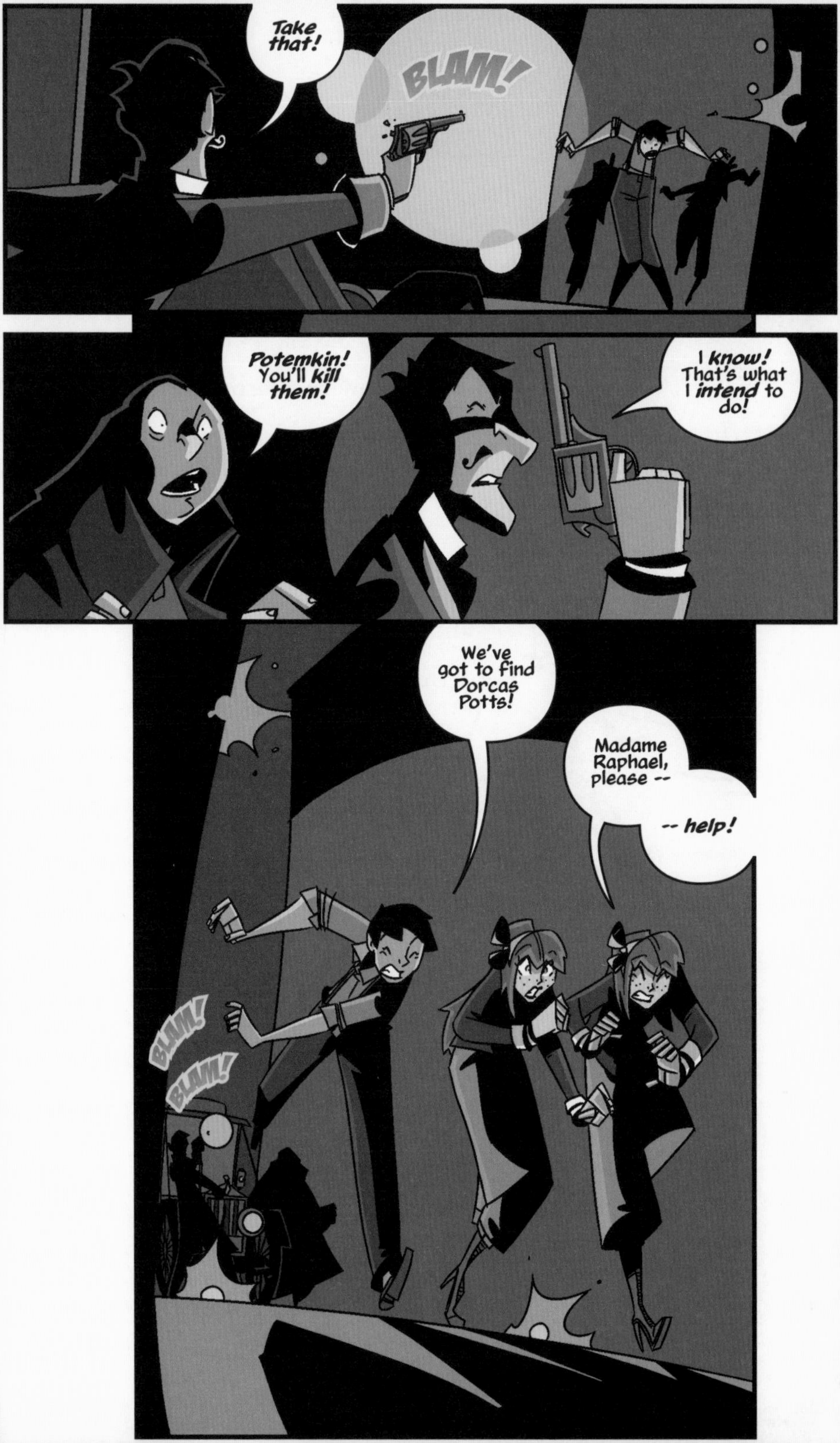
Take that!
BLAM!
Potemkin! You'll kill them!
I know! That's what I intend to do!
We've got to find Dorcas Potts!
Madame Raphael, please --
-- help!
BLAM!
BLAM!

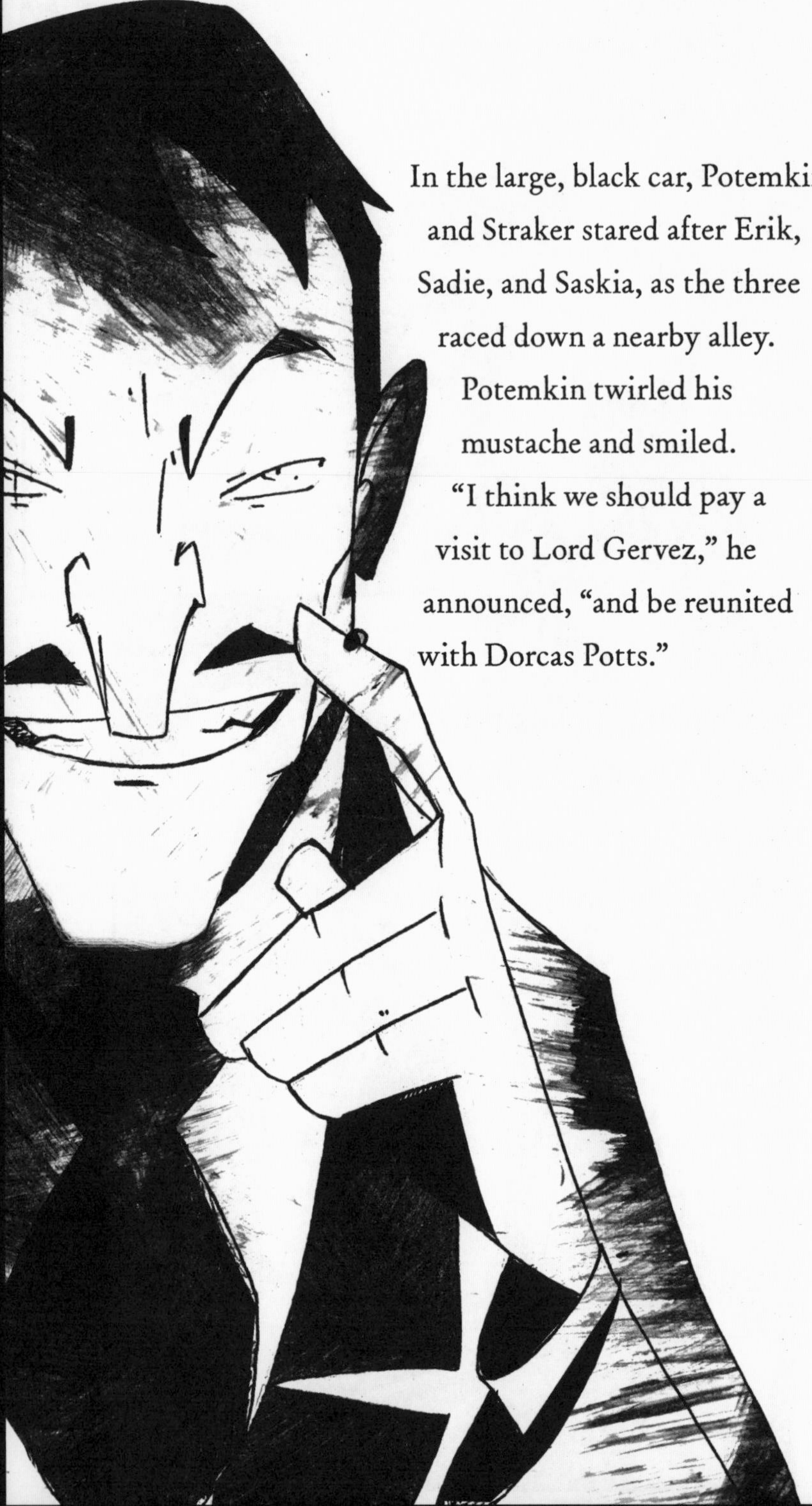

In the large, black car, Potemkin and Straker stared after Erik, Sadie, and Saskia, as the three raced down a nearby alley. Potemkin twirled his mustache and smiled.

"I think we should pay a visit to Lord Gervez," he announced, "and be reunited with Dorcas Potts."

Chapter Nine
Break and Enter

THEY KEPT TO THE ALLEYWAYS, where they knew the car couldn't follow. At every road they crossed, Erik stopped and looked out. Making sure the car was nowhere in sight, he motioned for Sadie and Saskia to hurry across the street and dart for the darkness of the next alley. All the while they made their way back toward Isambard Dunstan's, closer and closer to Gervez's house and Dorcas Potts.

The streets were empty, and they saw no one. The constable who usually stood on the corner of East Park Road was oddly absent. Skirting through the trees that bordered the park, the three slowly made their way up the steep hill.

"What will we tell Dorcas Potts when we find her?" Sadie asked. "She wasn't exactly pleased to see us in Gervez's house."

"We'll tell her that Rimmer's behind all this," Erik answered confidently, "and that Potemkin admitted it himself. Gervez told us Dorcas Potts has been trying to solve the crime—she'll want to hear our information."

A car with its headlights on came slowly by, and Erik, Sadie, and Saskia ducked into the hedgerow.

"It wasn't them," Erik said as the car went down the hill. "I can tell a Rolls-Royce anywhere—all you have to do is listen to the engine."

They crept back out of the hedge and carried on up the hill. They were almost at the school when Erik stopped so quickly that Sadie and Saskia nearly ran into him. The Rolls-Royce was parked inside the gates of Lord Gervez's house. It was dusty black with glowing white powder in the arches of the tires.

"We're too late," he said in a whisper. "Potemkin got here first. Look—405 SBH."

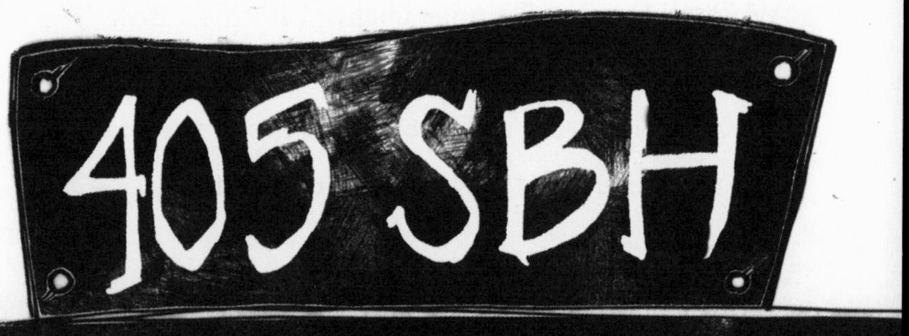
405 SBH

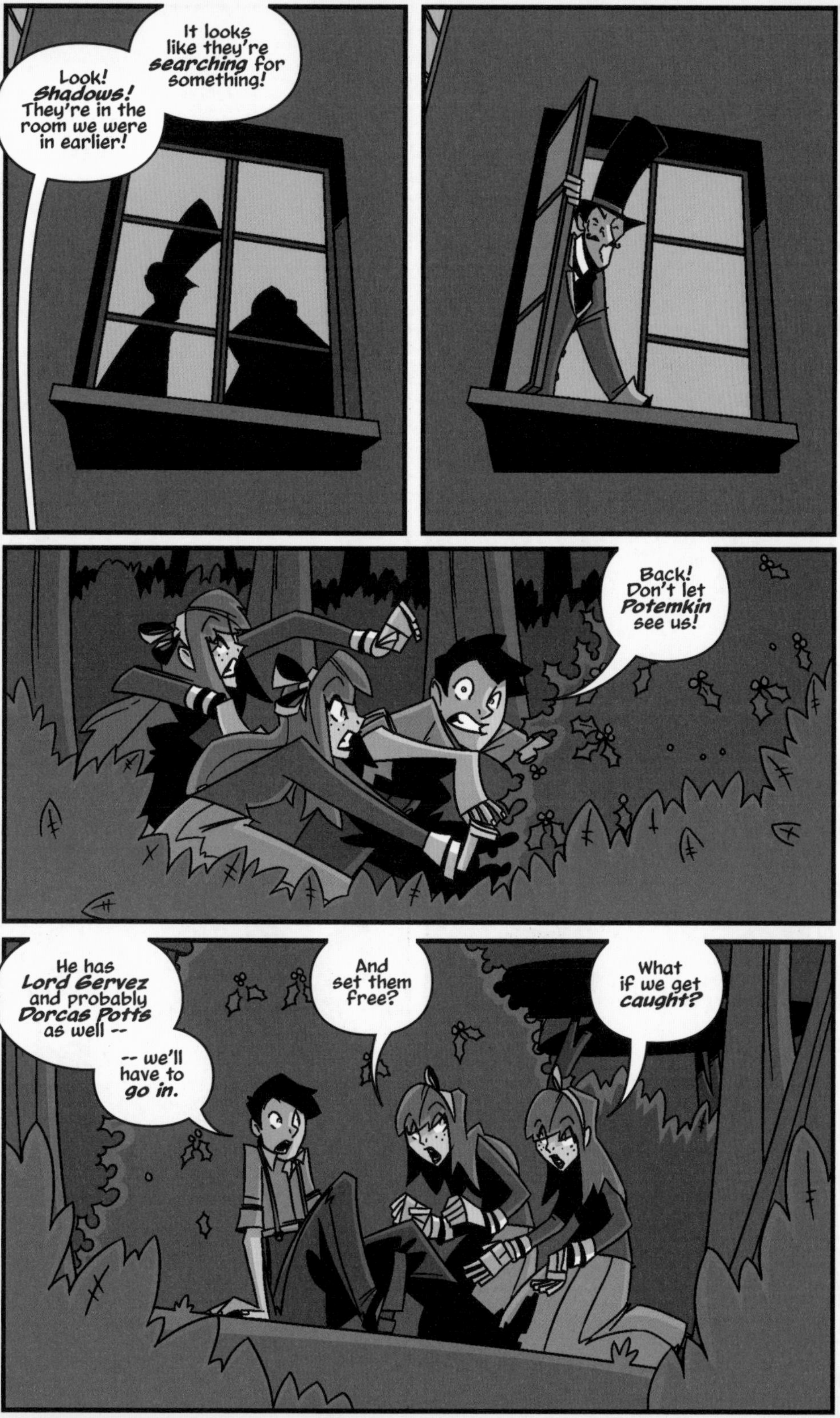
Look! Shadows! They're in the room we were in earlier!
It looks like they're searching for something!
Back! Don't let Potemkin see us!
He has Lord Gervez and probably Dorcas Potts as well --
-- we'll have to go in.
And set them free?
What if we get caught?

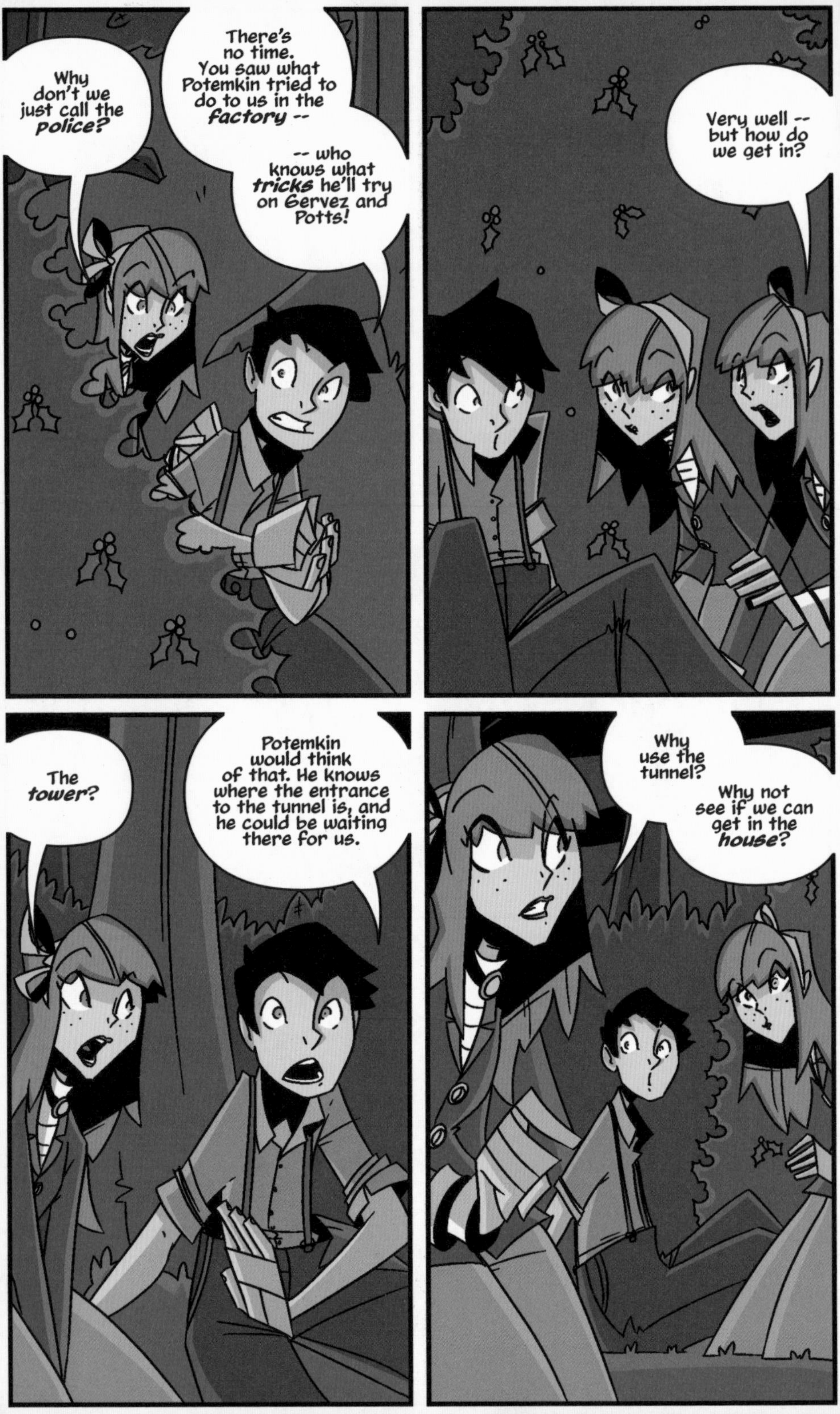
Why don't we just call the *police?*
There's no time. You saw what Potemkin tried to do to us in the *factory* --
-- who knows what *tricks* he'll try on Gervez and Potts!
Very well -- but how do we get in?
The *tower?*
Potemkin would think of that. He knows where the entrance to the tunnel is, and he could be waiting there for us.
Why use the tunnel?
Why not see if we can get in the *house?*

"We could," Erik said, annoyed he had not come up with the idea first. "My father said these places always have a window or door open at the back because the servants are too lazy to lock them."

"All right," Sadie said. "Let's get on with it. We can't leave old Gervez and Dorcas Potts to Potemkin. I'm sure you haven't forgotten how to break and enter."

Her words were cold, just like her smile. It was as if the mention of parents turned her heart to ice. Saskia looked at her sister with sympathetic eyes. She turned to Erik. Just for a moment he seemed far away, like a lost boy searching for a home.

Erik had been left behind just as Sadie and Saskia had, but unlike them, he wasn't usually bothered by the thought that he might never see his father again. He had been warm every night since he had been dumped at Dunstan's. No one at the school forced him to sneak through open windows or steal anything. It had been the stealing he had hated most—those pangs of guilt creeping through his thoughts like pointing fingers in his mind.

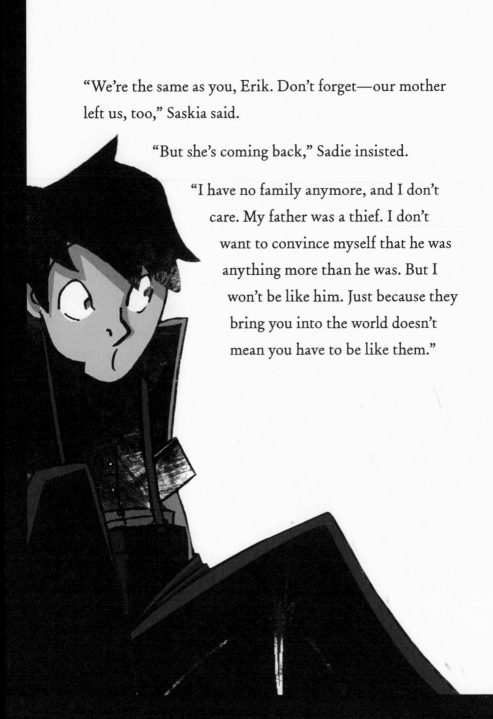

"We're the same as you, Erik. Don't forget—our mother left us, too," Saskia said.

"But she's coming back," Sadie insisted.

"I have no family anymore, and I don't care. My father was a thief. I don't want to convince myself that he was anything more than he was. But I won't be like him. Just because they bring you into the world doesn't mean you have to be like them."

Erik's words sounded rehearsed. They brought a harsh silence that no one wished to break.

The three stared across the darkness at the house and watched the shadows move about in the upstairs room.

"I'll go alone. Better to risk only one of us getting caught. You two can wait for me here," Erik said firmly.

"We should all go together," Saskia replied.

"Erik's right—one of us should stay outside. We can't all risk getting caught," said Sadie.

"But—" Saskia tried to protest.

Erik cut her off. "Don't worry, Saskia. You stay here. Sadie and I will go around the back and get in."

"I don't want . . ." she tried again. But before Saskia could say another word, Erik tugged Sadie by the arm and the two set off toward the house. It was as if they hadn't heard her at all.

". . . to be alone again," Saskia finished quietly. Her words fell onto the damp ground.

The next moment Erik and Sadie ran across the road into the shadows and dissolved into the darkness. Above, in the front room of Gervez's house, the shadows skirmished with one another.

Saskia waited, biting her lip in frustration.

On the drive of Lord Gervez's house, the car suddenly sprang to life. The doors rattled, the engine shook, and there was a sudden ominous crunching of the transmission. The vehicle lurched forward, quickly picking up speed as it hurtled toward the door.

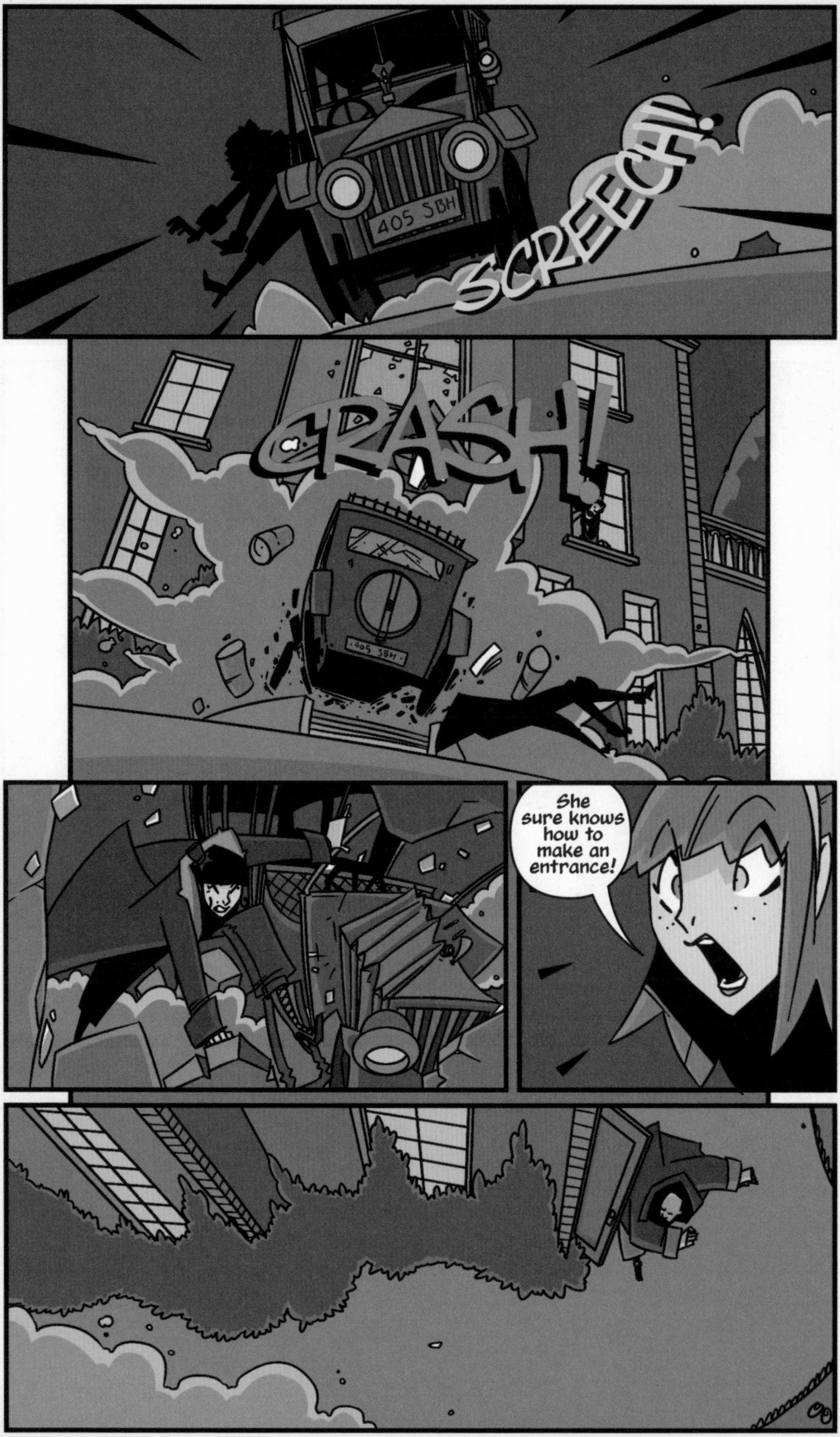
405 SBH
SCREECH!!
CRASH!
405 SBH
She sure knows how to make an entrance!

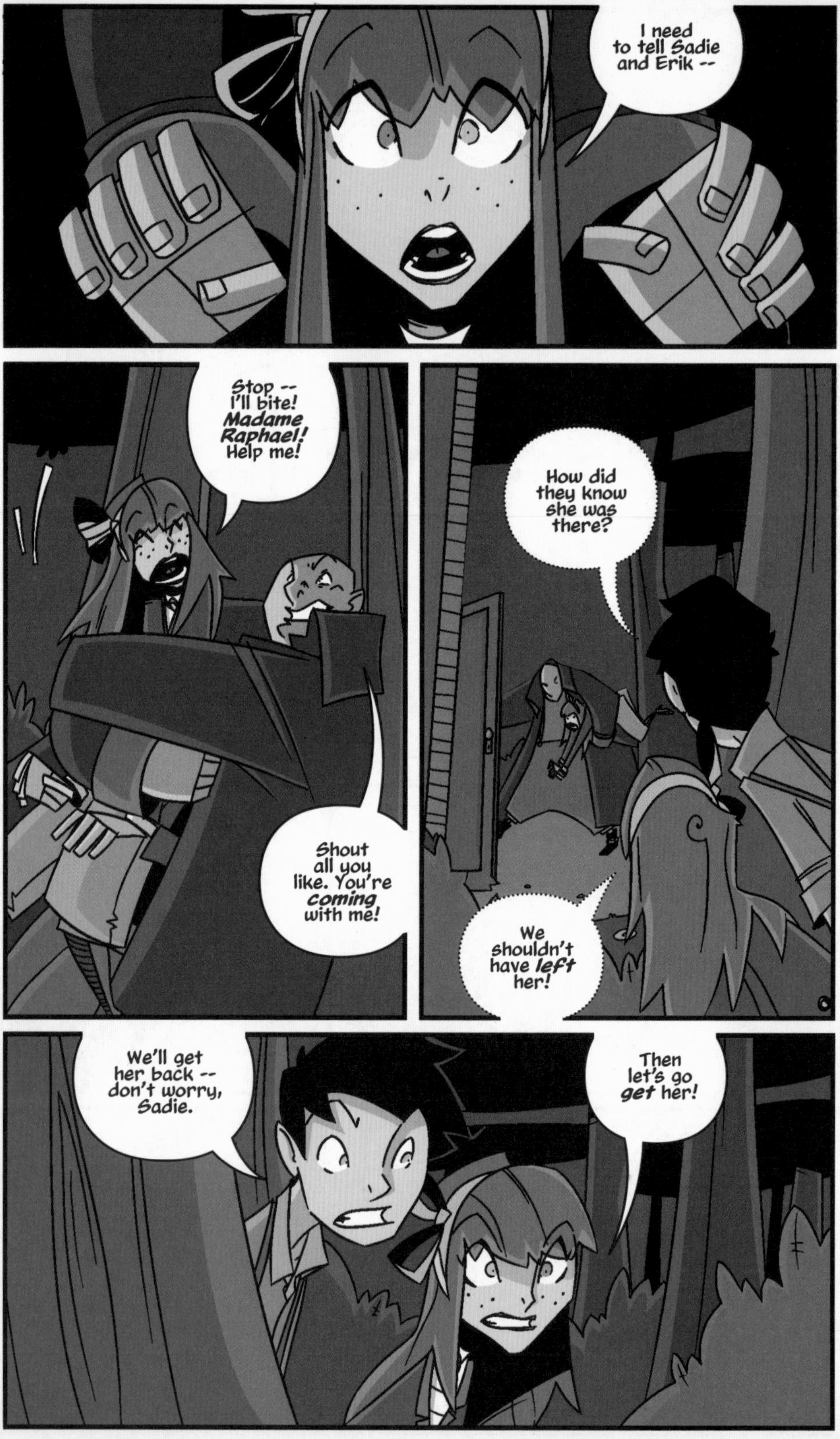
I need to tell Sadie and Erik --
Stop -- I'll bite! Madame Raphael! Help me!
Shout all you like. You're coming with me!
How did they know she was there?
We shouldn't have left her!
We'll get her back -- don't worry, Sadie.
Then let's go get her!

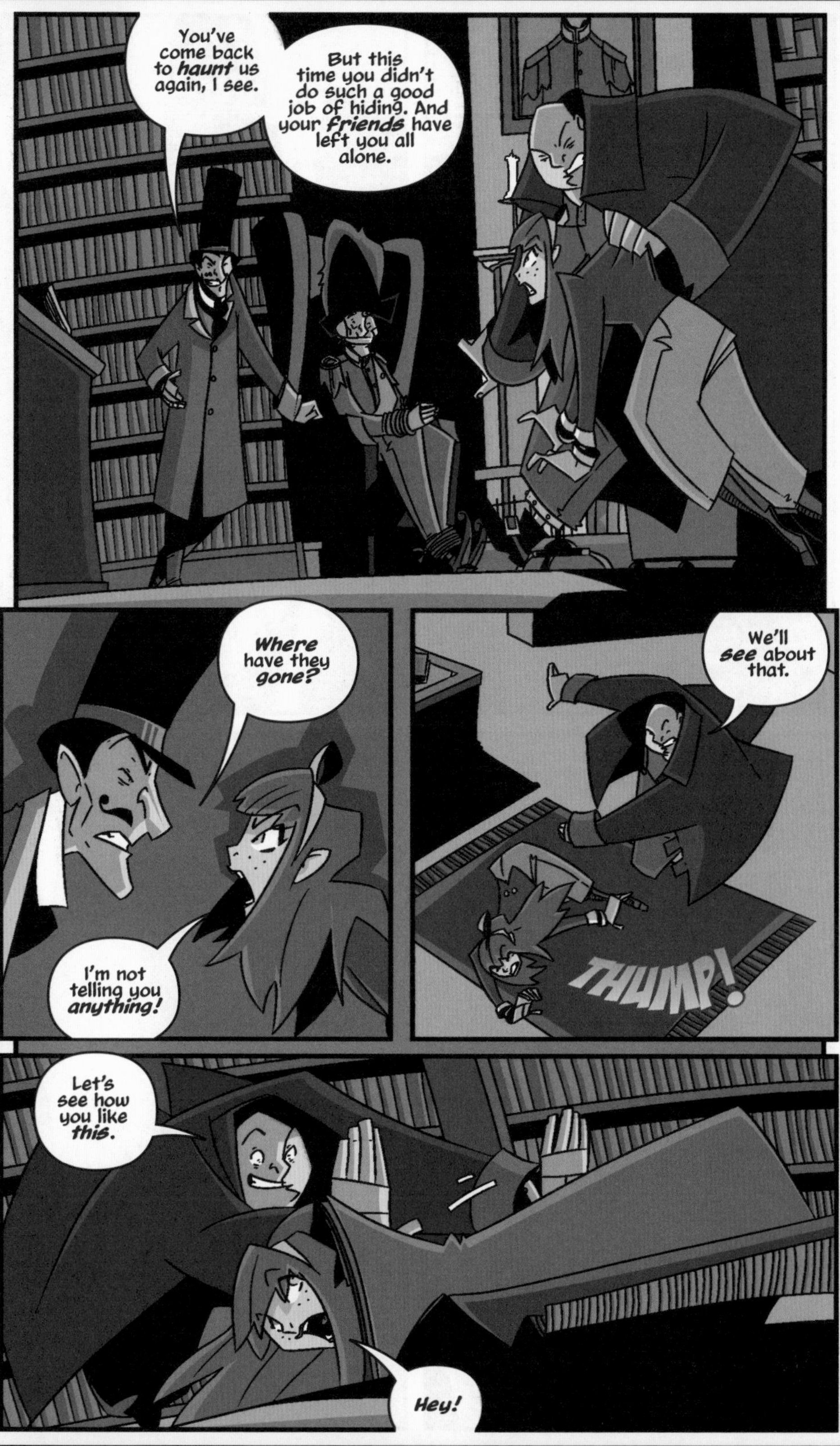
You've come back to *haunt* us again, I see.
But this time you didn't do such a good job of hiding. And your *friends* have left you all alone.
Where have they *gone?*
I'm not telling you *anything!*
We'll *see* about that.
THUMP!
Let's see how you like *this.*
Hey!

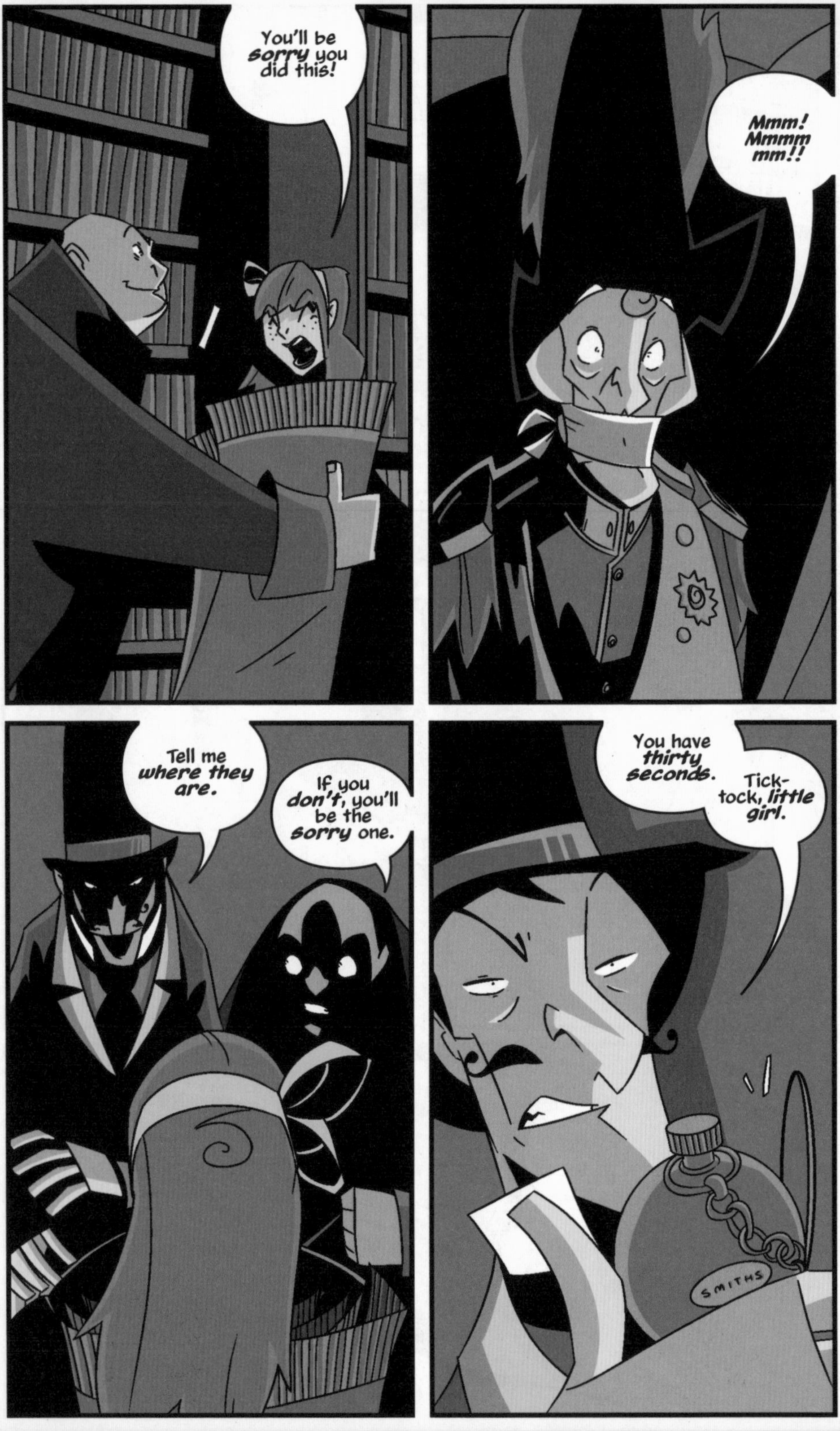
You'll be *sorry* you did this!
Mmm! Mmmm mm!!
Tell me *where they are.*
If you *don't*, you'll be the *sorry* one.
You have *thirty seconds*.
Tick-tock, *little girl*.
SMITHS

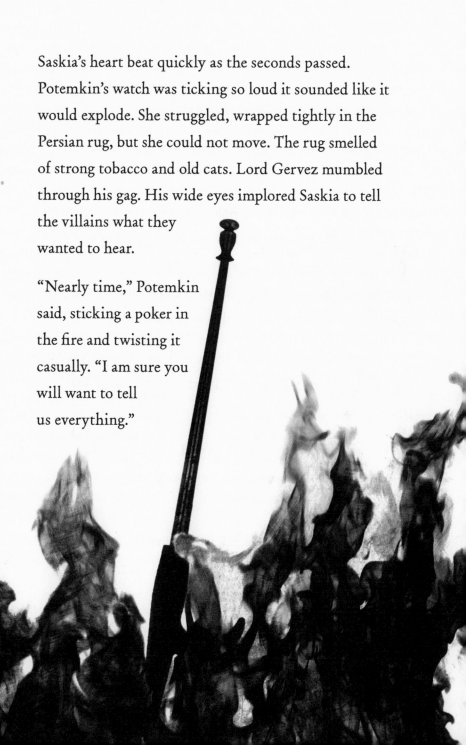

Saskia's heart beat quickly as the seconds passed. Potemkin's watch was ticking so loud it sounded like it would explode. She struggled, wrapped tightly in the Persian rug, but she could not move. The rug smelled of strong tobacco and old cats. Lord Gervez mumbled through his gag. His wide eyes implored Saskia to tell the villains what they wanted to hear.

"Nearly time," Potemkin said, sticking a poker in the fire and twisting it casually. "I am sure you will want to tell us everything."

"You're going to get caught—sent to prison. That's all you need to know," Saskia blurted defiantly.

"Ha!" Potemkin chortled. "Tell me, my dear, where are they, and what do they intend to do?"

He took the hot, smoldering poker from the fire and held it in front of him as though poised to conduct a grand orchestra. Suddenly he shoved the poker into the wall just by Saskia's face. She flinched. The poker slowly burned a hole in the wall as Potemkin stared unblinkingly into Saskia's eyes.

"Do what they say," Lord Gervez said, as he managed to spit the gag from his mouth. "Dorcas will save us—tell them where your friends are."

"Why don't you ask the woman you work for? Miss Rimmer will tell you—she knows everything," exclaimed Saskia.

"Miss Rimmer? Do you think we are mad?" Potemkin asked. He gargled with laughter as he placed the poker back into the embers of the fire.

"I heard you—you said the headmistress was your boss."

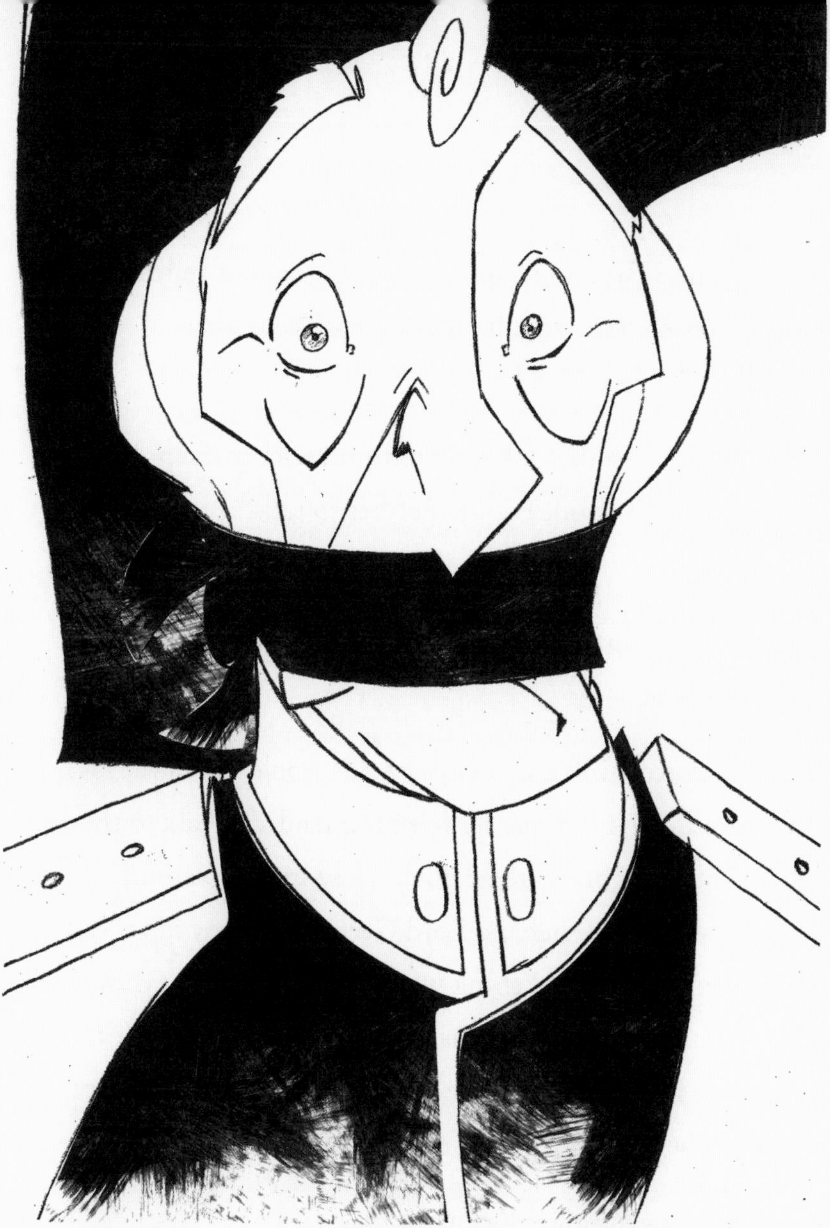

"Tsk-tsk. Has no one taught you the dangers of eavesdropping, my dear girl?"

"You can find Erik and Sadie yourself—I'm not telling!" Saskia shouted defiantly, hoping against hope that someone outside would hear her.

"Can I do it?" Straker asked Potemkin, taking the poker from the fire. "I think I could get her to talk."

Potemkin paused and thought for a while. His shrewd eyes watched the wisps of smoke spiraling from the burning tip of the fire iron.

"No . . . I don't think it is necessary. She would not have come here alone if she and her friends intended to talk to the police. The other brats are no doubt close by and planning some mission to free her and Lord Gervez. The boy never can resist playing the hero. I think we will give them what they want and use this little thing as bait for the trap." Potemkin stopped and eyed Lord Gervez angrily. "Did you think there was only one way into 'your' secret passage?"

Lord Gervez grumbled forlornly.

"The architect who built this place left some very detailed plans of your house—sold them to the highest bidder—

with every brick marked and every passageway revealed. He linked every house he built in Hampstead with a secret tunnel—so vast you could hide an army in it . . . and I know every inch." Potemkin proudly pulled a long, thin book from the top pocket of his coat.

"That architect was a scoundrel," Gervez said as he watched Potemkin leafing through the pages.

"And a very rich one at that. It was his intention all along to relieve you all of your money. Fancy houses upon the heath—each ready to be robbed. He sold the plans and the whereabouts of every tunnel to my employer."

"He didn't build Dunstan's school," Saskia said. She struggled to free herself from the rug.

"That he did not. It appears that he simply added on the link to the school in the disguise of a long-overdue sewer."

"That was done twenty years ago when my house was built," Gervez said in surprise. "You waited all that time to rob me?"

"It was obviously worth the wait."

"And wait you did until I had a house full of treasure. What part did you play in this?" Gervez asked Potemkin in disgust.

"Very little," he replied, twisting the wax on his mustache. "Mr. Straker and I met shortly before my brief time in prison. I am a newcomer to this sort of employment."

"He's a magician," Saskia said, in the way she might describe something she had found on the bottom of her shoe.

"And I would have been even greater had it not been for your sister and her interfering friend," Potemkin replied. "But no matter. With the treasure we've collected I have a practically endless supply of material to create new tricks."

"Will you let them live?" Straker asked.

"For the time being—until we get further instructions," Potemkin replied.

"You don't have to live this way," Saskia said, squirming in the rug to try to loosen it.

"Innocent words, Miss Dopple, innocent words. But very stupid ones," Potemkin gloated. "Let us take her to the tunnel, Mr. Straker. I shall prepare a place. A trap of traps, a contraption of the miraculous. Should your friends find you, they will wish they hadn't."

"She is but a child—leave her be," said Lord Gervez, his face reddening.

"She has gotten in the way." Potemkin snorted. "I am not one for wanting to settle old scores, but your sister and her friend have caused me much heartache and embarrassment. I think all three of you deserve to be punished."

"Don't worry, girl. Dorcas will help us," Lord Gervez said to Saskia.

"Dorcas Potts will be the death of herself. She has interfered too much in my life. I remember what she wrote in the TIMES about me when I was imprisoned: 'failed magician . . . child snatcher . . . robber of innocence.'" Potemkin sucked air through his teeth as he spoke. "Sticks and stones may break my bones, but calling names—" Potemkin stopped for a moment as he wiped a rolling tear from his sallow cheek. "They tear out the soul, Lord Gervez, tear out the soul."

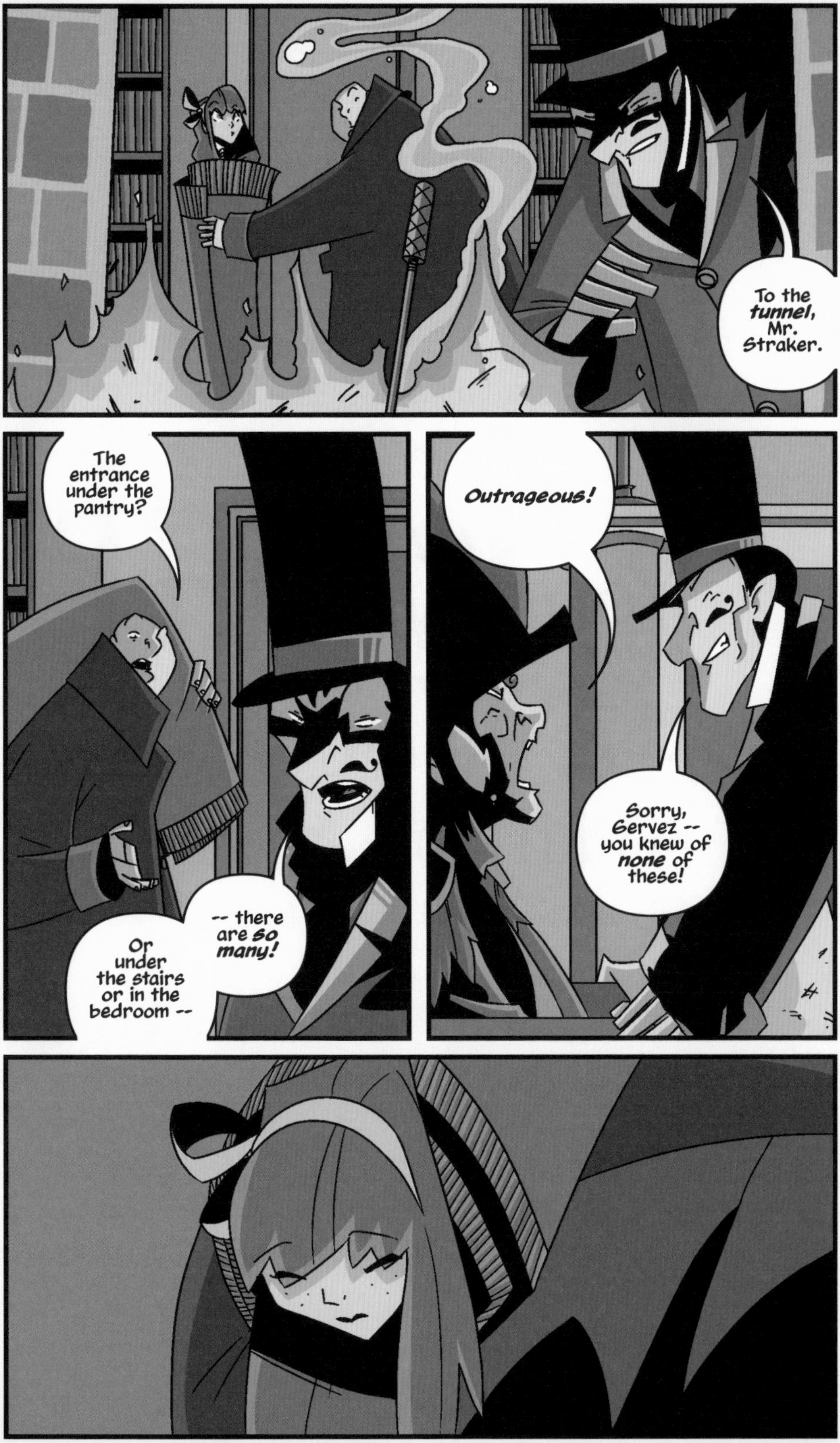
To the *tunnel,* Mr. Straker.
The entrance under the pantry?
Or under the stairs or in the bedroom --
-- there are *so many!*
Outrageous!
Sorry, Gervez -- you knew of *none* of these!

As Straker carried Saskia away over his shoulder, she caught one last glimpse of Lord Gervez struggling to get free of his bonds.

"You won't get away with this!" he called after them. Potemkin shut the door and turned to face his partner in crime.

"And now to deal with the interferers. Lead the way, Mr. Straker. We must set the trap and wait for our victims."

Chapter Ten

With Nail and Eye

ERIK AND SADIE found the window they had been looking for. It was narrow with cracked glass. The paint was peeling from the wood, and flakes of it lay about the brick pathway outside.

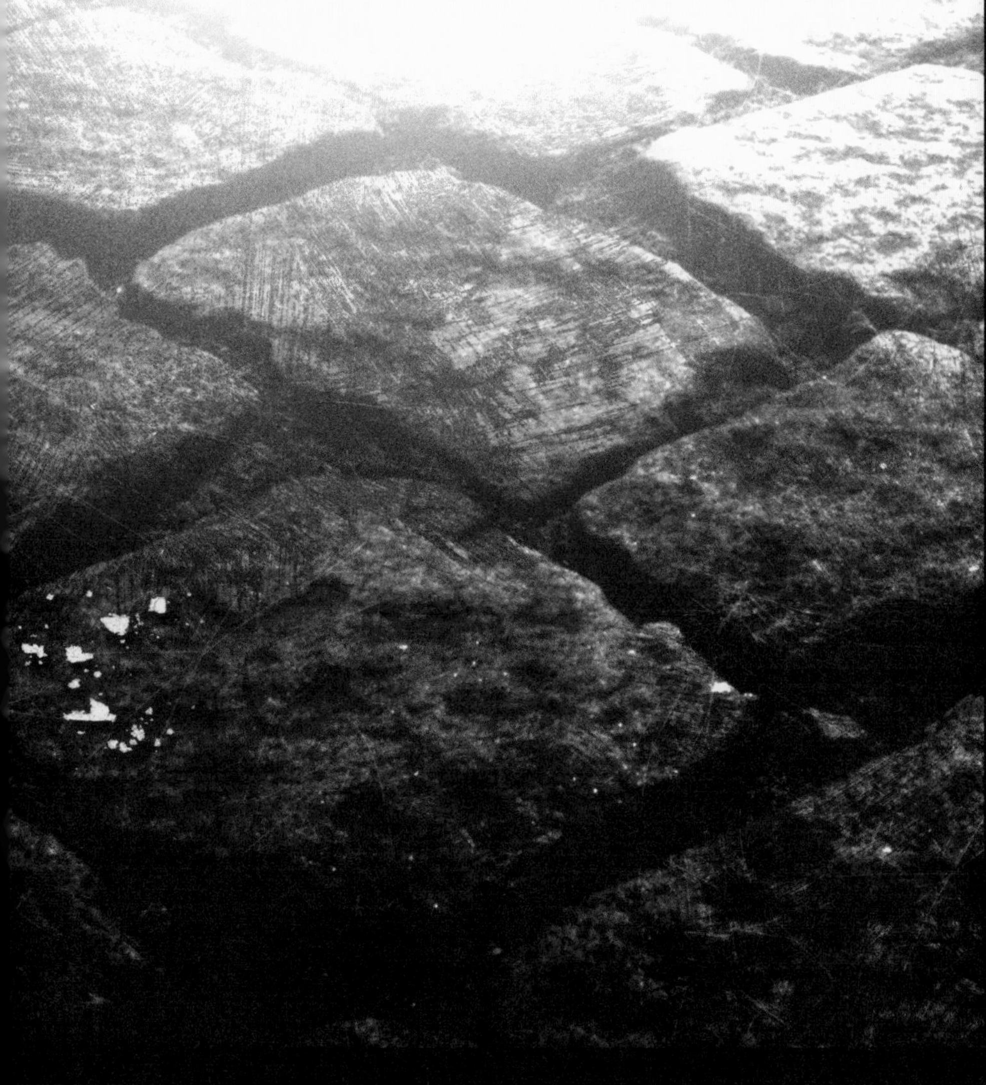

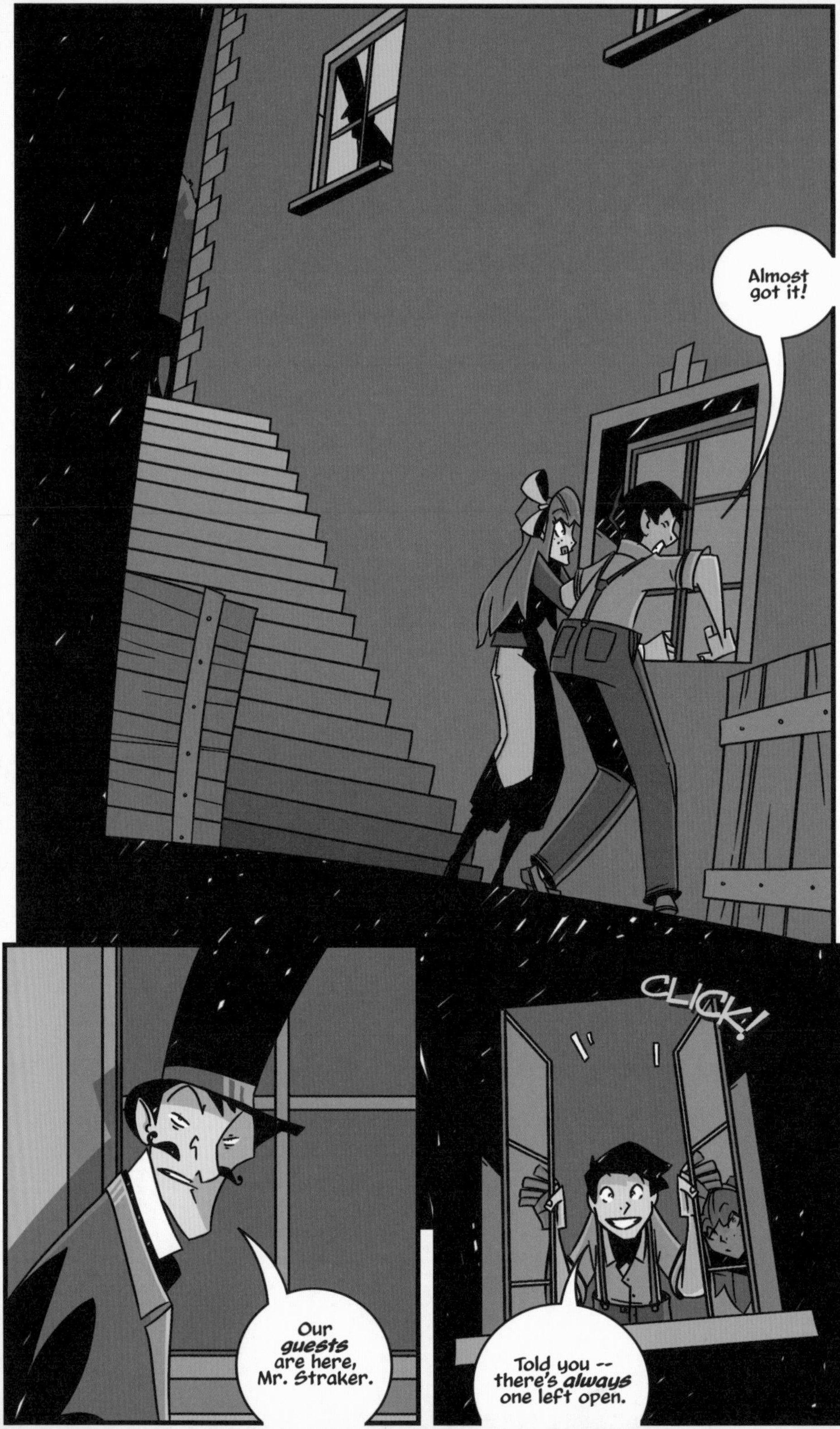
Almost got it!
CLICK!
Our *guests* are here, Mr. Straker.
Told you -- there's *always* one left open.

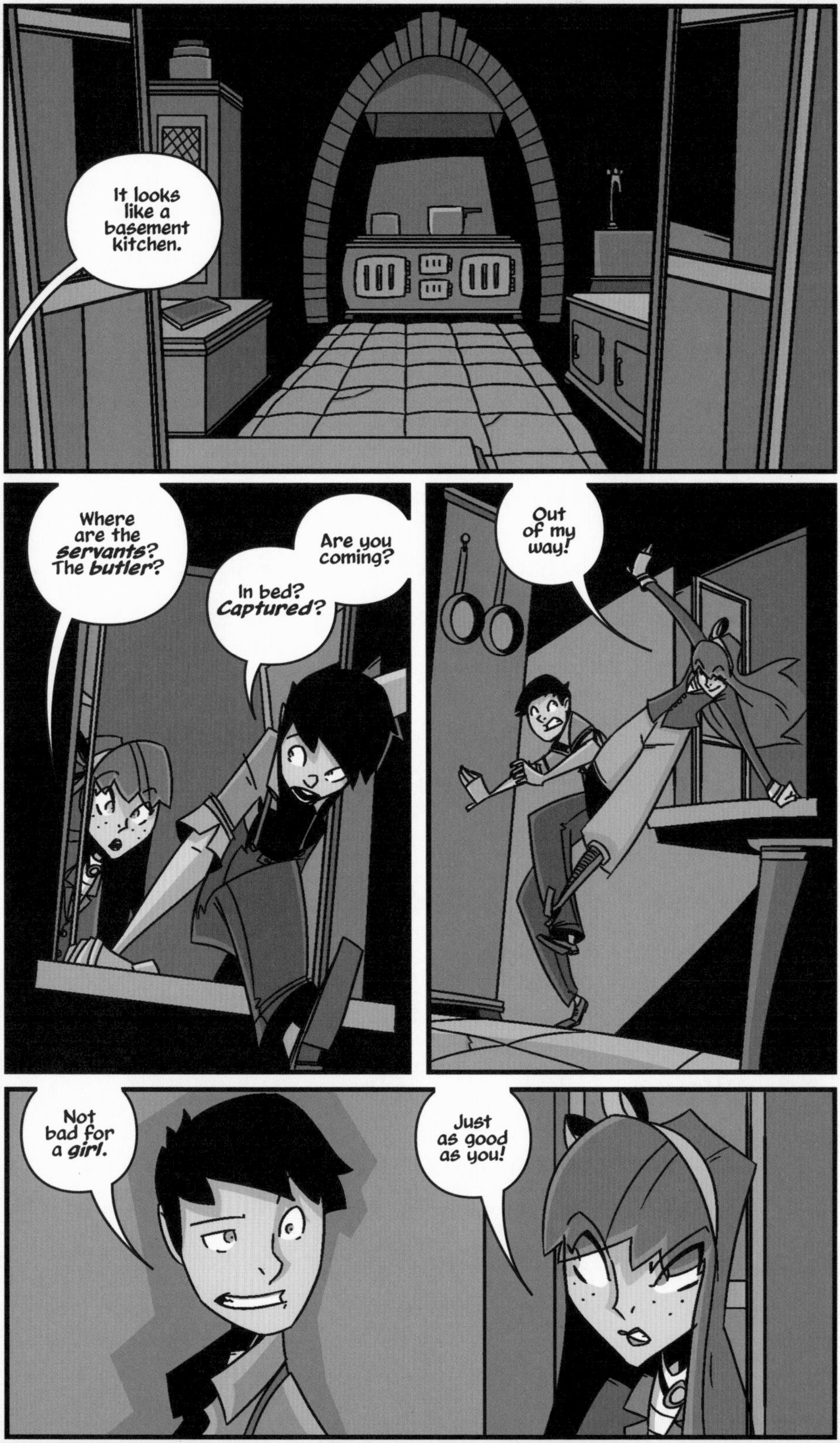
It looks like a basement kitchen.
Where are the *servants*? The *butler*?
Are you coming?
In bed? *Captured*?
Out of my way!
Not bad for a *girl*.
Just as good as you!

The kitchen was icy cold. Every sound they made echoed from wall to wall and was amplified by the high ceiling. There was not a single item out of place. Shelves of pans went floor to ceiling on one wall. To their right was a regiment of mixing bowls, all arranged by size. In a large wooden block were the handles of knives, their blades buried in the wood for safekeeping.

"Do you think they ever cook in here?" Erik asked as he made his way to the door and turned the handle. "Locked," he moaned.

"Locked from the inside? Are you sure?" Sadie grabbed the handle and tried to twist it, but it wouldn't turn. "What do we do now?"

Erik didn't speak. He looked along the avenue of countertops and drawers.

"There has to be one somewhere," he said to himself.

"What?" she asked.

"A drawer full of clutter. Every house I ever broke into had one somewhere—always in the kitchen and almost always by the door." Erik fumbled with several drawers. "Here we are," he said triumphantly. "Just what I need."

Sadie looked into the drawer and saw a jumbled mess. Old string, scissors, hat pins, nails, butterfly clips, and several buttons filled the tiny drawer.

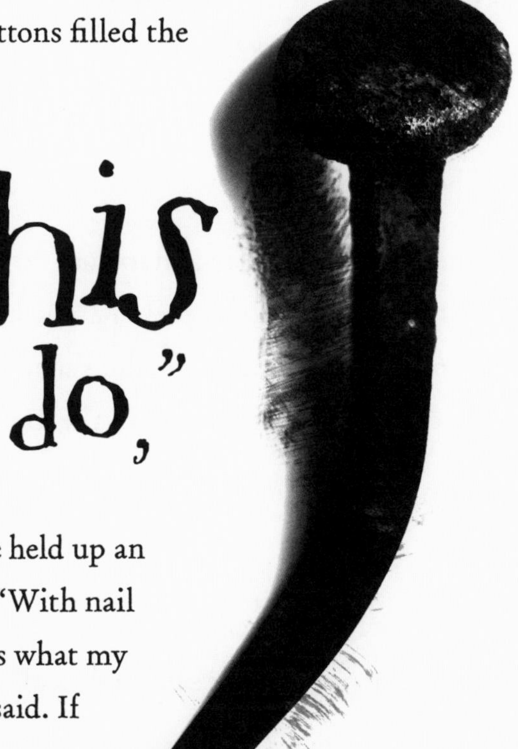

"This will do,"

Erik said as he held up an old bent nail. "With nail and eye. That's what my father always said. If you want to open a locked door, you can always do it with nail and eye."

Sadie watched as Erik looked through the keyhole and then skillfully pushed the nail into the lock and jiggled the door handle back and forth. There was a sudden and reassuring click.

"Done," he announced. "Never been stopped by a lock yet."

Erik opened the door slowly and looked down the corridor. As in every downstairs hall in a fine house, the lamps were always lit. They cast cold shadows on the polished floor as they shimmered in the draft.

"Where could they be?" Sadie asked. She slipped through the door behind Erik.

"Could be anywhere—we have to be on the lookout and take them by surprise," Erik said, frantically trying to think of a plan.

Erik and Sadie crept down the long corridor. The electric lights sent eerie shadows across the wooden-paneled walls. They passed cupboards with black metal handles.

In the darkness Erik could hear Sadie's teeth chattering.

"Cold?" he whispered.

"Sort of," she replied with a shudder.

Together they silently moved on. When they came to a set of stairs, they looked around the corner and up to a doorway.

"I'll go first," Erik said. He pushed by Sadie and crept cautiously up the stairs. When he got to the door he touched the brass handle as if it were the line of a fishing pole and he were waiting for a bite. He turned and smiled at Sadie, who had come up the stairs behind him. Then, carefully, he opened the door. On the other side was yet another passageway. They could just see the first turn of the stairs they had escaped by earlier that night.

"The front door is ahead. The stairs are on the right," Sadie whispered.

There was a sudden gust of wind. It blew through the passageway from which they had come and up the stairs.

The wind came again as if someone were opening and closing a door. Erik didn't dare move. He was completely mesmerized.

"What is it?" Sadie asked.

"The wind—it's just like the night I discovered the burglars in the tunnel. When they opened the door, it sent a massive wind up the tower."

"Do you think there could be another entrance to the tunnel downstairs?" asked Sadie.

"There's more than one entrance at Dunstan's," he replied.

Erik and Sadie looked at each other. Without speaking, they turned and headed back down the stairs.

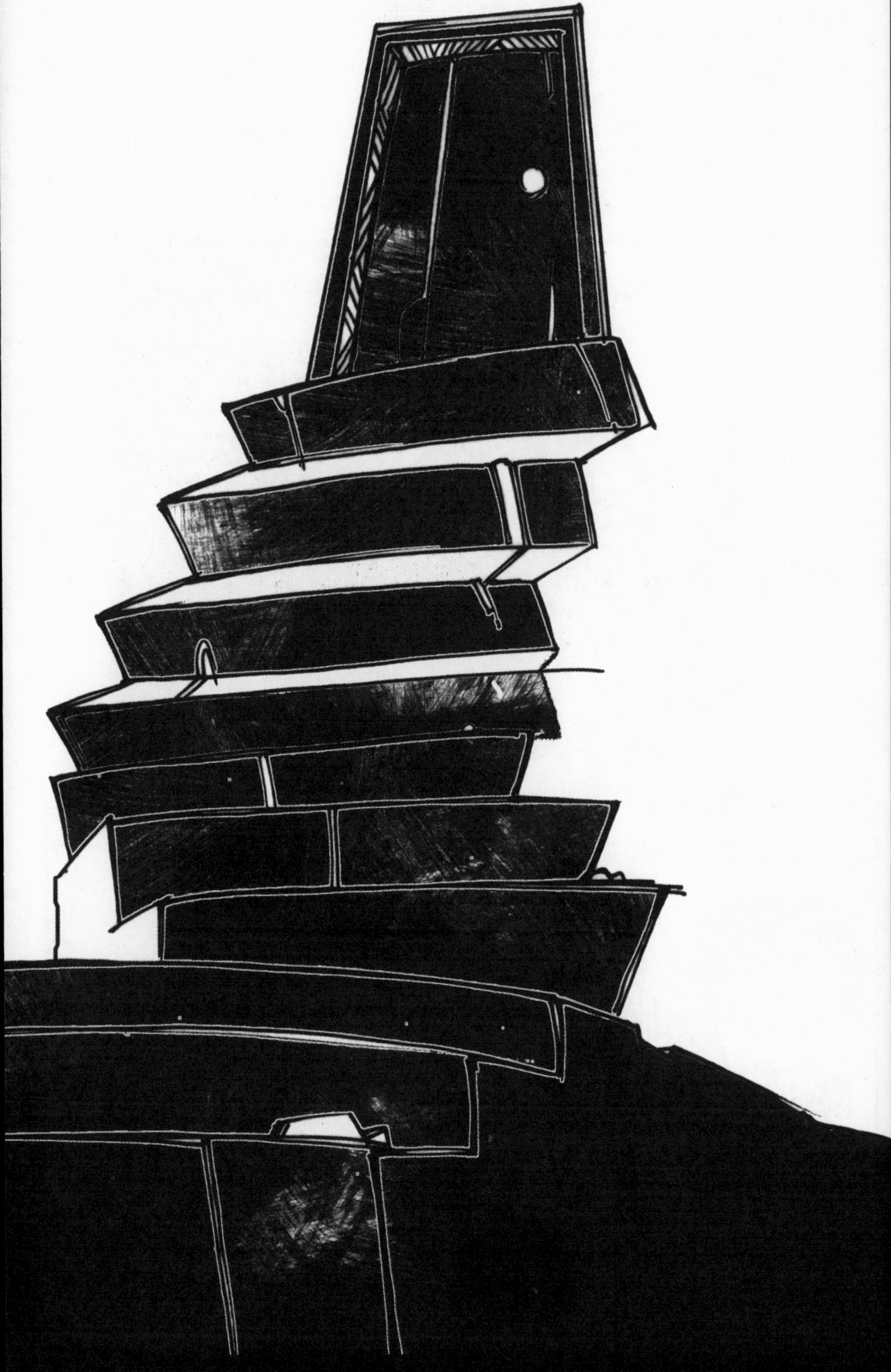

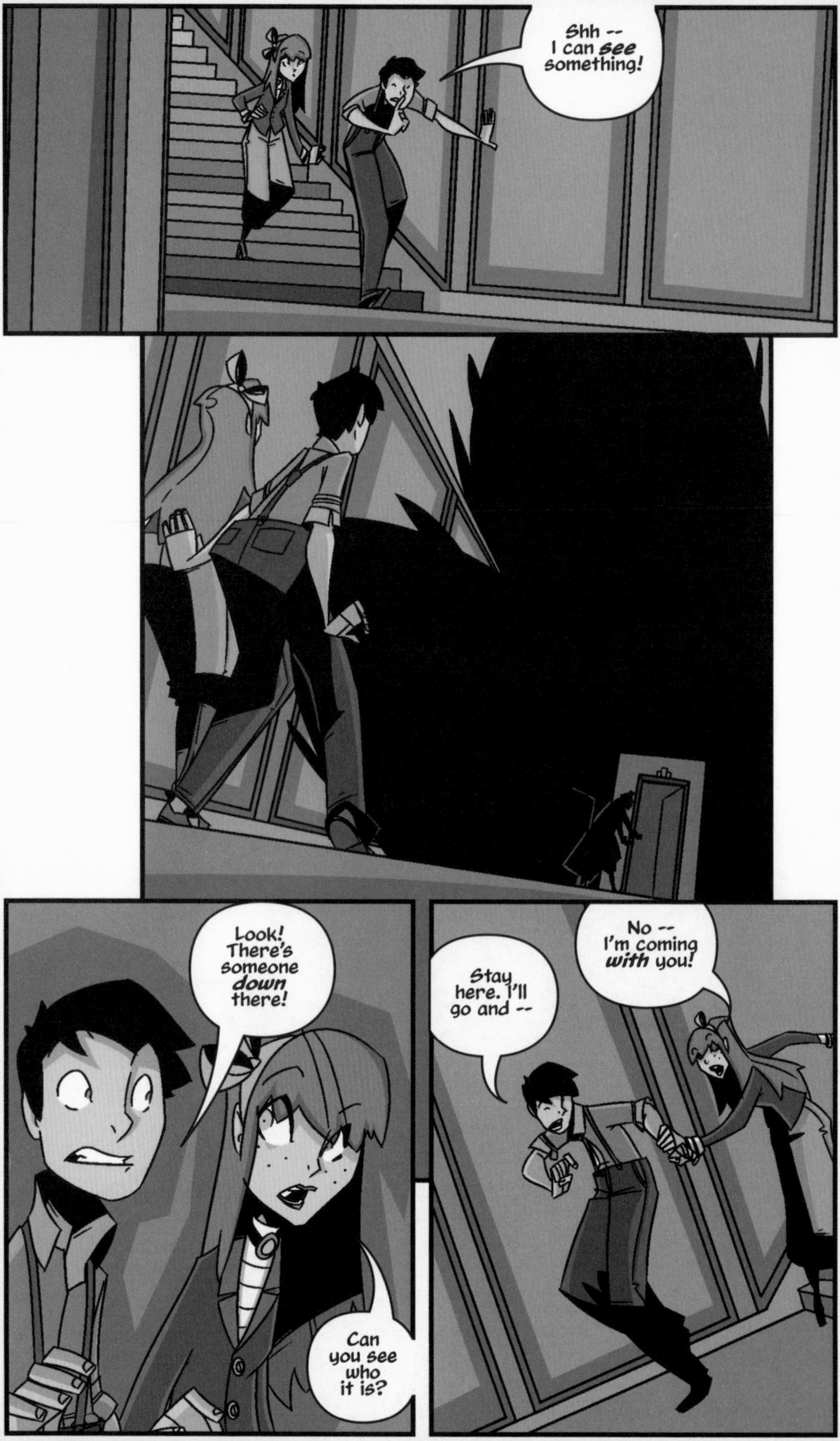
Shh -- I can *see* something!
Look! There's someone *down* there!
Can you see who it is?
Stay here. I'll go and --
No -- I'm coming *with* you!

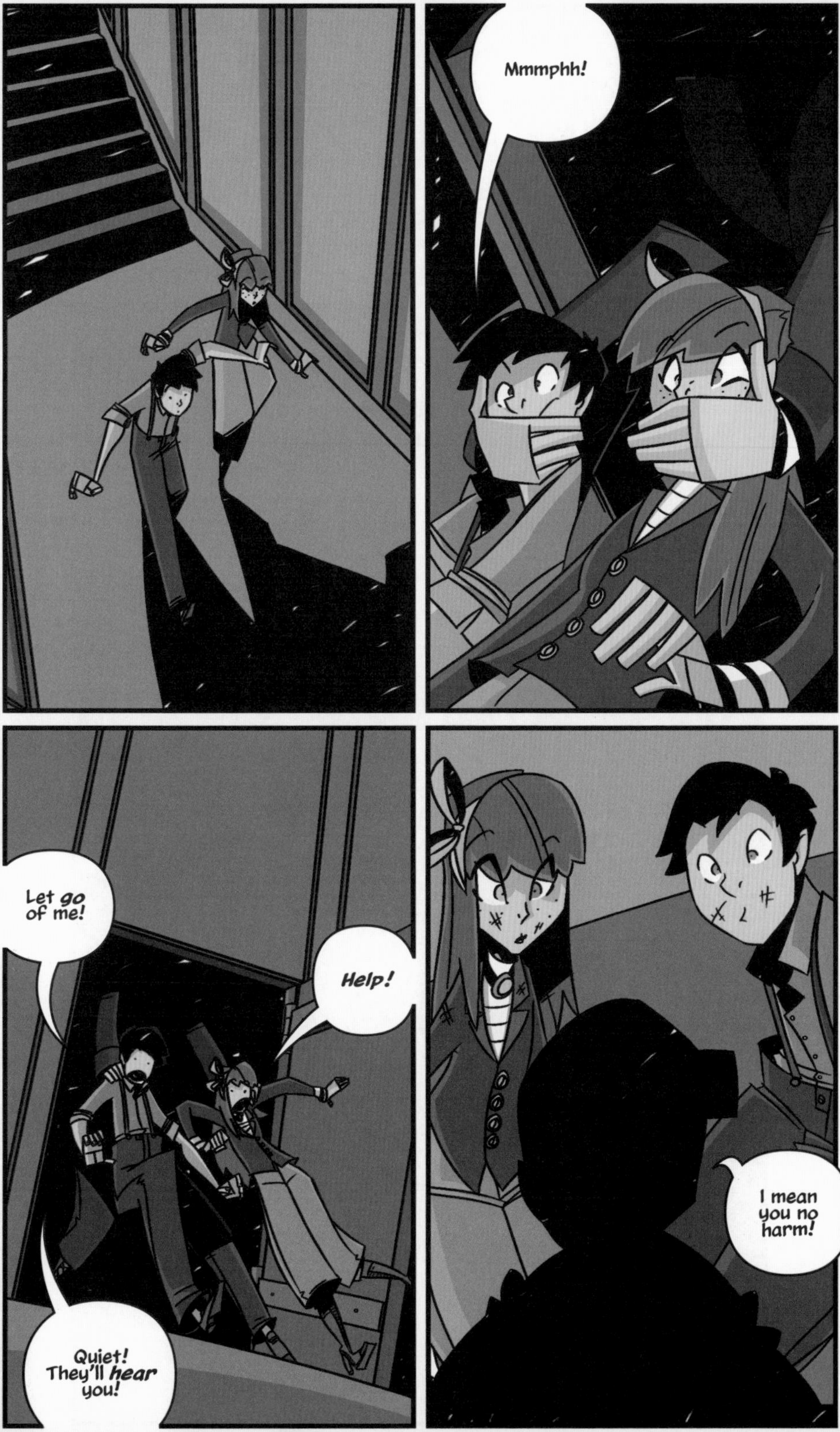
Mmmphh!
Let go of me!
Help!
Quiet! They'll hear you!
I mean you no harm!

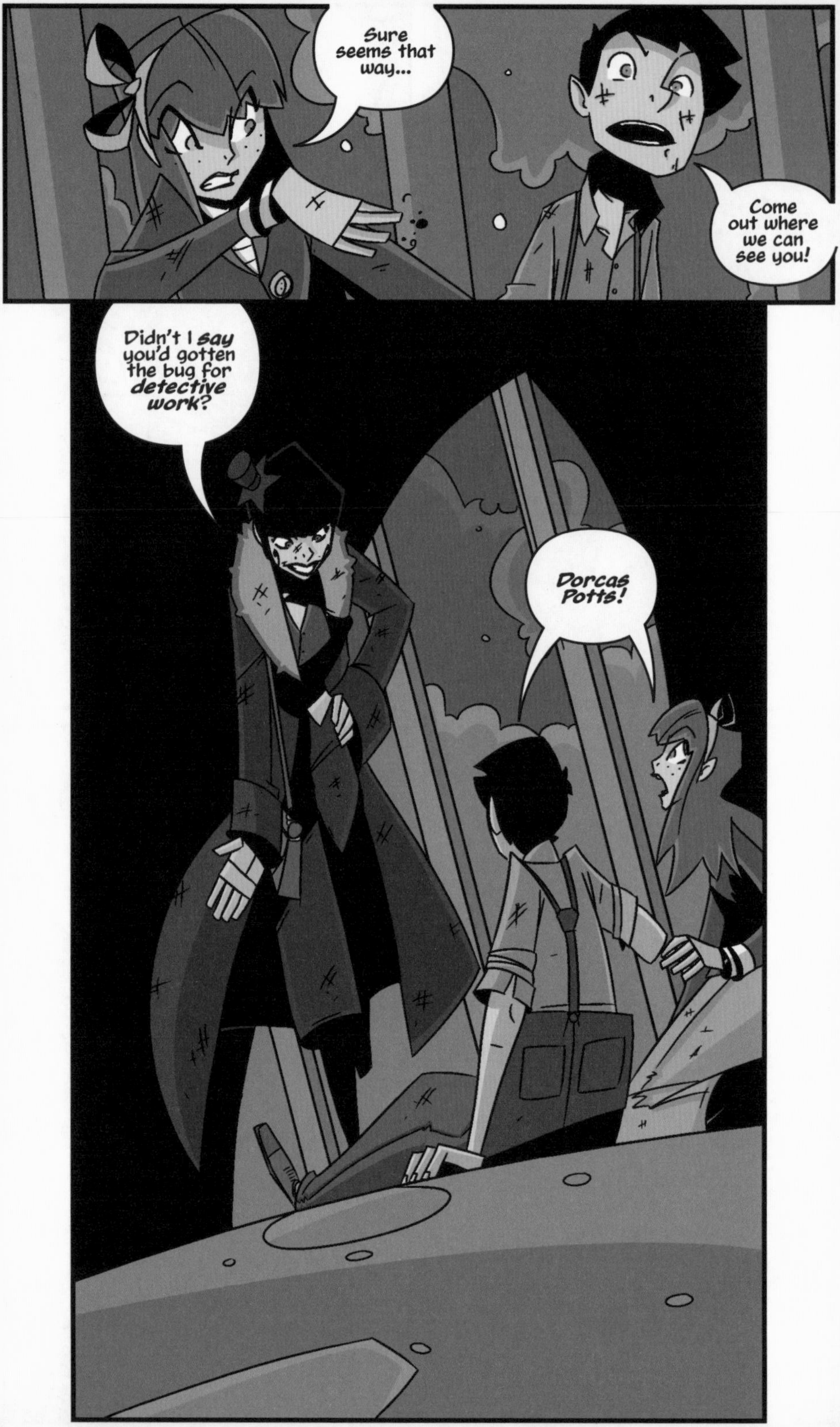
Sure seems that way...
Come out where we can see you!
Didn't I *say* you'd gotten the bug for *detective work*?
Dorcas Potts!

"And I wouldn't be in this mess if it weren't for you," snapped Dorcas Potts.

"What have we done?" Sadie asked.

"Done?" replied Dorcas Potts incredulously. "You have ruined everything. I would have found out who was behind the theft of my uncle's treasure."

"They've got Saskia," said Sadie.

"Just adds to the mess," came the curt reply. "I could have done without you kids getting involved—having you around just . . . complicates things."

"We could help," Erik said.

"Help? Help?" Her eyes widened and soot fell from her nose. "I had to crash a car into a house and climb the inside of a chimney to get here. I was on their trail when you two came my way—is that help?"

"I suppose—" began Sadie, but Dorcas Potts cut her off.

"Suppose? I suppose I should leave you both here and just get on with it. I have been on this case for a year and never thought my work would be ruined by a few schoolchildren."

"But you interviewed us," said Erik.

"I wanted to know if Miss Rimmer was involved in all this—there's something strange about that woman."

"She is involved! Potemkin said the headmistress was his boss—we heard him." Sadie rubbed a sooty handprint from her face. "That's why we came here—we were looking for you. We can't go back to the school."

"It's true," Erik said, seeing the look of disbelief on the journalist's face. "Lord Gervez told us about you—we knew you could help—we didn't mean to get in the way."

Dorcas Potts thought for a moment. She brushed another flurry of soot from her jacket and stared Erik in the eye.

"Very well, Erik Ganger with the missing father. I suppose you can help, but do what I say. I heard Potemkin in here with the other guy, but I couldn't see what they were doing. The tunnels go on for so long it could take weeks to find them."

"Erik and I could go one way and you another," Sadie suggested. "We'd at least have a better chance of finding them."

"And what if you get caught?" asked Dorcas Potts.

"Then it would be our fault and we'll take the consequences for getting involved," Erik said. "If that's what we have to do, then so be it. We have to find Saskia and your uncle—then we can get Potemkin."

"I like your style, but it won't be that easy," said Dorcas Potts, taking a pad of paper from her pocket. She began to sketch a map of the passages leading away from Gervez's house. "This is where you are. You two head this way, and I'll try going in this direction. If you get caught, say nothing.

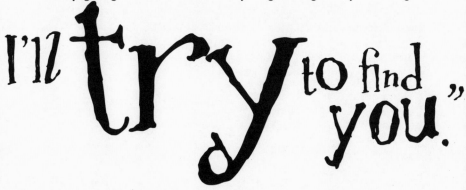
I'll try to find you."

In an instant she was gone, racing along the tunnel, her coat billowing behind her.

Sadie pulled the secret door of the paneled wall firmly shut. She turned to Erik. "Now we have to find Saskia," she said. "I'm not leaving this tunnel without her."

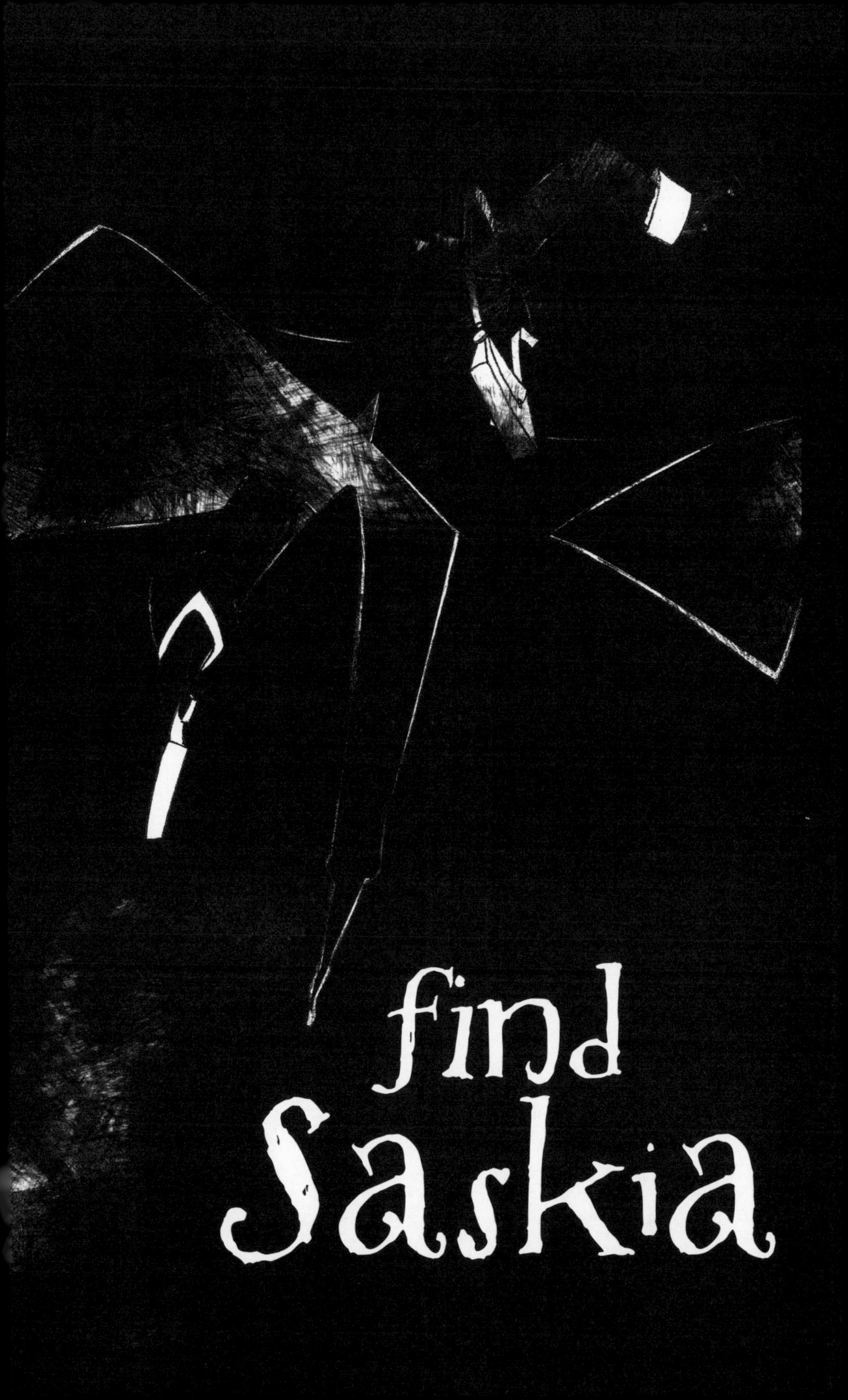
find
Saskia

Chapter Eleven
Beyond Locked Rooms

"IT'S NO USE STRUGGLING," Potemkin told
Saskia, as Straker forced her into yet another ancient
sarcophagus—this time with a cage for a front—on
the floor of a sewer vault deep under Lord Gervez's
house. A chain of feeble electric bulbs dangled like
grapes on a wire above them, barely lighting the room.
"I have left sufficient clues for your friends to find you,

and then—"

"You'll be arrested, Potemkin. Just like before," Saskia yelled. Her words echoed off the brick walls.

"By the time you are found we shall be long gone," Potemkin snarled.

Straker pulled on a metal chain. The coffin lifted from the ground and dangled several feet above the dirt floor.

"High enough?" Straker asked as he wedged the end of the chain between two metal clips on the wall. "Yet another use for Lord Gervez's antiquities."

"The iron doors will do the rest—this vault will be their resting place. She said there must be no loose ends."

"Tell Rimmer we'll track her down, no matter where she hides!" Saskia shouted. Her words echoed through the tunnel.

"Just as I thought," said Potemkin. "The squawking crow will bring her friends right to her."

Potemkin was about to turn when he suddenly stopped. "If only you knew the whole plan. You would be truly amazed."

"Let me out of this and I'll find out for myself!" screamed Saskia. She rattled the bars on the front of the coffin, trying to free herself.

"Feisty creature. Pity I will not be here to see her demise."

Straker and Potemkin began to walk away. Saskia dangled helplessly, suspended from the ceiling by the chain that was bolted into the coffin.

"I'll see you again, Potemkin," she screamed after him.

"Believe what you will; your fate has already been sealed." With that, the men disappeared into the dark tunnel.

The sarcophagus spun and twisted as a cold breeze blew through the tunnels. Saskia shivered. She wondered how in one night she had managed to get trapped in two different coffins . . . and whether she would make it out alive. Above her, she could hear the rushing of water. It gurgled and moaned like a draining bathtub with a half-plugged hole. As the coffin swung back and forth, Saskia saw several iron disks embedded into the vaulted roof. They dripped with green mucus that fell to the floor below.

Saskia heard, faintly at first, then slowly growing louder, the sound of approaching footsteps. Scuffed echoes of clumsy feet walking in darkness came ever nearer, their owners drawn like moths to the light of the vault. She thought of shouting or calling out for help, but she remembered what Potemkin had said about a squawking crow, and she did not want to bring anyone else into danger. The tunnel echoed with the sound of faint voices. Suddenly a face peered around the corner.

Erik! There she is!
Stay back -- don't come in! *Potemkin's set a trap!*
It stinks in here -- it's a *sewer!*
We'll get you down!
No -- find *Lord Gervez.* Have him call the police.
Just hold on, Saskia!
Stay away! I'm telling you, *it's a trap!*

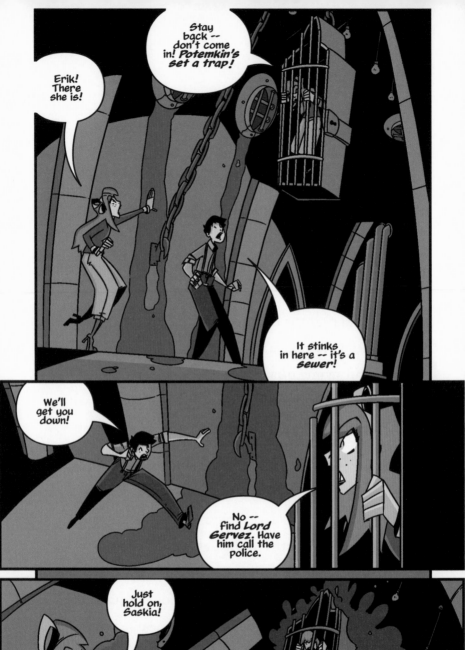

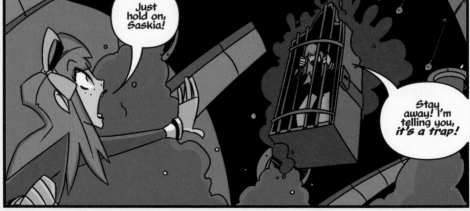

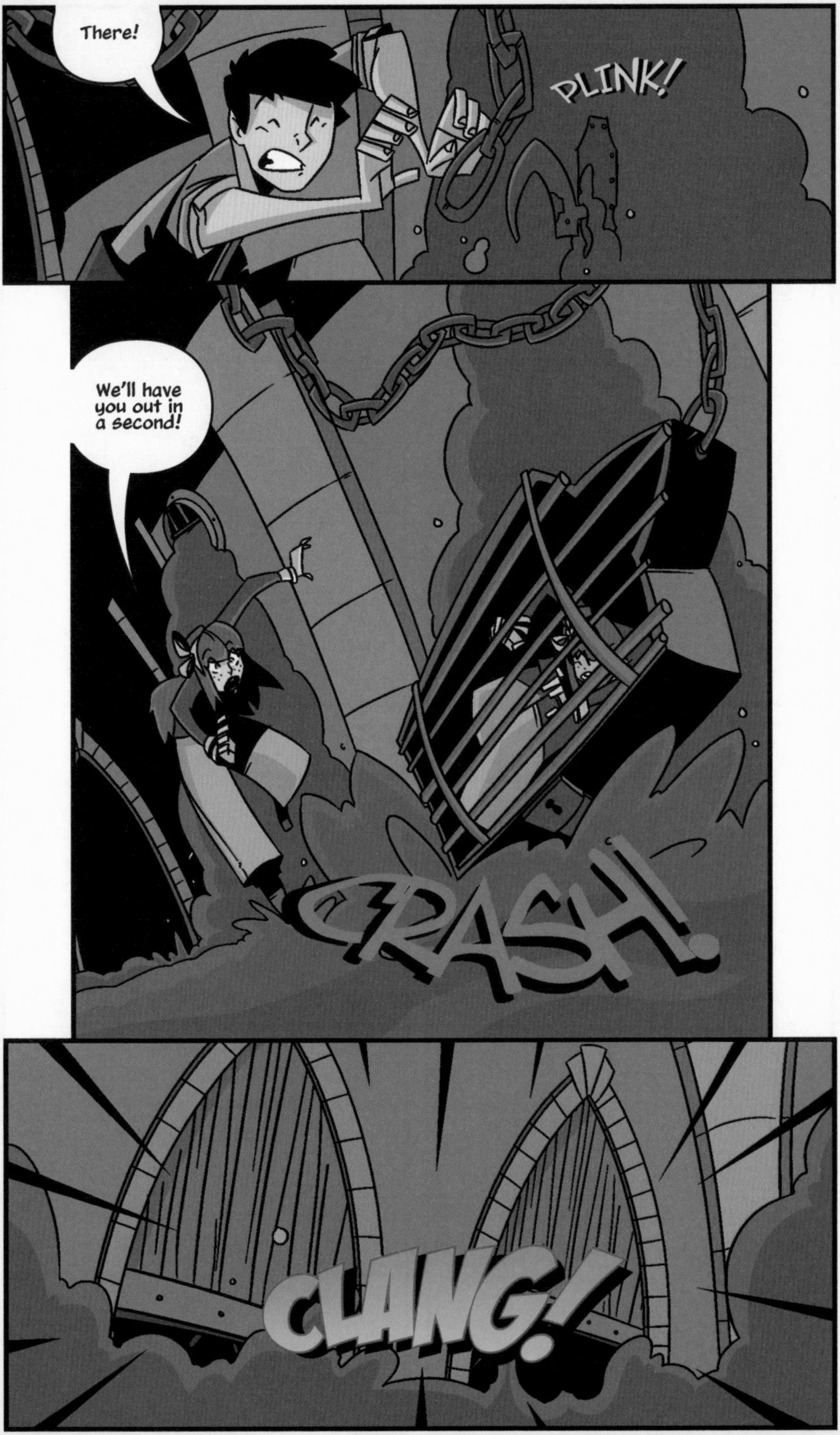
There!
PLINK!
We'll have you out in a second!
CRASH!
CLANG!

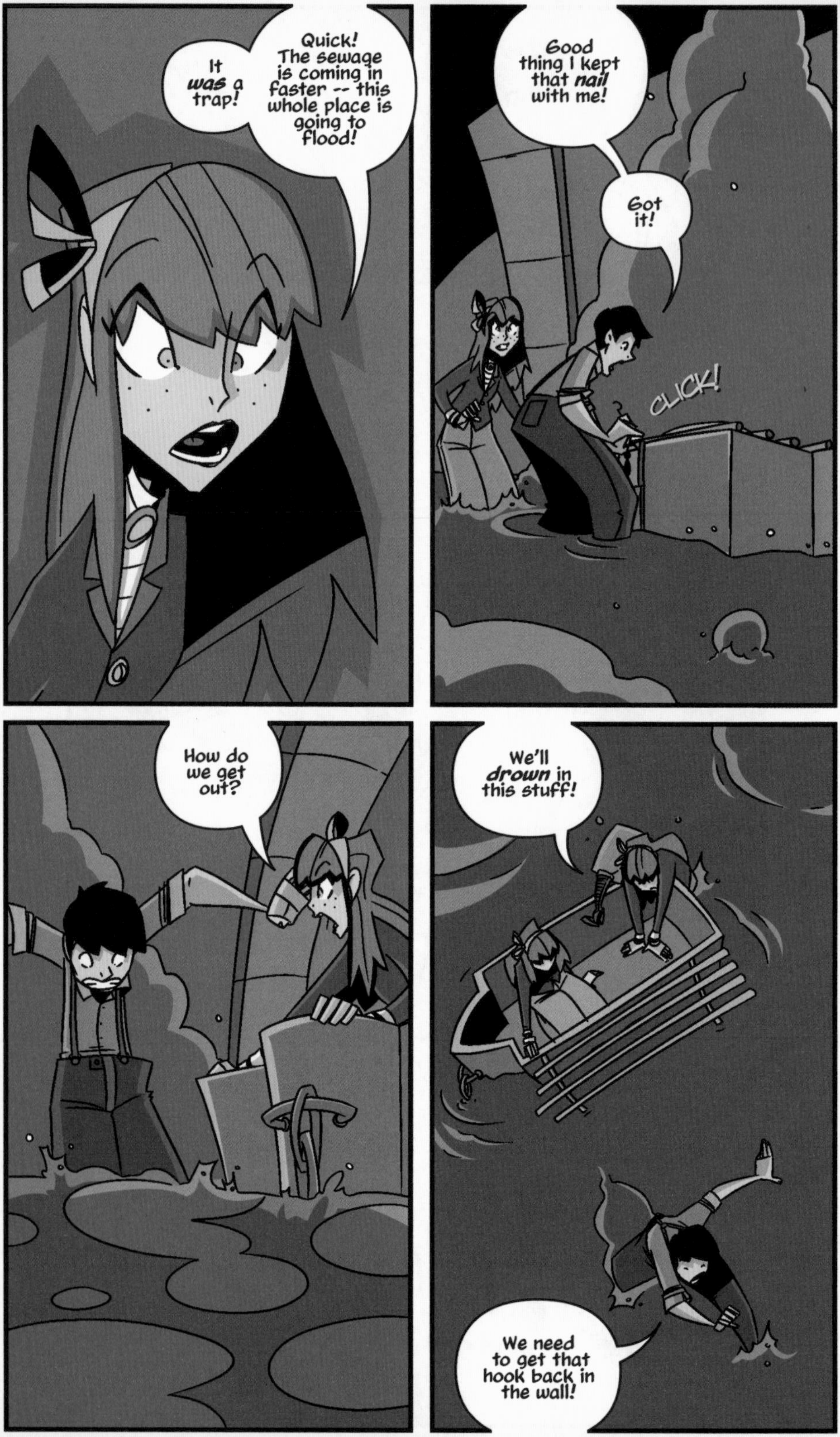
It *was* a trap!
Quick! The sewage is coming in faster -- this whole place is going to flood!
Good thing I kept that *nail* with me!
Got it!
CLICK!
How do we get out?
We'll *drown* in this stuff!
We need to get that hook back in the wall!

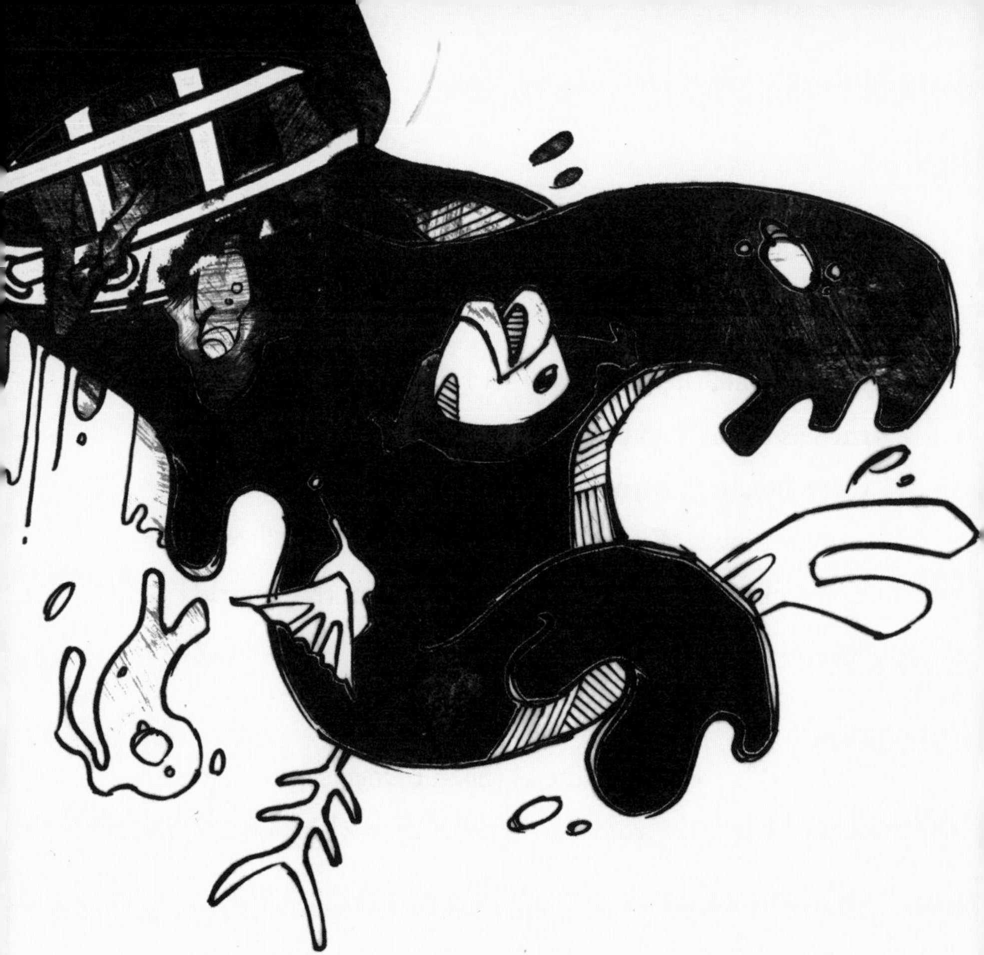

Erik waded through the waist-high vile liquid that spewed from the roof of the vault. He turned back and saw that Sadie and Saskia had climbed into the sarcophagus as if it were an upturned boat. It began to spin in the swirling green fluid. He waded farther and reached out toward the chain hook high up the buttress of the vaulted wall.

One by one, the iron disks set high in the roof began to turn as though an invisible hand twisted each one. The more the disks turned, the more furiously the sewage poured down. Within a minute, the liquid was touching Erik's chin. He pulled against the vortex that swirled against his feet and fought to keep from being dragged beneath the churning green slime.

"Hurry!" screamed Sadie as the upturned sarcophagus rocked violently from side to side in the whirlpool.

"Just stay where you are," Erik shouted against the pounding green surf. "If I can get to the—"

Erik reached out his hand. There was a sudden explosion of water from high in the vaulted roof. It crashed down on the sarcophagus, knocking Erik from his feet. Sadie and Saskia looked across the thunderous torrent. Erik was nowhere to be seen.

"Erik!" Saskia shouted.

"He's gone," wailed Sadie.

The sarcophagus had nearly reached the string of dim lightbulbs that dangled precariously from the ceiling. "If the water touches the lightbulbs, we'll be electrocuted," Sadie gasped.

Saskia looked around desperately. A small floating object caught her attention. It bobbed up and down in the grimy water, heedless of the raging whirlpool. As she stared at it, she realized what it was: an apple. She suddenly recalled her conversation with Madame Raphael. The angel had told her a story about an apple—something about it falling from a tree and hitting a man on the head. It seemed so long ago that they had spoken, yet Saskia knew only a few hours had passed. What was it Madame Raphael had said? "Sometimes to find wisdom you have to look beyond locked rooms." A sudden shriek from her sister broke Saskia's concentration.

"Erik!"

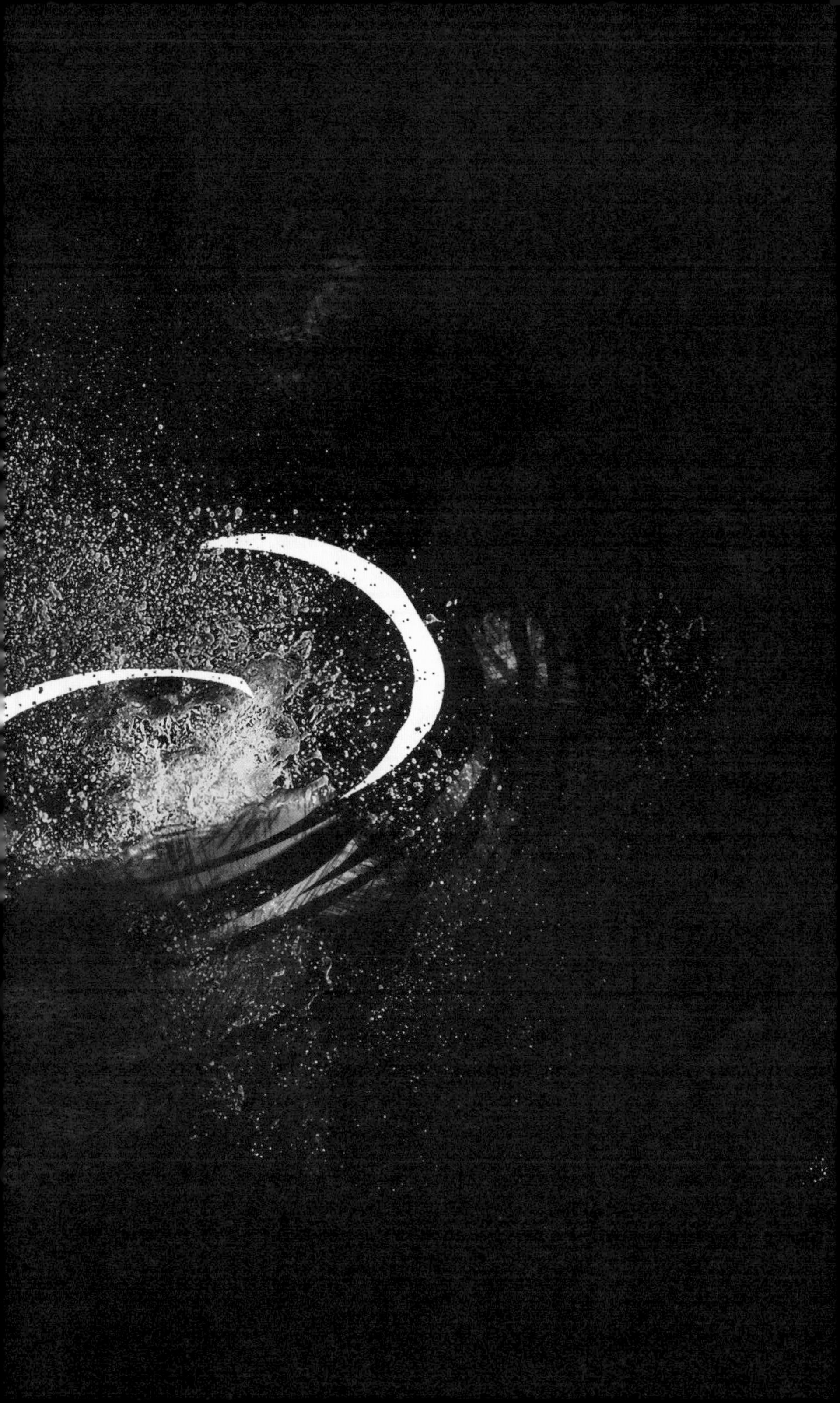

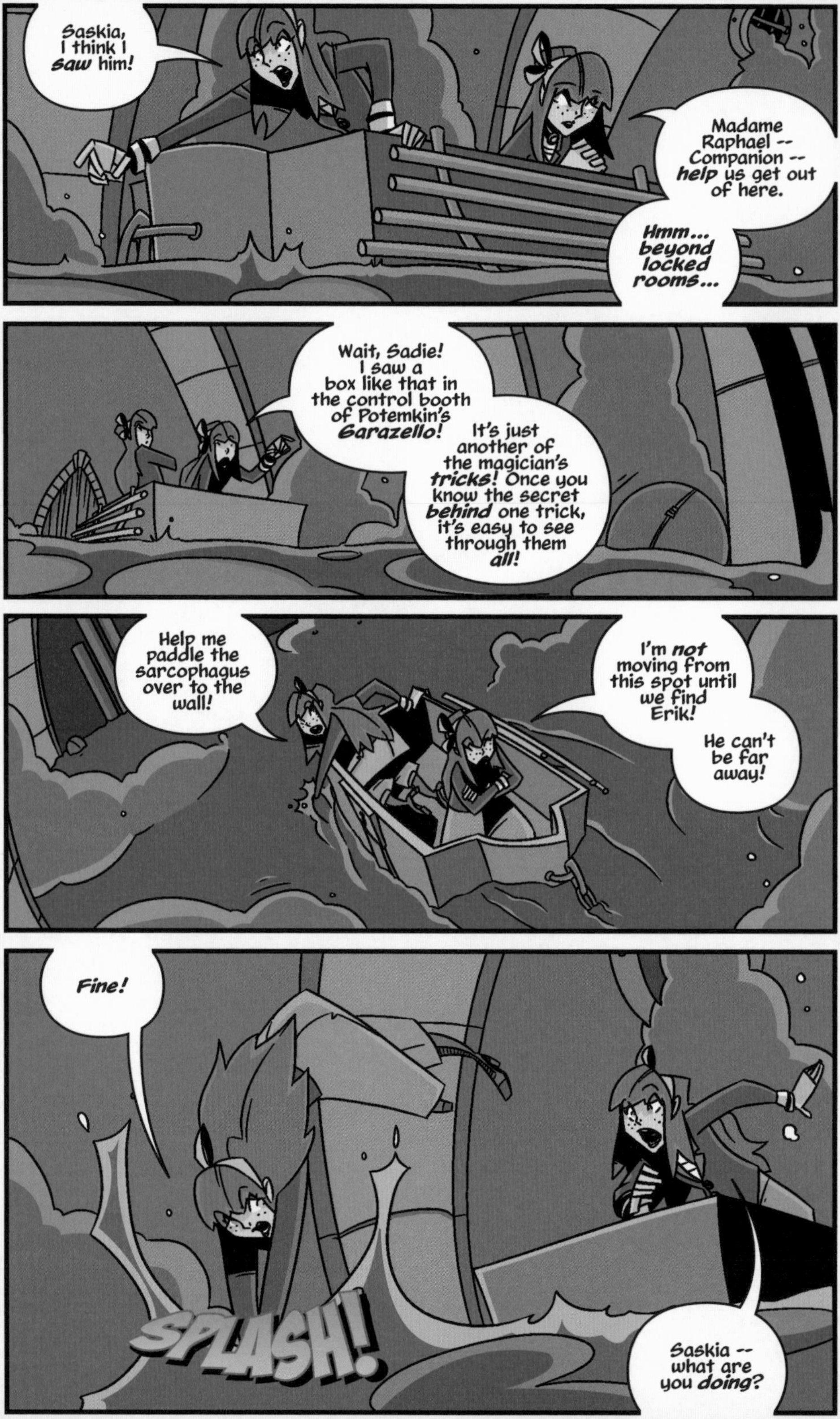

Saskia, I think I *saw* him!
Madame Raphael -- Companion -- *help* us get out of here.
Hmm... beyond locked rooms...
Wait, Sadie! I saw a box like that in the control booth of Potemkin's *Garazello!*
It's just another of the magician's *tricks!* Once you know the secret *behind* one trick, it's easy to see through them *all!*
Help me paddle the sarcophagus over to the wall!
I'm *not* moving from this spot until we find Erik!
He can't be far away!
Fine!
SPLASH!
Saskia -- what are you *doing?*

SPLASH!

Erik! Grab this!

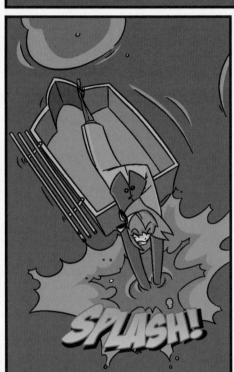

SPLASH!

Gasp! I turned off the control! Get inside, quick!

Cough -- cough!

SPLASH!

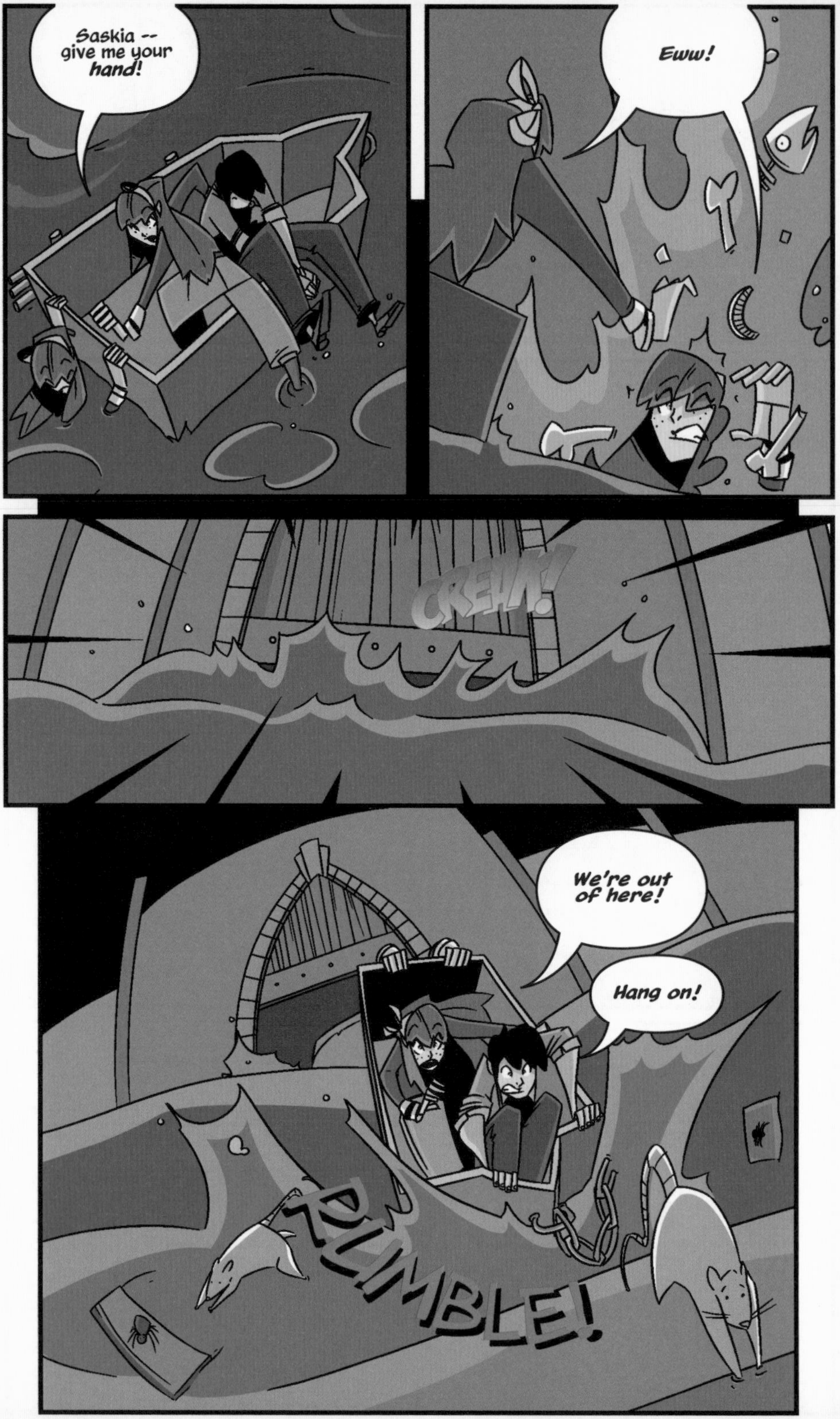
Saskia -- give me your hand!
Eww!
CREAK!
We're out of here!
Hang on!
RUMBLE!

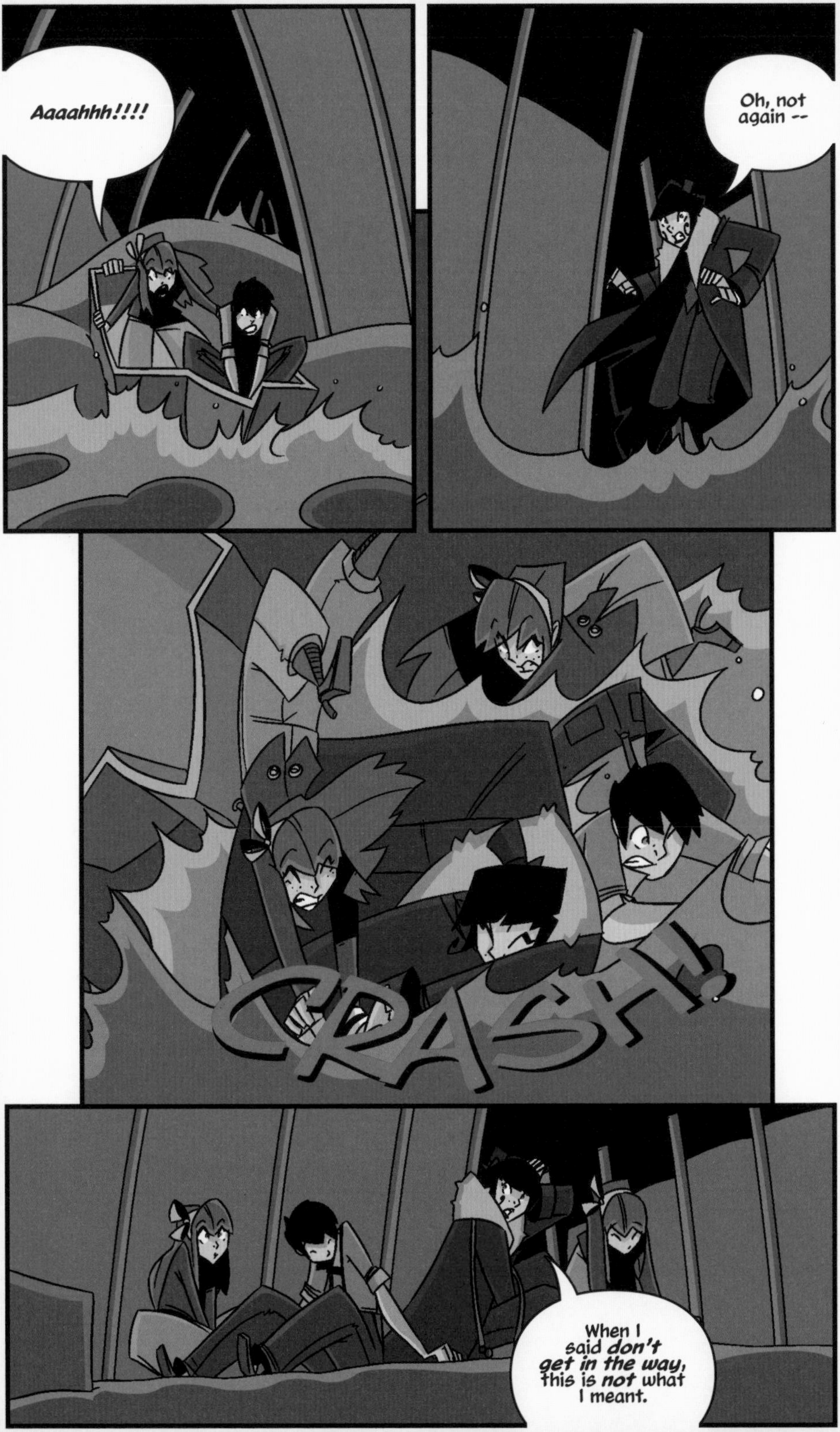
Aaaahhh!!!!
Oh, not again --
CRASH!
When I said *don't get in the way,* this is *not* what I meant.

For a moment, no one spoke. Saskia, Sadie, and Erik all gasped for breath. "Potemkin set a trap for us," Erik finally explained to Dorcas Potts. He turned to Sadie. "I thought I was going to drown. If it hadn't been for you, Sadie—"

"Saskia's the one who got us out of there," Sadie said quickly. "How did you know how to open the doors?" she asked her sister.

"I-I don't know," said Saskia quietly. "I just asked Madame Raphael to help me, and then . . ." Her voice trailed off.

"How could she help you?" Sadie said, just above a whisper. "She can't be real," she continued, almost talking to herself now. "Although . . ."

Sadie looked at her sister curiously. "Saskia," she said slowly, "you know that note—the one from, uh, Madame Raphael—that you found at Muzz Elliott's? Didn't it say something about an indigo moon?"

"Yes," replied Saskia. "Beware of the indigo moon."

"Well," continued Sadie, "when we were talking with Lord Gervez, he mentioned a person called Moon. He said that's who built all these tunnels."

Saskia gasped. "Potemkin talked about that man! He said an architect built tunnels connecting all the fine houses on Hampstead so he could rob them!"

"Indigo Moon is certainly a genius," said Dorcas Potts. The others turned to her. "He built all these houses and sold them to the wealthiest buyers, just so he could rob them. He also built a factory as a place to store the loot."

"The factory!" Erik cried. "The sign on it said Blue Moon Theatrical Supply!"

"Yes," said Dorcas Potts. "I followed you there earlier. You led me right to the treasure." Erik and Sadie stared at her in surprise. She continued, "Indigo Moon is the mastermind behind the plan, but I've known for some time that he is not the one who ended up setting it in motion."

"No, he's not," said Saskia quickly. "We heard Potemkin and Straker say Miss Rimmer—"

"So your friends have told me," cut in Dorcas Potts, "and now I must find my uncle and track down the other villains." She got to her feet and brushed herself off, meticulously picking the flotsam and jetsam from her long coat. Sadie and Saskia stood up as well.

But Erik stayed frozen to the spot by a sudden thought. "It's not Rimmer," he said.

"What?" asked Sadie. "What are you talking—"

"They didn't SAY Miss Rimmer. They said headmistress. We just assumed they meant Rimmer," said Erik. He searched his pockets and pulled out a soggy piece of paper with lines of ink running across it. The writing was now too blurred to read, but the last word could still be made out: "Olivia."

"I found this note in the tunnel the night I first saw the burglars," he explained to Dorcas Potts. "We thought it

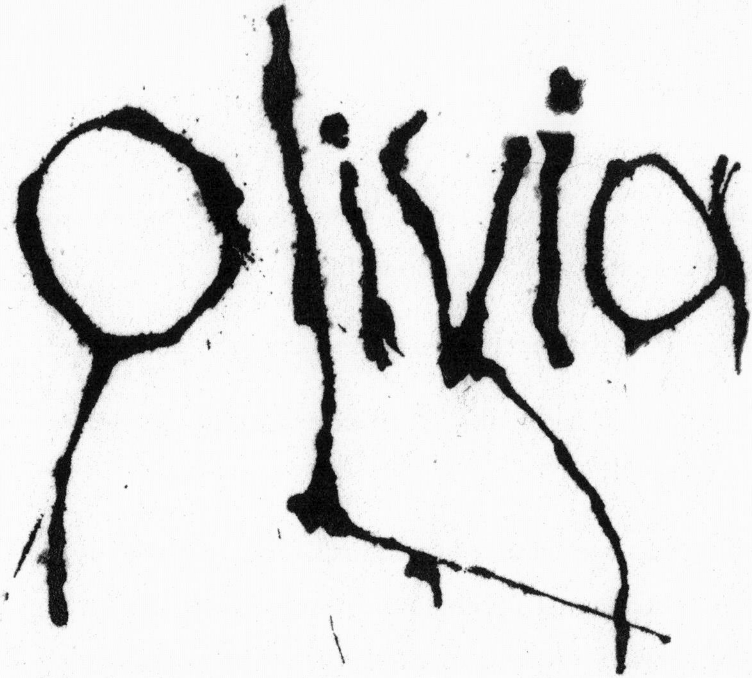
Olivia

was a warning from Miss Olivia; the note said someone had tricked her and that they were going to take her away. We thought maybe the burglars had kidnapped her," he continued. "But what if we were wrong? What if this note was her alibi to make the police think she had been kidnapped? She said she did it for the school, but she was lying. She did it for herself," he finished sadly.

"She could have been hiding in the tunnels all this time!" exclaimed Sadie. "She waited a year to get rid of the treasure and let the trail go cold. Everyone thinks she's long gone . . . or murdered."

"How could it be Miss Olivia?" Saskia asked. "She was so kind. She looked after us all so well."

"Do you think Rimmer is in on the robbery too?" Sadie asked.

"I don't know," said Erik. "She didn't like any questions about Miss Olivia."

"And she has been acting suspicious lately," said Dorcas Potts. "I intercepted a phone call from her yesterday in which she was secretly trying to get rid of some students. I thought that maybe some children at the school had found her out and she needed them gone. Unfortunately, before I learned any more, she heard me listening in on the line."

"We overheard the same phone call!" said Sadie.

"You've done your job well," said Dorcas Potts. "But now I suggest you go through the tunnels and get away through the school. You can go to Muzz Elliott's until all of this gets sorted out. From what you've told me, she'll gladly take you in."

"You mean, that's it?" Saskia asked.

"It's over?" added Sadie.

"It has to be over; it's far too dangerous for you to be involved. Potemkin has already tried to kill you, and I can't be responsible," said Dorcas Potts firmly.

"But we want to come with you—see it through to the end," Saskia argued. "We've gotten this far already."

"It's over, girl. I don't want you with me. Get out of here while you still can," Dorcas Potts said curtly and strode off.

"It's not over until the Valkyrie sings. That's what our mother said," Sadie replied as Dorcas Potts disappeared.

"Valkyrie . . . sings?" asked Erik, with a look that showed he thought Sadie had gone completely mad.

"The fat woman at the end of the opera—she sings the last song," Saskia chimed in. "We heard one once when our mother took us to a rehearsal at the theater where she was working. This opera ain't over."

Sadie and Saskia turned and marched after Dorcas Potts. When they had gone three paces, Sadie stopped, turned around, and looked at Erik.

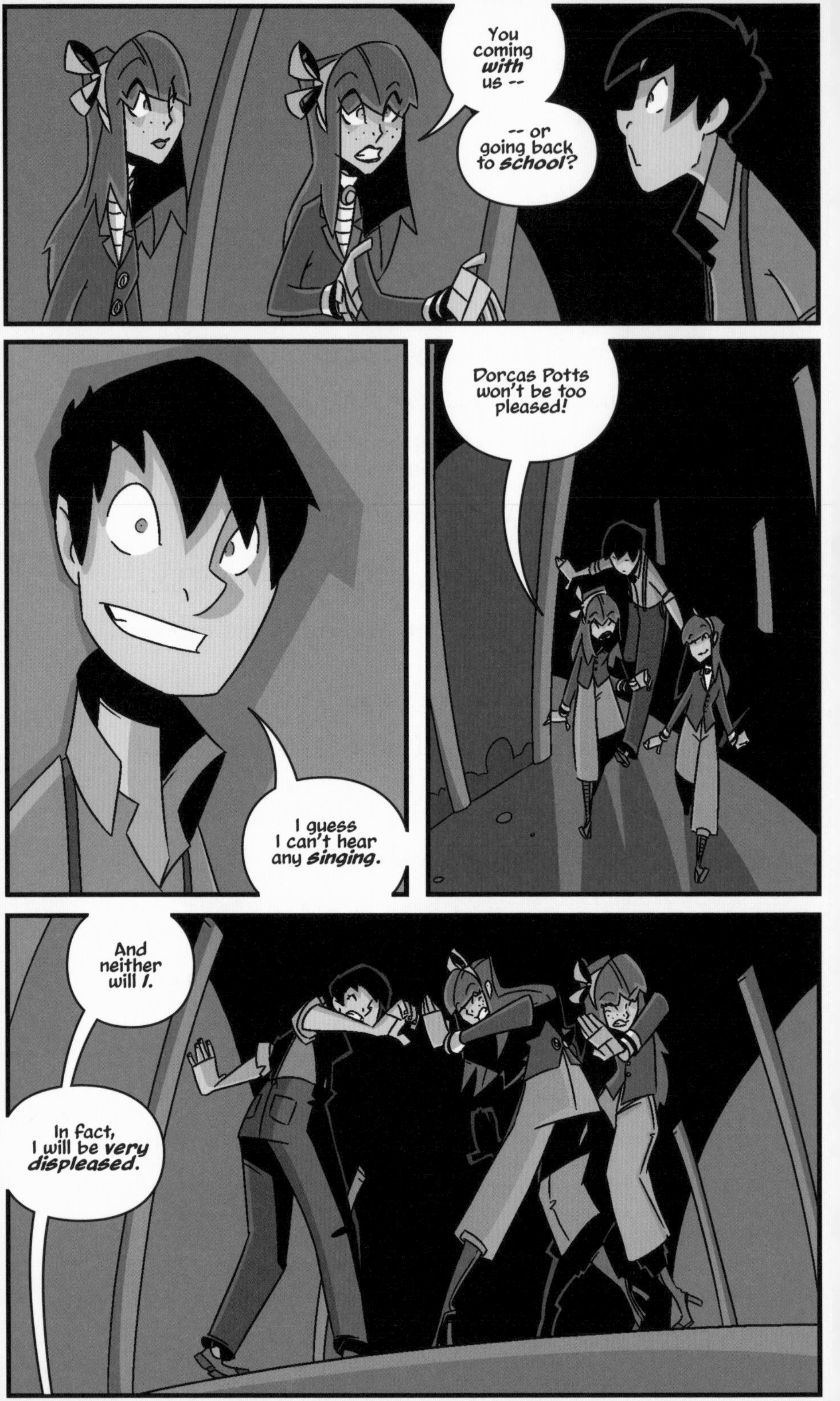
You coming *with* us --
-- or going back to *school*?
I guess I can't hear any *singing*.
Dorcas Potts won't be too pleased!
And neither will *I*.
In fact, I will be *very displeased*.

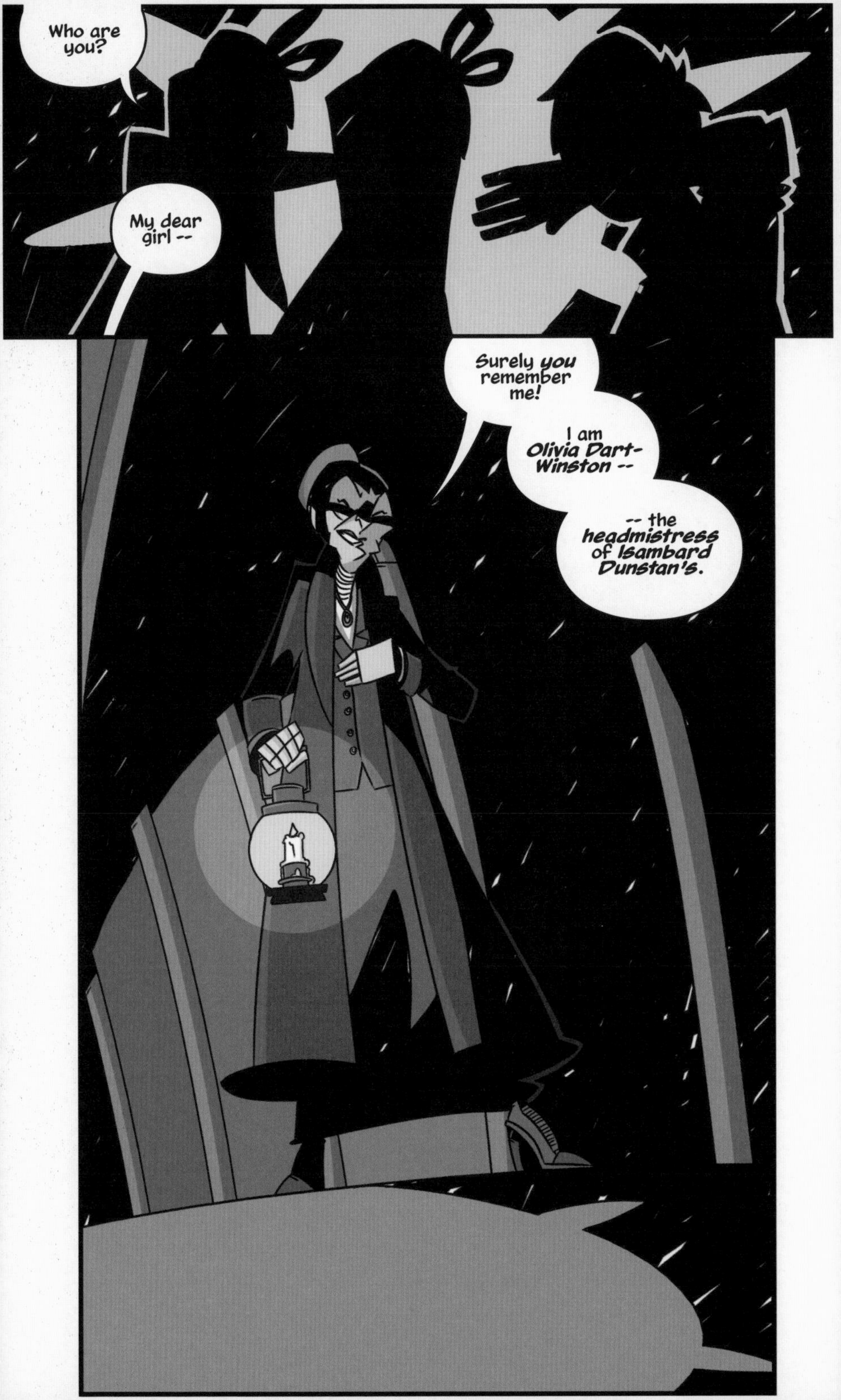
Who are you?
My dear girl --
Surely *you* remember me!
I am *Olivia Dart-Winston* --
-- the *headmistress* of *Isambard Dunstan's.*

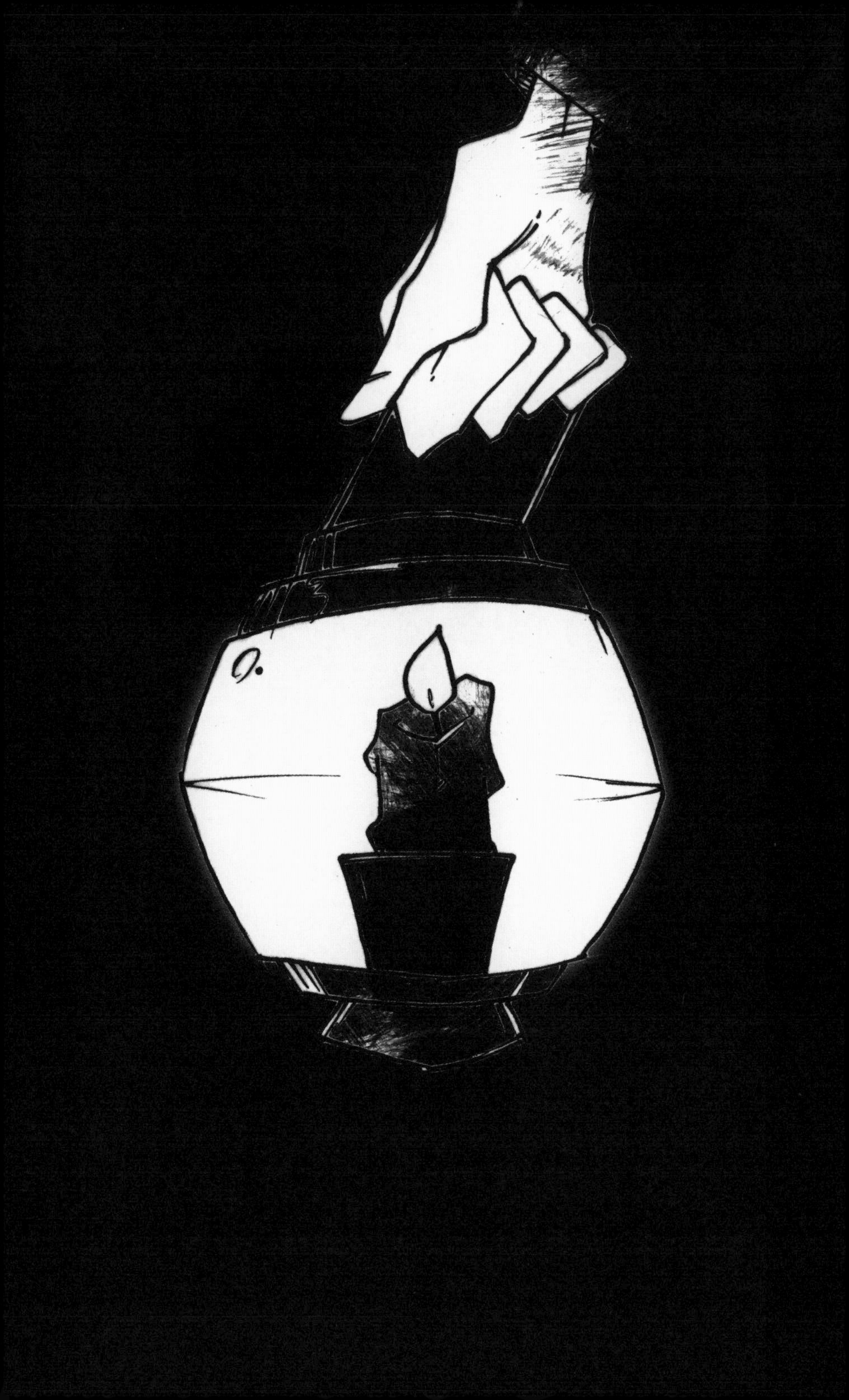

The woman slowly lowered the light so that the three could see her face. Miss Olivia seemed colder, gruff and angry, as though her crimes had taken the joy from her soul.

"M-M-Miss Olivia!" Saskia stammered. "What are you doing here? We heard you'd gone to Scotland."

"Saskia Dopple, I never believed you in the past, and I don't believe you now. I heard Erik's theory on what I'd done—isn't that true, Erik?"

"Yes, Miss Olivia," he said, just as he would have done in her days at the school.

"You leave me in a very difficult situation. I never intended for anyone to get hurt, but now I have no option. You'll be found in the Thames, another tragic accident. Three young people washed up on a lonely beach . . . oh how in life sad lessons we teach." She spoke her poem with a peculiar rhythm and laughed to herself.

"Why did you do it?" Erik asked. "If you're going to kill us, you can tell us—it doesn't matter."

Miss Olivia looked at him intently. "Like an honest thief, good things are hard to find. I came to the school for the purpose of robbing every house in Hampstead. My father bought the plans from Indigo Moon, but he didn't have the courage to go through with the heist. He's down here somewhere—but I forgot where I put him," she said eerily.

"That's not honest," Saskia said, trying to gain more time. She looked at Sadie and hoped her sister knew a way of escape.

"Honesty is not always the best policy, for as in life we are in death, you see. It's amazing what money can do for you."

"So you've lived down here for the last year?" Sadie asked.

"No, no, no. I have lived in a fine house on the other side of the park. A slight disguise, the odd dab of makeup—it's too busy in Hampstead to notice an old woman feeding the squirrels." The edge to her voice was like a sharpened knife.

"It was you—when we were looking at Potemkin—when they followed Dorcas Potts," Sadie said in amazement.

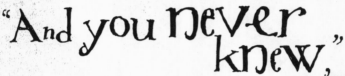

"And you never knew,"

Miss Olivia replied. "Enough of this merrymaking." She laughed again. "Straker, take them to my hideout. Have Lord Gervez join us, and see if Potemkin has tracked down Dorcas Potts. There is a stink around here, and I am not sure if it is the sewer or the children."

Straker stepped from the shadows.

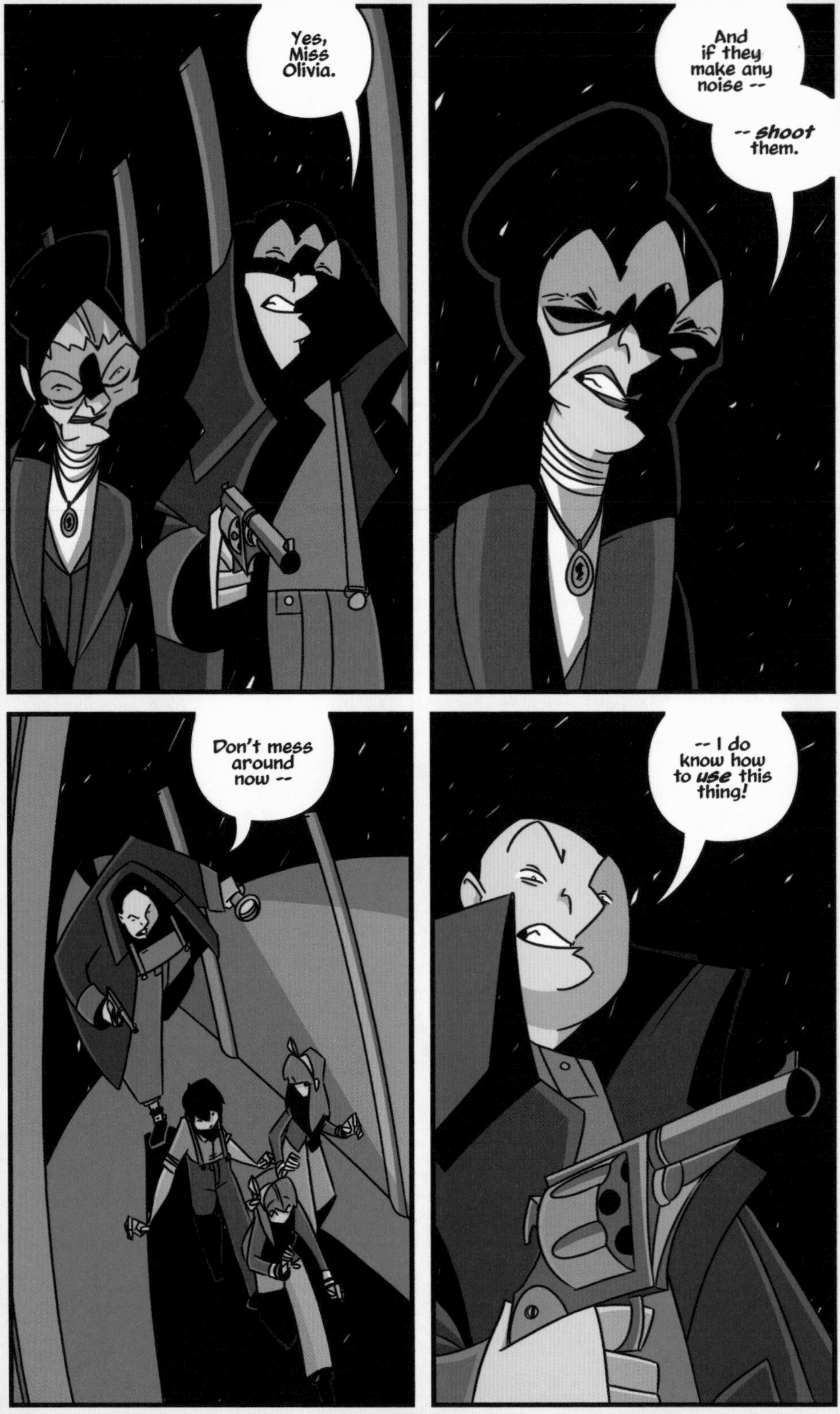
Yes, Miss Olivia.
And if they make any noise --
-- *shoot* them.
Don't mess around now --
-- I do know how to *use* this thing!

"Would you really shoot us, Mr. Straker?" Saskia asked as she walked in front of the burglar, carefully avoiding the end of his gun.

There was a long pause. "If I had to," came the gruff reply.

Saskia turned her head slightly to look at Straker—and noticed that the gun shook in his hand.

Straker snarled at her, "Just keep walking—and don't try anything."

Chapter Twelve

Flickering flames

THEY TRAMPED THE mile of dimly lit tunnel in wet
clothes that began to smell even more of rotten fish as
they slowly dried out. All the time, Straker barked orders,
nervously telling them to walk faster, turn left or right,
and keep their heads down. In places, the tunnel was only
wide enough to walk through in single file. Saskia went
first, her hands clasped together and her lips mumbling.

left
right

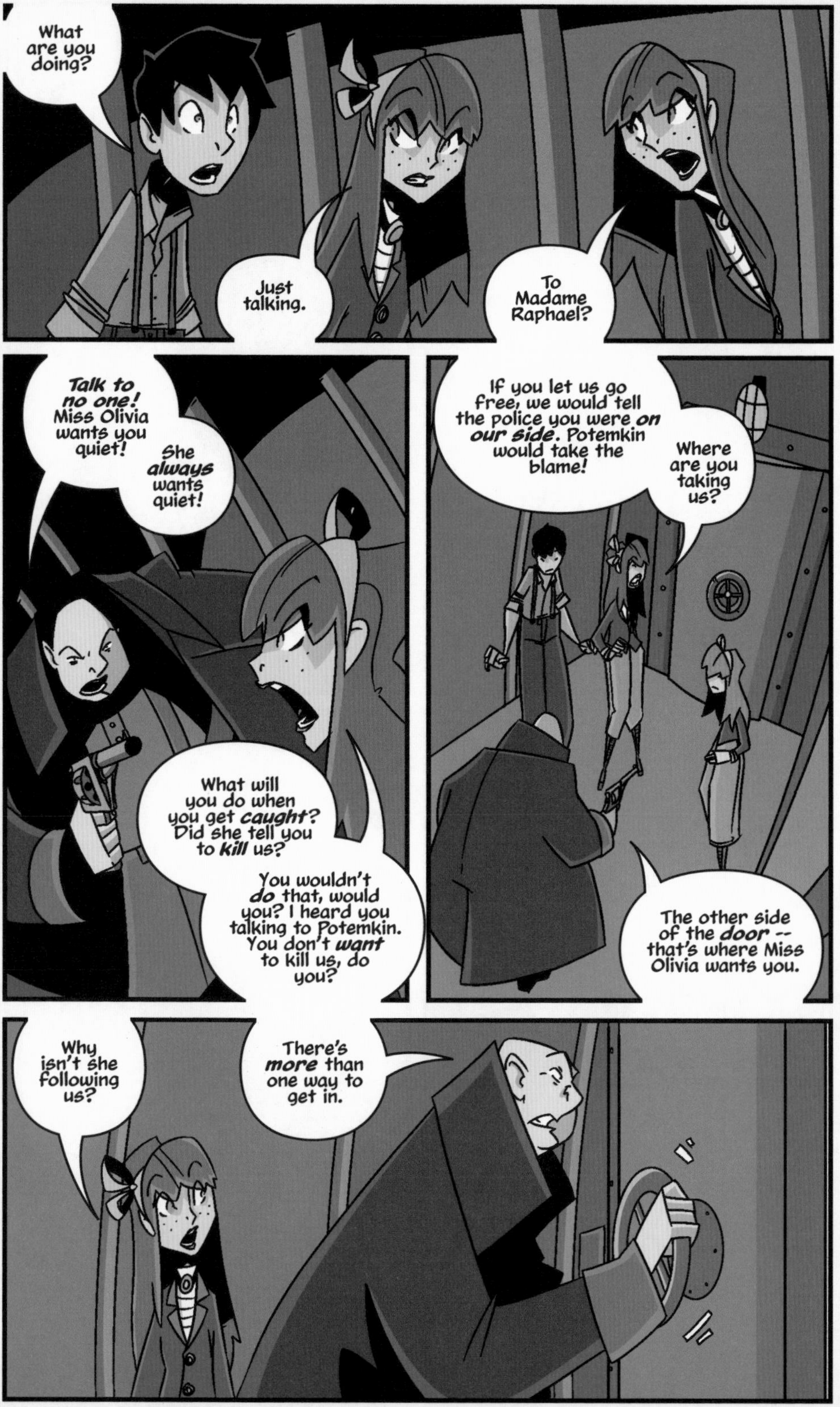
What are you doing?
Just talking.
To Madame Raphael?
Talk to no one! Miss Olivia wants you quiet!
She always wants quiet!
What will you do when you get caught? Did she tell you to kill us?
You wouldn't do that, would you? I heard you talking to Potemkin. You don't want to kill us, do you?
If you let us go free, we would tell the police you were on our side. Potemkin would take the blame!
Where are you taking us?
The other side of the door -- that's where Miss Olivia wants you.
Why isn't she following us?
There's more than one way to get in.

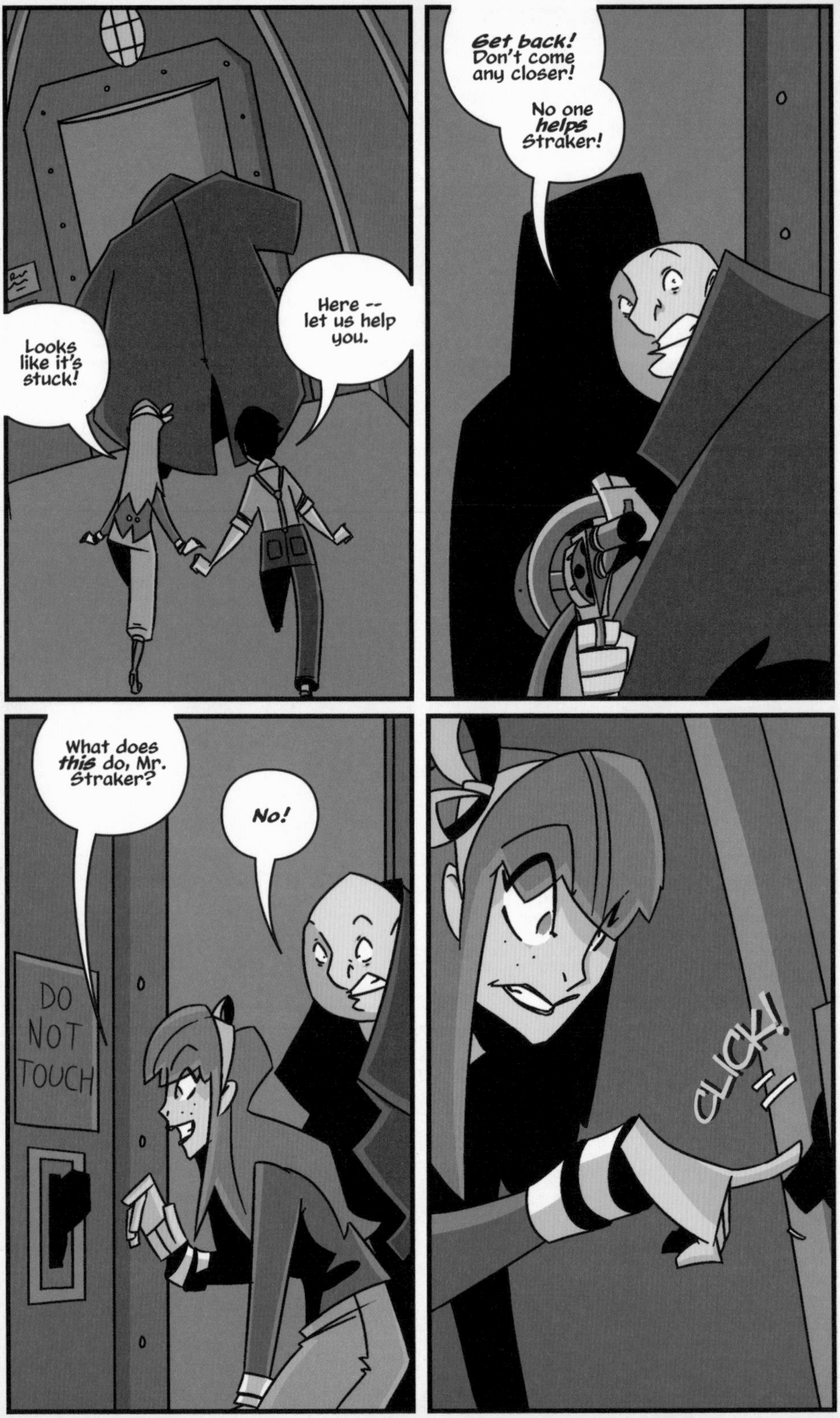
Looks like it's stuck!
Here -- let us help you.
Get back! Don't come any closer!
No one helps Straker!
What does this do, Mr. Straker?
No!
DO NOT TOUCH
CLICK!

The tunnel was plunged into darkness.

"There's someone coming," Erik shouted as they all fumbled in the thick, muddy black of the passage.

"Where is it?" shouted Straker. He felt around desperately for the switch.

There was a loud clatter. Erik stumbled over Straker, accidentally knocking him over. Saskia heard the sound of the pistol scraping across the floor.

"Give it back to me," Straker bellowed angrily.

"What?" asked Sadie, as she, too, fell over him. Straker made a dive for the place where he thought his gun had gone.

"I want it back!" he shouted, fighting them both.

Saskia waited a moment and listened to their screams before pulling the lever again. There was a crackling noise, and the lights came back on.

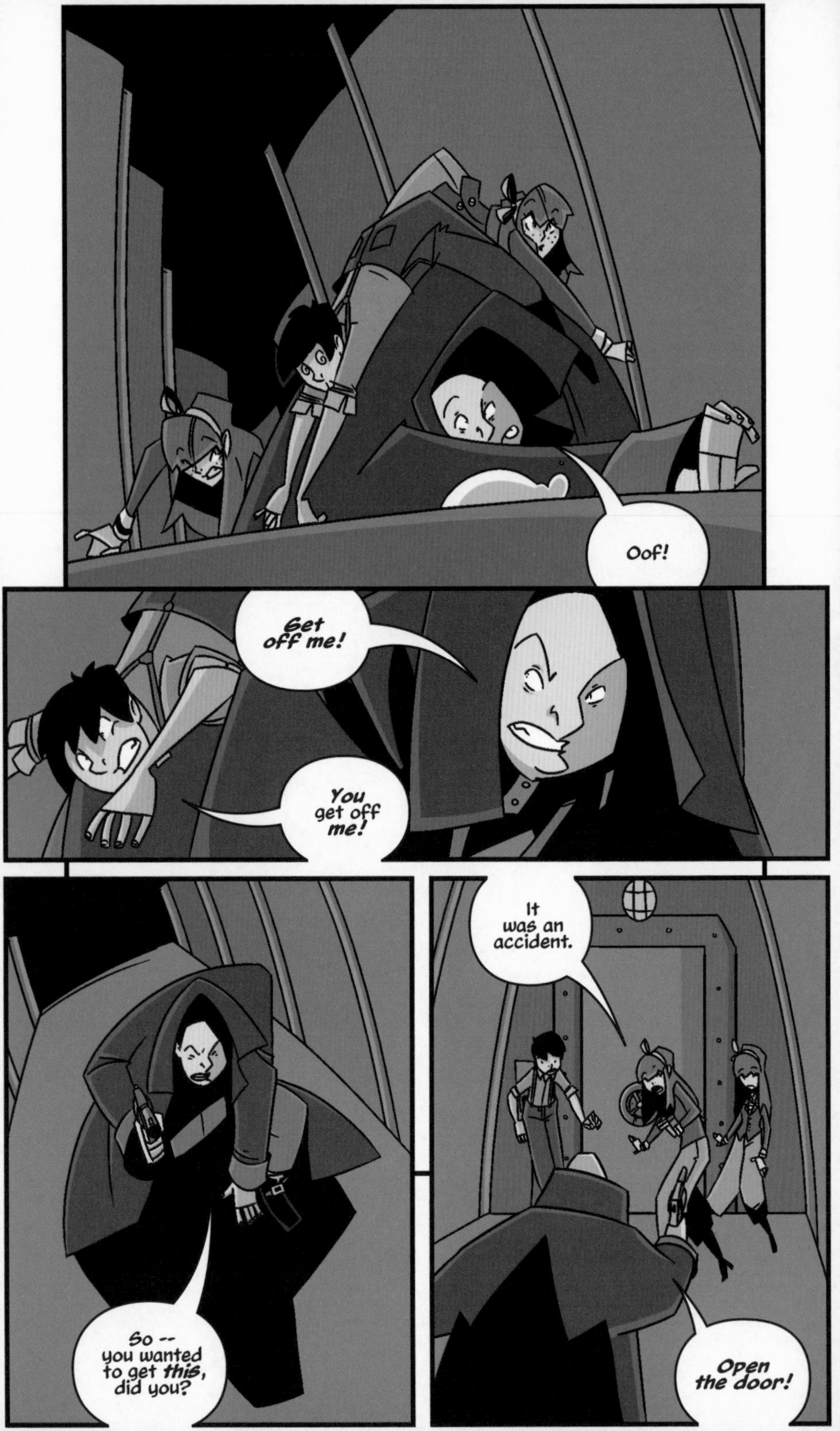
Oof!
Get off me!
You get off me!
So -- you wanted to get this, did you?
It was an accident.
Open the door!

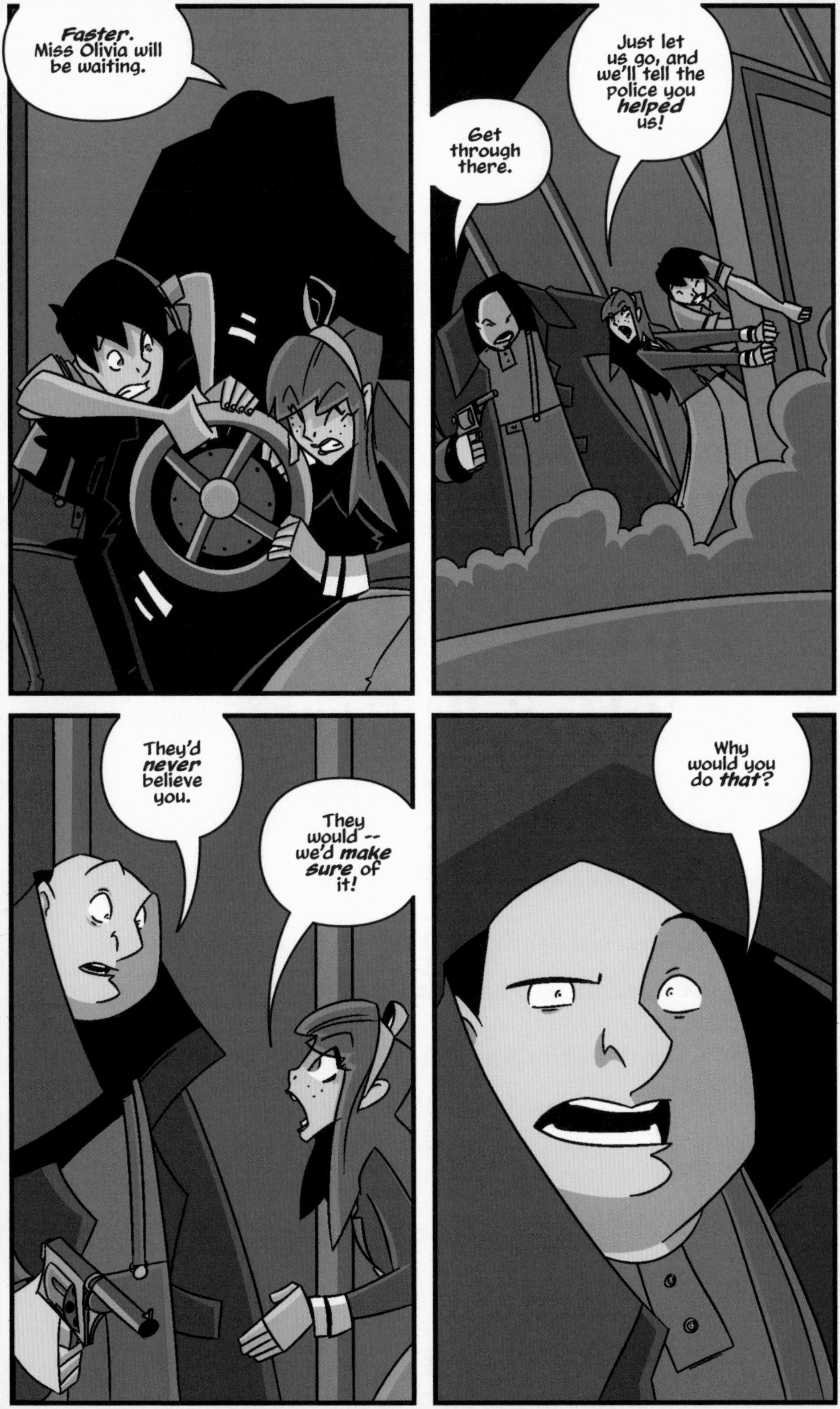
Faster. Miss Olivia will be waiting.
Just let us go, and we'll tell the police you helped us!
Get through there.
They'd never believe you.
They would -- we'd make sure of it!
Why would you do that?

Straker looked back and forth and then closed his eyes in thought. Sadie looked nervously at Erik and Saskia just as Straker began to speak.

"Couldn't trust you," he finally replied. "If I helped you, then you would break your promise, and I'd go to jail along with Potemkin and Miss Olivia."

"You don't like doing this, do you?" Saskia asked.

"It's my job. It's what I do," he replied. He waved the gun for them to go through the door.

"We'd keep our word. Just let us go—find a way for us to escape," Sadie urged him with a smile.

"Not worth it. Nothing you say can make me do that. Get inside. Miss Olivia should be waiting."

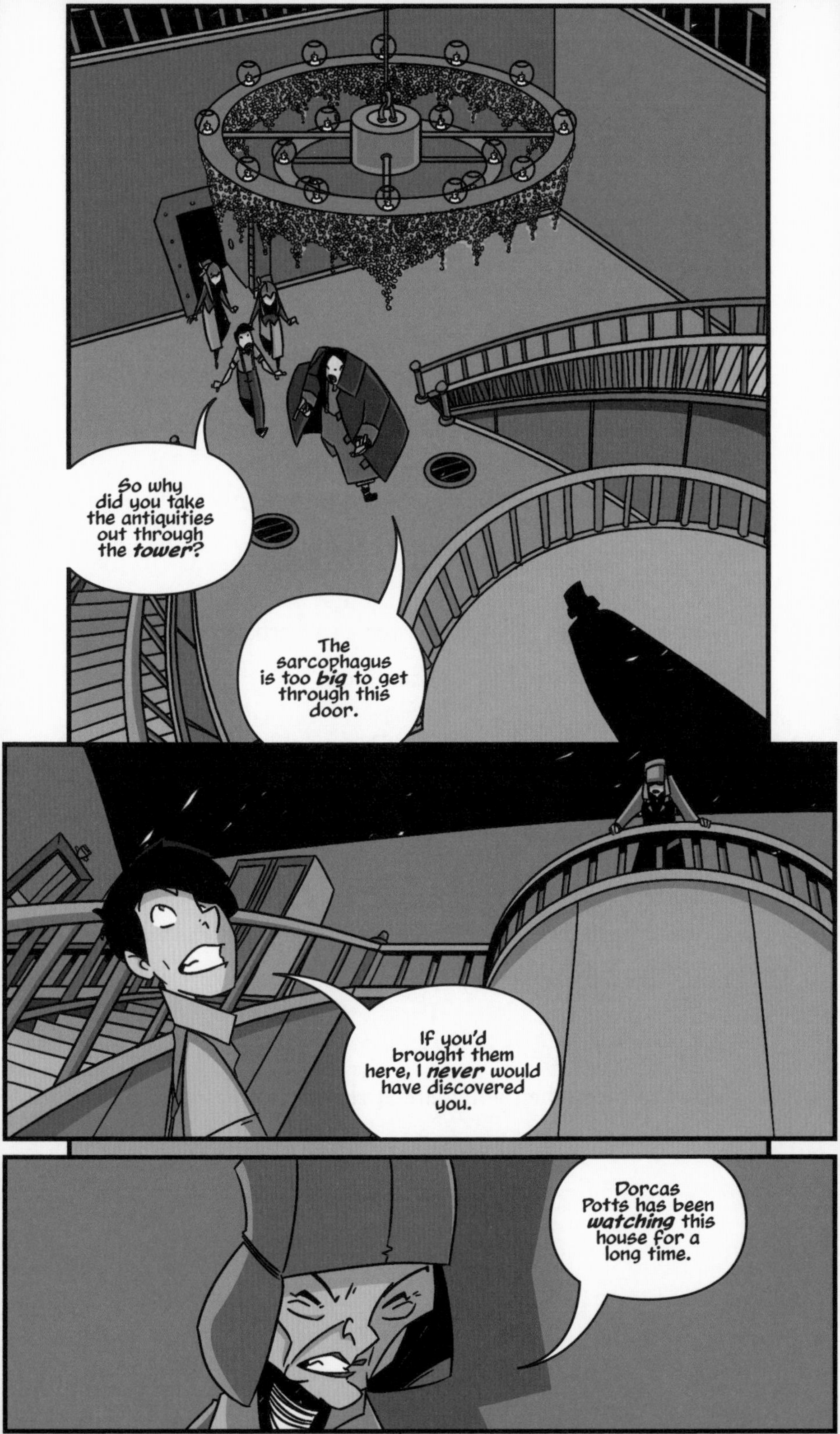
So why did you take the antiquities out through the *tower*?
The sarcophagus is too *big* to get through this door.
If you'd brought them here, I *never* would have discovered you.
Dorcas Potts has been *watching* this house for a long time.

Erik looked up. There, leaning over the ornate marble balcony high above him, was Miss Olivia. She had taken off her overcoat and was wearing a peculiar gentleman's hat that looked like the skinned head of a large, floppy-eared dog.

"I see you brought them here safely, Straker," Miss Olivia said.

"Ma'am," Straker replied with a nod of the head.

"Come up to me, all of you. I have something rather interesting I would like to show you."

With Straker still behind them, Erik, Sadie, and Saskia climbed the smooth marble steps and followed Miss Olivia through a theatrical doorway of carved clowns and into an even grander room. Lord Gervez was by the fireplace. In fact, he was almost IN the fireplace, propped against the wall and bound like a turkey ready to be roasted.

"What are you going to do to us?" Sadie asked. "You were always so nice when you were at the school."

"I resented every minute of it. Hated children, always have. I bided my time, knowing that one day I would have my revenge on everyone who had hurt me. The best way to hurt the rich is to steal what they have."

"But I never knew you," grumped Lord Gervez.

"Didn't have to. All your kind are the same. You never think of those below you. I wanted what you had—so I took the lot," she replied. "It was meticulously planned: came in at night by the tunnel you never knew about and stole all you had."

"Were you behind the other robberies in Hampstead?" Gervez asked.

"Me, me, and always me," Miss Olivia boasted. "I had to have help, and when the helpers had served their purpose, I did away with them in the tunnels below. Surprising how potent poisoned wine can be—and how greedy common thieves are to drink it."

"See, Straker, that's what she would do to you," Saskia said quickly. "You can't trust her. You'll be poisoned."

"Poisoned?"

muttered Straker. At that moment the door to the room opened and Dorcas Potts was thrown inside.

"Found her in the tunnel, Miss Olivia," Potemkin announced, strutting into the room after her.

"They were poisoned—the others—they were poisoned," Straker repeated in a daze.

"I know," Potemkin said without concern. "Miss Olivia has let me in on that secret already."

"She wants no witnesses. Not even you, Potemkin," Dorcas Potts said, looking about the room.

"Miss Olivia and I set sail from Southampton on April 10. A train will carry our treasure to the port, where it will be loaded onto the boat by unsuspecting dockhands. Soon we shall be long gone . . . and so will you."

Suddenly Potemkin snatched the gun from Straker's hand.

Saskia shouted. She pushed her hand deep inside her coat pocket.

"Told you, Mr. Straker!"

"Over there, Straker," barked Potemkin. "Your useful days are over. A shame, really—I was beginning to like you."

"Why are you doing this?" Straker asked, his eyes wide like a lost dog's.

"Because you don't have the heart for this. I can see that so clearly. You will meet your end like the rest of them."

"And what will that be?" asked Dorcas Potts.

"You will be locked in this room, and as Miss Olivia and I drive away, the house will mysteriously go up in flames. I'm sure there will be a front-page article about it in the TIMES," Potemkin said coldly.

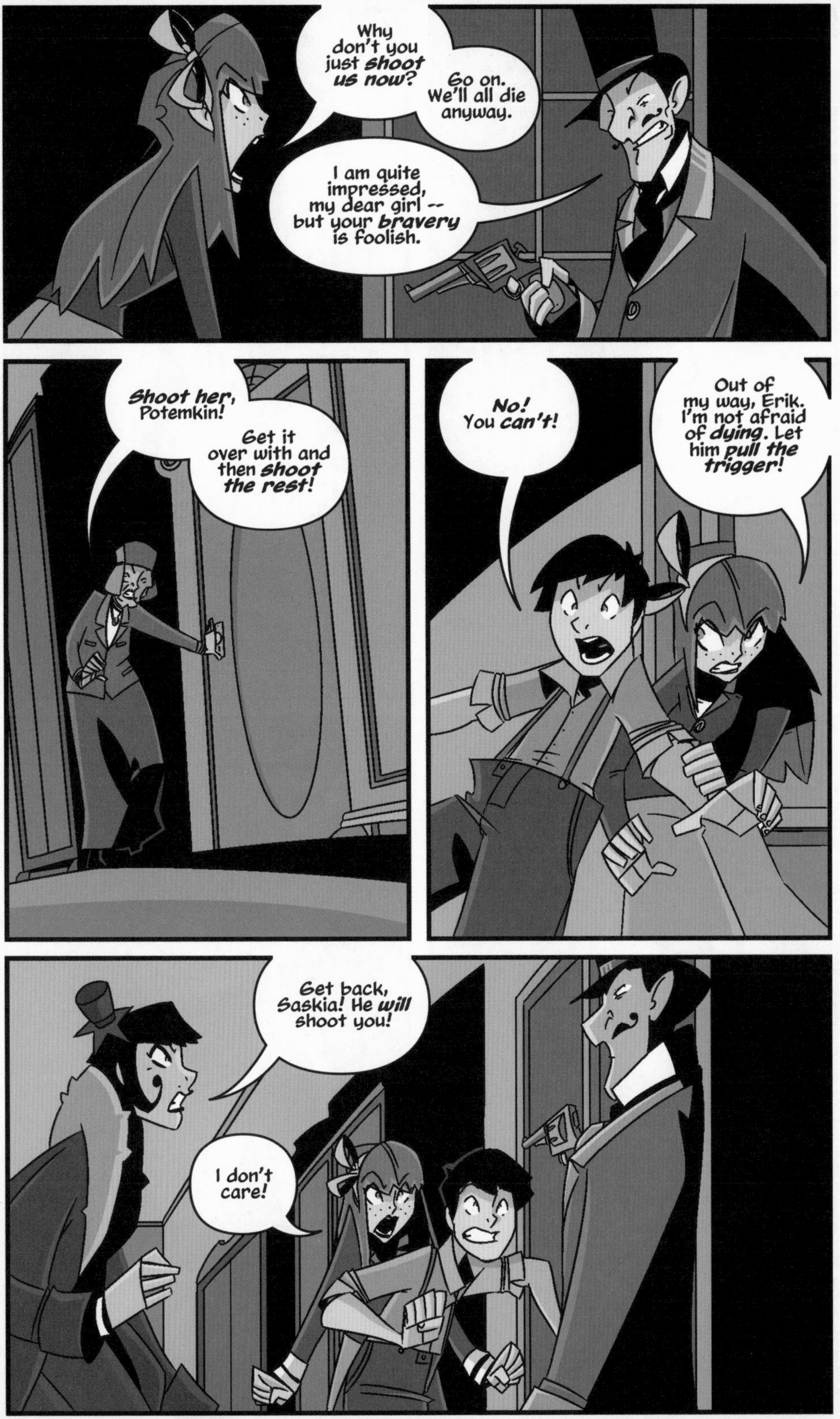
Why don't you just shoot us now?
Go on. We'll all die anyway.
I am quite impressed, my dear girl -- but your bravery is foolish.
Shoot her, Potemkin!
Get it over with and then shoot the rest!
No! You can't!
Out of my way, Erik. I'm not afraid of dying. Let him pull the trigger!
Get back, Saskia! He will shoot you!
I don't care!

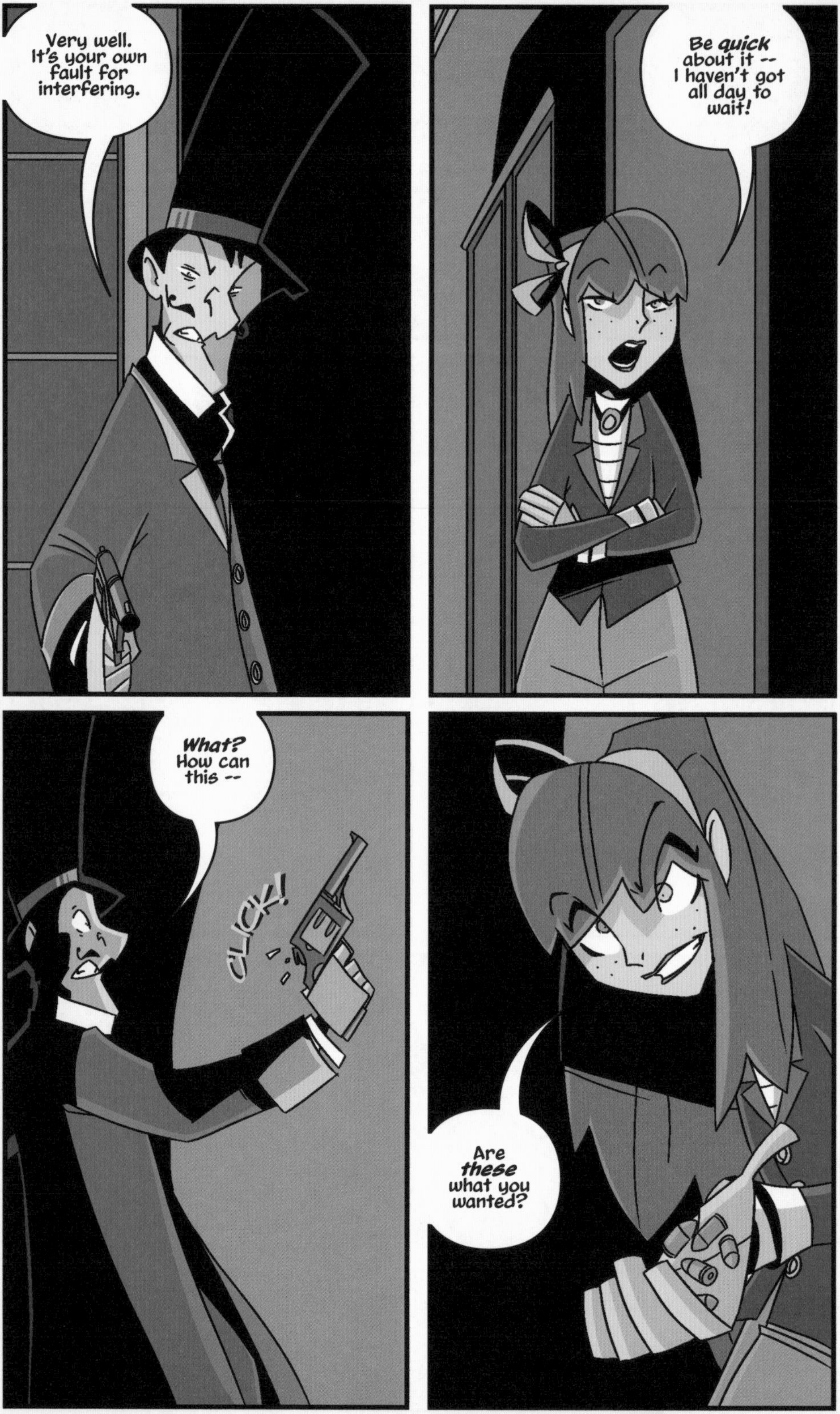
Very well. It's your own fault for interfering.
Be quick about it -- I haven't got all day to wait!
What? How can this --
CLICK!
Are these what you wanted?

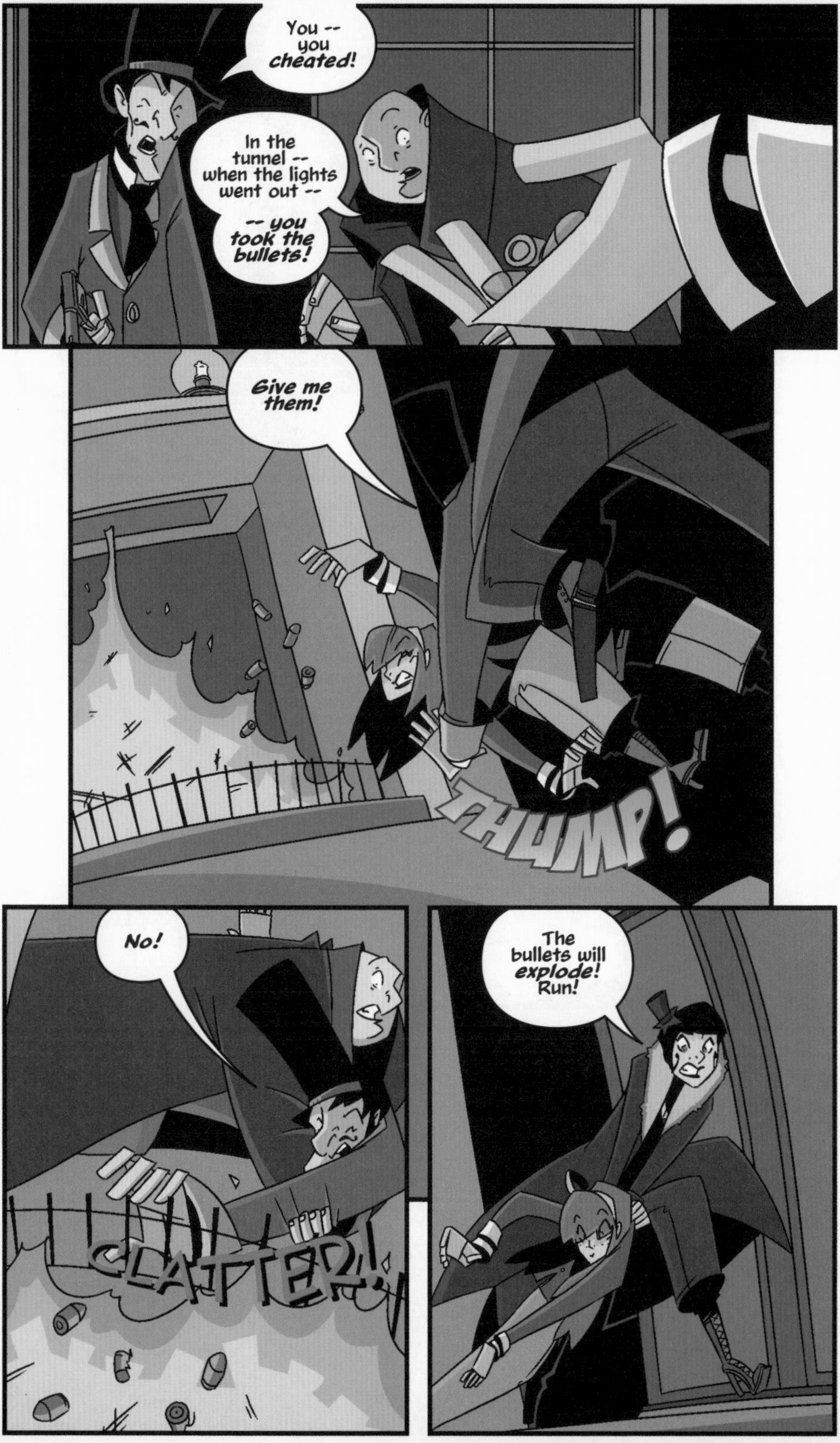

You -- you *cheated!*
In the tunnel -- when the lights went out --
-- you took the bullets!
Give me them!
THUMP!
No!
CLATTER!
The bullets will *explode!* Run!

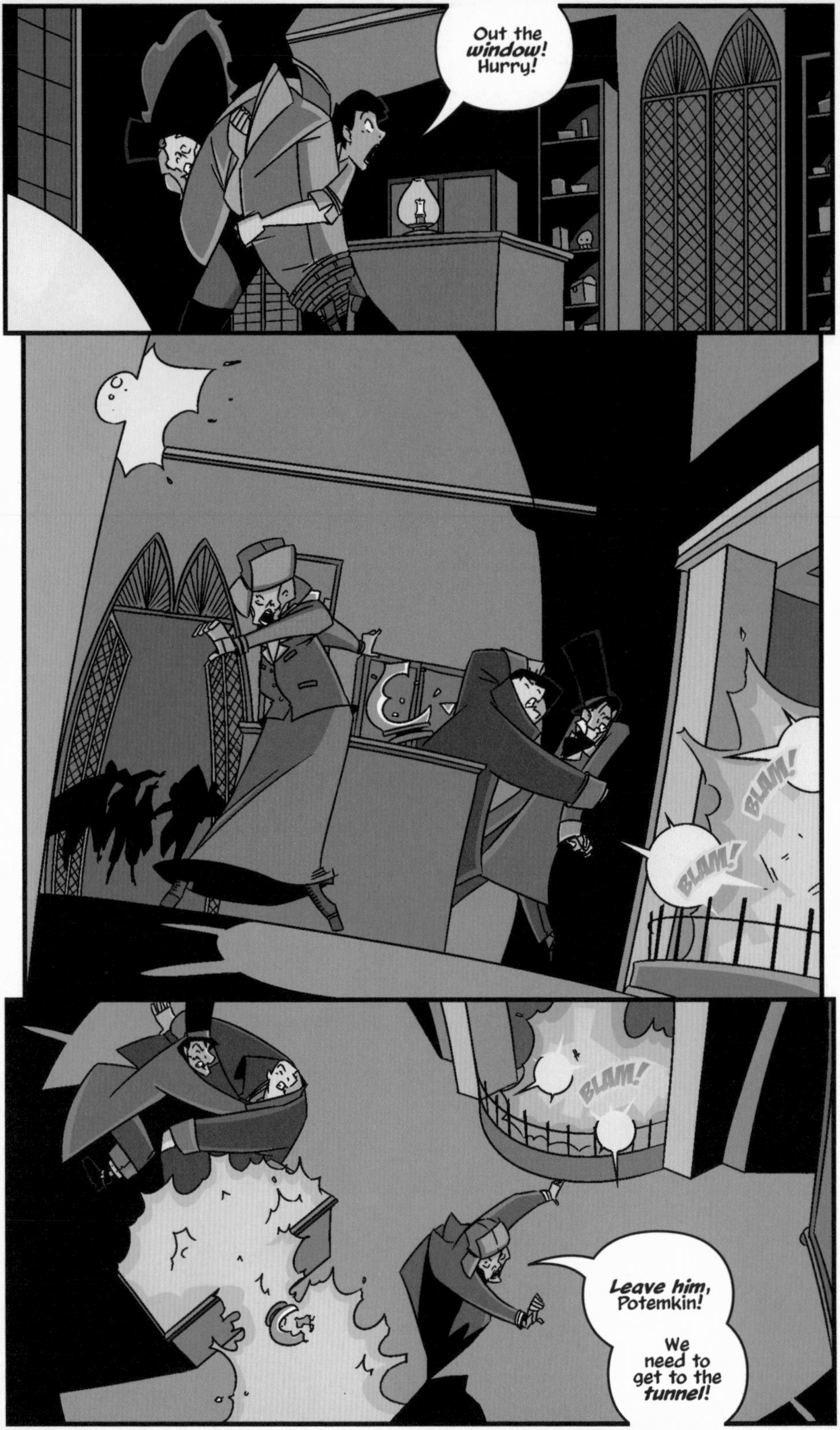
Out the *window*! Hurry!
BLAM!
BLAM!
BLAM!
Leave him, Potemkin!
We need to get to the *tunnel*!

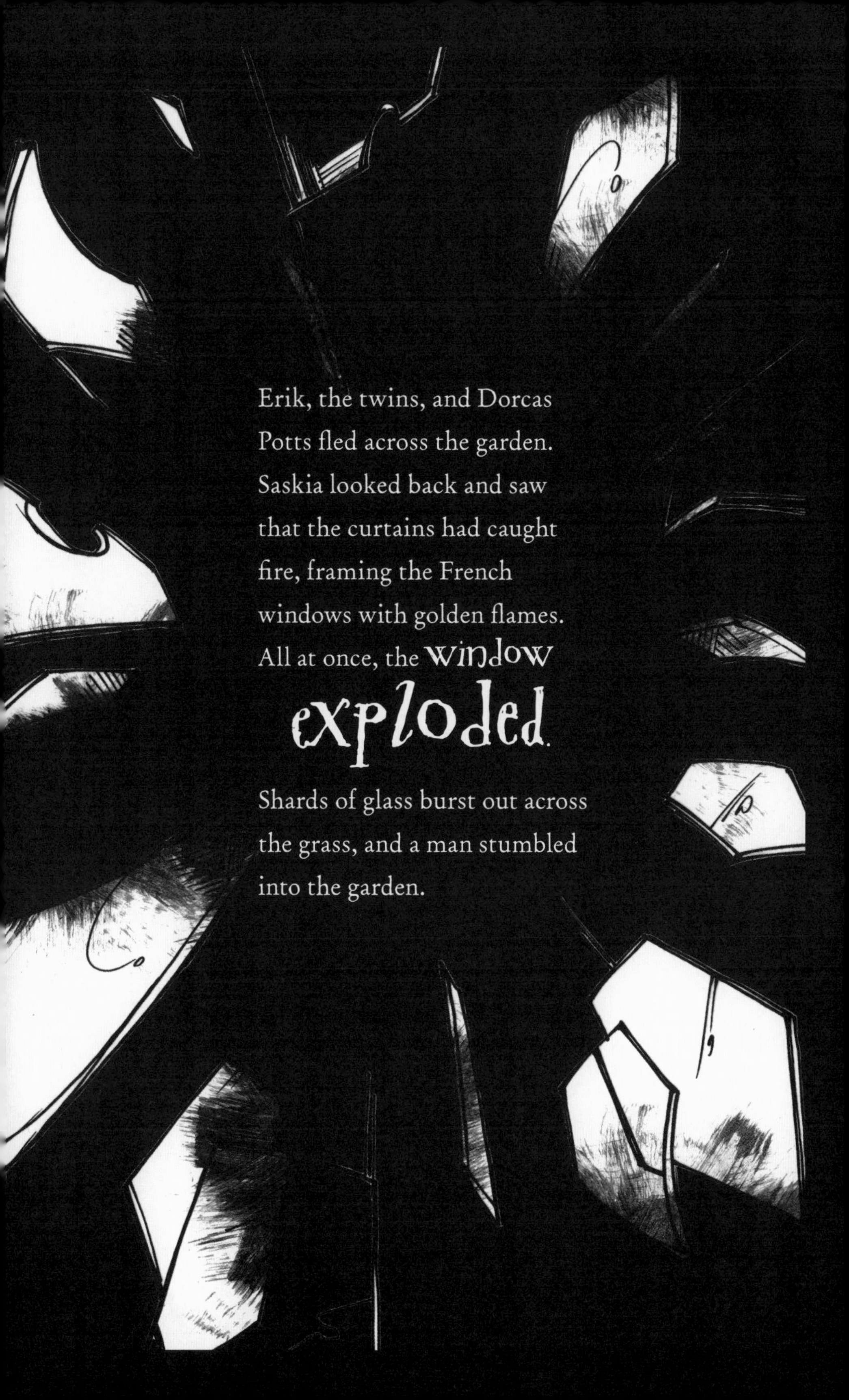

Erik, the twins, and Dorcas Potts fled across the garden. Saskia looked back and saw that the curtains had caught fire, framing the French windows with golden flames. All at once, the window

exploded.

Shards of glass burst out across the grass, and a man stumbled into the garden.

He coughed violently and fell to the ground. The light from the fire reflected off his large, bald head. In two seconds, Dorcas Potts was at his side.

"Gone," choked Straker. "They've escaped down the tunnel."

"Should we go after them?" asked Erik, coming up behind Dorcas Potts. Lord Gervez was still slung over his shoulder.

"No," said Dorcas Potts firmly. "The police can take it from here. We have our star witness who'll tell them the whole story—won't you, Mr. Straker?"

Straker nodded and whimpered at the same time.

"Where are we?" asked Sadie.

Erik set Lord Gervez down gently and looked up at the lights of the town in the distance. "The other side of Hampstead

Heath. Near Spaniards House," he said. "That tunnel brought us right across—Indigo Moon was a genius." He began to untie Lord Gervez.

"You have saved my life, young man," said his lordship. "There is always room in my house for the likes of you. When you are too old to live at the school, I'd be happy to give you a home."

Though grateful, Erik didn't know how to respond, so he simply shrugged his shoulders.

"My uncle is getting older and could use the company, Erik," Dorcas Potts added, taking one of the cords that had bound her uncle and tying Straker's hands securely behind his back. "I'm frequently away on assignment and don't have the time to look in on him as often as I'd like."

"Older?" Lord Gervez laughed. "Well, I suppose I am. Dorcas could teach you to be a detective when she comes to visit too. It's obvious you have the heart."

Erik blushed and looked at the ground. "Could I . . ." He hesitated. "Could I come and live with you right away? I don't really want to go back to the school. It was a good place to live for a time, but I want to be getting on with my life," he finished hurriedly. Then a new thought occurred to him. He turned to Dorcas Potts. "Besides, didn't you say Miss Rimmer could be involved with the burglaries? I've spent enough of my life living with a thief already."

Lord Gervez opened his mouth to answer, but everyone was surprised when Straker spoke up. "Miss Rimmer never had anything to do with it. She may be a tyrant and a lousy schoolteacher, but she's innocent of this crime."

"Then what was she talking about on the phone?" wondered Saskia. Then she looked at her twin, and her eyes grew wide.

Sadie caught her meaning and looked shocked. "You don't think she was trying to get rid of US, do you?" There was an uncomfortable silence.

"I'm not sure I want to go back to the school either," said Saskia finally. "Maybe we could ask Muzz Elliott to let us live with her again."

Dorcas Potts spoke up. "You could ask her tonight." She pointed in the direction of Spaniards House. "Do you think Muzz Elliott would mind our intruding at such a late hour?" she asked Saskia. "We need to call the police before Potemkin and Olivia get too far."

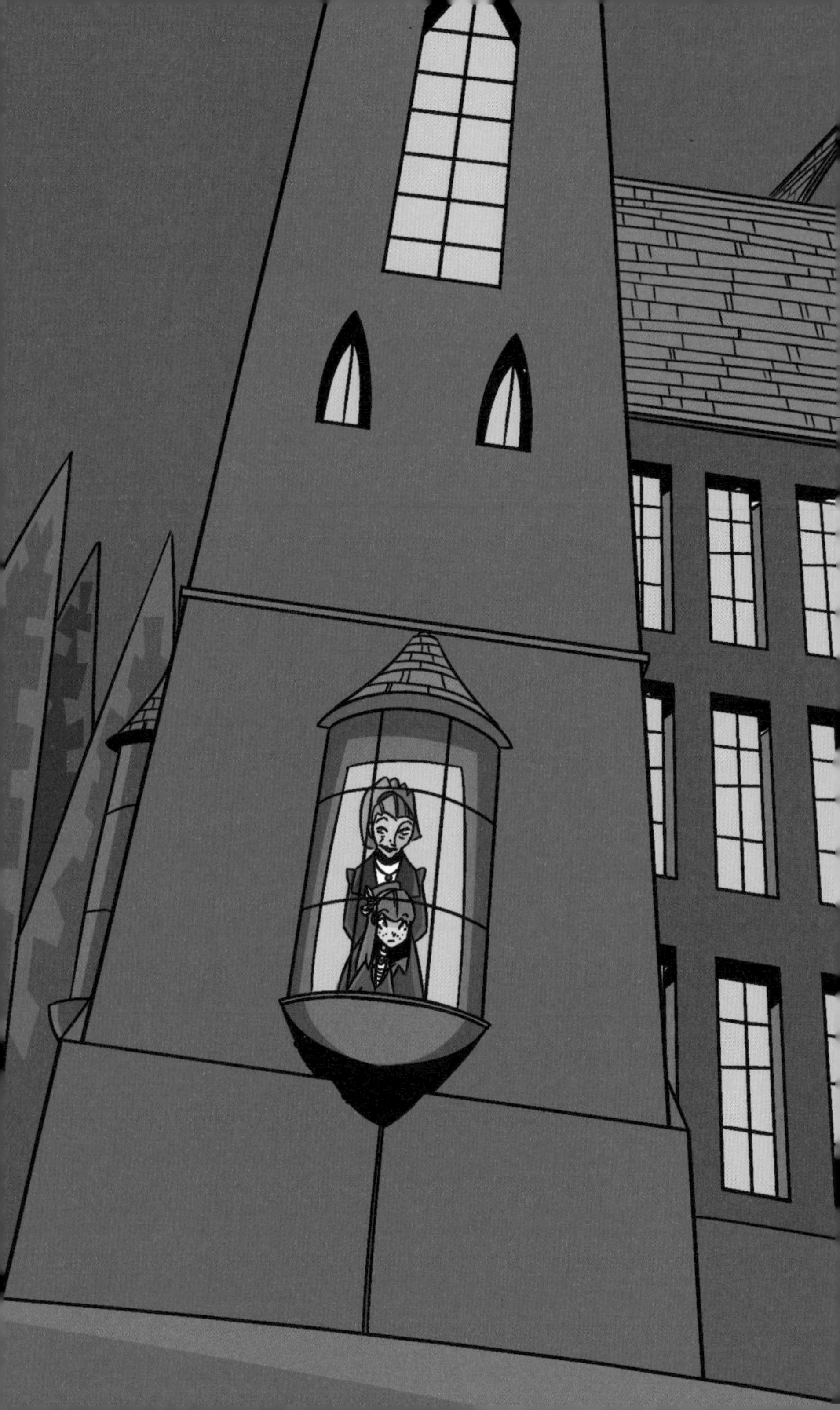

Chapter Thirteen
The Man of Good~Bye Friday

"SOMETIMES SAYING good-bye is a very hard thing to do," said the voice behind Saskia.

"Will we see him again soon?" Saskia asked as Lord Gervez's car drove away from Spaniards House with Erik frantically waving from the backseat. Muzz Elliott had been kind enough to let her and Sadie stay the night, and she had promised to talk with them in the morning about their future.

"I think that is a distinct possibility," Madame Raphael replied.

"Madame Raphael, there's something I've been wondering: how can I see you when no one else can?"

"Some people have a desire to search for the truth, and others do not. The Companion is all around us, yet many people go through life unaware of who he is," she replied.

"I think Sadie might believe that you're real now—at least, she remembered your warning from the note. But Erik still says you're a ghost." Saskia waved a final time at the disappearing car. She knew Erik couldn't see her, but something in her heart made her want to wave once more.

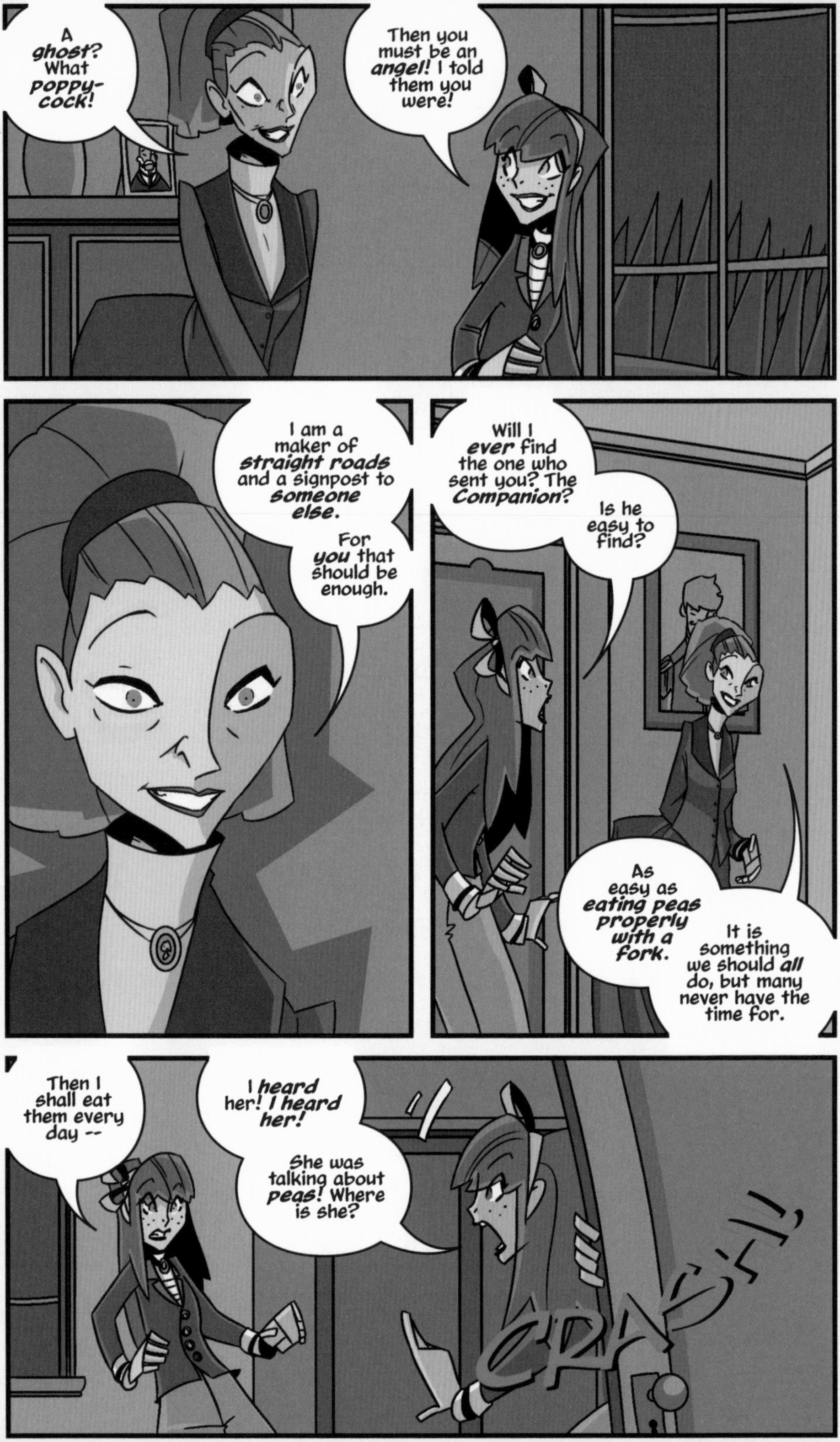
A ghost? What poppy-cock!
Then you must be an angel! I told them you were!
I am a maker of straight roads and a signpost to someone else.
For you that should be enough.
Will I ever find the one who sent you? The Companion?
Is he easy to find?
As easy as eating peas properly with a fork.
It is something we should all do, but many never have the time for.
Then I shall eat them every day --
I heard her! I heard her!
She was talking about peas! Where is she?
CRASH!!

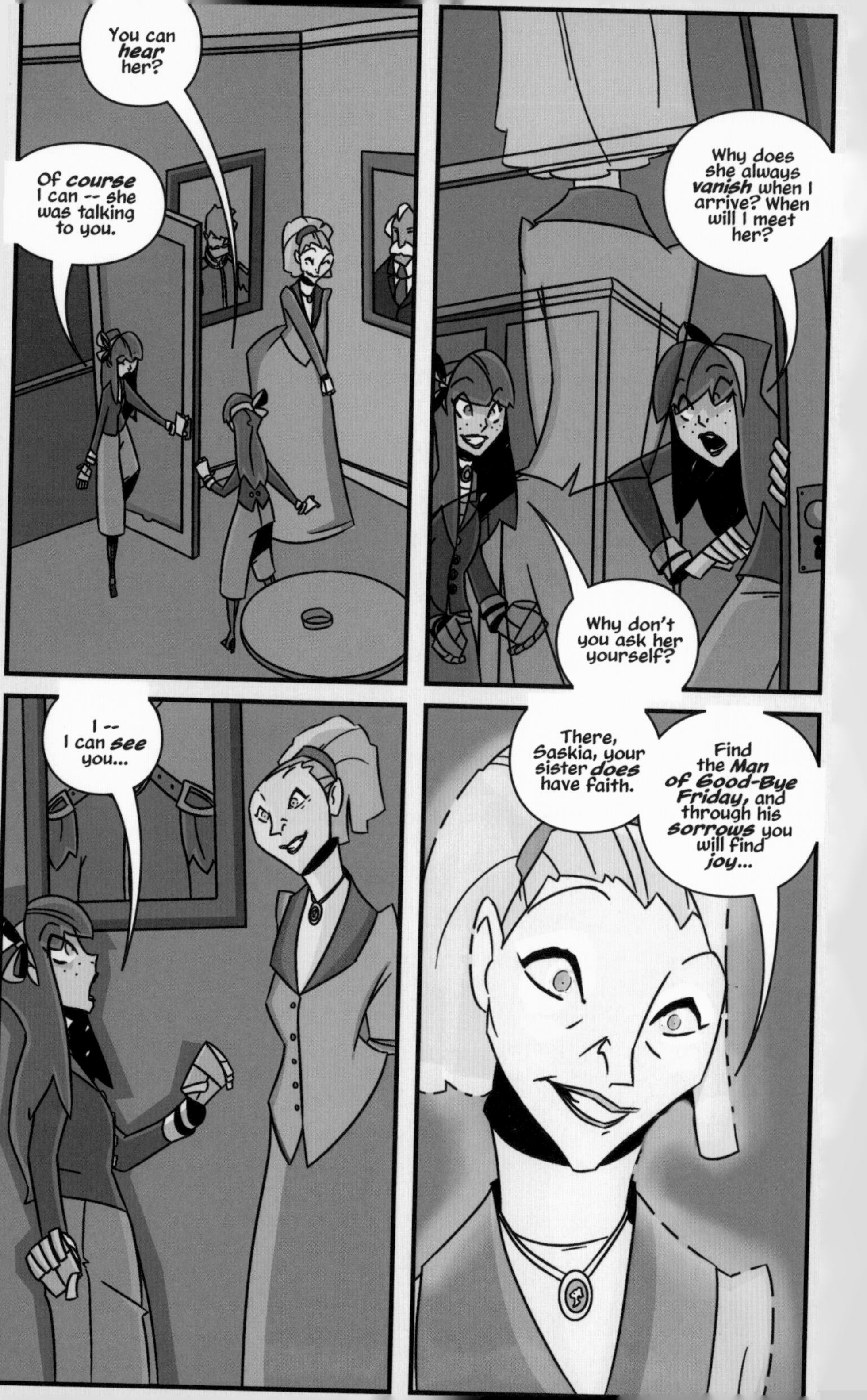

You can *hear* her?
Of *course* I can -- she was talking to you.
Why does she always *vanish* when I arrive? When will I meet her?
Why don't you ask her yourself?
I -- I can *see* you...
There, Saskia, your sister *does* have faith.
Find the *Man of Good-Bye Friday*, and through his *sorrows* you will find *joy*...

Sadie stared at the spot where Madame Raphael had just been. She looked disappointed. "Does she always speak in riddles?" she asked her twin.

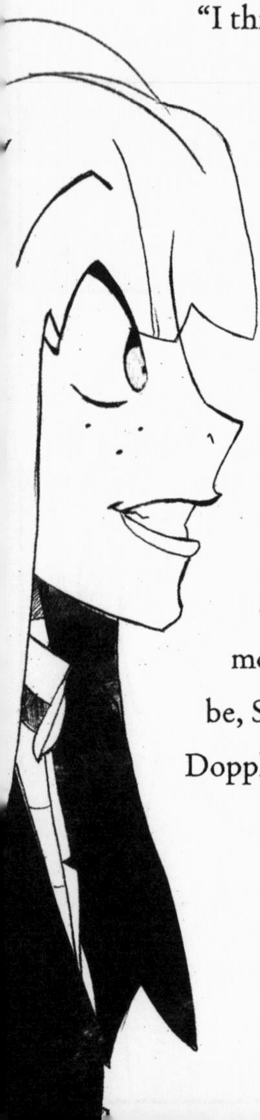

"I think it's her way not to explain everything," answered Saskia. "I think . . . I think it might be important sometimes for us to discover what she means on our own."

"I wish she'd told us how long we'd have to wait before seeing Erik again," murmured Sadie.

"She did say we'd probably see him again soon." Saskia looked at her sister thoughtfully. She wasn't used to hearing Sadie long for anyone else, except perhaps their mother. "It won't be that different than it used to be, Sadie. It's always been just the two of us: the Dopple twins against the world."

Sadie smiled wistfully at her sister. "It's not just us anymore, though, is it? There's Erik and Madame Raphael."

The two gazed at each other, as always not needing words to share their thoughts. "It's not quite the same," Saskia finally admitted. "But I think it can be even better."

Sadie's smile turned into a grin. "We ruled a school with no help at all," she reminded her sister. "Just imagine what we can do with a thief and an angel on our side!"

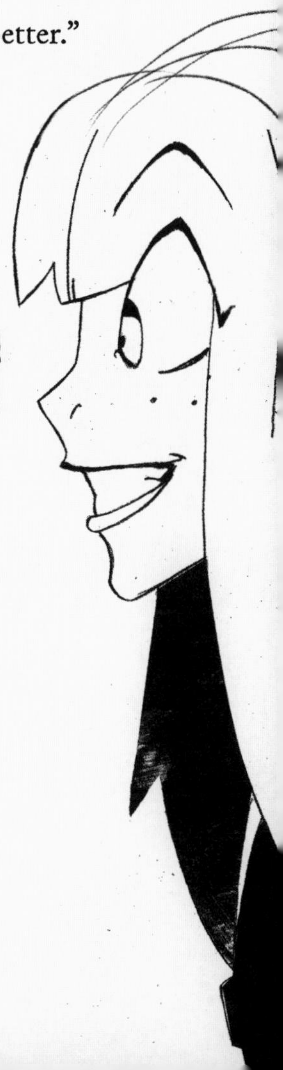

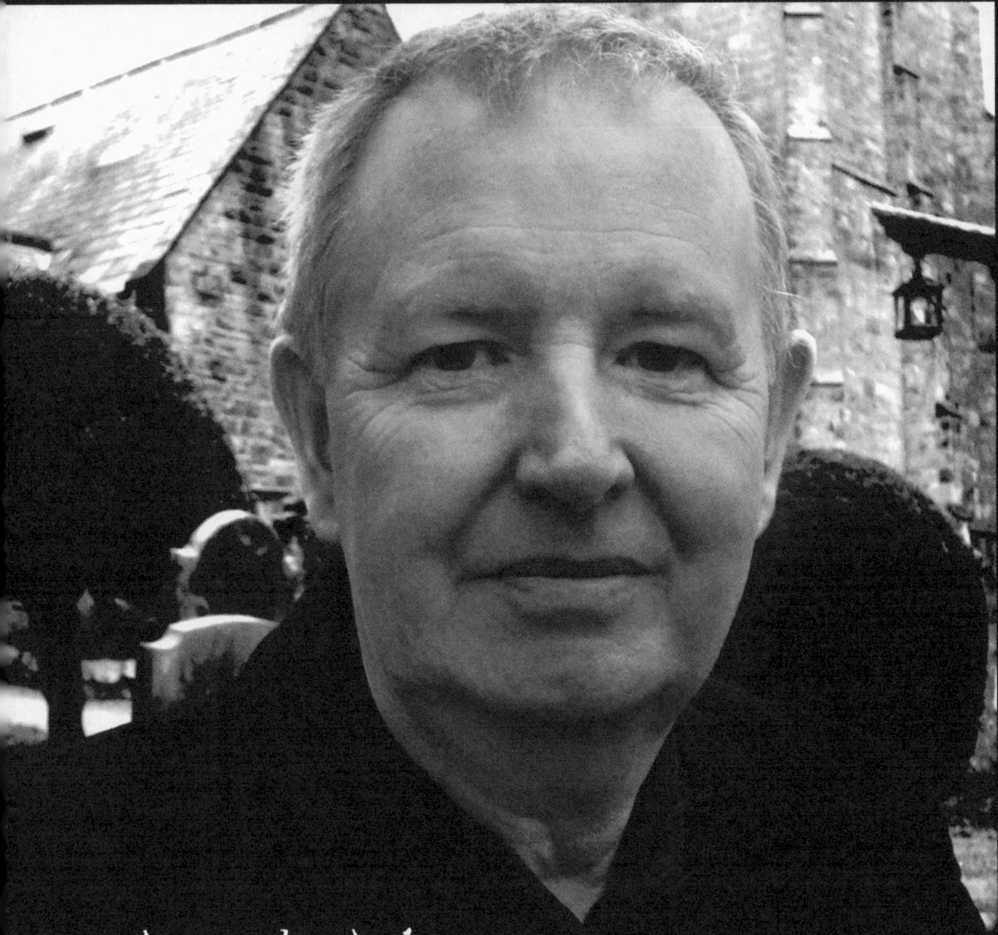

About the Author

A motorcyclist and former rock band roadie turned Anglican minister, G. P. Taylor has been hailed as "hotter than Potter" and "the new C. S. Lewis" in the United Kingdom. His first novel, SHADOWMANCER, reached #1 on the NEW YORK TIMES bestseller list in 2004 and has been translated into forty-eight languages. His other novels include WORMWOOD (another NEW YORK TIMES bestseller, which was nominated for a Quill book award), THE SHADOWMANCER RETURNS: THE CURSE OF SALAMANDER STREET, TERSIAS THE ORACLE, MARIAH MUNDI: THE MIDAS BOX, and THE FIRST ESCAPE. Worldwide sales for Taylor's books now total more than 3 million copies.

G. P. Taylor currently resides in North Yorkshire with his wife and three children.

About the Artists

DANIEL BOULTWOOD was born in London. He studied
illustration at Richmond College and went on to work in computer
game concept design. From there he moved into flash animation,
creating games for DreamWorks and Warner Bros. It was here that he
refined his style to the animation-inspired work it is today. He lives in
London in a shed with two cats.

LUKE DAAB grew up in Holland, Michigan, and received his
BFA in graphic design from the University of Michigan School of
Art and Design. In 2007, Luke founded Daab Creative, an award-
winning graphic design and illustration agency in the western
suburbs of Chicago. Luke currently resides in Winfield, Illinois,
with his wife, Jenny, and their pet rat, Rebekah. He enjoys reading
comic books, drawing superheroes, writing music, and collecting
action figures.

TONY LEE (adapter) began his career in games journalism and
magazine features, moving into radio in the early nineties. He
spent over ten years working for television, radio, and magazines
as a feature and script writer, winning several awards. In 2005 he
adapted G. P. Taylor's SHADOWMANCER novel into a graphic novel
for Markosia.

Other Books by G. P. Taylor

Shadowmancer

Wormwood

The Shadowmancer Returns:
The Curse of Salamander Street

Tersias the Oracle

Mariah Mundi: The Midas Box

The Dopple Ganger Chronicles
Book 1: The First Escape

Continue the adventure

with Erik, Sadie, and Saskia. . . .

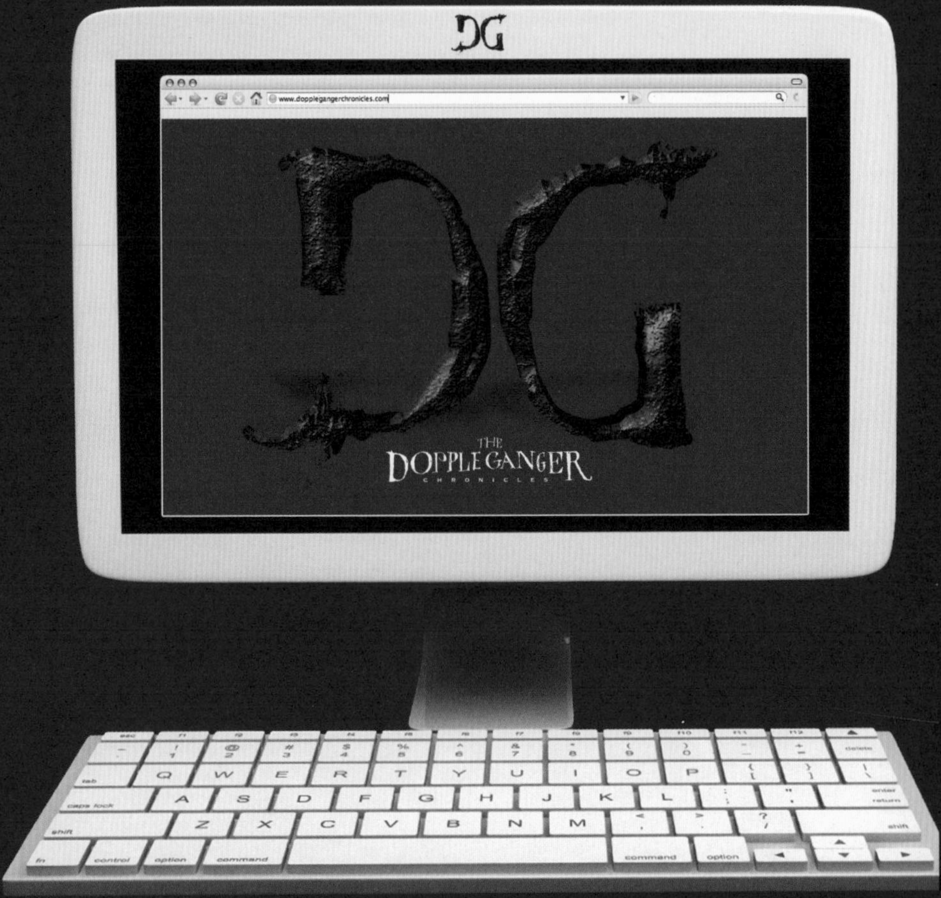
DG
www.dopplegangerchronicles.com
THE DOPPLEGANGER CHRONICLES

VISIT

WWW.DOPPLEGANGERCHRONICLES.COM